EARLY BIRDS

EARLY BIRDS

Peta Tayler

HEADLINE

First published in 1999
by HEADLINE BOOK PUBLISHING

10 9 8 7 6 5 4 3 2 1

British Library Cataloguing in Publication Data

Tayler, Peta
Early birds
I. Title
823.9'14[F]

ISBN 0 7472 2059 X

Typeset by Avon Dataset Ltd, Bidford-on-Avon, Warks

Printed and bound in Great Britain by
Mackays of Chatham PLC, Chatham, Kent

HEADLINE BOOK PUBLISHING
A division of Hodder Headline PLC
338 Euston Road
London NW1 3BH

To all my swimming relations and friends, chiefly Alan, Freda and Jean, Michèle, Bill and Joanna;

but not forgetting Anthony, Brenda, Josie, Dinah, George, Michelle, Jane DePinner, Jane Collins, Claire (who taught us the crawl), Claire (who lost and found her engagement ring), Jill (and Polly!), Sean, and all the other Early Birds and staff at the Dolphin Centre whose friendship and dedication has been an inspiration – even at six thirty in the morning!

Chapter One

T hree minutes to go.

The queue was shorter than usual. At three minutes to seven on a bitterly cold morning in late January, it wasn't very surprising. From her place at the tail end of the line, Maggie Whittington thought that the only surprising thing was that there was anybody there at all.

Three weeks of the kind of weather that makes even the most rabid Anglophile think about emigrating to the West Indies had soon weeded out the less committed. The New Year resolutions, the 'I must get rid of those pounds I put on over Christmas', had melted away much faster than the thin icing of snow that still lay in shaded corners around the Leisure Centre. Only the diehard few remained – those who turned up every morning whatever the weather, united by self-discipline and common suffering into a group that tried, with varying success, not to appear smug. And then there was Maggie.

Maggie was a newcomer. Like so many others, she had started coming to the Early Birds swimming session after the New Year holiday, but unlike them she was still there. Not because she was desperate to lose weight or to get fit, but merely because she found, greatly to her surprise, that she enjoyed it.

Sport had never featured in her life as something pleasurable. When Maggie was a child at school it had been a necessary evil, to be avoided if possible or endured if not. At her husband's insistence she had tried both tennis and golf, but in spite of the most expensive coaching she had proved to him what she already knew, which was that she was embarrassingly bad at ball games. Even the motionless golf ball seemed to take on a perverse life of its own when she approached it, and it seemed that nothing could cure her of closing her eyes and ducking at the sight of an approaching tennis ball. Turner had been irritated, but even he could see that Maggie would do his business interests no good on court or course in either club.

It was not in his nature, however, to give up. At Christmas, with a grin of triumph, he had presented her with a small envelope and

1

a large box. The envelope contained a gold card with a holographic logo which entitled her to use, at any time, all the facilities at the Health and Beauty Leisure Spa which had just opened in part of his lavish new hotel, The Grange. The box held a selection of tracksuits, leotards, tights and trainers, all emblazoned with designer labels.

Maggie tried to appear suitably grateful. Later, standing in front of the bathroom mirror and tugging at one of the leotards – was it really meant to be *so* skimpily cut? – she reflected that the breadmaking machine she had vaguely been hoping for would not have done her figure any favours. It wasn't that she was fat, exactly, merely that twenty years of enjoying cooking had left their mark. Turner, who had worked so hard to achieve his considerable success, was telling her that he needed her help again. Not, this time, as an unpaid secretary, or book-keeper, or general dogsbody, but as a glamorous accessory. If she could not network for him at the tennis club or the golf course, then she might do so in the multi-gym, or the whirlpool spa, or the sauna.

Dutifully, three days after Christmas, Maggie presented herself at the Spa.

'It was awful,' she said later to Julie Corre, her cleaner. 'Just awful. I felt totally humiliated.'

'What a shame,' said Julie, flicking through the glossy brochure that lay on the table between them. 'It looks lovely. All those things to try . . . did you go in the Sauna? And what about a massage, and a facial? I've always wanted to have a facial, and they say a massage is really relaxing.'

'I didn't get that far,' said Maggie gloomily. 'I didn't actually get to do anything much. They just showed me round – a girl, and a young man. They were so perfect – like *Baywatch* or something, those bodies that look as though they've been sculpted out of high quality plastic, all tanned and glowing and hairless.'

'What, even him? I couldn't fancy a man who shaved his legs.'

'Well, maybe not, but you know what I mean. And they had those Lycra clothes, and she wore one of those cut-away leotards that go into your . . . between your . . .' Maggie gestured to her well-rounded bottom. Julie giggled.

'Up your crack,' she suggested.

'Well, yes. And when you think how uncomfortable it is when your knickers do that . . . How do they stand it? Anyway, I felt all lumpy and awkward, and I knew my legs were bristly because I forgot to shave them, and the *thought* of taking off my tracksuit made me go hot and cold all over. So I ran away.'

'Really?'

'No, not really. I said I had a lunch appointment.'

The sound of wheels on the drive made them both jump. Maggie

2

picked up her half-drunk mug of instant coffee and hid it in one of the kitchen cabinets, and Julie took hers to the sink. Turner had strong views about what he called 'hobnobbing with the staff', and had been angry with Maggie when he came home unexpectedly and found her sharing a cake and a mug of tea with Julie one afternoon.

'But it was her birthday. And besides, I like her. We're friends,' Maggie had said.

'You can't be friends with your cleaning lady. She won't respect you.'

'She won't respect me for being a snob, either. I can't suddenly turn into Her Ladyship, Turner, just because I've got a house with eight bedrooms and a tennis court. She's a nice woman, doing a good job with those kids of hers. I like hearing about them.'

This had been a master-stroke. Their childlessness was something they no longer spoke of. Exhaustive tests on both of them had revealed no physical reason for it, beyond a marginally low sperm count. By the time it had become clear that normal methods were not going to work they were already in their late thirties. Maggie, offered more drastic IVF treatment, had felt that her own commitment to parenthood was not powerful enough to carry her through this trauma. She saw from the relief in Turner's face that he felt the same.

'I don't have enough to do. I get bored, and lonely,' she had continued in the reasonable voice that usually worked with him. 'My old friends do their best, but they don't feel comfortable here, and they don't expect me to be comfortable with them any more. If it really bothers you, then you'd better sack Julie and let me do the house myself. I'd be perfectly happy to. In fact, I'd like it.' She half-expected this to provoke an explosion of wrath, but Turner had done one of his disarming turnarounds, and looked hurt.

'You know I only want a good life for you, for both of us. That's what I've – what *we've* worked for, all these years. Now we've got there, I want you to be able to enjoy it. You've earned it. I always said you were my queen, and that's what I want you to be.' His eyes had glazed with tears. Turner, a hard man of business who could sack an employee of twenty years' loyal service without a qualm, was easily moved by his own sentimentality. Maggie knew she was being manipulated, but was unable to continue the battle. After that, Julie called her 'Mrs Whittington' in front of Turner, and Maggie kept her distance, while he was around, anyway.

If Julie had not been a friend, and such good company, it was true that Maggie would have preferred to do her own housework. To clean a house – especially one as beautiful as this late-Georgian gem – was no hardship to her. She would have relished polishing the antique furniture and dusting the collection of porcelain;

3

washing the kitchen floor and scrubbing out the lobby would have held no terrors for her. But Julie had four children, and a husband whose idea of providing for them was to spend his days (when not on fortnightly visits to the Social Security Office to sign on) on his allotment, where he grew rows of fine cabbages, monstrous leeks and pumpkins – none of which the children would touch (other than the pumpkins at Halloween, and even then they wouldn't dream of actually *eating* them).

'Only the postman,' said Julie from her position by the sink. Maggie retrieved her coffee and they both sat down again. Maggie reached absent-mindedly for another biscuit, but fortunately it caught her eye before it reached her mouth, and she guiltily put it back.

'I'm going to have to do something,' she said gloomily. 'Turner will expect to see some results from his present. And I suppose I would like to lose a bit of weight. All my clothes are tight, and I must admit the elastic-waisted things don't look very great.'

'Couldn't you just use the swimming pool? You wouldn't have to wear an up-yer-bum leotard for that, and it's good exercise.'

'I suppose so.' Maggie looked depressed. 'But they'll expect me to do the other things as well. I'd rather just go down to the local pool, and swim there.'

'What a waste.' Julie stroked the brochure, which she had opened on the swimming-pool page. An impossibly svelte woman in a swimming costume that was very obviously not designed actually to get wet was standing on the mosaic-tiled shallow steps that led down to sparkling aquamarine water. Other incipient anorexics were posed like Japanese flower arrangements on white and gold loungers that were set between marble pillars and fringed by tropical trees in Roman style pots. 'Look, you don't have to take towels or anything, it's all provided in the changing rooms – hair driers and shampoo and perfumes and talc, specially from *Floris*. I had some *Floris* bath stuff once, it was wonderful. Just two or three drops, and the whole house smelled of it.' She spoke, as always, without envy but simply in astonishment that such things could co-exist in a world where buying a new lipstick in Superdrug was a major self-indulgence.

'You ought to go, instead of me,' Maggie said.

'Oh, don't!' Julie laughed.

Maggie looked at her with more attention. 'No, really, why not? You said it yourself, it's a dreadful waste. I know I shall never go – it's just not my sort of thing.'

'How d'you know it's *my* sort of thing? Anyway, it's in your name. They'd never let me.'

'Who's to know? They won't remember me – I was only there for half an hour, and I made about as much impression as a photo taken with the lens cover on. The card doesn't have my picture on, or anything. Just say you're me.'

'But I couldn't! And what about Mr W? What if he found out? He'd do his nut, big time.'

'He'd never know. He's busy with his new shopping mall project, never sets foot in the hotel now it's up and running. Oh, go on, Julie. I'd really like it. After all, someone's got to use the card, and why shouldn't it be you?'

Conscience fought a short battle with longing in Julie's face, and was quickly defeated.

'Well, if you're sure . . .'

'Of course I'm sure. And for goodness' sake take some of the leotards and trainers with you. It's a good thing we're more or less the same sort of size.'

'No, no.' Having given in once, Julie, was determined to make a stand. 'They're your Christmas present. I can't take them.'

'Borrow them, I meant,' said Maggie quickly. 'You must, really. He'll expect them to be used – I can say I'm keeping them there. The gold card entitles you to a personal locker, and surely it would be easier for you not to have to take them home?'

'Yes, I'm not telling our lot about this,' said Julie decisively. 'That Stephanie of mine, she'd have them off me in no time. I'll have to take them home to wash, of course.'

'Bring them here,' said Maggie. 'That way I can leave them around drying from time to time, keep Turner happy.' They grinned at one another. Keeping Turner happy, in the end, was what it was all about.

Maggie sometimes wondered whether she wasn't making a big mistake about that. Certainly her more feminist friends on the estate where they had lived before would have made it clear that she was letting the side down. The trouble was that they had been together for so long – it was twenty years since they had married – and she had married him so young. At the time, when she was a very immature twenty year old, his twenty-five years allied to his undoubted business skill and his driving ambition had made him someone to admire. Lacking ambition of her own, Maggie had seen her role as a supporting one. Now that he had achieved what he had set out to do, her place in his world had become fixed in his mind and, indeed, in hers too.

Mixed in with all of this was a kind of fear. Maggie, who was not introspective nor given to analysing her own feelings, preferred not to acknowledge its presence, but was always aware of it. It was not a physical fear – no one could ever call Turner a cruel man, either mentally or physically. It was more like the kind of unease that occasionally washed over her if she found herself in an unfamiliar place at nightfall, when shadowy corners could look romantic or sinister, according to her mood.

Maggie was aware that there were aspects of Turner that she did not like – as she did not particularly like everything about herself – and other aspects she did not even know about or understand. This did not particularly bother her; she was realistic enough to accept that total intimacy was rarely achievable or even wished for between couples. At the heart of her fear was an instinctive unease about how Turner might think or react to an unknown situation. Whether it was fear of him, or for him, or both, was impossible to say. As the years had passed the fear had grown, spreading its tendrils ever wider until it encompassed everything.

The admiration she had once felt for Turner had changed. Where once she had been dazzled, now Maggie felt a mixture of respect, love and anxiety. Respect for his achievements, and anxiety because she alone knew how many risks he had taken, was currently taking, and would undoubtedly take in the future. Risks that increased in their degree of severity in direct relation to the potential profits. It was this buccaneer attitude towards the world of business that Maggie had fallen in love with, all those years ago. In her private universe he had been every male icon she had ever needed: protecting father, encompassing lover and beloved child.

As for his feelings for her, she could only assume that Turner loved her, though in what way and at what level she could not say. The fact that they were still married was all the indication she should need. Certainly he was generous with her spending money, never querying how she used it. His gifts were frequent and opulent, and if they were not what she wanted, how many men could show a better record?

So now, if Turner wanted Maggie to slim down and glamourise her appearance a bit, she was quite willing to do it to please him. Now that the work of refurbishing and furnishing the house was done, Maggie had time on her hands. Turner seldom needed her in the office, and neither her charity work nor her social life were sufficient to use up her energy. Of her two oldest friends one had died three years earlier in an accident, and the other had moved with her husband to New Zealand. More recent friendships, as she had tried to explain to Turner, were not strong enough to survive her move. So she had little else to do, after all, and if she could regard it as a challenge, like learning a new language, it could even be fun. But she would do it in her own way, and on her own terms.

So here she was at the town's swimming pool, at two minutes to seven, waiting to go down to the changing rooms for her swim. Ahead of her the queue shifted edgily as the big hand clicked another minute forward. It all depended who was on duty; in general the young men went by the book, while the pretty girl with curly hair who Maggie had heard the others call Jane usually let them go to the changing rooms as soon as the requisite two poolside attendants were visible on the security screen.

They were all there, the regulars. Maggie checked them off in her mind, using the private names she had given them: The Keens, who were the men in the fast lane who churned up and down with style and dedication and seldom stopped to speak to anyone; Body Beautiful, always first in the queue, who spent more time flexing his gold-tanned muscles at the end of the pool than he did in swimming his flashy, splashy crawl in the fast lane; The Gossips, who swam side by side in the general lane, heads held high to protect their hair, and put all their energy into chatting; Grunter, who did a frantic breast-stroke with a Jimmy Connors' grunt every time he exhaled; The Dolphin, tall and slim as a model, her dark-skinned body cutting through the water as if it were her natural habitat, elegant even doing butterfly; Mr Aggressive, who refused to move out of anyone's way and simply swam straight through anyone foolish enough to confront him; Dogged-As-Does-It, the elegant breast-stroker in her sensible black costume and white rubber hat, who stayed in the slow lane but kept aloof from the repartee; Cheerful Charlotte, who was always in a rush but never without a smile and a greeting as she bounced past; and finally Little Bit Desperate, a plump unhappy teenager, who swam until her face was scarlet but always had old chocolate bar wrappers falling out of her swimming bag.

Maggie regarded herself as a spectator rather than a participant. Since there was an element of secrecy about her presence there – she was careful to park at the back of the building, in case Turner should happen to drive past and notice her distinctive car – she thought of herself as being invisible. She was surprised when The Dolphin, at the head of the queue, caught her eye and smiled at her. She smiled back with a lift of her spirits: The Dolphin's smile, wide and white and generous, was as warm and open as a small child's, and was bestowed as freely. At that moment the attendant picked up his hole punch to signify that he was ready to allow them in, and all attention was at once focused on him. Regulars, including Maggie, had cards entitling them to twenty-four swims that merely needed punching. Those with cash, and particularly those requiring change, were regarded with covert irritation. Two minutes, when you have dragged yourself out of a warm bed in the pitch dark of a winter morning in order to fit in a swim before work, can seem like an unreasonably long time.

Infected by the others' haste, Maggie hurried down the stairs to the recently refurbished changing rooms, or the 'Changing Village' as it was now labelled. The word 'village' signified not that it had a pub, a church, and a small shop, but merely that the rooms were unisex, with only the showers and the lavatory cubicles separated.

7

Maggie, used to the strict segregation of childhood pool visits, had at first found this worrying, but already she had established a cubicle in the corner as 'hers', and the previous week she had been amused to find herself quite put out when the locker she had become accustomed to using was taken by someone else.

Although the air in the changing room was warm, she still shivered a little as she stripped and put on her costume. Once she was in the pool, however, the warm water welcomed her, softening cold flesh and tight, goose-bumped skin. The darkness outside was easing to dreary grey, but inside the lights shone on the shaded blue of the walls, and on the brighter blue of the water itself that was already rippled and stirred by the first swimmers. Maggie pulled on her hat, more to keep her shoulder-length brown hair out of her way than to protect it, and adjusted her goggles. They were new, bought the previous day, and she had to tighten the rubber strap before they would hold comfortably to her face. She was rather proud of them, feeling that they made her look more like a proper swimmer, and she was looking forward to being able to put her face in the water instead of getting neck-ache from holding her head up like a periscope.

Putting her feet against the side, she pushed off. The difference was so startling that she continued to glide without attempting to move her arms and legs until she suddenly realised she was completely out of breath and had to raise her head for a great gasp. At once, she put her head down again, turning it from side to side as she swam a leisurely breast-stroke, feeling that she had discovered a whole new world.

The goggles, new and crystal clear, showed her exactly what was happening under the water. He own arms, for the first few strokes, were silvered with little air bubbles that fascinated her. The kicking of Mr Aggressive in the fast lane next to her created a blinding cloud of froth so that for a moment it was like swimming in a washing machine. The Dolphin, behind him, made no splash at all and her dark skin looked exotic so that everyone else, for a moment, appeared pallid and anaemic. Other swimmers, previously identified by their swimming hats or their hair, suddenly had bodies much fatter or thinner than Maggie had realised, and a range of screw kicks and sideways wriggles that made her sure that she, too, was swimming very awkwardly.

The variety of swimwear, she found, was fascinating. The younger women were sleek or businesslike in one-piece costumes, legs cut high to the hip-bones but shoulders firmly strapped. Older women went for longer cuts or even, in two cases, little ballet skirts that pulsated as they swam like the movement of jelly-fish. And the men . . . Maggie found herself eyeing up those in the tight trunks that left nothing to the imagination, and averted her eyes hurriedly.

The baggy shorts were in any case more amusing, since they frequently trapped bubbles of air that wobbled as they moved, like the deflated hump of a dromedary.

The pool was unusual in having two shallow ends, so that the deep part was in the middle. There were large SHALLOW WATER signs on the walls, which in her bleary early-morning state Maggie always read as 'Swallow Water', a command she did her best to disobey. She enjoyed the way that the blue colour intensified and lightened as she went down the pool, and could scarcely bear to do the return length on her back, as she generally did because she felt it exercised her tummy muscles more.

Around her, the other swimmers were slotting into their accustomed positions. For the early swim the pool was divided up by coloured ropes with floats. A fairly wide slow lane down one side and a narrower fast lane in the middle had signs enforcing swimming in a clockwise direction. The rest of the pool was more chaotic, but Maggie preferred it as she was certainly not fast enough for the fast lane, but felt that in the slow lane she would drift along without getting any exercise. It was all relatively decorous; there were no children, for one thing, jumping and diving and swimming widths instead of lengths. The only contretemps occurred when people swimming on their backs, like Maggie, veered into the path of someone coming the other way, and even those accidents were rare.

Maggie, therefore, was astonished when halfway down her fifth length she suddenly saw The Dolphin's slim figure beneath her, swimming along the bottom across the lanes. Maggie turned her head to watch her and, distracted, crashed headlong into someone coming the other way. Treading water she straightened her goggles, which had been knocked askew by the other person's arm, and looked round to apologise. It was, she was relieved to see, Cheerful Charlotte.

'I'm so sorry,' she gasped. 'I'm afraid I wasn't looking where I was going at all.'

'Nor was I,' the other admitted. 'I was watching Stella. What on earth is she doing?' They both turned to look at the dark girl, who had pulled herself out of the water with no apparent effort, springing from the deepest part as if jet-propelled. Stella, thought Maggie. I like that. A shooting star, no less.

'I call her The Dolphin,' she admitted. 'She swims so beautifully.'

'Yes, doesn't she? Puts us all to shame. Mind you, she's about a hundred years younger than us – well, than me, anyway.' They swam together to the end, somehow bonded by mutual curiosity, and stopped at the wall. Stella, having talked for a moment to the poolside attendants, had run through to the changing rooms. After a few moments she came back, shaking her head.

'No sign of it,' she called to the attendants. Her usual happy smile was quite gone, and she sat on the edge of the fast lane, drooping disconsolately.

'What's the matter, Stella?' Maggie's companion called across. Stella raised tragic brown eyes to her.

'I've lost my engagement ring. I suddenly thought I didn't remember taking it off, and it's not there. I've looked in my bag, but I think it must have slipped off my finger.'

'Oh, poor Stella! Not the one that was your grandmother's?'

Stella nodded, pulling her goggles down from her forehead where they had left pressure marks like frowns.

'I must find it,' she said desperately. 'I just have to find it.'

'We'll all look,' said Cheerful Charlotte. 'If it's there, we'll find it, don't you worry. You'll help, won't you – sorry, what's your name?'

'Maggie,' said Maggie breathlessly. 'Of course I'll help.'

'Great. I'm Celia,' said the other. 'Why don't you check along this side of the rope, and I'll have a word with the people in the slow bit on the other side. They're the most likely places, near the fast lane.'

'Right,' said Maggie, content to be organised. Thank goodness I've got my goggles, she thought. I'd have been no use otherwise. How lovely if I could find it.

She took as deep a breath as she could hold, and pushed gently away from the side, paddling herself slowly along as she scanned the pool floor. Through the new, unscratched lenses every tile was clear. Twice she dived down, once for a flaw in a tile that her fingers scrabbled at fruitlessly, once again in a deeper bit for something which she was fairly sure was an old plaster, but which she checked anyway. It *was* a plaster, and she would have dropped it in disgust if it had not occurred to her that someone else might be deceived by it too.

At the far end of the pool, one of The Gossips spoke to her.

'What's the matter? Are you looking for something?'

'Stella's lost her engagement ring,' Maggie explained.

'Oh, poor girl! Not her grandmother's one?'

'I believe so. I don't know much about it,' Maggie admitted.

'They've just bought a little house, and they're saving for the wedding in May,' said the second Gossip, 'so they couldn't afford very much. Stella's mother gave them the ring that had been her own mother's – Stella's grandmother, that is. It's bad enough losing your engagement ring anyway, but when it's a family thing as well . . . Come on, we'll look too.'

By the time Maggie reached the near end of the pool again, the whole character of the place had changed. As word spread, each swimmer abandoned his (or her) usual stroke and floated slowly along, scanning the bottom. Even those without goggles were feeling along the edges with their feet, or checking the gully along the wall that was formed by the projecting handrail. The usual splashes were gone, and even Grunter was silent; only low murmurs and the occasional flurry as someone dived down disturbed the hush.

A collection of hair clips and elastic bands, old plasters, metal rings from locker keys (which caused much disappointment) and even the little gold butterfly clip from the back of an earring, built up on the tiled surround. People were beginning to shake their heads – every inch of the pool had been inspected without success. Even the grilles protecting the outlets of the filtration system had been checked, in case the gaps were large enough to allow the ring to go through. Maggie had seen Stella head down in the water, her eye up against the grille while the rest of her body hung vertically above her. She looked just like a fish in a television documentary, feeding on a coral reef. As Maggie watched she let go of the grille, and swam up to cling, breathless, to the side. She pulled off her goggles and rubbed her eyes like a tearful child. Maggie swam over to her.

'If it's gone through there, they'll be able to find it. There'll be a fine filter, I'm sure they can check that.' Turner had thought of installing a pool in the garden; for weeks the house had been littered with brochures and technical specifications, so Maggie spoke with authority.

'It's gone,' said Stella helplessly. 'We'd have found it by now, if it were in the water. You've all been so kind . . .' Her voice wobbled.

'Forgive me,' said Maggie tentatively, 'but you are quite sure you had it on this morning, aren't you? Only I know how easy it is to think you've done something, when really you did it the day before.'

'Yes, I thought of that. But I know I did, because Colin saw it lying in the bathroom, and gave it to me. If only he hadn't! And one of the others said she'd noticed it catch the light as I got into the water.'

Maggie looked at the slim brown hand clutching the ledge. There were several rings on it.

'It could have been one of those she saw. Tell me, what do you normally do with it? You don't usually swim in it, do you?'

'No, never. I take it off, and put it in my purse. Only I've looked there, tipped everything out, and it's not there.'

'Could it have fallen out of the purse and into the bottom of your bag? Only we've looked everywhere else.'

'It's worth a try, I suppose.' Stella, with a kick and a pull, was out of the water. She looked back at Maggie as if hoping the older woman would go with her. Maggie moved hand over hand along the wall to the ladder, and climbed out. Together they went to the Changing Village and into the Group Change room, where Maggie

11

had never been. Stella pointed to her sports bag, hanging lopsided on a hook.

'I emptied it right out,' she said. 'I don't think it's there.'

'Let's have a look anyway.' Maggie remembered how often she had sworn something was not in her handbag, only to find the missing article caught in the lining or at the bottom of a pocket. She began to take things out one by one. Deodorant, hair conditioner, make-up bag – clear plastic, but they emptied it anyway. The purse, that held no more than the swim card and a few bits of small change for the hair driers. And . . .

'What's this?' Made of the same patterned material as the purse, but longer, and with the same snap fastening at the top.

'My glasses case. For my specs.'

Maggie felt inside through the soft fabric, and smiled. Without a word she held it out to Stella, who took it with hands that shook and opened it. She turned it upside down.

'Careful!' Maggie was just in time to catch the glasses as something small and sparkling tumbled into Stella's waiting palm.

'It's there! You've found it! Oh, thank you, thank you!' Half-laughing, half-crying, Stella flung her arms round Maggie. Maggie hugged her back and patted her soothingly, the lithe young body smooth and cold and wet as a fish to her touch, though the clasp of the strong arms was full of warmth. Stella caught her breath as she released Maggie, then sniffed and wiped her eyes.

'We must go and tell everyone. Oh dear, they'll all be so cross, I've been so stupid.'

'It'll be fine, they'll all be happy for you. I'm sure they've all done the same sort of thing themselves. Come on.'

It was rare for Maggie to find herself in charge, almost unheard of for her to take the initiative. The pleasure of having been instrumental in finding the ring was enhanced by a novel feeling of power, of being able to make something better. She felt as if she were glowing, shining with a kind of inner light that illuminated her surroundings.

Chapter Two

As Maggie had predicted, the other swimmers were delighted for Stella. It was part of the girl's charm, Maggie thought, that she had no idea how attractive people found her friendly smile, and how popular she was in consequence. Most of the men, having made jocular remarks along the lines of 'Typical – just like a woman', returned to their swimming, but the women clustered round Stella assuring her that of course they hadn't minded looking for her ring, that they were relieved it was found even if it had never truly been lost, and that they had all done something similar just the other week.

Maggie, too, found herself something of a heroine. Cheerful Charlotte – or Celia, as Maggie had to remind herself – said: 'Well done, Maggie, that was really sensible of you. I should have thought of that myself, it's just the sort of thing I'm always doing.'

'It would have turned up anyway,' Maggie pointed out. 'She'd have found it as soon as she needed to use her glasses.'

'Yes, but it wouldn't have been here – she only wears them for reading. And then we wouldn't have *known* it was found, so it wouldn't have been the same. Goodness, look at the time,' said Celia. 'I must get going, I've got to be at work. Are you coming, Maggie?'

Maggie knew she probably should do a few more lengths, but she felt cold and the effort was too great. A hot shower was much more appealing. Together they left the water and joined the group of women waiting for a shower to be free; normally people got out at different times, but today most people, like Maggie, felt the lure of hot water. The steamy air was lively with voices, mostly telling of their own mislaid and suddenly found objects. As they collected their clothes from the lockers afterwards Maggie and Celia were still talking.

'Come in the Group Changing, why don't you? Those cubicles are so small, I always bang my elbows when I'm trying to get dressed. You're not shy, are you? We're all made the same, more or less.'

'Some of us rather more than less,' said Maggie.

'Oh, nonsense. Your figure's better than mine. My boobs are practically pimples, and my bum's too flat.' Maggie, eyeing Celia's enviably trim shape, wondered whether any woman was ever satisfied with her own appearance.

'What do you do? You said you had to get to work.'

'I teach part-time in the local Sixth Form College. French and Spanish. It used to be full-time, but wouldn't you know it, they're cutting back, and naturally languages was one of the things they're economising on, in spite of the EU. You?'

'I'm not working at the moment.' Maggie was slightly ashamed of her answer, in the face of Celia's energy.

'Well, it's not easy, is it?' Celia was tactful. 'I was lucky to get mine, even though it's gone part-time. As a matter of fact, I don't really mind from my point of view, as it gives me more time for other things. It's the kids I care about. I just don't feel they're getting a fair deal.'

Brisk as ever, she was wriggling into her clothes as she spoke. By the time Maggie was dressed, Celia had put on her make-up, packed up her things and was fishing for a coin for the hair drier. Maggie, who didn't bother with make-up until she got home, was ready to leave at the same time, and they walked out to the car park together. They said goodbye and Maggie saw Celia driving out in a shiny Peugeot Estate as she herself was getting into her little Morris.

There had been trouble with Turner over the Morris. He had recently bought her a spanking new Range Rover, the latest in a succession of increasingly expensive vehicles that he had felt appropriate to his rising status.

'Now, you can't complain that *this* is impractical,' he had said triumphantly, referring to Maggie's discomfort over a sports car that had been so low-slung she had found it almost impossible to get in and out of the thing. 'Take you anywhere, this will. Rough tracks, the lot. Bags of room. And high. You can see into people's gardens.' Maggie had had to smile, remembering how she had once confessed to him that she liked to travel on the top deck of buses, for that very reason. She felt a bit of a fraud, however, in the Range Rover. A vehicle like that should contain children, dogs, Wellingtons and perhaps a selection of hard hats and a bridle or two. Maggie, who only really used it for shopping trips, found it heavy on petrol and awkward to park, and soon returned to the Morris.

She loved her little car. She had bought it herself, many years earlier, with her first earnings as a secretary. It had been a classic 'one elderly lady driver' car – actually true, in this case – and Maggie had been enchanted by it; she had taken pride in keeping the paintwork polished, and the leather seats smooth and gleaming. She had never been able to part with it, and had persuaded Turner that it was a collector's item. Fortunately, enough people had admired it in his hearing for him to accept that such a car carried a certain *chic*. He continued to buy her what he considered to be more suitable vehicles, but Maggie was glad to come to the pool in the Morris. She had no wish to appear as 'Range Rover Woman' in someone else's list of nicknames.

At home, Maggie changed out of the tracksuit that was convenient for going to the pool, and put on a new (and expensive) suit and a carefully applied layer of make-up. Turner was taking potential investors to view the site of his new out-of-town shopping mall, and had said he might bring them back for lunch.

'Nothing formal – we'll just drop in if we're passing,' he had said with a wink. Maggie knew what this meant; although no table should be laid or meal too obviously prepared, there should still be something quick but impressive to be brought out – by Julie, naturally – and she herself should be looking smart. She went downstairs to prepare salads and check that there was enough bread to go with the smoked salmon, the *foie gras* and the selection of excellent cheeses, reflecting as she did so that to present an appearance of casual elegance was almost more work than preparing a formal three course meal.

Fortunately, there was plenty of food, because at half past one, when she had just begun to hope that they might not turn up after all, four large cars rolled into the sweep of the drive. Maggie greeted Turner with appropriate surprise and pleasure, and welcomed his guests, relieved to see that they were all men. Businesswomen in their own right were fine – they were so busy proving they were as good as their competitors that they never tried to help, but accompanying wives usually insisted on coming to the kitchen and getting in the way.

The visitors were all very cheerful, and Maggie guessed that their late arrival was because they had visited Turner's hotel for the Whisky Mac he invariably offered on cold days. The thought reminded her that there would be drivers, and she sent Julie out to invite them in for their share of the goodies. Everything was well under control, and there was no excuse for lingering in the kitchen. Pulling in her stomach – really, this skirt *did* feel looser, perhaps the swimming was doing the trick? – she went to the drawing room.

As she had expected, Turner was pouring more drinks – champagne, this time – and the group had gravitated naturally in front of the large open fire where big logs crackled and scented the room. Inevitably, since the whole focus of the room's decoration was designed to lead the eye to it, one of the men remarked on the painting displayed over the marble mantelpiece.

'It's the love of Turner's life,' said Maggie. 'He bought it several years ago. He likes to pretend it's a hedge against inflation, but I suspect we'd have to be begging on the streets before he'd sell it, and even then . . .' She gave a rueful smile that raised the expected laugh.

'Well, I had to have it,' said Turner. 'After all, it's got my name on it!' This time the laughter, primed by Maggie's earlier sally, was louder. Maggie reflected that it was fortunate that Turner's painting style was so immediately recognisable even to the least artistic.

'It's an unusual Christian name.' One of the visitors sipped his champagne with a nod of approval for its quality. 'Were your parents interested in painting?'

'Unfortunately not. It was horses that my father loved.' Turner never mentioned that it was this love of horses, or rather on betting on the more three-legged of the breed, that had brought his father to unemployed homelessness and his mother to an early grave. 'It's what they called me at school. "Turn Again, Whittington", you see – shortened to "Turner". Lucky, really, it's quite a good name. They started by calling me Dick, and worse, but I soon put a stop to that.' One look at him was enough to see that he would be capable of stopping most things he didn't like. He was neither tall nor heavily muscular, but his well-built frame was fizzing with energy and enthusiasm. His movements were controlled, without unnecessary gestures. His curly hair, dark brown beginning to be attractively flecked with grey, was kept trimmed short and below it, his face had a rugged, outdoor look. His eyes were very bright and direct, and though he could not have been called handsome, his face was one that it was easy to like. He had the knack of always appearing interested in what people were saying, and the ability to hide his own thoughts without appearing wooden.

The lunch went on a long time. Walking in the cold at the site had sharpened the men's appetites, and the champagne on top of Whisky Macs made them garrulous. Maggie's pâté, salmon and cheeses were much appreciated.

'I did think of giving you lunch at the hotel, but there's nothing like a bit of home cooking, is there?' Turner raised his glass, now filled with red wine, to Maggie and the guests followed suit. Maggie smiled back, wishing she hadn't drunk any champagne, which didn't agree with her at the best of times, and was particularly disastrous in the middle of the day. Her face felt stiff, and the effort to hold the smile was making it ache. It was a relief when, after lingering over coffee and cigars, the visitors all finally left and Maggie was able to kick off her shoes and pad into the kitchen, where Julie had long since finished the washing up. She normally left at lunchtime – she and Maggie quite often had a snack together first – but today had stayed on, as Turner liked her to do, to help. The kitchen was immaculate, and Julie had also worked her way through a pile of ironing.

'You shouldn't have worried about that,' said Maggie, stacking the coffee cups in the dishwasher.

'It's got to be done some time,' Julie pointed out, 'and you know me, I can't bear to be doing nothing. Anyway, you're paying me a fortune to be here.'

Maggie thought, not for the first time, how very lucky she was to have Julie. Turner, as a matter of course, expected anyone he was employing to work at top speed every minute he was paying them as, to be fair, he had always done himself; however Maggie knew that many people would have regarded their work as finished once the lunch was cleared away, and would have sat down with a cup of tea or coffee.

'Well, leave that now, and let's have a cup of tea. Unless you'd rather have champagne? There's an open bottle hardly touched. Or have you got to get back to the kids?'

'Tea'd be lovely. Champagne gives me hiccups. No, the kids'll be fine. Steph said she'd be home and make them some tea.'

'That's nice of her.' Unusually so, Maggie didn't say. Stephanie, at fourteen, was beginning to rebel from her responsibilities as the eldest.

'Yes, well.' Julie looked shamefaced, 'I said that as I'd be getting extra money for doing today, she could have some of it towards that pair of trainers she's been wanting.'

'Fair enough,' said Maggie mildly.

'You don't think that's bribery?'

'Not really. They say it's better to reward good behaviour than punish bad, don't they?'

'No taste in nothing, my granny used to say. Anyway, I really wanted to tell you about the Spa; we never got round to it this morning.'

'The Spa? Oh, the Health and Beauty thing. Are you enjoying it?'

'Enjoying it?' Julie's voice rose in a screech. 'I can't believe you don't want to go there. It's . . . it's *heaven*! I can hardly bear to leave it to go home – I've been late back twice. *Surely* you want to use it!'

'Not really. I'm rather enjoying going down to the local pool in the mornings. The people are really nice, very friendly, and I think I've lost a bit of weight already.'

'Yes, I believe you have.' Julie put her head on one side and considered Maggie. 'You look different. Happier. Not that you didn't look good before, but you know . . .'

'I know. And I do feel happier, somehow. There was a funny thing at the pool this morning . . .' Maggie recounted the story of the lost engagement ring. 'And it was all so friendly,' she concluded.

'Good for you, to meet a few more people – though I still don't see why you couldn't have met them at the Spa. Honestly, they're really nice, and they're not all model types by any means. Still, if you're making some friends . . .' Julie stopped out of delicacy, Maggie knew. Although she might complain constantly about her four children, and seldom mentioned them in any but critical terms, Maggie knew this hid enormous pride and satisfaction in her family, and that Julie regarded Maggie's own life, however luxurious and easy in practical terms, as empty and meaningless.

There had been very few times when Maggie had felt the same. In the past, when they had been less wealthy and had lived on a pleasant estate in a town about twenty miles away from their present home, she had felt herself to be increasingly isolated as one friend after another became pregnant and started a family. She was Godmother to four of them, and appreciated the generosity behind this sharing gesture, but as conversations revolved more and more round teething, and potty training, and later around schools, she had inevitably found herself slightly excluded. Working for Turner had been a welcome distraction, but she had been glad when they moved away.

Maggie felt slightly ambivalent about her childlessness. There were times when the sight of a mother cradling her baby made her want to dissolve into tears of self-pity. Then again, someone's toddler having a full-blown tantrum in the supermarket queue inspired relief that she didn't have to cope with that. At Christmastime she and Turner frequently went away to somewhere exotic. Maggie knew that at her age, the attack of Biological Clock anxiety was to be expected, but so far she had reached forty without feeling any insatiable urge to be pregnant before it was too late. Indeed, the arrival of her period each month was accompanied by a feeling of relief – they had long since ceased to take any contraceptive precautions. Maggie, who regarded herself as a passive rather than an active member of the human race, secretly felt that she was incapable of giving a child the kind of care she thought it needed, and would deserve. Turner, like her an only child, seemed similarly unaffected. Certainly he showed no signs of wishing to found a dynasty: there was no frantic urge to add '& Son' to his letterhead.

Maggie supposed that neither of them had enjoyed the kind of childhood that you would want to inflict on anyone else. Turner's parents had fought constantly. His mother's never-ending nagging about his father's betting and drinking was only too understandable, but its effect had been to drive him to the very places she hated as he took refuge in pub or betting shop from her vitriolic abuse. She had left school at fifteen, an intelligent girl frustrated by what was then the unknown condition of dyslexia, and she bitterly resented the fact that Turner's father had gone to grammar school and then failed to use the advantages his education should have conferred. One get-rich-quick scheme after another floated up like a hot air

18

balloon and exploded or simply vanished in a little puff of smoke, and the life of luxury he had promised her turned out to be no more than a succession of council flats and a cleaning job.

Turner's parents died soon after he and Maggie had married, his mother of a stroke and his father after a fall (when drunk). There had certainly never been any pressure from them to produce grandchildren. The first few years of that marriage had been so busy, both of them working together to build Turner's business, that for Maggie pregnancy would have been a disaster. Later on, when things were easier, the expected pregnancy never happened. By the time Maggie realised that there might be a problem, their pattern of life was so established and so pleasant that she had been unable to feel too much urgency.

Then Turner had seen this house, the kind of dream home he had always wanted, and they had moved. Furbishing the new house had occupied her energies for some time, but now that was done she was slightly at a loss. There was no doubt that having children, apart from filling one's mind, heart and time, gave opportunities for meeting new people. Maggie had never been a churchgoer, nor was she someone who liked to join things. The usual advice to the lonely – 'Go to evening classes' – was impossible for her. Turner relied on her to be there in the evening so that he could go over the day's events with her. Not that he wanted her advice, rather the contrary; he often became irritable if she suggested anything. It was simply that he found it helpful to use her as a sounding board. The very act of putting the day into words for her clarified his mind, so that things made connections and fell into place.

Maggie's old friends, beside being rather too far away for casual visiting, were uncomfortable in her new house. They had all come to see it, had made all the right appreciative noises, but Maggie noticed that they had stopped inviting her to visit them, although she was freer than they to take days out. She understood it, though she regretted it. She was not unhappy, and had not been conscious of being particularly lonely, but it was true that being accepted as part of the group at the pool that morning had been very pleasant.

Maggie's life, up to now, had in any case been relatively solitary. So much of her social life had been tied up with Turner's business, and she had learned very early on that it was better not to allow any but a superficial friendship to grow in that shifting world. The friends on the estate had been the friends of propinquity rather than deep choice, and she had no old childhood or schoolday friends.

The only child of elderly parents, she had always felt faintly apologetic about her existence. They had said, very often, how astonished they had been when she had come along, and although it was never spoken or even implied in the tone of voice, she had felt that her parents' astonishment had held more dismay than delight. They had always been kind to her, but it was with the kindness of duty rather than of love. Maggie's life with them had been a kind of endless apology; she had felt herself so peripheral to their relationship that she was like a bit of space debris, held in an orbit so distant from their planet that only the weak remnants of gravitational pull stopped her from drifting off altogether.

Maggie's father had died, quite suddenly and without any warning symptoms, just after her fifteenth birthday. She had come home from school to an empty house, not in itself a remarkable thing but unusual because the table in the kitchen still held the evidence of her mother's half-eaten lunch. The sight of a cold pork chop, with much of the meat still untouched, abandoned with its accompanying portions of mashed potato and sprouts in a layer of congealed gravy, had brought Maggie up short in the kitchen doorway. Vivid memories of rationing during what Maggie's mother always referred to as THE WAR – previous and subsequent conflicts having appeared, to her, as no more than minor skirmishes – ensured that no scrap of food was ever left on a plate to be wasted. Nor, in all her fifteen years, had Maggie ever known her mother to leave the house without ensuring that every room was spotlessly clean and tidy.

Maggie had cleared and wiped the table, covering the food before putting it in the fridge and washing up everything else, then had settled as usual in her room to do her homework. For once she had neither switched on the transistor radio (kept at low volume on her desk), nor shut the bedroom door to prevent any other escape of sound. Two hours later, when the homework was finished and the daylight was beginning to fade, Maggie had finally heard what she had been listening for, the sound of a key in the front-door lock. Her mother told her that her father had collapsed at work from a heart attack. He had been rushed to hospital, but in spite of their efforts had been pronounced dead a few hours later. It had not occurred to Maggie's mother to telephone the school so that Maggie could be there.

After her husband's death, Maggie's mother had dwindled, almost overnight, into a querulous old woman. She resisted any attempt to comfort her as if it were an insult, and displayed fierce resentment at any appearance of cheerfulness in others. She was by turns angry and bewildered, and when she was diagnosed with cancer eighteen months later seemed more relieved than frightened. She endured an operation and underwent all the subsequent treatments with the air of one humouring a helpful child, but showed no real interest in fighting the disease. Its rapid spread surprised her doctors, but not Maggie, who knew that her mother was merely living through the time, rather as she had through

20

Maggie's own early childhood, until she could be alone with Maggie's father again.

Maggie left school an orphan, relatively secure financially but with poor A-level grades because she had been preoccupied with her mother's illness throughout the course. To go to university seemed pointless. She knew that they would make allowances for the grades, but she herself felt so old, compared to those others she saw leaving, wide-eyed, for the big adventure of campus life. Maggie thought that university would be a postponement of adult life, and since childhood had not seemed to her to be a particularly enjoyable state she felt that she might as well move on straight away. She took a secretarial job with a firm of architects, which was how she first met Turner.

Turner was the first man to show any interest in her as a woman. There had been dates, but the young men who invited her to the pub or the cinema never repeated their invitations, and Maggie did not regret it. None of them seemed to her to be properly grown-up. Their conversation was still full of school and university, of games of football or rugby, of cars and holidays and tales of drinking bouts. They regarded their jobs as the means to achieve more of the same, and they made it clear that they thought Maggie dull company.

Maggie had been torn between envying the simplicity of their world-view and dismay that she herself seemed to be so dissimilar from her peers. She felt, increasingly, that she had been born in the wrong time, the wrong place, or perhaps even the wrong universe. With the self-consciousness of her youth, she felt that everyone else had learned some secret, mastered some kind of lesson, that she herself had failed even to notice. It did not seem to her that she could alter herself, since she had no idea of how she should be, and it never occurred to her that she could do anything to change the world.

Unconsciously, she had seen herself (and still did) as a two-dimensional being, all but invisible from some angles and distorted from others. Her ability to influence others, which appeared to her as the shadow she cast, was similarly affected. Peter Pan, that arch-manipulator, could detach his shadow, an apt metaphor for his separation from the everyday world. Maggie, though inexorably fastened to hers, perceived it as scarcely more than a thin line, an attenuated thread that revealed nothing of her actual shape.

Then she had met Turner. He, by contrast with the other young men and also with her, had been burning with energy and ambition. When he realised that Maggie was genuinely interested in what he had to say, the words poured out of him. His plans, his hopes, his successes and his failures, all were presented for her consideration. He was realistic, for all his enthusiasm, and Maggie had found it all more romantic than any amount of flowers and candles. He had not attempted to hide the fact that he was interested in her little nest-egg of capital – she had sold her parents' house without any sentimental regrets, and invested what was left after buying a small flat.

Maggie did not find him mercenary – but respected his practicality and his honesty. She never regretted using her nest-egg to help fund his first big building project, and he had been both scrupulous and generous in repaying her with interest. He paid her well for the work she did for him, too. Maggie knew that she had only to express the mildest wish for something for him to buy it for her, funds permitting. She also knew that he regarded money spent on her appearance and on that of the house as a legitimate business expense.

'Better be getting back, I s'pose,' said Julie reluctantly, breaking into Maggie's reverie. 'Mustn't put too much onto Steph – she'll be demanding another fiver off me, if I'm not careful.'

'Will you take the rest of the pâté back? Turner doesn't really like it, and I mustn't undo all the good of the swimming by eating it. Will your lot touch it?'

'Not if I tell them what it is. I'll say it's meat paste, or something. You know what Tim's like about liver. And mushrooms, come to that.'

'Mushrooms?'

'There's truffles in it,' Julie pointed out. 'Criminal, really, wasting it on a bunch of ungrateful brats. Are you sure you can't use it?'

'Positive. I'll put it in a container for you. Did you come in the car?' Julie and her husband owned an ancient Ford, which she usually only used when the weather was really bad.

'No, my bike. I've been using it more, recently, since I got that helmet. They love it down the Spa.'

'You ride it there? Doesn't that make it all rather exhausting, if you're exercising when you get there?'

'No, it's great. Besides, I don't like to turn up in the old rattletrap, not when I'm supposed to be you. They'd smell a whole sewer full of rats then. No, I sail in on the bike and they reckon I'm really cool, doing my bit for the environment, keeping extra fit, everything. In fact, there's a couple of others have taken to doing it. I reckon I've started a trend!'

'Good for you. And of course you'll have to keep going for ever, now. I can't possibly turn up on a bicycle, I'm hopelessly wobbly. I don't think I ever felt safe after they took the stabilisers off, and as for giving hand signals . . .' Maggie shuddered.

'Nonsense. Everyone can ride a bike, you just want practice. It's as easy as falling off a . . . well, dead easy, anyway. I'd better go before I tie myself even more into knots. Bye, see you tomorrow!'

The door closed behind Julie, and Maggie was alone in the house. She wandered through to the drawing room, where she twitched the cushions straight and emptied a cigar-butt-filled ashtray into the embers in the grate. The fire was dying down and she added more logs – Turner liked to come home to a log fire in the winter. Maggie suspected that he liked the excuse to stand in front of it, admiring his Turner painting. The after-effects of the champagne were making her feel sleepy, and she thought that she might take a nap on the sofa – there was plenty of time before she needed to start supper. Or rather dinner, she reminded herself. Turner was busy re-modelling himself to fit his surroundings.

She had noticed him doing it before; he had an almost chameleon-like ability to take on the mannerisms of people he was with. It looked like snobbery, but Maggie thought it was less conscious than that. It was more that he felt uncomfortable being different. He made no attempt to change or hide the kind of person he was, merely adding a veneer of language and behaviour to the basic Turner.

Maggie lay down on the sofa, and tucked her feet under a cushion. This skirt is definitely looser, she thought sleepily. I couldn't have done this a few weeks ago, not without undoing the waist-band.

She felt warm and happy. Julie was enjoying the Spa, she herself was enjoying swimming at the pool, and Turner's lunch had gone well. Nevertheless, there was something, some little disquiet niggling at her mind. What was it? She fought sleep off until it came back to her. Turner had introduced her to the prospective investors as 'my wife, Margot'. Not Maggie, but Margot. She woke up again.

I don't feel like a Margot, she thought. Margot is tall and slim and elegant, she speaks fluent French and probably rides, hunts with the local pack, even. I'm Maggie, just plain Margaret.

She had never had strong feelings about her name, as some people did. She had been called after her father's mother, who had died a few months after her son's sudden demise. They had shortened the Margaret to Maggie to avoid confusion. No, Maggie had never really given a thought to her name. She was Maggie, and that was that.

Margot, she thought as waves of sleep came rolling back like sea fog. I suppose it's not too bad. It makes me think of Margarine. I always prefer to say that with a soft G, so perhaps I could be Margery? But didn't someone tell me you were supposed to say it with a hard G, because the man who invented it named it after his wife? And her name was Margaret, so if they'd called *her* Maggie

23

we might all be talking about Maggierine, and I wonder how Mrs Thatcher would have liked that . . .?

She just had time to recognise that her mind had taken on that free-fall that meant she was about to be asleep, before she slept.

Chapter Three

With each day that passed, Maggie became more at home at the pool, more a member of the group. When she arrived in the morning there would be cries of 'Morning, Maggie!' from those already in the queue. She had to set her mind to learning their names in return, but although to their faces she called them Rob, or Sue, or Debbie, most of them were still more real in her mind as their nicknames. Grunter, who swam in the fast lane, turned out to be married to Lisa who swam a neat breast-stroke in the general section, and Maggie couldn't help thinking of her as 'Mrs Grunter'.

Inevitably, it was the people in her own part of the pool that she got to know the best. The fast lane was a world of its own, where the young men timed their lengths and took sips of isotronic drinks, or battled to prove who was the fastest or had the most stamina. The slow lane, though very sociable, was isolated by being on the other side of the fast lane – rather like knowing someone who lived quite near but on the opposite side of a motorway, Maggie thought.

Of the people in the general lane, it was Celia who had become the nearest to a proper friend, so much so that Maggie had quite forgotten ever calling her Cheerful Charlotte. Three years younger than Maggie in age, she seemed in some ways ten years older. Not in her looks or in her manner, for she had the energy, and the skin, of a twenty-five-year-old, but simply in experience. For the first time Maggie began to regret that she hadn't gone to university. Celia's casually dropped remarks about what she had learned there, both educationally and socially, were occasionally quite startling.

Like Maggie she had married relatively young, having met her husband at university. They, too, had struggled through the early years to relative prosperity now: Celia's husband had trained as a Chartered Surveyor, and was now employed by the Town Council. The difference was that they had travelled. As students they had back-packed round Europe and the States; after taking their degrees and getting married they had, to both their families' despair, taken a year to make their way overland to India, reasoning that if they waited until they could afford it they would no longer be young enough to be prepared to travel rough and camp out.

'It was wonderful,' Celia said, pausing as she briskly dried her legs and feet. Her face, as she remembered, was dreamy. 'I couldn't do it now, of course. I'm too hooked on my creature comforts. I couldn't do without a shower, and a proper bed, and proper loo paper. When we were in the wilds of Turkey, and we both had the runs, we completely ran out of loo paper and had to use fig leaves. Awful! Stiff, and sort of shiny! But we survived.'

'It gives you a whole new slant on Adam and Eve,' said Maggie.

'Doesn't it just! Still, I'm glad we did it when we could. All those trips, so many memories. And then the boys came along, and of course that put an end to it. Nothing but buckets and spades to come for a few years yet.' Celia had twin sons, William and Edward. They were so alike that Celia admitted that even her husband sometimes had trouble telling who was who.

'It's all right if they're together, because then you can see that Will's hair is a tiny shade darker, and Ed's is a bit curlier. But when they're apart, even I have to look carefully. It drives their teachers mad.'

'Do they make the most of it? It must be very tempting.'

'Of course they do, the little devils.' Celia, like Julie, masked her adoration behind an exterior of apparent despair. 'The boys just run rings round them. Nothing really serious, thank goodness, just mischief, but we're forever getting notes at home begging us to get their hair cut differently, or put them in different coloured shirts, or something. Trouble is, if it's clothes they swop them round all the time to keep everyone guessing, and when I tried a different haircut they both went off and had their heads practically shaved. That *did* make me cross. My mother-in-law was coming to stay, and she did nothing but go on and on about how they looked like convicts, and had they picked up ringworm or nits, and how it was a pity I couldn't control them better, and how ashamed I must feel. So then, of course, I said I wasn't ashamed in the slightest, and that I thought their hair looked great, which I didn't at all, but they heard me so it made it impossible to tell them off when the old bat had gone.'

'Bit of a problem, is she?' Maggie, with no in-laws or parents of her own, was fascinated by other people's.

'You can say that again. I call her the Mugger-in-Law, or at least I used to before the boys got old enough to start copying me. That's mugger like the Indian alligator – or is it a crocodile? I never know. Anyway, not the kind of mugger that hits you over the head and steals your handbag, though I wouldn't actually put it past her. The only good thing about her is that she lives in Spain, so at least she's not turning up on the doorstep every five minutes. The trouble is, when she does come she comes for weeks, to justify the expense of the flight. I can't tell you how I dread it.'

26

'What about your father-in-law?'

'Oh, she killed him off years ago. That's why she moved to Spain. Phil always says she was too mean to spend the money on an electric blanket, so once she hadn't got his Dad to warm her feet on she had to go and live somewhere hot.'

'Do you get holidays out there? Where in Spain is she?'

'Near Alicante. Costa Geriatrica, they call it, it's full of old dears whooping it up on their pensions. No, we don't go much. She's in a one-bedroom flat, so there isn't room for us even if she wanted us, which she doesn't. One time we rented a flat for a couple of weeks, but it was a disaster. She'd saved up a lot of jobs that she wanted Phil to do, and shopping trips to other towns. The boys were hot and bored and made it clear they hated it. The people at the club made a frightful fuss of them when we went there, and she didn't like that either. I think the boys got more attention than she'd ever had, and it rankled. Ma-in-law was livid, because she had at least to pretend to be fond of the little monsters. She took it out on me, and then of course Phil went for her, and it all became very tight-lipped for the rest of the time. We haven't been since. The visits to us are bad enough.'

Maggie felt that she was scarcely contributing to the exchange of information.

'My father-in-law was a drinker and a gambler,' she offered hopefully. 'He died years ago, soon after we married.'

'Just as well, by the sound of it. I hope he didn't pass it on. Oh sorry, that was a bit over the top. I mean, I'm not being nosy or anything.'

She was obviously dying to know, and Maggie laughed.

'No, it's fine – I've got nothing to hide! Turner does drink, but not much and mostly socially, and he certainly doesn't gamble.' She pulled herself up, realising that it wasn't really true at all. Turner's whole business life was a gamble. 'At least,' she amended, 'not on horses. It's funny, I'd always thought that his father had given him a horror of gambling. Well, it did of that kind of gambling, but I suppose there's something there in the blood . . .'

'Taking risks? It's in most men's blood, I've always thought.'

'Perhaps. I don't know.'

'What does he do?'

'He's in the building trade.' Maggie turned away on the pretext of looking for her towel, to hide her face. It wasn't that she was ashamed of Turner or what he did – far from it, she was proud of his achievements, and the day when the new hotel had opened had been wonderful. It was just that it was so nice to be, as before, just Maggie Whittington, rather than the wife of millionaire businessman Turner Whittington.

Celia noticed nothing.

27

'That's a good thing to be in at the moment, isn't it? I know the past few years have been pretty tough – how did he find it?'

'Hard work,' said Maggie truthfully. 'But he likes that. His idea of hell is a holiday on a beach with nothing to do but laze about in the sun! We tried it once. He started by clearing the whole beach of rubbish, and when he'd got that under control he made a huge sandcastle, a really complicated one, had every kid within a half-mile radius wanting to help him. He got very cross, because they didn't do the building work up to his standards. He had to teach them how to mix the sand and water to the proper consistency. They loved it.'

'Sounds fun.'

'Yes, but it wasn't enough, he was still bored out of his mind.'

'Not enough risks, with sandcastles.'

'D'you know, you could be right.' Maggie was much struck. 'I hadn't thought of that before.'

It was surprising, Maggie thought, how well you got to know people in the small conversations between swimming, and the slightly longer ones in the shower and the changing room. It was a curious relationship – intimate, as was bound to happen when they were all in various degrees of nakedness most of the time – and yet limited. It was rare, for instance, to know anyone's surname; first names were the rule. Nor, generally, did one learn where people lived, although their jobs were generally known. Husbands and children were much discussed, but they remained faceless beings. No one brought photos to the pool, they were too vulnerable to wet.

Of Stella The Dolphin, for instance, Maggie knew that she was engaged to Colin who played football and cricket but whose job had never been mentioned. She knew that he liked to cook, as Stella did, and that they often went to London to buy the ingredients for the Afro-Caribbean food of her childhood. For some while Maggie assumed, rather foolishly, that he was black, and was ashamed with herself when from a chance remark she learned that he had blond hair and blue eyes. She didn't even know what job Stella did, because what they mostly talked about was The Wedding.

Maggie had been delighted to hear that this was to be a full, formal event. She had already been imagining how beautiful Stella would look with a traditional white dress and veil contrasting with her skin that was the colour of expensive milk chocolate.

'It's crazy really,' Stella admitted. 'All that money just for one day.'

'I'm sure nobody grudges it,' said Maggie. 'I think it's lovely, if it's what you want. Not that there's anything wrong with *not* having a white wedding, of course, but I know if I had a daughter, I'd be thrilled to bits if she decided to do it.'

Stella's smile flashed out.

'My mum's thrilled to bits, too. Of course, we're not letting them pay for it – at least, only a little bit. It wouldn't be fair, with three more sisters at home. Colin's parents are helping the same amount, and we're working to get the rest together. We found this great place – you can pay your money in bit by bit, as you get it, and they organise the whole thing. You choose the dresses, and the flowers and the cake and everything for the reception, right at the beginning, and they tell you how much a month you need to put in, and by the end it's all there for you.'

'Sounds good,' said Maggie, with a small quiver of disquiet. 'Where is it?'

'That new hotel, The Grange,' said Stella happily. 'You have the reception there. It's lovely, have you seen it? There's a big room opening onto the garden, with a terrace where you can have drinks and things if the weather's good, only if it isn't it doesn't matter, because there's so much room indoors. Do you know, when they plant up the big pots on the terrace, they use mostly foliage and things with white flowers, then they just put in whatever colour you're having on the actual day, so it goes with the flowers inside. Isn't that a brilliant idea?'

'Brilliant,' said Maggie hollowly. It had been her idea. In fact, the whole wedding package had been her creation. They had offered it at discounted rates, at the start, and as a result it was losing a fair bit of money. Turner had frowned over the figures only last week, and said that he wasn't sure they were going to get enough business, at the realistic rate, to make it worthwhile.

'Yes, I'm having red,' enthused Stella. 'Not a bright red, but that really deep colour you get in roses, and those dark lilies. That's what they're going to put in the planters – the lilies, and in the indoor flowers too, so it'll smell lovely.'

'And look lovely too. I'm glad you're not going for the pale colours, though they're always pretty, but you can take something dramatic,' said Celia. 'I had pale pink, and it was fine except that practically everyone else I knew had the same. In fact, we shared the bridesmaid's dresses round, two other friends and I, so it worked out pretty well until someone spilled red wine down one of them.'

It'll be fine, Maggie reassured herself. And I can keep an eye on it, too, make sure nothing goes wrong. She was thinking about it as she swam along, and was startled when she crashed into a body moving fast in the other direction. She took in a gasp of air and water, and choked as she threshed to tread water in the deep centre of the pool.

'Sorry, Maggie. My fault, I was miles away.' It was Celia, her face red with effort, grasping Maggie's arm to support her as she caught her breath. Maggie coughed, and shook her head.

'So was I.' She coughed again. 'Bother.'

'It burns in your chest, doesn't it?' said Celia sympathetically. 'Come to the end, and we'll both have a break for a couple of minutes. I could do with one too, I'm boiling.'

'Yes, you do look hot.' They swam to the far shallow end.

'I am, but I didn't mean that. I'm boiling inside, that's why I was swimming so fast, I was trying to burn it off.'

'What's the matter?'

'My bloody mother-in-law. She rang up last night, and announced that she's giving us the pleasure of her company for a month. A month! Arriving on Tuesday. It's a disaster.'

'Tuesday? You mean, like in five days' time? That's not much notice.'

'You can say that again. And what's really so maddening is that she's been planning it for weeks, and waited until now to spring it on us. Apparently they've got the decorators in her block, doing up all the paintwork on the stairs and so on inside, and the outside of all the windows. Last time it was done they just gave them a quick lick, but this time they've got to strip right back to the frames, so it means keeping the windows open for days and having men up and down scaffolding peering in. And of course, the old bag's convinced that every man in Spain is lusting to view her English Rose body, so she's refusing to stay in her flat until they've finished. Four weeks, and probably longer. I mean, when did you ever know workmen who finished a job like that on time?'

Maggie thought privately that Turner always made sure that his did, but of course this wasn't something she could tell Celia, nor would it have helped if she did.

'What a bore. Is she going to spend the whole time with you?'

'Yes. She's fallen out with all her old friends because she kept on at them about how stupid they are to stay here, and how much better life is in Spain. And my sister-in-law, Phil's brother's wife in Nottingham, refuses to have anything to do with her since she was so rude to her parents at their wedding, and told Phil's brother that if he didn't divorce her at once she'd cut him out of her will.'

'Goodness! She does sound awful!'

'Well, she certainly believes in plain speaking – but only when she's doing it. I once tried giving her a taste of her own medicine, and practically started World War Three. It sent her blood pressure soaring, and she kept telling me if she had a stroke it'd be my fault, and I had visions of having to spend the rest of my life nursing her, so in the end it seemed easier to back down and grovel.' Celia shivered. She was beginning to cool off, and even in the warm air it was cold standing still. She crouched down in the water, and floated her legs out behind her to kick. Maggie did the same, so that their heads were both on a level with their hands on the ledge.

30

'You poor thing. And to think I've often regretted not having any parents-in-law.'

'Well, they don't have to be like that. My parents adore Phil, think the sun shines out of him and he can do no wrong, and I've got several friends who get on really well with their mothers-in-law. I always tell myself that Phil's so super it's worth putting up with his mother for a few weeks every year. It's just that this is an extra visit, and it couldn't have come at a worse time. My cleaning lady is going into hospital to have something done to her foot – not anything very big, but she won't be able to stand or walk on it for several weeks, so she'll be completely out of action. And guess which day she goes into hospital?'

'Monday?'

'Of course. Somebody up there hates me. We've got the second-year kids at college about to do their Mocks, and needing all the help we can give them. I'd arranged to take on a few extra classes at home, out of school hours, just to give them a bit more practice in conversation. Not a hope of doing that now.'

'Couldn't she help out? Spanish conversation, for instance? Make her feel useful?'

Celia laughed so much she had to stop kicking for a moment. 'Spanish? Not a chance. She doesn't speak a word.'

'How does she manage?'

'Oh, she hardly ever talks to anyone local. She shops in a supermarket, and if she has to say anything she just shouts it slowly. Of course, they all speak such good English, it puts us to shame. And the thing is, I wasn't charging any fees, it was just a special thing for the students, because I want them to do well. After all, if they don't, it's my job that's on the line, so it's worth it really. Only she's not going to see it like that. What she'll see is that the house is a tip, the meals all come out of the microwave, and I'm neglecting my husband and sons to do a pointless job that I'm not even properly paid for.'

Maggie had never known Celia to sound so depressed.

'There must be something we can do. Can't you find another cleaning lady, just someone temporary?'

'I did wonder about that. There is an agency, I remember using them once before when I was desperate, but it was fiendishly expensive, and I got a different person each time so they never knew what needed doing, or where everything was. And the old bat is always so rude to people like that, I don't think any of them would stay. There isn't time to advertise, and if I did people don't want just a few weeks' work. No, I'll have to manage. I'll give up swimming, for a start. That'll give me an extra hour a day, and I suppose housework is exercise.'

She was making an effort to sound positive. Maggie felt a rush of

31

almost motherly affection which surprised her.

'Couldn't I do it?' The words slipped out. Celia, who had given up on kicking and couldn't be bothered to swim any more, was already turning towards the steps to get out.

'That's so sweet of you.' She gave a wobbly smile to Maggie. Her eyes, dark-ringed from wearing goggles, looked suddenly a bit red and watery. 'But ridiculous. You couldn't possibly.' She pulled herself up the steps, her knuckles white as she gripped the handrail. Normally, she jumped herself out without bothering with the steps, but today she had no spring in her. Maggie thought that if she had tried, she would have ended up flat on the tiles, like a landed fish. Maggie followed her into the showers, and was glad to see that they were empty.

'Why not?' she said. Had Celia guessed about her circumstances?

'Well, because . . . I don't know, because it would be so awful for you. I mean, you're a friend. I can't have you cleaning up after me and the boys, and putting up with the Mugger. It's not fair.'

'Can't people be friends with their cleaning lady?' Maggie thought of Julie.

'Yes, of course. I'm devoted to mine, though I wouldn't say we're really friends – she's so much older than me, and of course I don't see much of her in termtime, we just leave each other notes. But it's different when we're already mates. I mean, I know you want to help, but . . .'

The idea, which Maggie had come up with so impulsively, began with opposition to look more attractive. After all, she had been feeling that her days were too empty. And how many times she had regretted not being able to clean her own house? It would only be for a few weeks.

'I'd like to do it,' she said, and Celia could hear the sincerity in her voice. 'I'd really like the work.'

Celia looked at her. Maggie knew that her swimsuit, after several weeks of daily immersion into the strongly chlorinated water of a public pool, had faded and stretched. She could see Celia reviewing the elderly tracksuit that Maggie wore to come to the pool, and the ancient Morris Minor that she drove – beautifully cared for, but undeniably almost an antique.

Maggie felt embarrassed, thinking that she was putting unfair pressure on Celia and that obviously she didn't like the idea. Celia took the embarrassment to be caused by Maggie having had to admit that she was hard up, that she really needed to earn some money. Her own face flushed in turn.

'It's all right,' said Maggie. 'It was just a thought.'

'It was a wonderful one,' said Celia slowly. 'If you really mean it, there's nothing I'd like more.'

They smiled shyly at one another. Celia saw how Maggie's face lit up, and was ashamed of her earlier reluctance.

'Can you come round later this afternoon? I'll make sure I get out of college on time. We could have a cup of tea, and I'll show you where everything is, all that kind of thing. And give you a key. You can't rely on the Mugger to let you in, she wakes up and wants a cup of tea at about six, but she never gets up before ten. Insists on breakfast in bed, and then complains about the toast crumbs. Not that you have to do her breakfast in bed, of course.'

'Why not? If I'm there, I might as well. You must have enough to do in the mornings. I could go straight along after my swim – it won't be worth going home again. How many hours does your usual lady do?'

'Four, usually, three days a week.'

'That would be fine. I can easily manage that, and I'd still have the other two days. I could do more if you'd like, but you probably don't have that much needing doing.' Maggie thought belatedly that Celia might not be able to afford any extra time. 'I could do the same number of hours, but spread it through the week, if it would help. That way I could do her breakfast every day.'

'If you could really manage three hours every day it would be a Godsend. It's what I've always wanted, but Tommy – her name's Mrs Tomsett, but the boys started calling her Tommy and it stuck – was already going to someone else for the other two days when she started with me. And I'm afraid you're not likely to run out of things to do! I do try to chase round after the boys and get them to tidy up their things, but Phil himself is horrendously messy and I've given up any hope of changing him. His mother did everything for them when he and his brother were little, you see, and he's never managed to get out of the mindset that when you take your clothes off, you drop them on the floor. It makes it difficult to train the boys.'

They went through to the changing room. Celia, who had recovered her usual bouncy energy, was soon dressed.

'I'll go in a bit early, get some form-filling done, that way I'll be able to get away quickly. Oh Maggie, are you really sure? I'm so afraid she'll be horrible to you.'

'Of course I'm sure. And I shan't mind what she says to me. She's not *my* Mugger-in-law, her teeth won't hurt me.'

Celia, like Stella before her, flung her arms round Maggie in a quick, hard hug.

'Thank you, thank you,' she said, unconsciously echoing Stella. 'You're wonderful, it's going to make all the difference. I'll see you later – goodness, I haven't given you the address! And I haven't got any kind of pen in my swimming bag, only in the car.'

'Write it when you get outside, stick it under my windscreen wiper,' said Maggie. 'I'll be out in a few minutes, and it's not raining today.'

'Right, okay. I'll expect you at four-thirty. If by any hideous chance I'm late, it'll only be a few minutes.'

'I'll hang on, don't worry. It's all going to work out just fine.'

I hope I'm right, thought Maggie. It's going to be quite fun, for those few weeks. Even the Mugger. I'd better not start calling her that, even in my mind. It's sure to slip out at the wrong moment. What should I wear? I don't suppose Celia would mind, but the M— – her mother-in-law might. A sensible skirt and blouse. And perhaps some kind of overall . . .

Maggie laughed at herself even as she thought it, but somehow the idea of dressing for the part had a lot of appeal. It reminded her of childhood; her mother had not approved of dressing-up games, since to her fantasy was at one remove from lying, but she had allowed Maggie a little nurse's outfit which had for several years persuaded Maggie that she would grow up to be a nurse. Now, feeling that she would be playing a part, it seemed right to throw herself into it thoroughly. She knew perfectly well that scarcely anyone bothered with overalls now, but the idea of one was an expression of light-heartedness, almost of playing. It would be practical, and she could keep it in her swimming bag. Turner would never see it.

Turner. Maggie found she had said the name aloud, and was glad nobody else was there. What was she to tell Turner? To say that he would be mortified to think of her cleaning someone else's house, even for just a few weeks, was an understatement. He would have no way of understanding why Maggie wanted to do it, and he would be bitterly hurt. She would have to think up some story, and what was more, she'd have to tell Julie to cover for her, too.

What kind of job would he regard as suitable? Charity work? That was promising, and had the benefit of being marginally true. After all, Maggie was really doing it to help Celia in a time of crisis, wasn't she? Turner would be happy with charity work. In his mind, it was what ladies of leisure did, sitting on committees, going to coffee mornings. And, of course, making useful contacts among other similar people. As long as she could keep it fairly vague, Maggie felt sure she could do it. And with Turner so busy setting up funds to buy the land for the shopping mall, he would be too preoccupied to make enquiries. It would all work out fine. Nothing could possibly go wrong.

Chapter Four

The following day was Friday. Maggie didn't go swimming at the weekends. On Saturday the pool was closed until twelve, while various clubs and classes used it. On Sunday even Turner usually had a day off, and what he really enjoyed was a leisurely late breakfast while he worked his way through the business and money sections of the weekend papers – the nearest he ever got to relaxation. So next time I come swimming, thought Maggie as she pulled on her hat and adjusted her goggles, I'll be a cleaning lady, in a hurry to get to work.

Tea with Celia yesterday had been fun. She had liked the house, which was an old cottage that they had renovated and enlarged.

'We bought it when the twins were babies, because it was what we'd been wanting for ages, and they don't come up all that often. The timing was appalling. We could only just afford it, and we were both permanently exhausted because what with the babies taking it in turns to wake and setting the other off, we got hardly any sleep. I sometimes wonder if that isn't the reason the boys are so untidy now – for the first few years of their life their home looked more like a building site than a house. Other toddlers had wooden bricks and sandpits – they had great heaps of sand and gravel, and real bricks! Not to mention the wood, and all those lovely shavings and offcuts and sawdust, and nails and screws and tiles, and scaffolding and ladders instead of climbing frames. It's amazing they survived with all their extremities intact, really. I kept telling myself it would be worth it in the end, and of course it was, though I couldn't go through it again.'

Maggie checked where all the cleaning materials were kept, learned the vagaries of the vacuum cleaner ('it *loves* the boys' Lego'). She was introduced to the dog, an elderly retriever bitch who was happy to offer her belly to be rubbed by anyone, and the cat. 'The Mugger doesn't approve of animals in the house, so naturally they always behave particularly badly when she's here. The dog makes smells all the time, and the cat leaves unsavoury bits of mouse just where she's bound to find them, or tread on them. I try to keep them out of her way as much as possible, but really at this time of year I hate to shut them outside. Of course, she's usually here in the summertime. Last year she came in August, and we'd booked our holiday for just after she went back, so I put them into kennels a couple of weeks early. I reckoned the extra expense was worth it, to give her one less thing to moan about.'

'Didn't the animals mind? They don't usually like going to kennels much.'

'Do you know, they looked positively grateful! She'd already been in the house for ten days or so, and in that time she'd trodden twice on the cat, shut the dog's tail in the back door, and of course kept them out of their usual daytime sleeping places. I could swear a look of relief came over their faces when they got to the kennels and saw their nice peaceful cages.'

Maggie made notes as they went round, feeling sure that she would never remember what needed doing where.

'Don't worry about it,' said Celia. 'Just do whatever you think are the most urgent things, and don't worry too much about the bits that don't show.'

'From what you've said, I'd have thought you mother-in-law was the kind of person who checks inside cupboards, and runs her fingers along the top of the pelmets.'

'In white gloves! Yes, that's just her style. Only once she opened a cupboard in Will's room and found his grass snake. It gave her the most terrific fright, and he's assured her that it's impossible to control the snake and he never knows where it might end up, so she's much more wary about poking around. Oh, don't worry!' Celia caught sight of Maggie's face. 'He hasn't had the snake for ages. We made him let it go on the Common when he went back to school the next term.'

Maggie swam through the warm water, thinking of the antique pieces in the sitting room that it would be a pleasure to polish, the kitchen with its friendly clutter and cupboards plastered with the twins' paintings where she would have her coffee.

'For God's sake,' Celia had said, 'make sure you sit down and have a break, help yourself to biscuits and things. The Mugger will be appalled, but take no notice of her. I know she thinks cleaning ladies should never be allowed to sit down, we've had that one out before. If she had her way you'd drink it on the hoof; she'd be balancing it on the lavatory cistern while you did the bathroom, or wanting you to drink it out in the garage, or something.'

Maggie didn't think of herself as particularly forceful, but she thought she could be more than a match for Celia's mother-in-law. The fact that she was doing the work out of friendship, that she didn't need to earn the money it would bring her, gave her a kind of strength. She was even looking forward to her first encounter, feeling that nothing that was said to her would be able to hurt her, and that there might even be a kind of perverse amusement in it all.

Reaching the near end of the pool, Maggie paused for a moment to allow The Gossips some room. They liked to swim side by side, and since both did a wide-reaching breast-stroke they took up a considerable width of water. They smiled and nodded at Maggie, and turned without a break in their conversation. Maggie caught a few words:

'. . . a face-lift, but what I always say is, what about the bunions?' and they were gone.

There was a gasping splash beside her as someone lunged for the rail. It was the girl Maggie had named 'Little Bit Desperate', and she was looking even more desperate than usual. She crouched low in the water, breathing hard, her plump face pink with exertion as she struggled for breath. She peered round the pool, her eyes red-rimmed from the chlorine and screwed half-shut. She seemed to be focusing on the fast lane. Just then, she gave a little moan and shrank lower in the water, pulling herself into the wall as if trying to make herself invisible behind Maggie. Maggie followed her stare, but could see little more than spray as someone did a showy crawl. After the swimmer had turned and was splashing away, Little Bit Desperate scuttled to the steps and clambered hurriedly out. She ran towards the showers, still half-crouching, and dived into the opening like a rabbit into its burrow.

'What's the matter with her?' Stella paused in her swimming. 'Is she all right?'

'I don't know. She seemed to be worried about someone in your lane.'

Stella looked around. 'I never really notice the others,' she said vaguely. 'I can't see them much without my specs, I just keep going and swim underneath them if they're going too slow. You don't think she was, well, molested by one of them, do you? There was a man used to come here some years ago, he used to put his hands on the girls as he swam by them, and always said it was just an accident. They finally caught him drilling holes in the wall that separated the men's from the women's cubicles to look through at them changing.'

'You're kidding!'

'No, honest, I didn't come here then but I know someone who did. She actually saw the drill bit come through.'

'Well, I don't *think* this was anything like that. She seemed to be frightened at the sight of him, and trying not to let him see her.'

'Perhaps we'd better go and check that she's okay.' It was typical of Stella, thought Maggie in some shame, that she should at once abandon her own swim to make sure a girl she didn't know was all right. *I* should have spoken to her, she thought guiltily. I really ought to stop being just an observer. She had time to be surprised by the thought, which had never occurred to her before.

Together, she and Stella left the water. The showers were empty, and a quick look round the changing area revealed no sign of the girl.

'She'll be dressing by now,' said Maggie quietly. 'Don't get cold.' Stella was shivering. 'You haven't been swimming long enough to get properly warm. I'll keep an eye out for her.'

Maggie put her towel round her shoulders, and walked round the changing area again. Several of the cubicle doors were shut, and she wondered what to do. Knocking at the doors seemed rather awkward, particularly in a unisex area, and after all, she reasoned, she couldn't even be sure that the girl would welcome what she might consider an intrusion. Still, she had seemed distressed, and she was very young . . .

Maggie sat in an open-doored cubicle within sight of the exit, and huddled her damp towel round her. A few latecomers bustled in, and one young man in a business suit left in a hurry, his shoes clacking purposefully on the floor. The changing area was silent. No showers ran, no lavatories flushed, there was no sound of movement, of drying and dressing. Maggie found that she was shivering quite hard, in spite of the warm air. She waited another five minutes by her waterproof watch, then went back to the pool.

Her blood felt congealed in heavy limbs so she swam hard to get it going again. Recently she had been finding that she was moving through the water quite a lot faster, partly because using the goggles gave her a better body position but mostly, she liked to think, because she was getting fitter. Certainly her stamina was improved, and she rarely needed to stop for a breather. She rather regretted not having weighed herself after Christmas. She was sure she had lost weight, but had no idea how much. Her clothes, though, were much looser, and she was sure she was an inch, if not two, less round the waist.

Such cheerful thoughts kept her going purposefully up and down the pool, until she was tapped on the shoulder as she came up to the turn. Standing up, she realised that everyone else had left the water, and that the session was over.

'Sorry,' she said to the poolside attendant. 'Miles away. I didn't realise it was so late.'

'It was a shame to disturb you, but we've got the SS arriving soon, and a school class.'

'The SS?' Maggie pulled herself out of the water. 'That sounds ominous.'

He looked abashed. 'I shouldn't have said that. It's what we call them, the Senior Citizens. You know they get their free swim at nine, before the schools arrive.'

'Oh yes, them. We call them the Geriatric Hooligans.' Maggie had seen them arriving, giggling and shoving at one another, calling out insults and generally behaving like a bunch of noisy school-children. She had envied what seemed to be a carefree existence, and admired the way they joked about their hip replacements as they took their crabwise path down the stairs. She exchanged a smile of complicity with the attendant, and went out to shower.

The women's showers and lavatories were next to one another in the part of the changing area nearest to the pool. Maggie went to put her towel, hat and goggles on the shelf by the basins. Since there was nobody there she stopped for a moment to look at herself in the mirror, turning sideways and sucking in her stomach. There was no doubt about it, she was definitely slimmer. Her hips, too . . . she ran her hand down over them, remembering how a few weeks earlier the flesh had bulged out beneath the elastic sides of the costume. They still bulged a bit, but not nearly as much, and she didn't think she was imagining it when she thought that her bottom was firmer as well.

A little sound made her start guiltily, not wanting to be caught preening in front of the mirror. She glanced round, but nobody had come through from the changing rooms. Most people were dressed and gone; only the sound of one of the hair driers at the far end showed that there was still somebody about. The sound came again. This time Maggie recognised it as a kind of sob, the noise of someone who had been trying not to breathe because to do so would be a betrayal, but who had been forced to take that sharp, hiccupping gulp of air. It came from one of the lavatory cubicles, and Maggie wondered why she hadn't noticed that one of the doors displayed a red panel on the lock.

She stood still, listening. The sound came again, more freely this time. An explosive exhalation, followed by a fractured, snuffling gasp. Maggie went to the door, and knocked gently on it.

'Are you all right?' The question came out automatically. Stupid, she thought. Stupid question. Of course she isn't, poor thing. There was the sound of one convulsive movement and a bang as an elbow or a knee hit the partition, then frozen silence. Oh dear, thought Maggie. She thought there was nobody there.

It was too late to creep away, and Maggie couldn't reconcile it with her conscience to do so. She tapped again, very softly, and put her head close to the door.

'It's all right,' she said in as soothing a voice as she could find. 'There's nobody else here. It's only me, Maggie Whittington. Dark blue costume, blue hat, in the general lane.' She offered the description as a kind of guarantee of respectability.

'It's okay. I'm all right.' The voice was trying hard, but with a betraying tremor.

'I don't think you are, you know. Won't you come out?'

39

'I *can't*!' It was a desperate, unfeigned sound, followed by another sob.

'Well, you can't stay in there for ever,' Maggie pointed out reasonably. 'Aren't you well? Is it an upset stomach? Or your period? There's a machine out here, and I've got some change, if you need anything.'

'It's not that. I'm not ill.'

'Well, I can't go away and leave you there, I'd be worried about it for the rest of the day. Won't you just unlock the door? I promise I won't make a fuss, or do anything you don't want.'

There was a silence, broken only by a few sniffs. Then came the sound of paper being pulled from the dispenser, and a tremulous nose blow. At last, after more hesitation, the bolt was released.

Maggie put her hand on the door, half-expecting some resistance, but it swung open quite easily. It was, as she had suspected, Little Bit Desperate who sat huddled on the lowered lid of the lavatory. Her plump face was pale with cold and misery; only her puffy eyes looked hot and red, and she had her arms clasped protectively round her body which was bent forward so that her elbows rested on her plump thighs. As soon as she had seen Maggie, her head drooped down to her knees.

Maggie crouched down to bring her head nearer to the girl's. She put her hand on the smooth shoulder, feeling the flesh cold almost as death beneath her fingers. Little Bit Desperate shivered at her touch as if it were even colder, and Maggie saw that the girl's whole body was convulsed with shaking. Awkwardly she put her arms round her, hoping that no one would come through from the changing area at this delicate moment.

'You're frozen,' she said. 'Come on. You can't stay here.' The girl pulled away, from the suggestion more than from the embrace, Maggie thought.

'No, no! I don't want to go out there!'

'Everybody's gone,' said Maggie. 'There's nobody there.'

'You can't be sure . . .'

'Well, I can go and check. But will you at least come as far as the showers?'

The girl seemed to shrink into a tighter, more desperate crouch. 'Go and see . . .'

Since there was no point in arguing, Maggie went. None of the cubicle doors was locked, but she pushed each one open just to be sure. She glanced into the group changing room, and listened at the door of the men's group changing room, then went back to the lavatories.

'It's completely deserted,' she assured the shivering girl, 'but it won't be for long. Don't forget, the old dears will be in quite soon.'

The girl lifted her head. 'I don't want to see anyone.'

40

'You don't have to. Come and have a hot shower and warm up a bit, then you can get changed in the group room. They never use that one, and once they're all in the water we can leave.'

'All right.'

The girl stood up, and padded her way to the showers. Maggie pressed buttons, and put a squeeze of shampoo into her hand.

'Shampoo?' she offered the bottle.

'I don't usually.'

'Oh, go on. It's good one, and it smells lovely. It might help to cheer you up a bit.'

'Take more than a bit of shampoo,' she replied ungraciously, but she accepted the generous dollop that Maggie squeezed onto her palm and rubbed it into her hair. Maggie had noticed that the girl's shoulder-length rust-coloured hair always looked greasy when she stood in the queue in the mornings. It generally hung in lank, tangled curls round her face, or rather against it, since she habitually stood with her head lowered. Maggie had thought, privately, that the dirty hair must be a contributing factor to the crop of spots that glowed on her pale face. Today, at least, Desperate's hair would be clean and sweet-smelling.

They stood under the hot water, turning front and back to warm each side in turn, reluctant to leave the soothing flow.

'Right,' said Maggie at last. 'We'd better get going, I can hear the SS coming.'

If Maggie had hoped that this would spark some curiosity in the girl and give her a chance to repeat the jokey name, she was disappointed. Desperate seemed not at all surprised to hear that Hitler's Blackshirts were on the prowl: presumably to her all arrivals were equally unwelcome. With an anxious glance towards the door she scurried through to the group changing room. Maggie, following her, found her seated on the bench and tugging at the locker key that was attached to her wrist by a stout rubber band. She tugged at it so fiercely that the band broke, and she gave a little whimper of pain and frustration as the rubber snapped against her skin.

'Do you want me to fetch your things?' Maggie saw that the girl was making no move to stand, merely looking in despair at the key in her hand. Wordlessly, the key was held out to her.

The girl dressed clumsily, turning her back and trying to keep her towel modestly around her as she struggled into her underwear. Maggie tactfully turned her back also, but because she didn't worry about keeping herself hidden she was dressed long before the other had finished, and when she turned back to her, Desperate was still in her underwear. Maggie was relieved to see that that, at least, was well cared for, the nylon petticoat creased but clean. Her school shirt, though crumpled from having been carelessly thrust into a plastic bag, was equally spotless. Maggie glanced at her watch.

'I'm afraid there's no hope of you getting to school on time. It's practically quarter to nine.'

Her only answer was a shrug.

'So, if you're going to be late anyway, why don't we go and have a coffee when we've dried our hair?'

'I don't dry it.'

'In this cold weather? How can you bear it? Don't you get frozen?'

Another shrug.

'Well, I have to dry mine. I'd get a dreadful headache if I didn't. Won't you dry yours too, just this once?'

This time the shrug was of acquiescence. Not agreement, more in the way of 'Oh, all right then', but better than the earlier 'So what?'. Maggie fished in her purse for 10p coins. The bustle of arrival as the Senior Citizens went for their swim had died to a background of splashing and laughter, and when Maggie opened the door the changing area was once more empty.

At the row of hair driers Maggie blow-dried her hair with her usual care – it wouldn't do for her to go home looking dishevelled after she was supposed to have been pampered at the Spa. Desperate took the coin Maggie offered, then stood with her back to the mirror and simply pointed the hair drier at her head, her other hand hanging by her side as she made no attempt to brush or otherwise control her hair. Maggie, whose straight hair dried fast, was soon ready. She never wore much make-up, a touch of foundation and powder, a brush of mascara and some lipstick were the furthest she usually went. In the past she had played around with blushers and shapers, but she had long since decided that her rather round face was better when allowed to be itself. Her skin was clear and still unlined, and her eyelashes long and thick enough, with mascara, to need no further assistance from eyeshadow.

Maggie pushed in the two combs she often used to hold back her dead straight hair, and eyed Desperate's drying technique.

'So curly!' she marvelled. 'Doesn't it get tangled?'

A twitch of the shoulders, which Maggie interpreted as a token shrug.

'Haven't you a brush? You can borrow mine.'

A shake of the head. Maggie saw that the curls, as they dried, looked redder than she had ever seen them before. Soft and clean, as it dried the hair grew in volume, the curls springing up with a life of their own like speeded-up films of flowers growing and opening, or like milk foaming up in a saucepan. By the time the money ran out and the drier clicked off, the girl's head was haloed with curls.

'How lovely!' exclaimed Maggie with unfeigned pleasure. 'Oh, don't!' as Desperate, after one glance at the mirror, dug in her pocket and pulled out a rubber band with which she ruthlessly confined the frizzy hair into a tight ponytail at the back of her neck, where it sat like a round toadstool on a tree stump. A pair of glasses, with one arm held in place by a large safety pin, was pulled from the plastic bag that now held her swimming things, and pushed ruthlessly on, the ear-pieces dragging through the tightly fastened hair. Through the thick lenses, Maggie saw that there were once again tears in the eyes whose blank gaze, she now realised, was more myopic than stupid. Don't comment, Maggie told herself, remembering her own awkward adolescence when even a compliment felt like a kind of criticism. 'What about that coffee, then?'

She received a look of wary suspicion.

'Why?'

'Why not? It's a horrible morning, you've been upset, and this is my last chance to do anything like this. I'm starting a new job on Monday.'

'What as?' Maggie took the abrupt question as a good sign, that the girl was showing some slight interest in another person.

'A white slaver, of course,' she answered briskly. 'I kidnap young girls and sell them to evil men from foreign lands. But I haven't started yet, so you're quite safe for today.'

'Who'd want me?' The simplicity of the reply stunned Maggie. She wondered for a moment whether the girl had actually believed her.

'Plenty of people, I'm afraid. But as a matter of fact, I'm just a cleaning lady.'

'Pity. I might have come and found you, on Monday.'

It was obviously an attempt at a joke, and Maggie smiled broadly though, inside, her mind was filled with pity at the bitterness behind the words.

They went up the stairs. When, a few years earlier, the old municipal swimming pool had been re-vamped and face-lifted into a Leisure Centre, a new wing had been built on two levels that incorporated a large indoor court and two smaller ones, with above them a gym for weight training and a fitness suite. The central area that joined old to new had squash courts and rooms for a crèche and a youth club on the ground floor, while the reception desk was at the top of the stairs. The large space behind reception, with windows looking down to the pools on one side and the large court on the other, was arranged as a cafeteria which, with a bar for the evenings, did a thriving trade and tempted those who had burned a few calories to replace them at once.

At that time of a weekday morning they had the place to themselves. The coffee machine scented the air, and there was an unbroken display of buns and cakes. Seeing how the girl's eyes lingered over these Maggie took a piece of flapjack to go with her coffee, and nodded to her companion to help herself. She took a doughnut and then, with a defiant look, an iced bun. Comfort food, thought Maggie. Poor child. They sat at a table where they could look down at the pool, in which the elderly swimmers were disporting themselves with varying degrees of friskyness. Maggie sipped her coffee, and took a bite of flapjack.

'What did you say your name was?'

'Maggie,' said Maggie indistinctly through her mouthful of oats. 'Maggie Whittington. Oops. Sorry.' A crumb of flapjack shot across the table, narrowly missing the girl. 'And you?'

The girl grimaced. 'Primrose.'

'Pretty name.'

'For someone like me?' The girl gestured at her body. 'Primroses are small, and delicate. I'm not a flower.'

'What are you, then?'

'I dunno. A vegetable. Potato? Cabbage? Carrot?' She raised a hand to her hair.

'It's beautiful hair. A wonderful colour, and those curls . . . surely they're really fashionable at the moment?'

'Only if they're not natural. If you had them done at the hairdresser, and it took all afternoon and cost a bomb, then it's cool. But if it's just like that, and always has been, and ever since you started school they've been telling you you've got hair like a pan scourer, that's not so cool. And if you're fat, and wear glasses, and have red hair – well, that's about as far from cool as you can get without exploding.' Primrose bit hard into her doughnut. The red jam spurted out down her chin but she ignored it, chewing on her mouthful with miserable relish. When the doughnut was finished she scooped the jam up with one nail-bitten finger, and licked it off with what looked like deliberate inelegance.

'They tease you?' Stupid, Maggie told herself. Of course they do.

'What do you think?' Primrose picked up the iced bun, and started to nibble the icing off the top.

'That's why you were upset this morning, is it? Someone from your school was here?'

'Yeah.' The rest of the bun was being crammed into Primrose's mouth, and her voice was muffled. 'I might not have seen him, only he kicked me as he went by so I stopped and looked at him when he was coming back. I saw his face.'

She stopped. Her plate was empty, but she stared down at it, running her licked finger round and round to pick up sugar from the doughnut.

'He's one of the ones that tease you?'

'What do you mean, "the ones"? They all do it. But he's one of the worst. In fact, the worst of all, really. He's clever, too, so of course he's better at it, thinking up things to say and do.'

'Are you clever?'

'Oh, yes.' It was spoken carelessly, as an irrelevance.

'Doesn't that help?'

'Not really. Who's going to like you for being clever?'

'Your teachers?'

Primrose raised her eyes. Behind the thick lenses, they blazed with contempt.

'They don't care. They see what everyone sees. I used to think they could help – you know, stop the others, like they say. But it's all "Sticks and Stones", and "How would you like it if people treated *you* like that". What good does that do?'

'Not much. But if you're being bullied . . . What about your parents?'

'Parent. Mum went off – five, six years ago. I live with my dad. He does his best, but he's got to work. He worries about losing his job all the time, worries about money, worries about the future, worries about me . . .' Maggie saw that Primrose couldn't see any point in adding to his worries. 'I once said I didn't like being so fat, but he just told me it was puppy fat and not to mind, it would all disappear in a year or two. I think he was afraid I'd start dieting and getting anorexic. Anorexic, me! So now I tell him everything's fine,' said Primrose.

'And he believes you?'

'I think so. I'm a good liar.'

Maggie nodded. She could see that Primrose would need to be.

'And how long have you been coming here to swim?'

'Since the beginning of the Christmas holidays. New Year Resolution, and all that shit. You know, get in shape, get fit, all the stuff they tell you in the magazines. I thought I'd be safe coming here, nobody else would know about it. Now I'll have to stop. Not that it was doing any good. I just felt even more hungry afterwards.'

'I know. I did too. But it wears off.' Only I, Maggie thought, can go home to my nice safe house and eat exotic fruit and expensive salads. I don't have to spend the day among people who bully me, surrounded by shops and cafeterias selling food like this.

'If you say so. Only it won't get a chance to now, will it? I'm not going to keep coming here if there's any risk of Dez seeing me.'

'But he might never come again.'

'Can't risk it. You want the rest of that?'

Maggie absently pushed the remains of her flapjack across the table, and thought.

'Look,' she said, 'give it a few days. I'll keep an eye out for him – Dez, is it? I'll try and find out. Get one of the fast swimmers to have a word with him, see if he's likely to turn up often. It would be a shame for you to give up if that was just a once-off. I'll phone you, or you can ring me if you prefer, round the end of next week.'

Primrose studied her suspiciously. 'Why should you? You a lezza, or something?'

'A what? Oh, no. Nothing like that.' Maggie was more amused than upset by the question. No one had ever before asked her if she had lesbian tendencies. 'I just want to help. I didn't like school much either, though I didn't have as bad a time as you. But I remember what it was like.'

Primrose considered her. 'All right, then.' It was grudging, but Maggie well-remembered the teenager's reluctance to accept adult help.

'I'll give you my number.' Maggie scribbled it down on a blank page torn from her diary. 'There you go.' She glanced at her watch. 'Heavens, you'll be dreadfully late for school.'

'I shan't go now. Easier to take the whole day off. I can take a note tomorrow, forge my dad's signature – they never check.'

'Where will you go?' Horrid visions of malls and shoplifting floated into Maggie's head.

'Library. They know me there. I go there a lot, it's nice and quiet. Better than school; they let you read anything you like. See you.'

She ambled away, without thanking Maggie. Maggie didn't mind. The final 'See you' had been spoken in an almost friendly way. Goodness, she thought. My social life is filling up. A job, and a bullied teenager. Whatever next?

Chapter Five

It was a strange weekend. Maggie was secretly rather excited about starting her cleaning job on Monday. It was ridiculous, she knew, but to be doing something so different, to be working in someone else's home, even to be dealing with the mother-in-law from Hell, made her feel quite young and impulsive. More so, really, than when she *had* been young. Then, she would have been terrified to act on a whim. Now, it suddenly seemed not only desirable but normal.

For once, Maggie had little attention to spare for Turner. He, fortunately, seemed very preoccupied. He spent Saturday morning on the telephone and Saturday afternoon on the golf course. He had recently worked hard at his golf, fitting in lessons with the pro three or four times a week, and Maggie knew that the game that afternoon was as much to do with work as if he had spent it at the office. For Turner, no social occasion was without its financial subtext. Maggie, knowing him well enough not to need telling, made sure that there was a hot meal ready for as many as might happen to return for a spontaneous supper.

It was lucky that she did, for six slightly inebriated and very noisy men eventually came back with him, all crammed hilariously into his large car. They came into the house enclosed as it were in their own eco-system, cocooned in an almost visible effluvium of cigar and cigarette smoke, beer, whisky and the stale memory of fried bar food. Maggie set out a buffet of cold meats and cheeses, and was thankful to leave them to it. It was three in the morning before they left, in several taxis, their loud goodbyes and even louder shushings and laughter waking Maggie from a dream of cleaning the swimming pool as if it had been a giant bath.

Not very surprisingly, Turner slept late the following morning, and when he did get up showed little inclination to do anything more than read the papers. Maggie pottered in the garden and the house. Already, although she had not yet started work, she felt she had moved on. The house felt unreal; it might as well have been a museum, or a showroom. From time to time Maggie stood outside the closed door of the study, but there was no sound from within and the closed door meant that he didn't want to be disturbed.

What was he doing in there, Maggie wondered? The obvious answer was of course that he was indulging in a quiet doze over the newspapers. Maggie found it hard, however, to envisage Turner doing such a thing; in his book, sleeping in the daytime was strictly for babies, the elderly, or the sick. It was a measure of Maggie's ambivalent attitude to Turner that she could as easily imagine him transformed, in his sanctuary, into some kind of alien creature as think of him quietly studying the financial reports. The thread of fear that wove through her feelings for him was like a fishing line, transparent almost to invisibility, but unnaturally strong.

Turner's silent presence in the study seemed, perversely, to make the house feel emptier. Maggie flung open windows in sitting and dining rooms to clear the lingering smell from the previous evening, thankful that the log fire had already drawn much of it up the chimney. When the windows were closed the air, warmed by super-efficient central heating to an almost summery temperature, was flat and dead tasting and Maggie almost wished she had left the bar smell, which at least was alive. She thought, fancifully, that the house was marking time just as she was, waiting for some unknown future event that she could not guess at.

On Monday morning, Maggie left early for her swim. In a separate bag she carried what she had already settled upon as suitable clothes: a sensible skirt, blouse and cardigan, and a nylon overall. She was particularly pleased with this, and had several times surreptitiously tried it on, as a kind of dress rehearsal. It had been surprisingly difficult to find, and she had ended up making a special trip to the nearest large town where she remembered seeing the kind of old-fashioned shop that sells not only knitting wool and haberdashery but wool vests, long-legged knickers, and hefty replacement suspenders. Amazingly, the shop had still been there although both its neighbours had turned into charity shops. She had picked an overall on which improbably fat roses rioted in cheerful pinks and blues, and had been complimented on her choice by the elderly proprietor.

'Nice large pockets on that style,' she said approvingly, stroking the slippery nylon. 'Very handy. You've always got what you want, if you've got nice large pockets.' Maggie, who had never considered the subject, could see that this would be so.

At the end of Monday's swim, Maggie suddenly remembered her promise to Primrose. She felt a bit awkward about speaking to the fast-swimming young men in their lane. For one thing, they rarely stopped, and she certainly couldn't bring herself to accost one in mid-turn. As she hesitated, she saw one of the older men stop. He leaned against the wall and lifted his goggles to the top of his forehead, so he was obviously not going to swim again straight away. She drifted nearer.

'Good morning!'

'Morning.' He looked surprised, but answered civilly enough. She saw, now that she was nearer, that he was the one she had called Body Beautiful, but it was too late and in any case, there was nobody else.

'Quite crowded in your lane,' she ventured, as a lead in.

'Yes, it's often busy on Fridays,' he responded. 'Not too bad, as long as you know them.'

'I suppose that does make it easier, if you bump into them.' Goodness, she thought, I hope he doesn't think I'm trying to pick him up or anything. He smiled.

'No, I mean that you're less likely to bump into people if you know how fast they swim. If you know who's slower than you, and how much, then you can work out where to swim.'

'Yes, I suppose so.' Was it typical of him, she wondered, to mention only the people who were slower than him? He had a pleasant smile, though, and seemed friendly. 'Have you been swimming here long?'

'Only a couple of years.' For some reason the simple answer was made sheepishly. Maggie hastened to get to the nub of her conversation.

'Two years is quite a while. There was a boy yesterday I hadn't noticed before, rather a splashy swimmer. He must have been difficult to swim with.'

'Oh, that one. Yes, he wasn't nearly as fast as he thought he was, but he wouldn't give way to anyone.'

'Irritating. He kicked a friend of mine, which was why I noticed him. She was quite upset, actually, said she wouldn't come here any more if he was going to be here.'

'Bit over the top, for one kick. And he's not here today. I don't think I've ever seen him before, though I don't see too well when I'm swimming.'

'Goggles always steam up, don't they? No, the trouble was she knows him a bit and doesn't like him. I said I'd find out how often he was likely to be here, if I could.'

He nodded. 'If he comes again, I'll ask him, if you like.'

'That's very kind of you.' Maggie was surprised that he was so helpful. Perhaps, she thought, you couldn't judge people's characters by their swimming styles. Certainly Body Beautiful was more helpful than his look-at-me narcissism had led her to expect.

It seemed strange to let herself into someone else's empty house. Maggie felt compelled to ring the doorbell before putting the key in the lock, just in case somebody should be there. As soon as she stepped over the threshold she could feel that the house was empty. It had that abandoned, echoing silence that homes have while their occupants are out, as though the furniture were holding its breath. Maggie disarmed the burglar alarm – a far less sophisticated one than hers, but then not everyone has to worry about a Turner over the fireplace – and stayed on the mat to change her outdoor shoes for lighter indoor ones. Then she carried the outdoor ones to the lobby outside the back door. The dog looked up at her and thumped a lazy tail; there was what could only be described as a dog-flap in the outside door so that she could go out to the garden, and the door to the kitchen was well locked. Maggie gave her a quick fuss, then hung up her coat and slipped on the overall. Buttoning the crisp nylon she stepped purposefully back into the kitchen.

Celia had warned her what to expect.

'It's always the most fearful rush in the morning. We don't go in for cooked breakfasts – just as well, or I'd never have my swim – so we all help ourselves. I just have a cup of tea, and eat a quick bowl of muesli in the staffroom when I get to College, the boys have cereal and Phil has toast. It doesn't sound much, but whatever I do they all seem to be incapable of even *thinking* about putting their bowls and plates in the dishwasher. I don't like to nag Phil, because I'm so grateful that he drops the boys off for me so I can get to the pool, and the boys always have some excuse to be late, like last-minute homework or a missing football sock. I'm sorry . . .'

She had seemed so worried that Maggie hastened to reassure her.

'There's no point in being a cleaning lady if you don't have anything to clean.'

Now, she was rather pleased to see that the table was littered with packets of cereal, (all open and one tipped on its side so that some of the contents had escaped), spilled sugar, abandoned bowls and mugs, and a marmalade-covered knife that had somehow spread itself generously. Obviously, all three had opted for toast that day. Maggie set to with gusto, thinking how much more interesting it was to clean someone else's house than your own. She found herself humming as she wiped down surfaces and washed the floor, and once she had moved out of the kitchen and had the vacuum cleaner going, she allowed her hum to burst into full-blown song.

By the time she stopped for coffee she had finished the downstairs rooms. The sitting room was easy, needing no more than a vacuum and a dust, but the little family room had been more challenging. Piles of magazines and books, a half-finished model car, and a complicated Lego construction – all of these were obviously in use, and must not be disturbed more than necessary. She felt that the risk of breaking the model or the Lego was worse than inadequate cleaning, and ended up blowing the dust from round them and hoping for the best.

After a cup of coffee – drunk, as ordered, sitting in the kitchen – she tucked her dusters into one pocket and the spray cleaner into the other (how right her friend in the shop had been, she thought gratefully) and carried the vacuum cleaner upstairs. Afterwards she wondered if she had been led by some kind of premonition, but by chance she started with the guest room and its little en-suite bathroom. The cat was cosily nested on the bed, and resented being ejected, but Maggie carried her firmly downstairs and put her in the lobby.

The clean sheets were soon on the bed, the bathroom scrubbed and shining, and she even took the time to run out to the garden for a handful of evergreen leaves and some delicately scented viburnum to put in a little vase on the table. Satisfied, she moved to Celia and Phil's room, leaving the boys' rooms until last as the most challenging and, therefore, the most interesting, and she was soon singing lustily to the rhythmic roar of the vacuum. It was not until she stopped to move some furniture that she heard the prolonged ring on the doorbell, accompanied by a furious clatter of the letter box and the sound of urgent barking.

'Coming!' she called as she ran down the steps. The letter box continued its furious rattling, and there was another assault on the bell. Maggie flew to the door, wrestling with the safety chain which she had almost undone before realising that she ought to keep it on until she had discovered who was so eager to gain admittance. She undid the latch, and the door was immediately pushed so hard that if the safety chain had not crunched into position she would have received a sharp blow.

'Open this door. Open the door *at once!*' The voice was elderly, but undoubtedly vigorous. 'I have been standing here in the cold ringing the bell for *hours.* I shall catch pneumonia, at least. Open this door, I say!'

Maggie peered through the narrow opening. A small, slightly stooped figure in a fur coat, surrounded by several large and expensive suitcases, stood on the step. Behind her, a taxi was pulling out of the drive rather faster than was really safe. Oh no, thought Maggie. Surely she was supposed to arrive tomorrow? 'May I ask who you are?' she enquired, feeling that there was no truly polite way to put such a question.

'I'm Mrs Draper, of course. Who are you, and what are you doing in my son's house?'

'I beg your pardon, Mrs Draper. I understood you weren't arriving until tomorrow. If you'll just give me a moment . . .'

'I've waited out here long enough already. What are you doing?

How dare you shut the door in my face, young woman? Open it at once!'

Maggie, struggling to push the door shut so that she could undo the safety chain, was torn between pleasure at being called 'young woman' and appalled amusement at the thought of Celia's horror when she arrived home and found the Mugger already in residence. As she had jumped out of the pool that morning, she had grimaced at Maggie.

'Last day of freedom! Last night of peace! I'm going to cook us a special steak supper tonight, and open a good bottle of wine.' Mrs Draper, meanwhile, was strenuously foiling Maggie's attempts to shut the door. She might not be very big, but she certainly is forceful, Maggie thought.

'If you will allow me to push the door to, Mrs Draper, I can undo the safety chain,' she said breathlessly.

'What's that? I can't hear you. I warn you, young woman, that if you do not instantly let me into my son's house, and give me a proper explanation of what you are doing there, I shall be calling the police.'

With one last heave, Maggie shoved the door closed and wrenched the safety chain free. She flung the door open just as a shrill cry of 'Police! Police!' rose from the step.

'Do come in, Mrs Draper. I'm Maggie Whittington, the cleaning lady.'

Stopping in mid-screech, Mrs Draper looked at her with suspicion. 'Where's what's-her-name, then? You're not the person my daughter-in-law normally employs.'

'I'm afraid she's had to go into hospital. I'm taking her place, just temporarily.'

Mrs Draper sniffed, but she stepped into the hall.

'Well, you couldn't be any worse than the other one, I suppose. Useless, fly-by-night creature she is, just the kind of person my daughter-in-law would choose. Perhaps you would be kind enough to bring in my luggage. Be careful with it, it's expensive.' The polite words were spoken sarcastically. Maggie, who was already wrestling with two of the cases, wondered whether they were weighted with gold bricks, they certainly felt heavy enough. 'Hurry up, that open door is letting all the warmth out, such as it is. Why this house is always so cold I cannot imagine. Draughts, I suppose. English houses are always draughty.'

Maggie, who had vivid memories of being very cold indeed when staying in Spain in a cold snap one Easter, said nothing, but pushed the door shut behind her by leaning on it.

'Your room's all ready,' she offered. 'I'll take your luggage up in a moment. Do you want to go and freshen up after your journey? I'll make you a cup of coffee. That'll warm you up.'

Unconsciously, Maggie found herself speaking more in the tones of a mistress of the house than of an employee. Mrs Draper looked at her sourly.

'You seem to be very much at home here, I must say. I'll have a cup of tea, if you please. The English never know how to make coffee. You can bring it up to my room, since you say it's ready for me.'

'Certainly, madam.' Is that over the top, Maggie wondered? The older woman gave her a suspicious glance, but Maggie busied herself with the luggage and in the end they went upstairs without incident.

Once the cases were arranged to her satisfaction – 'I said the *big* one on the stand, not that one! And the little one on the chest near the bathroom, of course!' – Maggie withdrew to the kitchen. She rubbed her back, feeling the strain of carrying such unaccustomed weights. I hope I haven't damaged anything, she thought. I'm out of practice for that kind of lifting.

She laid a tray with the best china that Celia had shown her the previous week – 'You have to use this for her, she gets insulted if she has to have the everyday stuff' – and hunted through the drawers for a tray-cloth, an item which she suspected Celia's mother-in-law would regard as a prerequisite of civilised living. Not finding one, she improvised with an embroidered napkin and, while getting the milk from the fridge, checked quickly to see what there might be to make a suitable lunch for the old tyrant. Celia, she knew, intended to shop on her way home, so she wasn't very surprised to see that there wasn't a great deal there.

The rest of the morning had perforce to be structured around the new arrival. Maggie managed to do a rapid clear-up of the boys' rooms while the visitor was unpacking, and could only be thankful that the doors had been shut earlier so that the chaos within had been invisible. A quick forage through the freezer revealed a stray lamb chop, and blessing the wonders of modern living Maggie defrosted it in the microwave, and was able to mollify Mrs Draper with a three-course meal of home-made soup (from some left-over vegetables in the fridge), the grilled chop, and ice cream. Mrs Draper thawed a little, particularly as Maggie continued to address her as 'madam', and said that it was pleasant to eat English lamb again. She then went upstairs, saying that while she disapproved of sleeping in the daytime, her journey and its early start had exhausted her and she supposed she had better rest before she had to deal with her grandchildren, whom she referred to as 'those boys'. The adjective 'wretched' was implied but unspoken.

Maggie cleared up the lunch, and prepared to leave as it was already later than she had meant to be. Once her little car was out of the drive, however, she pulled into a side road and rummaged in the bottom of her bag for her mobile phone, thankful that Turner had insisted that she should always carry one with her.

'If you must drive around in that old heap,' he had said, 'then at least let me make sure you've got some way of calling for help when the wheels fall off, or the engine drops out.'

Now, she called Directory Enquiries and asked for the number of the Sixth Form College where Celia worked.

'I'm afraid she's teaching at the moment,' the secretary told her, 'and I'm not supposed to interrupt a class unless it's an emergency.'

'Well, it's not that, but it is quite important. What about after the class? Isn't there somewhere a message can be left for her?'

'Yes, of course, but the problem is she's not very likely to see it. This is her last class of the day, and she always goes off in a rush to pick up her boys from school, so she dashes straight off from her class. You'd do better to wait a bit, and reach her at home.'

'But I need to speak to her before she gets home . . . What if I came down to the College now? I could catch her as she leaves.'

'Safer to go to the school, I should think. You might easily miss her here, it all depends where she found a space, but if you go straight to the school now you can be sure of being in time.'

That sounded like sense. Maggie drove to the school and, being early, managed to park nearby. She got out, and went to stand by the gates, looking through them with interest. Without children of her own, and with few local friends as yet, she had never really been particularly aware of it except as an area to avoid at dropping off and picking up time. It was built on a large open site at the edge of the town, and housed both the Middle and the Senior schools in separate sets of buildings, each with its own entrance.

The College secretary had told Maggie that the Middle School came out at three-fifteen and the Senior at three-thirty, in an effort to stagger the traffic problems. There were also large signs by the gates, firmly stating that they were for the younger children only, and that Senior pupils, even older brothers and sisters, *must* use the other gates. Maggie was surprised, therefore, to see a near adult-sized figure in school uniform approaching her at a swift walk that was just short of breaking into a run. Because it was an unexpected sight Maggie watched more closely, then as the girl drew level with her she recognised Little Bit Desperate.

'Hello, Primrose!' The girl flinched and half-turned away. 'It's me, Maggie. From the swimming pool, remember?'

Primrose glanced round in a hunted fashion, and scurried through the gates.

'What are you doing here?' she hissed. 'How did you know I'd come this way?'

Maggie, who naturally had little to do with teenagers, was amused and touched by this typical assumption that the world revolved around Primrose. Or was it, she wondered, merely paranoia?

'I didn't. In fact, I didn't even know you were at this school. I'm waiting for someone else.'

'Oh. Well . . .' Primrose, though obviously eager to go, still hesitated.

'He wasn't there this morning,' said Maggie kindly. 'And I had a word with one of the men in the fast lane, and he said he'd try and find out for me.'

'Oh. Thanks.' It was ungraciously spoken, but genuine.

'Did you get away with skipping Friday?'

A swift smile transformed Primrose's round face. 'Yes, just! I'd forgotten that my English set had a visit to the Library that day. Luckily it was first thing in the morning, so I just played dumb and said I'd thought we were meant to be going straight there. It was just another Rolling Stone thing.'

'Rolling Stone? Like the band?'

'No. Like gathering no moss. Take too long to tell you.' And it wasn't a friendly nickname, Maggie felt. Primrose was glancing back at the school again.

'You'd better go. The Middle School will be coming out in a moment.'

'Yes. Thanks.' This time her voice was gruff rather than surly. Maggie wasn't altogether sure why she was being thanked again, unless it was for not asking more about the nickname, or about why Primrose was leaving half an hour early and through the wrong gate. No need to ask, Maggie thought, watching the girl cross the road with scarcely a glance for the oncoming traffic. The way she walked, the hunched shoulders and dipped head, showed too clearly that she was escaping, evading her tormentors.

More and more cars were beginning to collect, and groups of mothers drew into chatting clusters fringed with small children. Maggie watched out for Celia's car, and soon saw her standing by it talking to another woman who had arrived on foot. Maggie hurried over. Unwilling to interrupt, she hovered until Celia saw her.

'Maggie! Is everything all right?'

'Oh, yes. At least, nothing's wrong with the house. I tried to call you at College, and they suggested I catch you here. I thought I must warn you – your mother-in-law's arrived.'

'What? Already?'

'Yes, this morning. I've given her some lunch, and she's having a lie down, but I didn't want you to get home and find her already there.'

'Isn't that *typical*! She does it to catch me out, I'm sure. So much for our Last Supper. I'll have to stop on the way back and get another steak for her – pretend I intended it for a welcoming meal.

Oh Maggie, thank you! You've saved my life. Thank God you warned me.'

Maggie was pleased. 'Well, I did rather get the impression she wanted to steal a march on you. Luckily I'd finished downstairs and done her room, and the boys' doors were shut, so it looked all right.'

'Bless you! That's several less things for her to moan about. What about lunch? I know there wasn't much in the fridge, except tonight's stuff. Has she eaten one of the steaks?'

'No, I found a lamb chop in the freezer and cooked her that. She probably won't be able to manage a steak tonight as well.'

'Don't you believe it! You wouldn't think it to look at her, but she eats like a horse. Especially if someone else is providing the food. Oh well, I'd better go home and see her, get it over with. The boys won't be very pleased, they're supposed to be going to a friend's house after school.'

'I shouldn't stop them. After all, you're not supposed to know she's there, so there's no reason why they shouldn't go. And I got the impression . . . well, I don't think she's in any rush to see them. She's a bit tired, after the journey,' Maggie concluded tactfully.

Celia's face brightened. 'Good thinking. I'll drop them off and whizz round the supermarket. I can go back laden with goodies that I've bought for her visit, and she can see them being unloaded. She can't complain at that, can she?'

'Well . . .' Maggie dragged the syllable out, and they both laughed.

'Seriously, Maggie, thank you so much. Was everything all right this morning, apart from the Mugger?'

'Yes, fine. I enjoyed it.'

Celia looked sceptical, but it was true. Maggie had even enjoyed dealing with Mrs Draper. The problems and challenges of her own life were so small, so empty and flat, that the morning she had passed had been like entering into a soap opera.

When she arrived home, her own house felt dead. Julie had been and gone, leaving a scrawled note on the kitchen table. It was Maggie's only regret that she would inevitably see little of Julie for the next few weeks, while she was going to Celia's every morning.

She had been reluctant to tell Julie what she was doing. She was aware that although Julie was her friend, although she liked working for and with Maggie and was grateful for the relatively high pay, nevertheless she felt deep down that the job was demeaning. She always referred to herself as a 'housekeeper', in tones redolent of *Upstairs, Downstairs*, and made no secret of the fact that if she weren't restricted by having young children she would be working at something much more high-powered.

Maggie sympathised. She, too, felt that Julie was fitted for something more stimulating than cleaning someone else's house.

She herself did not regard it as demeaning work, but then she wasn't doing it out of necessity but merely because it amused her. She thought that this Marie-Antoinette-type attitude to what Julie regarded as drudgery might upset Julie quite a lot, and in the end had decided against confiding in her. It made things more difficult, but after all it was only for a few weeks. Julie could be told that Maggie was helping a friend, which was only true, and could console herself for working in an empty house by visits to the Spa.

Turner was home by six, which was early for him.

'This is a nice surprise,' said Maggie. 'Is everything all right?'

Turner kissed her absent-mindedly. 'I tried to ring you today,' he said. 'Julie said she didn't know where you were.'

There was no suspicion in his voice. Obviously, thought Maggie with a little gnawing of regret, I'm not the kind of woman who would be likely to be having an extra-marital affair. Honesty compelled her to admit that this was so: on the whole, very good-looking men made her nervous, and since her marriage no one had ever shown even the most fleeting interest in making romantic or sexual advances to her. Even so, she knew that she was lucky not to have a husband who invariably assumed the worst. A former neighbour had been married to a man who was suspicious of even the most innocent encounter, and so possessive that in the end she got bored with trying to prove her loyalty, and went off with one of his friends.

'I went to a friend's house,' said Maggie, who had already chosen her words. 'Someone I met in the swimming pool.'

She had expected Turner to be pleased – that, after all, was why he had wanted her to join the Spa – but he merely nodded.

'I wish you'd switch on that bloody mobile I gave you,' he said peevishly. 'What's the point of carrying it around if you never use it?'

'Well, I did use it today, as a matter of fact, but I'm afraid I didn't leave it on. I always think it's rather embarrassing if it rings when I'm having coffee with someone. I'm sorry if you wanted to speak to me, though. Was it anything urgent?'

'No.' He sounded vague again. 'But I might have wanted to bring someone back for dinner. I didn't, but suppose I had?'

'I expect I'd have coped,' said Maggie calmly. 'You know I always have things in the freezer for emergencies like that.'

'Yes. I know you do.' She felt that he had needed to talk to her during the day, perhaps not for anything important but simply to touch base, as it were, and she felt guilty.

'I promise I'll make sure I keep the mobile on in future. I'll even remember to recharge the battery,' she joked, reminding him how he had teased her at the beginning for always leaving the battery flat.

'Right,' he said. Maggie realised that he was scarcely listening to her, and his mind was elsewhere. She went to check the supper.

Turner ate a large meal, but without any visible sign of enjoying it. He looked, Maggie thought, like someone stoking a furnace, or even taking necessary but unpleasant medicine. When Maggie spoke to him he looked at her as if surprised to find her there. She knew that he was preoccupied with business – such absences in the past had presaged a new project – and left him to his thoughts. Her own, in any case, were also removed from present reality to that other world which already, though based on a lie, seemed to comprise a more cogent reality.

Chapter Six

By Thursday morning, Maggie felt she had settled into a proper routine.

'I don't know what you're doing, but it's definitely working,' Celia said in the changing room as they stripped off. 'The Mugger's positively *gracious* about you, says she can't think how I've managed to find such a treasure. I reckon she thinks you're far too good for me – which of course you are!'

'I just call her madam, and agree with everything she says. Well, not everything, but if I disagree I try to make it sound as though I don't, if you know what I mean.' Years of being tactful with the people Turner brought home had made this almost second nature to Maggie. She could as easily chat to a multi-millionaire as to a scaffolder, and had long since learned to tailor her remarks to fit in with what people wanted to hear. 'I'm a crawler,' she added cheerfully.

'Well, it certainly works, as long as you don't mind too much. Heaven knows what she'll say next time she comes, when we're back to usual.'

They were hurriedly hanging up their clothes as they spoke, and rummaging in their holdalls for hats and goggles. Even before she had a job to hurry off to, Maggie had found herself rushing to get into the pool: there was something in the atmosphere generated by people who have made an effort to leave their warm beds early and who don't want to waste a second of swimming time.

There was also a race, unspoken but real, to be the first into the water. Maggie, who had only managed it once, thought that the need lay not so much in wanting to win as in the seductive sight of the water, limpid and calm, its smooth surface marred only by the movement of the filtration, like the faint quivering of a jelly from a nearby footfall. To be the first one to slip into that stillness, to see the ripples of one's first stroke spreading their way down to the far end and catching spangles of light as they did so, was to know a second of pure joy.

'Oh, damn it, I've forgotten my knickers *again*!' Celia's anguished voice broke into her reverie. 'That's what comes of putting your costume on under your clothes. It saves time when you arrive, but I simply can't endure the thought of teaching all day with no knickers on. Not that anyone will *know*, of course, but I will just feel so insecure! And if I were to slip, or be knocked over . . .' she shuddered '. . . I'd have to give up my job. In fact, I'd have to move to another town. I'll just have to cut short on the swimming and rush home first before I go to College. Heaven knows what the Mugger will make of that; she already thinks it's dreadful that I come swimming instead of giving the boys a cooked breakfast.'

'Calm down,' Maggie broke in, laughing at this recital of disasters. 'I can give you a nice clean pair of knickers. Only the paper ones, but better than nothing. I keep a packet in my bag, just in case.'

Celia stared at her in admiration. 'What are you doing, cleaning my house? You should be running a company. Or the railways. Or the country, why not? Oh, thank you, Maggie! Magic Maggie! Magic Maggie with her paper pants!' She was chanting it as they went through the shower area to the poolside, and several people turned to grin.

'Steady on,' said Maggie. 'They'll all want some.'

A few minutes later, Maggie lifted her head to breathe, and was slapped in the face by a small wave. She drew in a breath that was half-water, and choked. Luckily she was still in her depth, so she stood up while she coughed and spluttered. Not greatly to her surprise, she saw the boy from Primrose's school – what was it she had called him? Of course, Dez. Easy to remember because it could almost have been a shortened form of Desperate, Maggie's nickname for the girl.

Thursday, she thought, as she swam on again. It was Thursday when he came last week. Maybe that's the only day he's going to be here. That would be good news for Primrose. Body Beautiful was there, too, ploughing vigorously in Dez's wake. Would he remember offering to help? She could only hope so, but was delighted a while later to see the boy and the older man leaning against the far end of the pool. With her goggles slightly steamed over, Maggie couldn't tell whether they were speaking or not, but at least they had both stopped swimming at the same time. She swam on.

Towards the end of the session the numbers thinned down. Celia had left, and so had most of the people who had to get to work. Maggie didn't rush. Mrs Draper always slept late, and never wanted her breakfast until ten, so Maggie found it was better for her to arrive and leave later, which meant she was there to make lunch as well. Body Beautiful was once more punishing the water in the fast lane, but at last Maggie saw him stop and lean, panting, against the side. She swam back, and moved over to where the dividing rope was fastened to the wall.

'Morning!' He seemed pleased to see her – a good sign.

'Good morning! We're the ones with the most stamina this morning. Or is it that we don't have to rush?' Maggie didn't like to go straight into asking whether he'd remembered to speak to Dez.

'I run my own business, so it's up to me if I'm a bit late. I think it's important to keep in peak condition, don't you?' Almost unconsciously, Maggie thought, he stood up straighter and sucked in his stomach.

'Well, I don't know that I've got anywhere near peaking yet, but I do enjoy my swim in the morning, and luckily it doesn't matter if I start work a bit later. And it's so nice when there are only a few people in – not so splashy, for one thing.'

'Yes, I noticed you getting a lungful of water from our young friend. I did have a word with him – at least, I did the words, and he grunted. Anyway, I did find out he's only going to come on Thursdays, so that's good news for your friend.'

'Oh, thank you! It is good of you to have asked.'

He grinned again – a surprisingly boyish and attractive grin that assorted strangely with the rubber hat that wrinkled his forehead.

'Braver than you realise, in fact. I think he thought I was trying to chat him up.'

'Oh, Lord!' That hadn't occurred to Maggie. 'I'm so sorry.' She couldn't help giggling, and he laughed in sympathy.

'You can laugh, but we all have to be careful nowadays. Anyway, I told him straight that he wasn't my type, that I'd been married for two years and that my wife is only twenty-four and looks like a model. That shut him up. Then I told him I only wanted to know so I could avoid him, because he swam like a fish. I didn't tell him I meant like a landed fish, all struggle and flop.'

'Goodness, that was clever of you. Had you worked it out in advance?'

'No, it's true. About my wife, I mean.'

'I meant about the fish,' said Maggie, quickly and untruthfully. Embarrassed, she glanced up at the clock. 'Goodness, I must go. I can be late, but not *very* late.'

Going to the steps, Maggie waited while another woman climbed out. It was Dogged-As-Does-It, pulling herself up the handrails and pausing between each step. As she emerged from the water, Maggie saw that she had a large, irregular bruise on her leg, the skin inflamed in places where it was broken. Her movements were awkward, and at one point her foot slipped on the ladder-like step. Maggie put out a hand to steady her.

'Thank you.' Her voice was so soft as to be barely audible.

'That looks painful.'

'It is, a bit. But it's getting better, so . . .' She let the words tail off.

'How did you do it?'

Reaching the top, the other woman put her head down and scuttled off. As she went, Maggie thought she heard her say, 'It was the pig . . .' but the voice was so indeterminate that she could easily have been wrong.

As she cleaned Celia's house, Maggie thought about Primrose. She found that the physical activity of cleaning, particularly now that she had evolved a routine and knew the house better, left her mind free and even stimulated it. Using the vacuum cleaner, in particular, engendered a rhythmic humming that insulated her still further from the outside world, and left her imagination free-wheeling.

She found herself imagining scenarios. She saw herself winning Primrose's confidence. She saw Primrose coming to her for advice, listening, changing, being happier. It was surprising how involved she felt. Am I, she wondered, going through some kind of mid-life crisis? Is my character changing? Is it, perhaps, some form of biological clock? Am I sublimating a desire for a child of my own by trying to look after Primrose? She's scarcely a child, and I can't say I feel particularly motherly towards her. I just feel sorry for her, there's nothing peculiar about that.

Her impulsive offer to clean Celia's house, which had started more as a joke than anything else, had been something quite novel to her. She had never imagined that she could become so quickly involved in someone else's life. There was something very satisfying about making the old lady comfortable, in finding small ways to calm her irritable temper, like a mother soothing a fractious child.

Now, with her mind dwelling on Primrose, Maggie found herself musing on what a difference it would make if she could take the girl in hand. A sensible diet, for instance, might slim her down and, more importantly, improve both her complexion and her general health. Contact lenses, or a more attractive pair of spectacles, a good haircut, some advice on skin care – what the magazines called 'a make-over', in fact – Maggie was sure that all of these would boost the girl's confidence and enable her to fend off the bullies at school. No one with Primrose's undoubted intelligence ought to be short of cutting phrases or the ability to turn things into a joke, laughter being one of the best defences against the kind of verbal bullying Maggie thought Primrose was enduring.

It would be easy enough, of course, for Maggie to do all of this. She had the money; the cost of contact lenses and a good hair stylist, even a new wardrobe of clothes, would scarcely dent her bank balance. At the Spa there were beauticians, make-up special-ists, people who could advise on diet and work out a personalised exercise plan. However, Primrose would need to want to be helped, and to be prepared to accept someone else's charity. Maggie had only had two conversations with Primrose, but she thought she knew her well enough to be certain that any such offers would be rejected with fury and resentment. And if Primrose *were* the kind of person ready to take hand-outs, then Maggie knew that she herself would be less inclined to help her. It was, after all, only a day-dream.

The downstairs was finished, Maggie glanced at her watch. Coffee-time. As she washed her hands at the sink, she heard the creak of footsteps on the stairs and smiled to herself.

'Ah, Maggie!' The tone of surprise was nicely done, Maggie thought. As if she didn't know I was about to make a coffee. 'I didn't realise you were there.'

'I'll be out of your way in a moment, madam,' said Maggie cheerfully. She liked to tease Mrs Draper. 'I was just about to go and make a start on the bedrooms.'

'Already?' Mrs Draper glanced at her watch.

'Well, I've finished downstairs, and I thought I'd give Ed's room a bit of a turn-out,' said Maggie briskly.

'Edward is perfectly old enough to keep his room tidy for himself.' This was no more than a reflex response; Mrs Draper had more important things on her mind. 'Surely my daughter-in-law doesn't expect you to work all morning without any kind of break?' Her air of shocked superiority was nicely simulated. 'She hasn't told you not to have a mid-morning coffee, has she?' She spoke as though Celia was an acknowledged slave-driver, with the added implication that she herself was treated with equal thoughtlessness.

'She hasn't actually forbidden it,' said Maggie thoughtfully, 'but I don't know. Ed's room is quite bad.'

'You shouldn't be expected to run round clearing up after those boys,' said Mrs Draper crossly. 'I'll put the kettle on.'

Such an unprecedented offer disarmed Maggie completely.

'That's very kind of you, madam. Perhaps you'd like a cup as well? And I believe there's some of that orange cake in the tin, if you could manage it.'

'Well, I shouldn't really . . . The one with the boiled oranges?'

'Yes. It really needs eating up,' said Maggie. 'Mustn't let it go to waste. Although the boys will probably finish it when they come home from school.'

As she expected, such a dire threat immediately made Mrs Draper realise that she really should have some cake. It was true, as Celia had said, that she had an excellent appetite, and it was amazing that her spare frame never seemed to acquire one single extra ounce of weight. Celia's privately expressed theory was that her spitefulness burned up the calories, and it was true that the old lady was seldom still. She rarely went out, since she did not drive and would not spend money on taxis, but spent her days roaming the house and garden, examining and criticising.

It was easy enough to see that Mrs Draper was bored, and lonely.

'What would you be doing now, if you were in Spain?' Maggie asked. Mrs Draper looked momentarily affronted, as if this were rudely intrusive. Maggie brought the cake out and set it on the table, and the older woman's face softened.

'Oh, I don't know,' she said vaguely. 'Having a cup of coffee, I suppose, something like that.'

'With one of your friends? I expect you take it in turns, don't you?'

'Not really.' The response was disappointing. Maggie, who had hoped to encourage a cheerful conversation about Spain and its delights, persevered.

'I suppose the flats are rather small for entertaining, but surely there are lots of places to go? Isn't there a club you all belong to, where you go to play cards?'

'Yes, the *Real*. That means Royal, you know, not real. A lot of people don't realise that. Yes. I go to the club. It's quite pleasant, though perhaps not quite as exclusive as it might be. Some of the things they organise are really quite . . . And some of the people who have joined recently . . . And they go to one another's homes quite indiscriminately. I prefer to keep myself to myself.'

Maggie inferred that Mrs Draper was as unpopular in Spain as she appeared to be at home. It seemed like a sad, empty existence. She made the coffee – proper ground beans for Mrs Draper served in one of the best cups, and instant in a mug for herself. She had originally done this because although she loved the smell of fresh coffee, she found it didn't agree with her and she preferred a large mug of weak, milky instant. She suspected that Mrs Draper read into it what she considered to be a very proper sense of what she would doubtless think of as 'knowing her place'.

'Very nice,' said Mrs Draper approvingly. 'I won't put you to the trouble of taking it through,' she said graciously. 'Do sit down.' Maggie suppressed a smile, and did so. This charade had been repeated for the last three days, and it occurred to Maggie that the Mugger and her own husband Turner held disquietingly similar views about 'hobnobbing with the staff'.

'You are far too good to be doing this kind of work,' said Mrs Draper. 'I realise it isn't easy to find work in this country, but surely you could be doing something better than cleaning?'

'I'm not very well qualified,' answered Maggie truthfully, 'and I like doing this. Cleaning someone else's house is much more interesting than doing one's own. And this is a lovely house.'

'It's quite pleasant, I suppose,' was the grudging reply. 'And I imagine there's more to do here than you have at home.'

'Much more,' said Maggie, suppressing a giggle at the thought of how astonished and mortified Mrs Draper would be if she were to see where Maggie lived. 'And, of course, I don't have small children, so that makes a difference.'

'Well, children are a mixed blessing. Mine have been a great disappointment to me.' Mrs Draper spoke so calmly that it took a moment for the words to sink into Maggie's mind. She looked across the table, aghast, at the older woman who calmly sipped her coffee and took another mouthful of cake.

'But surely . . . I mean, here you are . . .'

'Yes, here I am. And am I with my son? Or his wife? No, they're too busy for me. Now, if I were with my daughter, things would be different.' Mrs Draper's voice sounded wistful. 'We would be doing things together. Going to London, looking at clothes, going to a show, maybe.'

Maggie, who had hitherto found Mrs Draper to be reticent to the point of obsession, was astounded.

'I didn't know you had a daughter.'

'I haven't. Just two sons.' Mrs Draper's voice expressed her disgust at this oversight by Providence.

'But if you'd had a daughter, surely she'd be working, too? I mean, most women have jobs now, don't they?'

'My daughter would make time for me. We would have the same interests, enjoy doing the same things.'

'Yes, of course.' In the face of such sublime confidence, Maggie couldn't argue. 'Um, what sort of things?'

'Fashion. I've always been interested in clothes.' It was true that Mrs Draper was always immaculately dressed. Maggie thought of Celia with her practical school clothes and realised that from that point of view her daughter-in-law was a disappointment. 'I'd never expected to have only *boys*,' continued Mrs Draper. 'I always thought . . . a little girl. I was very fond of smocking, at one time, and would have loved to make party frocks, ballet clothes, fancy dress – and later on, of course, there would have been a wedding . . .' Her harsh voice was wistful. Maggie thought, with sympathy for them both, that no daughter would have been able to withstand an endless torrent of smocking and tulle, and would doubtless have rebelled by refusing to wear anything but dungarees. Nevertheless, she felt the pathos of this lonely old woman who had never, it seemed, outgrown her desire to play with dolls.

'Boys like dressing up too, sometimes,' she offered.

'Not in costumes that I'd consider making. I did offer once, a few years ago, and all they seemed to be interested in was some turtles with peculiar names. No, I just sew for myself, now. At least that way I can get something I can do up easily, and feel comfortable in.'

Maggie blinked at her. 'Do you mean you make your own clothes? Which ones?'

'Most of them.' The reply was careless, but Maggie could see that the older woman was proud of her skill. 'This suit. And the blouse. Not heavy things like overcoats. Of course, I don't tell people. I wouldn't want anyone to get the wrong idea.'

'Of course.' Maggie was unsure what the wrong idea was, whether that Mrs Draper couldn't afford to shop in designer boutiques, or that she might be asked to make something for someone else. 'I really envy you,' she said with genuine enthusiasm. 'I'd love to be able to do something like that. I was only thinking, this morning, about Primrose . . .'

'I didn't know you had a daughter. What a pretty name! How old is she?'

Mrs Draper was leaning forward in her chair, her face lit up with interest and pleasure. Maggie opened her mouth to disillusion her, and paused. Why spoil the moment? After all, she was to a certain extent living a lie anyway – why not do it properly?

'She's thirteen . . .'

Later that afternoon, Maggie was in the kitchen at home when she heard the splintery sound of wheels on the frozen gravel of the carriage sweep. At five o'clock it was effectively dark, though Maggie tried to persuade herself that the February days were beginning to lengthen. She lifted the corner of the blind to look out, and saw Julie's battered Ford, floodlit like the star of a musical by the outside lighting. It was in the middle of the turning circle, and appeared to have stopped rather than have been parked. Julie herself erupted from the driving door which she slammed behind her so that a few flakes of rusty paint fell from the bottom of it. She marched round to the passenger door, wrenched it open, then bent and began to tug. She appeared to be trying to pull something heavy from the front seat, and Maggie was just about to go out and help her when she heard Julie's voice.

'Come on. Out you get.' Her words came clearly through the sealed unit glazing that had been specially made to fit the Victorian windows of the kitchen area. 'Yes, you bloody well are. If you want to go flinging accusations around like that, you've got to learn to take the consequences. Come *on*.'

Maggie watched as the tall figure of Stephanie, elegant even in school uniform, emerged reluctantly from the car. It was still surprising to Maggie, who tended to think of her as a little girl to see how she now topped her mother's height by half a head, the heavy soles of her shoes adding a further inch to her endless legs. Julie pulled and pushed her towards the back door, looking like a sheepdog worrying at a giraffe. Maggie dropped the blind, and went to unlock the back door that opened into a lobby so spacious it was practically a room.

'Sorry about this,' puffed Julie. 'Wipe those bloody clodhoppers of yours, Steph. I don't wash this floor for you to traipse mud all over it.' Stephanie promptly levered the shoes off without undoing the laces, which made her a bit shorter although Maggie still had to tip her head back to look at her.

'Hello, Stephanie. This is a nice surprise. Hi, Julie.'

'Hi,' answered Julie morosely. Stephanie looked down at her feet. Even without the shoes her legs looked as long as a wading bird's, an impression enhanced by the shortness of her skirt, the black tights, and the way she stood with her toes turned in. Julie poked her in the back, and she scowled.

'Hello,' she mumbled. Julie wiped her feet vigorously on the mat, and inspected them before stepping off it. She was in a tracksuit and trainers, and Maggie could see a glimpse of one of the high-necked leotards where the tracksuit jacket zip had caught. It didn't look very adequate for a day when the frost had never vanished even from the unshadowed patches of the lawn.

'Come into the kitchen, Julie. You must be frozen. I'll put the kettle on.'

Julie looked down at her bare hands, as if surprised to find that they were icy.

'We're not stopping,' she said. 'I've got supper to do, and I don't want to hold you up. It's just Steph. She's got something she wants to ask you.'

A mutter from Stephanie attempted to deny this, but Julie was having none of it.

'Go on, my girl! You weren't so shy just now, so go ahead. Ask her.'

'Why don't we go into the kitchen? It's chilly out here.' Without waiting for an answer, Maggie turned and went back, pulling chairs out from the table and sitting down herself. Julie, out of habit, sat in her usual chair and after a moment's hesitation Stephanie folded her long legs and sat. She instantly looked about five years younger, and far more vulnerable. 'What's the matter, Stephanie? If something's worrying you, you might as well ask me now you're here.'

Stephanie twisted her legs into a knot.

'Mum says she's been going to that health farm place at your – at Mr Whittington's hotel,' she muttered.

'Yes?' Maggie raised her eyebrows at Julie, who pursed her lips and shook her head. 'It was meant to be a bit of a secret. Not so much from you, as from Mr Whittington.'

'Why?'

'Why is it a secret, or why is she going? The same reason, really.

He gave me the membership for Christmas, but I didn't like it and didn't want to go, so rather than waste it I gave it to your mum. I just didn't want him to know, because it was a present and he'd be hurt.'

'Why'd she want to go, if you didn't like it?' Stephanie was still clearly suspicious. Maggie wondered why the girl seemed to mind so much.

'I don't know why I didn't like it. I just didn't, that's all, it's not my kind of thing. But why shouldn't your mum like it? Don't you think it's doing her good? I think she looks great.'

Stephanie's expression said clearly that mums weren't meant to look great.

'Did you think it was a bit unfair?' Maggie persisted. 'I suppose there's no reason why you shouldn't go too, sometimes. The card says family membership, I think.'

Stephanie looked surprised. 'She wouldn't want *me* there,' she said, sounding more and more like a small child.

'Oh? Why not?'

Stephanie undid her legs and re-twisted them in the opposite direction. She glanced sideways at her mother.

'My daughter,' said Julie, in tones that mingled exasperation, despair and amusement, 'my *oldest* child, who although she is sometimes a pain in the neck is, I used to think, relatively sensible, has decided that I have A LOVER.' She spoke the words impressively. Stephanie ducked her head. 'That is how my daughter sees me, as the kind of woman who goes out and picks up dirty old men. Or even dirty younger men. I mean – *look* at me!' Obediently, they both looked. Maggie smothered a laugh.

'There's no reason why you shouldn't attract a younger man – apart from the fact that you're married, of course.'

'Well, what was I supposed to think?' Stephanie was stung into defence. 'You're *always* going out, and you won't say where you're going, and you come back smelling all expensive and you keep having your hair done, and wearing special make-up, and don't tell me you haven't got some new clothes because I've *seen* them.' She came to a halt on a little snuffling hiccup, and ducked her head again.

'Oh dear! My Christmas present has really backfired, hasn't it? Listen, Stephanie, the new clothes are just the leotards and things that my husband gave me. I told Julie to use them so he wouldn't see them sitting in the cupboard. The make-up and hair dressing is all part of the Spa, it's included in the deal, and so are the body sprays and so on. That's why she's coming home smelling exotic.'

Stephanie was staring at her open-mouthed. 'How can you possibly *not* want to go? It sounds amazing!'

'I suppose I'm just not into being amazed. Anyway, if you are particularly nice to your mother for a week or two, she might consider taking you with her occasionally.'

'Would you really? Oh, Mum!'

'You'd need to be really nice. Unbelievably nice. For a long time.'

'I will! I will! I'll look after the brats, I'll do the washing up, I'll help you with the supermarket, I'll keep my room tidy, I'll—'

'Steady! There's more to it than that.' Julie and Stephanie looked enquiringly at Maggie. 'Do you know a girl called Primrose at your school?' Maggie continued. 'She's the year below you, I think. She's got red hair, very curly, and she's quite – well, plump.'

'Primrose? No, I . . . Oh, you mean RSJ?'

'RSJ?' It was Maggie's turn to be confused.

'Yes, that's what they call her. It started as Rolling Stone, I don't know why – something about her hair and being fat and gathering moss, that's RS, and then someone said it should be RSJ because that's what you call those big beams that carry a heavy load – you know.'

'Poor girl.' Julie was disgusted. 'I hope you had nothing to do with that.'

'Course not! I mean, she's not in my year, I don't have anything to do with her. I'm just telling you what they say.'

'Well, her proper name's Primrose. And I want you to make friends with her.'

'But – but she's *awful*! Fat and spotty and that hair, it smells, she doesn't wash it, and she thinks she's really clever.' Stephanie spoke the last word with all the disgust English people reserve for what Maggie had heard Stephen Fry call 'The C Word'.

'That's why she needs a friend.'

'But I *can't*! I mean, what would everyone think? And say? She's not even in my year!'

'I'm not saying you've got to make her your best friend. I just want you to be nice to her, try to help her.'

Stephanie looked mutinous.

'Well, there it is.' Maggie spoke with finality. 'If you want to go to the Spa, that's the deal. You have to earn it. It's entirely up to you.'

69

Chapter Seven

'Hello?'

Silence. Wrong number, thought Maggie. Or a nuisance call? 'Hello?' she said again, just in case.

'I can't remember your name.'

'Maggie Whittington,' said Maggie, recognising Primrose's voice. 'I hoped you'd ring me. I've been thinking about you.' She spoke warmly, as if to a relative or a friend, forgetting that any intimacy she had with Primrose was in her imagination, and in the mind of Mrs Draper.

'Why?' A wave of suspicion came over the telephone.

'Well, because I've found out what you wanted to know,' said Maggie calmly. 'That boy from your school – Dez – only comes swimming on Thursday. Someone asked him, and he said it was the only day he could manage.'

'Oh.' If Maggie had hoped for gratitude, or even pleasure, she was to be disappointed. 'Right.'

'So you'll be able to come on the other days,' pursued Maggie.

'S'pose so.' Primrose didn't sound very enthusiastic.

Don't give up now, Maggie longed to say. Keep at it, you can do it.

'I'd be sorry not to see you there any more,' she said mildly. 'After all, if you stop going, that's another win for Dez, isn't it? Even if he doesn't know it.'

'S'pose so.' The same words as before, but more thoughtfully.

'You know what they say – don't let the buggers get you down.'

Was that a little breath of laughter? Maggie preferred to think that it was, and not a bored sigh.

'Right. See you.' Primrose rang off. Maggie hoped that her closing words had some significance, and weren't merely a formula.

It was Saturday lunchtime. Maggie had expected that going out to work would make her appreciate her free mornings much more. Going to bed the night before, she had relished the idea of an extra hour under the covers, with no swimming or work to get up for. In the event, she had woken slightly earlier than usual and lay waiting for it to be a reasonable time to make a cup of tea, and feeling that

71

the day stretched emptily before her. Empty not so much of activity, for she could easily find something to busy her in house or garden, but of people. Maggie realised that she had all too quickly become accustomed to the stimulus supplied by the varied group of people at the swimming pool.

She spent much of the morning pottering in the garden, cutting branches from the evergreen shrubs and from the coloured dogwoods, and subsequently arranging them with bought flowers to decorate her house. It was one of her favourite jobs; the garden had been tended by generations of women who understood the need for a year-round supply of foliage, and even at this time of year she needed to buy only a few cut blooms for her displays.

Maggie hummed as she snipped stems and stripped away lower leaves, breathing in the spicy or astringent smells as her fingers crushed them, relishing their cool freshness that still carried a memory of crisp winter air. As she did so, she thought of her mother, who had never liked to have flowers in the house because, she said, they made a mess when they dropped. Maggie remembered the first time she had visited a house where every room had flowers, even if it were only a handful of buttercups and ox-eye daisies from the verge thrust carelessly into a jam jar. Her mother, she knew, would have sniffed at that and been scathing of bringing weeds indoors, but to Maggie it had been a revelation. Now, looking back, she felt pity for her mother, who had denied herself this pleasure for the sake of tidiness.

Turner had invited a group of business associates, and their wives, to spend the evening at the hotel. Maggie, zipping up her new evening dress (just bought, and a size smaller) was quite thankful that it wasn't at the house. She didn't mind cooking for such occasions, in fact she quite enjoyed it, but she was glad not to have to ask Julie to give up her Saturday evening. Nor, she thought as she fastened the clasp of her necklace, would she have to spend tomorrow morning airing the smell of cigars and cigarettes out of the downstairs rooms.

She went through the evening on automatic pilot. It was second nature to her now to make the right remarks, to ask the questions that would keep the conversation flowing smoothly and pleasantly, to keep an unobtrusive eye on the service of the food and, even more unobtrusively, on how much people were drinking. Turner was on his best form, with a fund of amusing stories that occasionally teetered on the edge of being offensive, but never quite slipped over into anything that might be unacceptable. Maggie watched him flirting mildly with the wives, feeling no jealousy because she had seen it before and knew it for what it was – as much a part of his business technique as his golf rounds with the husbands, or his occasional evenings with the workforce when he drank, and sang, and told filthy jokes without ever quite crossing that invisible line that made him the boss.

'That went well,' she said to him later, as he undid the safety chain of her necklace. He kissed the back of her neck.

'Thanks to you,' he said, as he always did. He kissed her again, unzipping her dress and pushing it down from her shoulders. His love-making recently had been more urgent, and more frequent, than for some years. She felt a difference in him. On the surface he was as he had always been, a considerate lover. He knew what pleased her, as she knew his likes and dislikes, the little signals that would encourage him and the words or movements that excited. Nevertheless, although what he did was familiar and pleasurable, she sensed that in his mind he was elsewhere, much as she had been at the dinner-table. It was as if he sought the momentary oblivion of sex as a child seeks the comfort and familiar safety of its mother's arms.

She had wondered, once or twice, whether he was being, or had been, unfaithful to her. Twice, in the past, his eye had been taken by another woman. Maggie had guessed what was happening, but had wisely said nothing, and the little episodes had very quickly died a natural death without going any further than a momentary flash of attraction. On both occasions, afterwards, he had been particularly affectionate, and their love-making had, as now, been more frequent and more exciting. This time, however, there was nothing to indicate any romantic interest. Whatever the problem, Maggie knew better than to ask him about it directly. Turner told her things in his own way and his own time, and would profoundly resent questions that he would see as interference, however lovingly meant.

On Sunday morning, Turner shut himself in the study with his account books. It wasn't unusual, although Maggie did notice that he had more paperwork than usual, a stack of ledgers and files.

'Can I do anything to help?' In the past, when the business was getting going, she had often taken over the routine drudgery of the book-keeping. He looked at her vaguely.

'No, don't worry, Mags. Just some stuff I need to get straight before tomorrow. I'll be busy until lunch, then we might go somewhere, if you like? One of your stately homes, get a few ideas?' Maggie was an enthusiastic supporter of the National Trust, and ever since they had moved into their present home it had been one of Turner's jokes to say that she was bent on turning it into something similar.

'Lovely. I'll do soup and cheese for lunch, and we'll eat this evening. I might just go down to the shops, get a few things, if you're sure there's nothing you want me to do?'

'No, that's fine, you go and shop.' His attention was already withdrawn; he seemed almost eager to be rid of her.

As she drove to the supermarket, Maggie pondered on the mysterious power of names. When Turner had called her Mags just now she had been quite moved, because it was what he had called her, jokingly, in the early days of their marriage. Then, she had hated the name, and he had used it to tease her with in intimate moments. Last night, she thought, he called me Margot again, when we were at the hotel. Today, for the first time in years, I'm Mags. Does it mean anything? Am I reading too much into all this?

Inside the crowded supermarket she paused with her hand on the trolley and tried to remember what she actually needed. With only the two of them, and no pets to feed, her weekly shopping was not particularly arduous. She ran a mental check on the basics: more washing-up liquid, she remembered, and some fabric conditioner while she was at it. Fruit, definitely, and vegetables. She pushed off into the crowded aisle like a swimmer breasting a rough sea, her trolley in front of her like a surfboard.

Two punnets of imported strawberries, some salad and a bunch of grapes went into the bottom of the trolley first, then Maggie picked up a pack of lemons. Decisively she dropped them into her trolley, realising too late that they had landed squarely on one of the boxes of strawberries.

'Stupid woman,' she muttered to herself, picking up the strawberries. A figure next to her turned to stare. 'Oh, not you!' Maggie apologised. 'I'm afraid I was talking to myself.' The other woman smiled. Her face was vaguely familiar.

'I do it too,' she offered shyly. 'My brother says people will think I'm barmy, but I find it helps. What lovely strawberries! I did look at them, but it seemed a bit...' She shook her head, implying extravagance, but her voice and expression were without any envy or disappointment, pleased that someone was going to enjoy the treat she could not afford, and Maggie was reminded of Julie.

'I'm not so sure about them now. They look lovely, but I don't know that I'm altogether happy about strawberries that can have four heavy lemons dropped on them and not even be bruised.' She looked again at her companion, the sense of familiarity niggling at her. 'I'm sorry, but haven't we met? I'm sure I recognise your face.'

The other woman smiled her shy smile. 'At the swimming pool,' she said. 'I come to the Early Bird sessions.'

'Of course! I'm so sorry, how awful of me. My memory is dreadful.'

'I think you're supposed to say "You look quite different with your clothes on",' said the other, and Maggie laughed perhaps slightly more than this mild joke warranted. She realised that she was actually talking to Dogged-As-Does-It, almost unrecognisable today in trousers and an elderly waxed jacket, with a woollen

74

headscarf tied beneath her chin. Within the blue and black checks her face had a scrubbed, weatherbeaten look, innocent of any make-up, and the hair that wisped from beneath it had a dull, dried-out finish. In the early-morning queue at the swimming pool she wore what Maggie always termed 'respectable' clothes: tweed skirts and twin-sets, and sensible shoes.

'I always admire your swimming,' said Maggie truthfully. 'You make it look so elegant.' A flush of pleasure rose beneath the chapped skin, and for the first time Maggie noticed how bright the eyes were beneath the untidy brows, blue and with the fresh, unmarked whites of a child that has never smoked, or drunk, or stayed up too late.

'I've always loved swimming. When I was younger I thought of taking it up competitively, but somehow it was never possible. Still, I go as often as I can. It's such a . . .' Such a what, Maggie wondered? Such a bore? Such a problem? Such a treat? 'And you're the one who found that girl's engagement ring, aren't you? I was so glad. She smiles at me, you know. Such a nice . . .' Her voice tailed off again, as if finding a word to describe Stella was beyond her.

She made being smiled at sound extraordinary, like winning the lottery.

'She's a lovely girl, isn't she,' Maggie agreed.

'She looks lovely. I don't really know anyone at the pool.'

'Nor did I, until that business with the ring. Of course, it's always a bit of a rush in the morning, isn't it?'

'Yes, I'm always in a hurry. I shouldn't really be going at all, my brother wouldn't like it if he knew, and it's not as if I need the exercise, but I try to fit it in because . . . well . . . you know . . .'

Once again she seemed unable to explain herself, but about her brother she spoke as calmly as if she were commenting on inclement weather, as though it were quite normal for a middle-aged woman to be dictated to by her brother about something so trivial as an early-morning swim. Maggie was fascinated. She knew, of course, that even in these liberated days there were plenty of women who were in thrall to their husbands' commands, but a brother? The temptation to learn more, to expand her knowledge of the characters of her own particular soap opera, was great. Maggie glanced at her watch.

'Have you got much shopping to do? Why don't we have a coffee, if you've got time?'

The other woman dithered anxiously. 'Well, I shouldn't really. My brother . . .' Maggie waited, feeling that too much encouragement might frighten her off. 'Well, a quick coffee would be nice. I don't have much to get, we grow most of our own food.'

'How fascinating,' said Maggie with sincerity. 'You must tell me all about it. I don't need very much, either. I'll put my stuff in the car, and meet you by the coffee shop. My name's Maggie, by the way.'

'I'm Dawn.' There was the usual embarrassing moment when British women wonder whether they should shake hands or not, but the trolleys between them solved the problem and they separated to their shopping. Half an hour later they were sitting at a table in the coffee shop attached to the supermarket.

Maggie had insisted on paying, since it was her idea. She had been vividly reminded of her coffee with Primrose by the sight of her companion looking with yearning at the display of cakes. Damn the diet, she thought, and took one since the other woman would obviously not like to otherwise. It was worth it to see the pleasure with which Dawn took a first mouthful of her slice of rich chocolate cake. A blissful expression spread over her face.

'Delicious! I'd forgotten how good chocolate is.'

'You don't normally eat it?'

'No, Gordon – that's my brother – doesn't approve of it. He says the chocolate manufacturers exploit the people who grow the cocoa beans, and that it's an unnecessary indulgence.'

'Chocolate contains iron,' Maggie offered. She had often found this an encouraging thought. 'And I can't see what good it does to the growers if we all stop buying it. Still, it's nice to hear of people with a social conscience. You're . . . close to your brother, are you?'

'Oh yes. He practically brought me up – he's a lot older than me, of course. My big brother.' Dawn smiled sadly. 'That's how I always think of him.' She said it with uncharacteristic firmness. Maggie wondered who she was trying to convince. 'Our mother died when I was quite young, and we've looked after each other ever since, really.' She took another mouthful, pausing to savour it. Her face was pink, as though the rich cake were acting like alcohol on a system unused to it. 'He was always a loner, always had – what did you call it? A social conscience. We've got a farm – well, it's more of a smallholding, in fact, but he doesn't like it called that.'

'A smallholding? What fun! And you grow all your own food?'

'Most of it. Not cereals, of course. It's not practical to grow wheat, for instance, so I buy flour.' She looked down at the bag at her feet. 'And oranges and lemons, and cleaning and washing stuff. We have our own vegetables and fruit, meat, eggs, milk and butter and cheese – and all organic, of course.'

'That's very impressive. It must be hard work.'

'It is.' An unconscious sigh, then she straightened her shoulders. 'But very rewarding.'

'Of course,' Maggie agreed.

'And I don't do it full-time. We have to have an income, you see – Council Tax, and electricity, all that kind of thing. We can't make enough out of what we sell to cover that, so I have a job at the Council offices.'

'Really? The friend I work for – she swims too, actually, you probably know her – her husband works for the Council. Draper – Philip Draper. Do you know him?'

'He's in Planning, isn't he? Yes, I know him by sight. I work in a different department. And you work with his wife? Small world.'

'Small town. And I work *for* her, not with her – I clean her house.'

'Really? I'd have thought you'd be doing something more . . . well, you know.' She blushed unhappily. 'I'm sorry, that sounds rude. Of course there's nothing wrong with cleaning a house. It's probably more interesting than what I do. Working in an office can be very dull.'

'I suppose it could be. But you're working with other people, at least. I should think a farm could be quite a lonely place, sometimes.'

'Yes, it is. Only the people I work with are all much younger than me, so of course we don't have much in common. They'd think I was mad if they knew I go and do the milking before I come to work, and then make butter and cheese when I get home. It's so . . .' An inability to bring a sentence to a proper conclusion was, Maggie thought, very much an indication of Dawn's lack of self-confidence.

'I should think they'd be riveted. I know I would be. I suppose I couldn't come and visit some time, could I? It all sounds fascinating.'

'Oh, yes.' She looked startled. 'It's not really very interesting to see, you know. We never seem to have quite enough money or time for extras like decorating, or new fences, or modern buildings for the animals. And Gordon is a great believer in recycling . . .'

Maggie could well believe it. Looking at her new friend, she thought that the policy must apply to her clothes as well, which had all the chic of jumble-sale bargains.

'Your brother's never married, then?' she fished carefully.

'No. He doesn't get the chance to meet many people, as he's always working. Sometimes I wish . . . but it would be strange, after all these years, to be living on my own, with nobody to look after.'

'It might be you who meets someone, instead of your brother.'

Dawn stared at Maggie as if the possibility had never occurred to her.

'At my age?'

'Why not? You're not old.' Maggie studied Dawn, revising her first estimate of her age. She had guessed at over forty, but now she saw that her skin, though weatherbeaten, was relatively unlined while her hair, obviously, was innocent of artificial colouring. 'People do. You could join one of those dating agencies.'

Dawn looked appalled.

'I couldn't do that! What would Gordon say?'

Quite a lot, obviously, thought Maggie. 'Sorry,' she said, seeing that she had gone too far. 'It was just one of those mad suggestions. After all, there's nothing wrong with not being married, is there? And better no marriage than an unhappy one.'

'That's what Gordon says.' Dawn sipped at her coffee. Following Maggie's lead she had asked for cappuccino. Maggie suspected that if chocolate was forbidden by Gordon then coffee must be under a similar embargo, and she was touched to see the look on Dawn's face as she licked the froth from her lips, and tasted the sprinkling of chocolate on it.

Maggie suddenly remembered her previous encounter with Dawn.

'How's your leg? You had such a nasty bruise on it.'

The other woman flushed. 'Oh, it's much better now, thank you. It wasn't as bad as it looked. At least . . .' Her voice tailed off. Maggie, remembering the soot-coloured bruise and inflamed skin, thought this unlikely, but let it go.

'Did I really hear you say it was the pig? At the time I thought I must have imagined it, but if you've got a farm, perhaps not.'

'Yes, it was the sow. I was mucking her out, and she was feeling a bit irritable. My brother usually does her, and she doesn't really like me. I'm a bit frightened of her, and animals always know, don't they?'

'So they say. But you don't usually have to do the heavy stuff, do you?'

'Well, not really, but there's always so much to do, I never seem to be . . .' Her words acting as a reminder, Dawn pushed her empty cup away and began looking round for her shopping. She appeared flustered. 'I must get back. My brother—'

'Of course.' Maggie could see that her companion was anxious to leave. 'I expect I'll see you at the pool soon. It's been lovely to meet you.'

Dawn pulled a pair of knitted gloves out of her pocket, dropping one in her haste.

'Oh dear . . . Yes, it's been . . . thank you . . . I expect I'll . . .' One of her carrier bags fell over, and oranges rolled everywhere. 'Oh dear . . .'

'Here, let me. There you are.' Maggie gathered up the straying fruit that people on nearby tables had picked up.

'Thank you. I'm sorry, but I really must . . .'

Dawn hurried off, and Maggie watched her go. How extraordinary people are, she thought. Who would have guessed that Dawn, swimming her decorous lengths of the pool, had such an unusual life? Memories of *The Good Life*, enjoyed on television so

78

many years ago, brought images of suburban self-sufficiency, improvident and cheerful as the Flopsy Bunnies, but she didn't think Maggie's existence was quite like that. For one thing, the fictional character played by Felicity Kendall had enjoyed the adoring attentions of a jolly Richard Briers, whereas Dawn seemed positively scared of her brother. Had the cherishing big brother grown up into a tyrant?

Maggie picked up her handbag, and made her way to the door. The coffee shop was crowded now. During the week it was much used by the pupils of the nearby Sixth Form College – Celia's pupils, Maggie reminded herself. Today the clientèle was different – young couples making use of the Sunday opening to do their weekly shopping, families with children who had been promised a bribe to keep them quiet while the trolley was filled, older couples regarding it more as an outing than a shopping trip. How many of them, she wondered, were as ordinary as their outward appearance would suggest? Not as many as she would once have thought, certainly.

Why didn't I ever realise, she wondered? Was I so wrapped up in my own life that I just didn't notice? How dreadful, if that were so. Yet the people I met before, neighbours and people at work – none of them seemed to be doing anything particularly unusual beyond the general round of work, marriage, children or divorce. Can it be that people who get up early to go swimming are a bit odd? Look at me – all of a sudden I'm a cleaning lady and pretending that Primrose is my daughter, perish the thought. Maybe they're putting something in the water, and we're all going down with Mad Swimmer's disease!

Chapter Eight

Driving home from Celia's one Monday, Maggie was amazed to realise that she had already been working there for three weeks. There had been few problems. Maggie's chief worry had been Turner, with his habit of bringing groups of people home for lunch at short notice. Fortunately he had not done that recently, and in fact appeared so preoccupied with work that he had scarcely noticed that Maggie was out every morning. She had been too thankful for this to wonder why it should be so and anyway, one of the reasons for Turner's success was his ability to immerse himself wholeheartedly in a current project.

It was quite sad to think that Maggie's time working for Celia would soon be coming to a close. Only one more week, according to the original plan, and Maggie found she was rather dreading a return to her previous existence. Once the routine had been established, the days had flowed past swiftly but imperceptibly. Like a holiday, the first few days had seemed long, the prospect ahead seeming to stretch to beyond the horizon, but suddenly there was so little time left before returning to reality.

Reality, thought Maggie. I'm not sure I know what that is any more. My old life would probably seem like a fantasy to most people, and the fantasy I'm living now is what most people would call normal life. After all, you can't get much more real than washing a kitchen floor. Even pretending that I've got a daughter seems real, when I'm talking to Mrs Draper.

Maggie had seen Primrose regularly at the swimming pool. She seldom did more than mumble 'Morning' in return to Maggie's greeting, but Maggie noticed that she had bought some goggles, and as a result was swimming better. Maggie had seen her watching Stella as she cut effortlessly through the water.

'I wish I could swim like that,' Primrose had burst out, as she and Maggie observed Stella execute a neat tumble-turn.

'Don't we all. You probably could, though, if you worked at it.'

'What, me?' Primrose gestured at her body, bulging out of an old black costume that only fitted her because the Lycra had perished enough to give it unlimited stretch.

'Why not? You could do classes, or join a club.'

Primrose's look, scathing even through the lenses of the goggles, showed what she thought of *that* idea.

'Going to school, with my clothes on, is bad enough. How do you think it would be at a club?'

Maggie could see that Primrose wasn't ready to try anything too radical.

'Well, why not ask Stella to give you some advice? She's very nice, I'm sure she'd help you.'

'I couldn't.' The words were flat, but the tone was wistful.

'I'll ask her, if you like. You could say she owes me a favour since I found her engagement ring for her. Not that she wouldn't have found it anyway, but she always behaves as if I performed some kind of miracle.'

'I don't mind.' Primrose, ungracious as always, swam away, but Maggie didn't allow herself to be discouraged. Primrose was so accustomed to rejection that she avoided any possible chance of being hurt. In the changing room Maggie spoke to Stella.

'Of course I'll help, if she'd like me to!' the young woman said immediately. 'Not that I'm an expert or anything, but I had a very good coach and I expect I could pass on some tips.'

'She won't ask you, that's the thing. She's a bit . . .' Maggie searched for a word to describe Primrose. Goodness, she thought, I sound like Dawn. 'A bit shy,' she concluded.

'I'll speak to her, shall I?' Stella gave her sunny smile, the smile of one to whom the possibility of rejection has never occurred.

Stella's magic worked. Primrose had developed the kind of admiration of Stella that in Maggie's schooldays had been termed 'a crush'. As a result, she worked hard at improving her stroke, practising with floats and concentrating on the economy of movement that characterised Stella's style. It was difficult to tell, but Maggie thought that inside the sagging old swimming costume Primrose was looking a bit slimmer.

Maggie felt that she was getting to know Primrose, and she was amazed by how much pleasure she had from seeing the girl enjoy her swimming. With Dawn, however, things had not been so successful, in spite of the promising start at the supermarket. At the pool Dawn was perfectly friendly, in her shy way, but she didn't come very regularly and when she did she was always in a hurry to get to work. Maggie had been hoping to visit the smallholding – or farm, as the brother liked it to be called – but Dawn had been evasive and Maggie didn't like to appear pushy.

Pulling into the drive, Maggie was surprised to see Julie's car still there. She glanced at her watch – two o'clock; normally, Julie would have left at one. Goodness, thought Maggie, I hope Turner didn't suddenly decide to bring people back, or something. No, surely they'd be here by now, if it were lunch. Still, it would be nice to see Julie. She had really missed her.

Julie had been ironing in the kitchen. As Maggie came in she was emptying the water out of the iron. A pile of neatly folded shirts on the table stood as mute witness to her industry, and the room smelled pleasantly of fresh linen.

'Julie! How nice to see you! I've really missed you, being out so much the last few weeks. Everything all right?'

Julie pressed the steam button on the iron to clear out the last of the water, and it hissed furiously.

'Yes, everything's fine. I just thought it would be nice to see you. I'll do a couple of hours less later in the week, to make it right.'

'Don't be silly, you don't have to do that. I'm always happy for you to do a bit more. Have you had any lunch?'

'I brought a sandwich with me, but I didn't get round to eating it.'

'You're not dieting, are you? You're looking remarkably svelte – is that the effect of the Spa?'

Julie looked down at herself, momentarily distracted.

'I am slimmer, aren't I? It's mostly the Spa, though I've been a bit off my food for the last few days. I could murder a cup of tea, though, if you'd like one? I'll put the kettle on.'

They sat at the table.

'What you been up to, then?' Julie eyed Maggie's clothes. 'Nothing very grand, is it?'

Maggie was amused. 'You could say that. It's sort of charity work, really, and it's better if I don't look too dressed up. It's fun, I'm quite enjoying it, but it's not really very interesting. I'd much rather hear about you. How are the kids? How's Stephanie? Has she recovered from thinking you've got a lover?'

Julie smiled, but it was not her usual cheerful grin.

'Steph's fine. I let her come to the club with me once a week and she adores it. It's made her much more helpful, too – she wants to keep on the right side of me, in case I change my mind about taking her! She's been doing her best with that girl at school – you know, Primrose?'

'Yes, that's right. Oh, that is good of her, Julie. I know how difficult it is at school to get to know someone in a different year, especially if it's someone nobody likes.'

'Well, you know our Steph. She likes going against everyone else. Anyway, she's quite grateful to you – this Primrose is supposed to be really clever, so Steph thought she'd start by asking some advice about her maths, as a way of getting to talk to her. She hates maths, always has done. So Primrose started explaining it to her, and at the end of it Steph said she suddenly found she understood it, which she'd never done before. Says Primrose made it really clear, which that teacher of hers has never done.'

'That's interesting. Being clever is one thing, but being able to explain things to other people is quite another. I wouldn't have thought she'd be like that – she's not exactly one of the world's great communicators.'

'Maths is different, though, isn't it? Not like English or something.'

'I suppose so. It's right, or it's wrong, and it's just a question of understanding the processes. Still, if it's helped Stephanie then I'm very glad. I felt rather bad about lumbering her with Miss Most-Hated.'

'Well, I don't know about her own year, but she's certainly much more popular with Steph's lot. Once they discovered how she'd helped Steph several of them asked her to explain things to them.'

'That's great. As long as they're not getting her to do all their homework for them.'

'There may be a bit of that, but not much. She may be clever, but she's in the year below so she hasn't done most of what they're working on. Anyway, I told Steph to ask Primrose if she'd like to come with us to the Spa some time. I thought you wouldn't mind. I can sign her in as a guest – gold card holders are allowed to do that on weekdays.'

'Julie, that's wonderful! I do hope she'll say yes, it's just the thing for her. She's very self-conscious about her appearance, though. I don't know whether she'd do it.'

'Worth a try. She's been back to the house once after school, had tea with us. Poor kid, she didn't know what had hit her with my lot all shouting and fighting and stuffing their faces; it must have been like feeding time at the zoo.'

'I expect she loved it. There's not much going on at home, by the sound of things. Her father works late most days, poor man, and by the time he gets home he's too tired to talk to her. You'll be doing a good thing if you can help her, Julie.'

'My good deed.' Julie smiled again, but there was still an underlying constraint. Maggie sipped her tea.

'Is there something wrong, Julie?' A horrid thought, born of the knowledge that Julie wouldn't have stayed late unless she really needed a proper talk, crossed Maggie's mind. 'It's not Turner, is it? He hasn't been making things difficult for you, has he?'

Turner's attitude to Julie was an unspoken thing between them. They both knew that his behaviour stemmed from the insecurities of his childhood, though Maggie thought that the fact that he showed none of this sharp snobbery towards his own workforce was more to do with a little bit of jealousy about his wife's friendship with her cleaning lady.

84

'No, it's nothing like that. I've not seen or spoken to him for weeks. No, it's Tom.'

'Tom? You mean your husband?'

'Mm.' Maggie's mug of tea had been too full, and some of it had spilled onto the table. Julie turned her mug in the puddle, and used it to make a circle on the varnished wood.

'What is it? Is he ill?'

Julie made a second circle bisecting the first.

'No. At least, I don't think so. He doesn't seem ill. Just . . . different.' Maggie waited. With immense concentration, Julie continued to mark wet circles until she had made a flower pattern. 'He's got a job.'

'Goodness! What kind of job?'

'At the petrol station. That new big one past the station.'

One of the things that Julie half-jokingly moaned about in Tom – apart from the huge inedible vegetables he grew – was that he never had a job. Having trained as a gardener, he had worked for a few years for the Town Council, but had been so miserable spending his days planting out bedding in neat, tight rows that in the end he had left. Since then he had done part-time gardening work, but since he regarded lawns and flower beds as a waste of good vegetable garden and was impervious to requests or even demands, he never did very well. Maggie would have been happy to give him some work in her own garden, but Julie, though grateful, had said no.

'Not that he isn't a good worker – he can get more done in an hour than most people in three – but he has to do it his own way. You might want to grow asparagus, or beans, but if he got it into his head that what the garden wanted was carrots and spinach, then carrots and spinach is what you'd get. I can't see that going down with Mr Whittington, somehow, can you?'

'The petrol station?' Maggie queried now. 'That doesn't sound like his sort of thing.'

'It isn't. He hates it – I just know he does. The hours are awful, it's all shifts and half the time he doesn't know whether he'll be on at six in the morning or midnight, and then he's spending hours stuck in a little cubby hole – they've got the tills all shut up behind strengthened glass, in case of robbers – and the other people all smoke, you know how he hates that, and he comes home all tired and grumpy and stinking of cigarettes . . .' Julie gave a gasp that was more than half a sob. 'The worst of it is, he didn't say anything, didn't discuss it, just took himself off one afternoon and came back saying he was starting the next day. I mean, it's quite well paid, but we were managing, with my money and the gardening; it wasn't great but we got by, have done all these years, so why? He hasn't got the energy for his allotment now, even if he had the time, and he won't tell me why he's done it!'

'You've asked him?' Maggie knew it was a stupid question. In Julie's family, everyone was very open, and there was never any problem about asking questions. If someone didn't want to answer they said so, but mostly they did.

' 'Course I have. And the kids have, and all. All he says is it's time he had a proper job. But why now? I mean, I've been nagging him for *years* to get a proper job, and he just used to smile and say, "What's proper?" It was a kind of family joke, that he wouldn't even get an *imp*roper job, let alone a proper one. I wouldn't mind, only he's so miserable! If it weren't for that, I might have wondered whether he's met someone else. Matter of fact,' she admitted, 'I did think it might be something like that, that there's some young totty who he's trying to impress, or he wants to have money so he can take her out. But he never goes out, except to work, so *surely* it can't be that.'

Maggie thought about it. 'You don't think . . .' she began, then stopped and tried again. 'You remember when you came round with Steph, the other week?'

Julie stared at her. ' 'Course I do, but . . . you don't think she said something to Tom? She wouldn't. I'm sure she wouldn't. Besides, that was all sorted out.'

'I know it was, and I'm sure she wouldn't have said anything to him. But supposing he's noticed something different about you? I mean, you were wondering about Tom, maybe he's wondering about you. And now he's trying to please you, do what he thinks you want.'

'But that's ridiculous! Besides, he never notices what I look like. I could dye my hair green and grow a second nose, and all he'd probably do is offer to spray my hair for greenfly.'

Maggie laughed. 'I'm sure he can't be that bad. Why not tackle him head-on? Ask him if he's seeing another woman. That should stir him up.'

Julie fidgeted with her mug, obliterating the flower pattern. 'What if he says yes?'

'It's not very likely, is it? Unless it's someone at the garage, I suppose.'

'There's only one woman works there, and she's about sixty.'

'Well, then. And if there is someone, what would you do about it?'

It was obvious that Julie had never seriously considered the possibility. She frowned.

'I dunno. Fight, I suppose.' She saw Maggie's expression, and laughed. In spite of their conversation it was her old laugh, open and full-blooded. 'I don't mean I'd go round and punch her lights out! Just that I wouldn't let him go easily.' Julie began a new pattern with her mug, this time a long shape like a worm. 'Thing is, I wondered, do you ever get petrol there?'

'Not very often. I could do, though, if you like.'

'Would you? Not if it's a nuisance.'

'Of course it isn't. I'm not sure what good it would do, though. After all, for one thing he'd recognise me, and for another he might not be on duty. What am I looking for – naked women?'

Julie grinned ruefully. 'Something like that. I know it sounds silly, but I can't keep calling in myself, and I can't leave it alone.'

Maggie nodded understandingly. 'Okay! The car's pretty empty, I'll go along tomorrow. Any idea what time he'll be there?'

'Afternoon, I think. Um, thanks, Maggie.'

'No problem – though I honestly don't believe you've got anything to worry about.'

Maggie thought about it the following morning as she was swimming. As usual, the rhythmic movement and the warm blue water worked on her mind like a comb on wet hair, easing the tangles out smooth and straight. As Stella had helped Primrose, Maggie had listened, watched and emulated, and as a result found that she too enjoyed her swimming even more. By now, the new goggles had lost some of their crystal clarity and tended to steam up, so that after the first two or three lengths Maggie saw everything through a haze, and this increased the feeling that she was in her own private world.

Something had gone wrong with the thermostat, and the water was unusually warm – getting in had been like climbing into a warm bath. It was too hot for the serious swimmers, most of whom had done a few lengths and got out. Even Maggie found the warmth enervating, so she gave up swimming properly and floated on her back.

It was the first time she had done that since childhood. Buoyed up in the womb-like warmth, doing no more than moving her feet or paddling with her hands to keep her body level, was as peaceful as she imagined floating in space might be. With her head back and her ears full of water the outside world came to her dimly through the sound of her own breathing. Through her misted goggles she could see the round lights set in the ceiling like little moons through thin cloud – even down to the shadowy craters. Dead flies, she supposed idly, but still . . . It was extraordinarily relaxing, the way she imagined people must feel while meditating.

Presently she rolled over and swam a slow length. A shape loomed up ahead of her. Maggie swerved, but unfortunately the other did too, and in the same direction. A collision was avoided by both of them stopping swimming and treading water.

'Sorry,' said Maggie automatically. 'Oh, hello, Dawn!'

'Hello, um, Maggie.' Maggie thought that the hesitation was more from indecisiveness than because Dawn had trouble remembering her name. 'I've left the slow lane because it's so crowded, and I'm afraid I wasn't really looking where I was going.'

'Me neither. Still, no harm done. How are you? How's the farm?'

Dawn looked startled. 'The farm? Oh, the same as usual, I suppose. It doesn't really . . . except for the seasons, of course, that makes a difference, but still . . .'

'I expect this is a busy time of year for you,' said Maggie tactfully. Dawn had been evasive about Maggie's visit the last time they had spoken, and it seemed impolite to mention it again.

'They're all busy,' Dawn responded, unusually brusque. 'But I was thinking – you said you'd like to come and see it. Do you still want to? It's really not very interesting . . .'

'I'd love to,' said Maggie decisively. 'I'm sure I wouldn't find it boring, and anyway it would be nice to see you, and meet your brother.'

'Oh . . .' Dawn flinched slightly, and a ripple of water splashed into her mouth. She choked. 'Sorry,' she gasped at length.

'It's not really the place for a conversation, is it? We'd better get to the side.'

'Don't you think that's a bit tricky?' Dawn looked dubiously at the number of people swimming past them in both directions.

'Yes, it is a bit like crossing a busy road. The end, then.'

At the shallow end nearest the changing rooms they met again.

'Now, where were we?' Maggie was determined to pin Dawn down to a definite arrangement. Until they had fixed a day and a time, she felt that Dawn would be likely to change her mind about the visit. 'When can I come?'

'Oh, well, I thought the weekend,' said Dawn. 'Saturday, if you can manage it. I'm working, you see, on weekdays, and it still gets dark so early . . . The only thing is, my brother won't be there. Saturday afternoon is when he usually goes out.'

'Never mind, it's you that I'm coming to see – and the farm, of course. What sort of time?'

'Could we make it half-past two? Then we'd have some time before I have to do the feeding and milking.' Maggie agreed, and Dawn gave her directions which Maggie muttered to herself, hoping it wasn't as complicated as it sounded. She was about to swim off when a body landed with a splash next to her.

'Celia! I thought you wouldn't be coming today, it's so late.'

'I know.' Celia was tugging on her hat. 'It's madness, I should have skipped it but I just felt I needed a quick swim to work off all the adrenalin or whatever it is. Oh Maggie, it's a disaster! I shall go mad!'

'What is it? Not the boys?'

'No, no.' Celia dismissed her beloved offspring with a flap of her hand. 'Much worse than them. It's the Mugger. She's just learned that her flat in Spain has been burned down.'

'Burned down? You mean the whole building? Good heavens!'

'Well, perhaps not the whole building. Just a bit of it. Those bloody painters, taking forever to do the work, and using one of those hot-air things to get rid of the old paint, stupidly left something smouldering in the flat below hers. The people there were away, like herself, so by the time the fire brigade got there it was all well and truly alight. So what with the smoke and the soot and the water, her flat's just about wrecked.'

'How dreadful! I'm so sorry! How has she taken it?'

Celia grimaced. Then: 'Surprisingly well. Angry, of course, and worried about her bits and pieces. Phil's going to fly out with her at the weekend, see what can be salvaged, do the paperwork, that kind of thing. And then, of course, she'll come back and stay with us until the flat's habitable again, which could be *months*! The twins are practically mutinying and I don't feel much better about it. Though to be fair, she hasn't been nearly as bad as usual this time, largely thanks to you, but . . .' She eyed Maggie dubiously.

'But what?'

'Well, I'm hoping you'll be pleased, but my Mrs Tomsett – you remember her, my usual cleaning lady – she more or less told me she didn't want to come back until the Mugger had gone, so . . . can you carry on, Maggie? I don't know how long for, and I'd be happy to give you a bit extra because I really think you more than earn it, soft-soaping the old battleaxe, and if you say no I just don't know how we're going to survive it!' She finished on a tone that tried to express mock-horror, but Maggie could see that in fact the horror was real. She thought rapidly.

'I'd be happy to stay. I enjoy the work, and Mrs Draper doesn't worry me. It's just my husband . . . I'm not sure whether it will be possible.'

'Oh dear.' Celia was too nice a woman to put any more pressure on Maggie, but her face spoke volumes. Maggie patted her arm.

'Don't worry. I'm sure we'll be able to work something out. I'll carry on for as long as I possibly can, even if I can't manage quite so many mornings, and maybe the flat won't take as long as you feared. The building is still sound, presumably?'

Celia nodded. 'It's really just cosmetics, apparently. Phil will have to throw his weight about a bit when he goes over, and perhaps go out again after a week or two. Meanwhile,' she glanced at her watch, 'we'd better do a length or two, or it will be time to get out.'

'It's almost too warm for swimming today.'

'Yes, it is, isn't it. Such a waste, really. Bless you, Maggie! I know it's a bit old-fashioned to talk about you being a treasure, but truly you are.' Celia gave Maggie a quick kiss, and swam off, her normal cheerfulness quite restored. Maggie followed more slowly, thinking as she swam. What had been possible for a few weeks, at a time when Turner was obviously preoccupied with business, would be more difficult to sustain for a longer period. Once whatever was bothering him was sorted out – and she had no doubt that he would sort it out, for he always did – he would be bound to want to know more about her mythical charity work. Could she carry it off, and was it right to deceive him like this?

Once again, the water had its usual calming effect. I won't make any decisions now, Maggie thought. What is it they say – Go with the flow? I'll go with the flow, and see what happens.

For the first time since her arrival, Mrs Draper was up and dressed when Maggie arrived.

'Oh Maggie, the most dreadful thing has happened!' She followed Maggie through the kitchen as she went to hang up her coat and change into indoor shoes. Maggie saw that she was enjoying the drama of it, and refrained from saying that she already knew. It would be pointless anyway, since Mrs Draper would undoubtedly wish to go through every detail again.

'Oh dear, Mrs Draper, what is it?'

She needed to say no more. It was a good thing that the house was still relatively clean from the day before, because very little work was done that morning. Mrs Draper was torn between the excitement of being the heroine of her very own drama, and worry about the contents of her home. Maggie listened, and commiserated, and encouraged. By lunchtime the old lady, pinkcheeked and stimulated, had talked her way round and through the event like someone in a maze, doubling back, taking the same path over and over again, and taking startling diversions that still, eventually, seemed to lead her back to the heart of the matter. She insisted on Maggie eating lunch with her and Maggie, feeling that all this stimulation might not be healthy to the blood pressure of one of her age, stayed.

'One of the good things to come out of all this,' said Mrs Draper, dismembering a Dover sole with skill, 'is that I shall be able to carry out a little idea I had, about Primrose.'

'Primrose?' Maggie was momentarily disconcerted by the sudden change of subject. 'Oh, you mean *Prim*rose.'

'Of course, Maggie. Your daughter, Primrose. Such a pretty name! I'd been thinking it would be fun to make her something to wear, something nice. Now, don't shake your head at me – you know how I like dressmaking, and you've made my stay here much more enjoyable than usual. In fact, if it weren't for you, I don't know how I'd have put up with the thought of staying all these extra weeks. So you see, I'd really like to do it, and I won't take no for an answer!'

Chapter Nine

O h good grief, thought Maggie desperately. What on earth do I say now? Talk about pigeons coming home to roost! How can I get out of it? Say Primrose has got mumps? No, that wouldn't last long enough, and the Mugger would probably just say she's had it, so it doesn't matter. Something worse? But then I wouldn't be here.

'How very kind of you, Mrs Draper. The trouble is, you know what these girls are like. I just can't keep pace with what's fashionable in their eyes, it changes so fast.'

'That's all right. If we go through some magazines, I'm sure she could find something she likes.'

'She's not a very easy girl,' Maggie confided. 'I think I told you she's, well, rather *big*. It bothers her, of course, and it means she tends to go for things that cover her up – lots of layers, that kind of thing. I'm afraid she'd be embarrassed to have anything made specially for her.'

'Just puppy fat.' Mrs Draper dismissed Primrose's shape as irrelevant. 'It's surprising what you can do with good cutting and fitting. And as for being embarrassed – an old woman like me! What is there to be embarrassed about?'

'Of course, she's very busy with her schoolwork at the moment . . .' Maggie was floundering, and knew it. 'She doesn't have much free time.'

'She must have some,' said Mrs Draper reasonably. 'It doesn't matter when, after school or at the weekend, just let me know. I've already bought several magazines – perhaps you'd like to take them home for her to look at, get some ideas.'

Maggie dithered. 'It's so good of you, madam, but—'

'Now, that's enough of that. I've told you I should enjoy it, and if she's a difficult shape, I shall just regard it as a challenge. One has to make allowances for these girls who are at an awkward age.'

Maggie thought that Celia would probably die of shock if she could hear her mother-in-law now. 'Make allowances!' Maggie could almost hear her shriek. 'Make allowances! The only allowance she's ever been interested in has been what was paid into her bank account! She's never made allowances for anyone in her life. When the twins were six, she knocked off points in Junior Scrabble for spelling mistakes!' Celia had, in fact, told Maggie this story only a few days earlier, as an instance of Mrs Draper's intolerance where the boys were concerned.

Mrs Draper, having for perhaps the first time in her life decided to do something for someone else, was flown with the novel feeling and not to be denied. She continued to insist until Maggie had run out of excuses and energy.

'Yes, of course,' Maggie said weakly. 'I'll see what I can fix up.'

As a result, she was loitering by the reception desk waiting for Primrose when she arrived at the swimming pool the following morning.

'Oh, Primrose, hello. Um, how are you?'

'Okay,' Primrose mumbled, hunting through her pockets for her admission card. She sounded surprised to be asked.

'There was something I wanted to ask you.'

Primrose picked up the swimming bag she had dropped while she looked for the card, and headed for the stairs. 'Yeah?'

'The thing is, it's a bit complicated to explain.' Maggie hurried after her. She was surprised by how fast Primrose took the stairs: of course, going down was always quicker than going up, but surely Primrose had never before moved so quickly? She was running, her feet neat and quick as a dancer's on the narrow treads.

'Leave it till later, then. Stella's giving me a lesson.'

'Is she?' Maggie was easily distracted by the pleasure of hearing that. 'Lucky you.'

Primrose dived through the swinging doors without bothering to hold them for Maggie behind her. The heavy doors would have crashed back in her face if she hadn't turned her shoulder to them. Ungrateful little wretch, she thought ruefully. It's only thanks to me that Stella ever spoke to her. Still, she mustn't keep Stella waiting, it's very good of her to bother.

'It's just for ten minutes,' Primrose shouted. 'Speak to you after.'

Surreptitiously surveying the lesson as she swam, Maggie thought how much better Primrose was looking. She was still large, but Maggie was sure she was less fat than she had been. Her flesh looked firmer, and now that her swimming style had improved her posture was better too. Her front crawl was economical, almost splash-free, as close an imitation of Stella's effortless elegance as she could manage, and she had taken to wearing a hat to keep her hair out of her mouth when she turned her head to breathe.

'That's lovely! That's *so* much better!' Stella's voice rang out like a bell, her smile a flash of delight. Primrose smiled back, and her face was transformed. Maggie thought that probably she might have picked the best possible moment to ask Primrose for a favour.

When Stella went off to the fast lane to do her lengths, Primrose looked round for Maggie. Her face was pink from exertion and pleasure, the expression softened from its usual fierce blankness.

'Your swimming's so much improved, you really could join a swimming club now,' Maggie said.

'That's what Stella said. I might think about it, some time, I s'pose. What was it you wanted?'

'Your help, really. I've done something really stupid, and I don't know how to get out of it.'

Primrose looked astonished, but not displeased. 'My help? What with?'

'Well, it's like this . . .' Maggie launched straight into her tale. Primrose's face was inscrutable as she listened.

'Let me get this straight,' she said as Maggie finally ran down. 'You've been pretending to this old lady that you've got a daughter, and I'm her. Right?'

'I know it sounds mad,' Maggie apologised. 'I didn't actually *tell* her I had a daughter, I just mentioned you and she assumed . . . I didn't expect her to stay for very long, so it didn't seem to matter as I'd probably never see her again. I was just trying to jolly her along, to amuse her.'

'Why me?'

'I don't know,' said Maggie honestly. 'We were talking about daughters, and she said she'd always wished she'd had one. For some reason I mentioned your name – just thinking about girls in general, really – and she immediately assumed you were mine.'

'You mean, you were going to tell her that having a daughter wasn't such a good thing, if she's like me.' Primrose spoke matter-of-factly, but Maggie was quick to deny it.

'No, not at all. You were just on my mind, because I'd been watching you swimming with Stella.'

'Whatever. And now she wants to make me a dress.'

'Well, she wants to make you something. Anything, really. She's got all these magazines.'

'It's a bit weird.'

'I know it is. I wouldn't blame you if you thought it was some awful kind of plot to kidnap you. After all, I did tell you I was a white-slave-trader! You could meet the old lady's daughter-in-law, though. She swims here, and she's a teacher at the Sixth Form College.'

'And you think that makes her respectable?' Maggie saw with relief that Primrose was making a joke.

'Certainly I do. So do you want to meet her? The only thing is, I'd rather she didn't know that I've done something this foolish, if possible.'

'Won't the old lady tell her?'

'Well, they don't communicate much. I know that Celia, her daughter-in-law, is always out on Friday afternoons, shopping and taking her sons to things, so it should be possible to do it without her actually seeing us. That is, if you're going to say yes, of course.'

'Well, why not? I get something new to wear, and it might even be good, you never know your luck. I think it's a bit of a laugh.'

'Oh, thank you, Primrose! I promise you, if what she makes you is awful, I'll take you out and buy you whatever you want instead, no expense spared.'

'Yeah? What with?'

Maggie pulled herself up short, remembering that she was a cleaning lady. 'Well, no expense spared, within reason. Are you sure you don't mind?'

Primrose pulled her goggles down over her eyes. 'No problem – Mum!' She dived like a porpoise and swam off.

The visit to Dawn and her brother's smallholding came as a welcome distraction.

'Dawn, it's lovely!'

The other woman looked around vaguely. 'Yes, I suppose it is. Not quite so lovely at six in the morning in the winter, when it's pouring with rain, or frozen solid.'

'No, I suppose not. But then nothing looks nice under those circumstances, does it? And in the summer it must look idyllic.'

Dawn nodded with an air of resignation. Maggie saw that however beautiful the place might be, that did nothing to mitigate the work involved. And there was no doubt that the work must be tremendous, and endless.

It was, in truth, an idyllic sight already. The weather had suddenly relented, and produced one of those soft winter days that feel like spring; indeed, there had been a border of snowdrops in full flower under the hedge along the drive. The gateway was narrow and unmarked, and in spite of Dawn's careful directions Maggie had driven past it, and been forced to back down the lane to return to it.

From the drive, where Maggie had parked, the house presented rather a blank face to the world. Though obviously old it seemed characterless, perhaps because it lacked the decorative adjuncts generally found outside a country cottage. The gravelled drive, neatly hedged, led to a plain turning circle. There were no flagstones, no flower beds or tubs of winter pansies, no climbing rose or wisteria trained artfully up the old brick wall so that the cottage had a bare look that was oddly unwelcoming, like an older woman whose sole beauty aid was a scrub with cold water and carbolic.

Following Dawn's instructions, Maggie had ignored the front door and gone through the solid wooden gate set in the tall hedge to one side of the house. Dawn, who had obviously been listening for her car, came out of the back door just as she did so. She found Maggie standing stock still and gazing about her.

It was certainly worth looking at. From the back it was possible to see that the little cottage was merely a third of the whole building, the other two thirds being largely hidden from the drive by the hedge. An ancient, timber-framed barn lay open on to a large, brick-paved courtyard. Down the side of the courtyard opposite to where they stood ran an equally old wall, the first part with wooden doorways in, and beyond that, fan-trained fruit trees, immaculately pruned, grew along it.

The courtyard was bounded by a continuation of the tall hedge, through which wide arched openings gave glimpses of a large vegetable garden, organised like a French *potager* with neatly arranged small beds intersected by paths. Most of them were empty, or mounded with rotted manure, but a few held immaculate rows of leeks, kale and sprouts, or were protected by cloches. Maggie noticed that the actual beds were as neat as any vegetable garden can be in the middle of winter, but unsightly compost heaps, piles of rotting dung, and a collection of old fence posts, rusting ends of chicken wire, sundry wooden boxes, broken pallets and heaps of bricks, tiles and breeze blocks, lay around the edges and in the corners of the courtyard.

Maggie walked down the hedge. The fourth side of the courtyard had a lower wall, no more than waist-height, and on the far side three ewes, almost barrel-shaped from pregnancy, nibbled unenthu-siastically at the grass beneath rows of fruit trees. Seeing her approach they ambled hopefully to the gate in the wall, bleating. The noise, which Maggie had always thought of as a tranquil country sound, was deafening, even aggressive.

'I'm sorry I haven't anything for you, ladies.' The ewes looked sceptical, like busy housewives being importuned by a doorstep salesman, determined to believe nothing they were told but still hopeful that there might be a bargain to be had. Dawn pushed them away.

'I'm afraid they're very greedy. They were orphan lambs origin-ally, we got them quite cheaply because they didn't look very strong, and we bottle-reared them so they think of people as food-providers. Not that any of the others are any better. The sow – well, you know about her. She's the one that bit my leg.'

'Bit it!'

'Well, more of a nip, really. I had thick overalls on over jeans, so it was only bruised. And the cow will only stand to be milked while she's got food in her trough. As soon as it's finished she kicks the clusters off.'

'Clusters?' Maggie visualised a posy of flowers.

'The bit of the milking machine that goes on her udder. We used to milk by hand, but I was always rather slow because my wrists aren't very strong, so we bought a little milking machine. Cleaning and sterilising it takes forever, so the whole process is no quicker, but it's much less tiring. Gordon still likes to do it by hand, though.'

'Where do you do it? And where's the cow?'

Dawn nodded towards the tree-covered wall. 'There's a paddock the other side of that; she's out there. Those doors in the wall, one of them goes to the milking parlour – we call it that although it's really not much more than a glorified loose box with running water. The second is to her shed, and the third goes to the pigsty. Would you like to see? It's a bit muddy round there . . .' Dawn, who was wearing Wellingtons, looked doubtfully at Maggie's feet.

'I guessed it might be, that's why I came in these old boots. They're not quite Wellingtons, but it doesn't matter if they get mucky.'

Fending off the sheep, Dawn led Maggie through the gate into the orchard.

'You can go the other way, from the barn, but this is prettier. All this stretch is ours, to that line of trees. We've kept the hedges and the old small paddocks, so we can use them in rotation.'

'It must look wonderful in the spring.'

'Yes, it does. I've put a lot of bulbs in the orchard – miniature daffodils, and narcissi mostly, so they go on flowering right through to almost the end of May. My brother doesn't like it, because he has to put the sheep out, but even he has to agree it's pretty . . . At least . . .' Mention of her brother, Maggie noticed, seemed to bring back Dawn's habit of letting her sentences tail off unfinished.

'What about beyond the trees? Is that more farmland?'

'Yes, at the moment. A big commercial farm, they've grubbed out all the hedges to make huge prairie fields, and they just grow things there's a subsidy on. We don't have much to do with them. They think we're cranks, and Gordon thinks they're a cross between Attila the Hun and Hitler. Still, bad as they are, it looks as though it could be worse. They're talking of selling off some of the land – the bit right next door to us, naturally – for a shopping mall. My brother's very upset about it.'

I should have realised, thought Maggie. I knew it was somewhere round here, only the way I came got me so confused that I lost track of just where I was.

'Oh dear,' she said inadequately. 'Um, would it be such a bad thing?'

'Well, Gordon disapproves on principle of shopping malls, because they encourage people to use their cars, and they kill off all the small town-centre shops. And of course he disapproves even more of people building on farmland, so you see . . . I mean, he

96

wouldn't like it wherever it was, but to have it on our doorstep, practically, well . . . Still, they might not get the planning consent.'

'Really?' In her surprise, Maggie spoke without thinking. 'I thought that was all settled.'

'Do you know about it, then?' Dawn looked puzzled.

'I thought I'd heard about it somewhere . . .' Maggie took refuge in a manner as vague as her companion's.

'At your work? I remember you said you work for Mr Draper's wife – perhaps he said something. Though he's not really supposed to discuss it, but still . . .'

'No, it definitely wasn't him. I must have been thinking about something else. Wasn't there a similar case in the paper recently?' It seemed a fairly safe bet, and fortunately Dawn nodded.

'I expect that was it. Anyway, let's not worry about the shopping mall now. Perhaps it won't happen.'

'Yes. I mean, no,' said Maggie with hollow cheerfulness. She forced her mind away from Turner's shopping mall, and concentrated on seeing everything on the farm. At her insistence, Dawn agreed to do the feeding and milking a bit early, and Maggie followed her round, carrying buckets as Dawn fed the pig and the hens, in their movable ark in the paddock. The cow, a placid Jersey, watched them, knowing her turn was coming.

'Doesn't she mind having the hens in with her?'

'No, I think she quite likes it. They're company, of a sort. Herd animals don't like to be on their own.'

'Can't you put the sheep in with her?'

'No, they eat differently. Sheep nibble the grass right down, the cow would starve. They follow her on, tidy up the grass.'

The barn was as untidy as the rest, with bales of hay and straw and a range of tools from spades and hoes to a small, ancient tractor. After the cow had been milked Maggie and Dawn went back into the house, where Dawn strained and cooled the milk, and set it in wide pans for the cream to rise. The pans had a sheet of metal protecting the lip, so that they poured from the bottom, leaving the cream behind. 'I've got a gravy boat like that,' Maggie remarked, 'but it's a nightmare to clean. These are much more sensible, with that bit coming out. And what a lot of cream! How tempting!'

'This is nothing,' said Dawn with gloomy pride. 'You should see it in early summer, when she's newly calved and there's lots of new grass. I cook everything in butter, we have cream till we're sick of it – thank goodness we take plenty of exercise, or we'd be enormous – and I make cream cheeses, but it still gives me nightmares. I give the extra milk to the pigs, but it seems dreadful to give them cream!'

'I suppose you can't sell it? Rules and regulations?'

'Bane of our life,' Dawn agreed. 'For the little we'd make, it's not worth all the forms and inspections and things. I sell eggs, and fruit and vegetables at the gate, and we mostly sell the calves, though they don't fetch much these days. We keep about one in three and rear it for beef, which lasts us for ages. It's all organic, of course. No worries about BSE, thank goodness.'

When the chores were finished, they had tea. Maggie, her appetite whetted by the fresh air, relished the freshly baked scones, with butter, cream and jam all similarly home-made.

'I should think you've got enough to do without making scones for me,' she said guiltily, 'but I must say they are delicious.'

'They don't take a moment. I make our bread, too. It feels all wrong to spread our own butter on supermarket sliced! Though occasionally I treat myself to a decadent white loaf, for a change.'

On her own ground, speaking of her day-to-day routines, Dawn was much less indecisive, Maggie noticed.

'Do you enjoy it?' Maggie asked curiously. 'I mean, it's your brother's idea, really, isn't it?'

Dawn poured more tea. 'I loved the *idea* of it,' she said carefully. 'It's what he always wanted, from when he was a teenager. He talked about it all the time – you could say I was brainwashed, I suppose. When we bought this place I was as enthusiastic as he was, maybe even more so. We went on courses, everything you can think of – pruning, and calving a cow, and cheesemaking – it was such fun. And of course I knew it would be hard work. I didn't mind that, and I still don't, really, but it's the *endlessness* of it that gets me down. You can never say, that's done, that's finished. You can't say "I think I'll have a weekend away", or even take a day off.' She looked at her hands and Maggie, looking with her, saw how worn they were, the skin stained and scored, the nails cut very short but with ragged cuticles. 'I don't want to stop,' said Dawn quietly. 'I don't think I could live any other way now. But I would love a break occasionally.'

'Of course you would. I suppose it's not easy to find anyone who would take over.'

'Impossible. Either they don't know what they're doing, or they want to be paid more per hour than I earn. Still . . .' Dawn paused though not, for once, because she was hesitating to finish her sentence. She was listening. 'That sounds like a car,' she said, puzzled.

'Another visitor?'

'We don't get many. It might be someone just turning round, though mostly they don't use us when they're lost because it's such a small entrance. I'd better go and . . . Oh, Gordon! What's happened?'

A man, so very much an older male version of Dawn that there could be no doubting who he was, had come into the kitchen. His face was scratched and he had a gauze pad taped to his forehead. He also had his left arm in a sling, from which the cuff of a plaster cast protruded. Dawn jumped up and went to him.

'Came off my bike,' he uttered laconically. 'Some idiot pulled onto a roundabout and didn't give me enough room. Bike's a wreck. Had to come back in a taxi.'

'Never mind the bike, what about you? Your arm . . .'

'Broken.' He sat heavily in a chair, and nodded to Maggie, his eyes glancing up to her and quickly away, as if she had no clothes on and he was embarrassed to look at her. 'I'll have a cup of chamomile, and some arnica for my head, if you wouldn't mind, Roar.'

'Of course, at once. I'm sorry, Maggie, I should have said, this is my brother, Gordon. Gordon, this is Maggie. We met in, well, in . . .'

'We first got speaking to one another in Sainsbury's,' put in Maggie lightly. 'I'll be going, Dawn, you'll want to look after your brother. It was wonderful to have seen the farm.'

'Don't go on my account,' he said heavily. 'I shan't be stopping. I like to walk round the place before it gets dark, check the animals are all right.'

'Is it really necessary?' Maggie ventured. 'Dawn's done the feeding and the milking, and you've had a nasty shock. You shouldn't risk making things worse. What about your head?'

'Just a bump.' He put up his free hand and touched it to the gauze, wincing. 'Arnica, that's the thing. They wanted to keep me in the hospital, but I told them I wasn't concussed, didn't need one of their scans to tell me that. They didn't like it,' he gave a dour smile, 'but they couldn't keep me.'

Maggie imagined the confrontation between this hard-bitten countryman and a tired junior doctor, and repressed a smile.

'I think you should be content with that victory, then,' she said. Dawn, who had put the kettle to boil and was hunting out the arnica, looked anxious, but after a moment Gordon gave a laugh that was almost indistinguishable from a cough.

'Well, maybe,' he said, grudging the words. 'It's going to be difficult enough as it is, with all the spring planting to do and me with only one hand. Better not risk anything else. Thanks, Roar.' He took the mug of herb tea that Dawn had made, and Maggie saw that his hand trembled a little. She guessed that he was more shaken than he cared to admit. She stood up.

'Well, goodbye, Gordon. I hope your arm mends quickly. Thank you, Dawn.'

'I'll see you to your car.' Dawn waited while Maggie put on the boots which she had taken off when they came indoors. By the car she dithered while Maggie hunted for her keys.

'I hope Gordon wasn't too – well, abrupt,' she said. Maggie was surprised.

'No, for a man who's just been knocked off his bicycle and then, I assume, spent some while hanging around in hospital in pain waiting to be treated, I thought he was remarkably calm.'

'Oh, Gordon never loses his temper. He just . . . goes on. Or goes silent. I never know which is worse.' She looked wretched. 'I'm going to have to stop coming swimming for a while. He'll need me there all the time.'

'Of course. I wish I could help. There ought to be someone . . . I'll rack my brains. Tell me, what was it he called you? It sounded like Roar.'

Dawn's cheeks went pink. 'It's what he called me when I was little. You see, my parents christened me Aurora. So ridiculous. I was rather a plain, lumpy child, not at all the Sleeping Beauty type. So when I grew up I changed it to Dawn, only he'd got into the habit of calling me "Rora" by then, and somehow it always stuck.'

As she drove home, Maggie took a detour to the main road that went past Turner's site. It was almost dark, and a light mist had come up so that the tall street-lights along the busy road shed triangles of pinkish-yellow, for all the world as though they were giant shower heads spraying glowing water. The site was unmarked, invisible. Maggie sighed, feeling her loyalties torn.

Remembering her promise to Julie, Maggie made another detour to the big new petrol station where Tom had his job. The tank filled, she went inside and was pleased to see that Tom was there, shut in the box that Julie had described and looking more miserable than Maggie would have thought possible. He was normally a gentle, slow-moving man with the patience of a gardener who is prepared to wait ten years for a plant to produce one flower, but the place was busy, queues of people jostling to pay for petrol, to buy crisps or sandwiches or lottery tickets. Tom was short with them, snapping his words off as if he were dead-heading roses, his eyes never reaching theirs as though the effort to lift his gaze was too great.

Maggie, queueing unseen behind a man who had ten lottery forms each of which, it seemed, had to be paid for separately, was irresistibly reminded of a battery hen in a tiny cage. She thought of Dawn's hens, scratching busily round the cow's feet, and felt the germ of an idea stirring within her. Once, she would have dismissed it, or at least taken a few days to think about it, but Maggie was changing.

'Hello, Tom,' she said briskly when she came up to the glass window. Slowly, frowning, he peered towards her.

'Mrs Whittington! I didn't think you usually came here.'

'I don't. Julie told me you were here.' His face, not usually expressive, showed a curious blend of embarrassment and misery. 'She's worried about you, Tom.'

'No need,' he said, sounding so like Gordon that Maggie could have laughed.

'Anyway, I've got a reason for coming here to see you. I've just been to visit some friends with a smallholding. A brother and sister, and he's just been knocked off his bike, broken his arm. They really need some help, and I thought of you.'

Chapter Ten

Four days later, on the following Wednesday, Maggie told herself that things were going surprisingly well. Julie had just telephoned her, so happy she was almost in tears.

'Maggie! You're a miracle-worker! I've never seen Tom so excited! He's had two days at the farm, and they want him to go every day so he's rung the petrol station to say he's giving up. That place – it's made for him!'

'I thought it might be. I know he hasn't much experience of looking after animals, but the gardening is just his cup of tea, I'd have thought.'

'It really is. He likes the animals, too. Brought home half a dozen eggs – beauties, they are – and a great block of butter, and cream. I'm going to have to spend even longer in the gym if he's going to keep bringing cream home!'

'It's all right, then, is it, if they pay him in kind instead of money? I wasn't sure how you'd feel about it.'

'All right? It's great! All the dairy stuff, as much milk as even my lot can drink. D'you have any idea what my milk bill comes to each week, with this lot guzzling it down all the time? Then there's beef, and lamb and pork, and they even make their own bacon. I never knew you *could*! And veg, of course, and fruit . . . Better than money for us, that is. And the best thing of all is to see him so happy.' She gave a sniff. 'We had a real good talk about things, did a good bit of sorting out.'

'I'm so glad, Julie.'

'Yes. And you were right about the other business, too. About why he got the job at the petrol station. I should've seen it myself, only I panicked a bit, I suppose. So I told him about the Spa, and he was a bit funny about it at first but he understands, now, that it's just to get fit, and for a bit of a laugh. Mind you, now he's going to the farm every day I don't think he'd have minded what I did! Well, within reason.'

Maggie put the phone down feeling positively elated. She had already heard from Dawn, when they met at the swimming pool, how well Tom and Gordon seemed to be getting on. An interest in organic vegetable-growing was the passport to Gordon's approval, it appeared.

Feeling for the first time in her life that she was someone who could be useful in the world, Maggie was humming to herself as she chopped onions and mushrooms which, with the addition of some salted black beans and some mushroom soy, would make a sauce to go with the steaks for supper. She jumped when someone knocked at the back door. Normally the sound of car tyres on the gravel drive alerted her to visitors, but she must have been too preoccupied to hear anything, she thought.

Switching on the outside light – at five o'clock it was nearly dark – she opened the door without checking through the spyhole, something which Turner was always warning her about. At the sight of the figure on the doorstep, beneath the bright beam of the overhead bulb, she checked. Her visitor stood, solid and accusing, glaring at her.

'Hello, Primrose,' said Maggie.

Primrose scowled. 'Is this really where you live, then? I didn't believe her when she told me.'

'When who told you?'

'Steph.'

'Oh, dear. I'm sorry, Primrose.'

'What are you playing at? You're rich, aren't you? Or do you work as a cleaner in this house, too?'

Primrose's voice was bitterly resentful. Maggie sighed.

'You know I don't. Look, I really am sorry. I'm not just playing games, I promise you. Won't you come in? It's pretty cold standing here with the door open, and if you want to be angry with me you might as well see what you're being angry about, and do it in comfort.'

Primrose shrugged, and stepped inside the door. She set her feet down firmly, almost stamping.

'Grinding your feet in the face of the idle rich?' suggested Maggie in a murmur.

Primrose glowered. 'If the cap fits.'

'Well, I don't see that I have to apologise for being rich,' said Maggie reasonably. 'My husband has earned the money for this house with a lot of hard work, and I've worked alongside him, since before you were born. It's not something I need to feel ashamed of.'

'So what are you doing working as a cleaner? Or is that a lie too?'

'No, it's not a lie. It sounds a bit silly, but I did it to help out my friend, Celia. It was only supposed to be for a few weeks, while her mother-in-law was over from Spain, but now there's been a fire at her mother-in-law's flat and she's staying on longer. She's the one I told you about. Of course, they don't know I live in a house like this, and if they did Celia would be embarrassed and uncomfortable about it, and so would Mrs Draper. I wasn't trying to trick them, or you either. I suppose you could say it's just a harmless deception that's got a bit out of hand.'

Primrose stared at her feet. Then she looked slowly round the kitchen, her eyes lingering on the expensive marble worksurfaces, the hand-finished cabinets, and the bank of gleaming pans. At last, reluctantly, her look travelled over Maggie herself and halted just below her face.

'I don't know...' For the first time since she had met her, Primrose sounded unsure of herself.

'Whether you can trust me? Well, nothing I can say is going to help you to do that, is it? What does Stephanie say?'

'She says you're all right.' It was grudgingly spoken. Maggie waited. 'Okay, then. I'll go along with it.'

'Thank you, Primrose. So, shall we have a cup of tea or something? And then I'll run you back. You didn't come on a bike, did you?'

'No, I walked from the bus. I can get myself back.'

'I know you can, but it's pretty dark by now, and I'd feel happier taking you home myself. Please, Primrose, as a favour to me.'

'You mothers are all the same,' Primrose growled, and Maggie saw that they had returned to their previous state of, on Primrose's side, wary acceptance.

'It looks okay!'

Maggie, who had been holding her breath without realising it, let it go in a rush. This was more than she had hoped for. Primrose, smiling – smiling! – was turning in front of a long mirror in Mrs Draper's bedroom, admiring herself from all angles. Mrs Draper tweaked at the jacket and adjusted the set of the shoulders, looking as pleased as Primrose herself.

'I always say a well-cut trouser-suit can be very flattering. It's lucky they're so fashionable at the moment.'

It was two weeks since Maggie had first taken Primrose to see Mrs Draper. The initial meeting had been awkward: Maggie had been nervous, still worried that she was behaving dishonestly in deceiving Mrs Draper. Her anxiety had not been helped by the strange look Celia had given her in the changing room that morning. Celia, direct as ever, had not wasted words.

'I didn't know you had a daughter. I thought you told me you didn't have any kids?'

'I don't,' said Maggie miserably.

'Then how come the old bat says you're coming round with your daughter this afternoon, and she's going to make something for her? I mean, I don't mind a bit – in fact I'm delighted, anything to keep her cheerful. Not that she *is* cheerful, but at least less crabby. It just seemed a bit funny, that's all.'

'Oh dear,' said Maggie. 'You're going to think I'm quite mad. It was when I thought your mother-in-law would soon be going back to Spain. She was – oh, a bit bored. Somehow or other she got the idea I had a daughter and I went along with it, because it was what she wanted to hear.'

'Yes, she moaned like hell when the twins were born, because they were boys. I don't think she's ever forgiven me for not having another go at producing a granddaughter for her.' Celia chuckled. 'So you told her the tale to keep her sweet, and now it's blown up in your face. What a nightmare!'

Maggie grimaced. 'Tell me about it! I nearly died! In fact, I nearly killed off my supposed daughter on the spot, only I thought it was a bit sudden, and she might think it rather strange that I'd come to work. I was so flummoxed I couldn't think of anything to say, and somehow I found myself agreeing to do it.'

'Where did you get the girl from?' Celia sounded rather admiring. Maggie glanced round, and lowered her voice.

'It's the girl who swims here most mornings, the one with red hair who's a bit, well, plump.'

'Goodness! Why her?'

'Well, I knew her slightly, because of talking to her here, and as a matter of fact when I told Mrs Draper about my daughter it was her I described. I thought it was more interesting, if I was going to have a daughter, to have one with problems.'

'My dear, if you had ever had a teenage daughter, you'd know that they've *all* got problems! And you managed to persuade her to go along with it. What did you do, bribe her?'

Maggie grinned. 'More or less. I said that if she really hated whatever was made for her I'd buy her something else, of her own choice. She thinks I'm mad, of course, but she thought it was quite funny. Heaven knows if we'll get away with it. If I get caught out, you'll have to sack me.'

'Sack you? You must be kidding! You can have a dozen children, real or imaginary, as far as I'm concerned. No, you go for it, and good luck to you – and to Whatever-her-name-is. The old girl can kit her out with an entire new wardrobe, and welcome, as long as it keeps her happy. I just hope it doesn't turn out to be too hideous. The things she makes herself are pretty good, to be fair, and beautifully finished, but I'm not so sure about a teenager . . . Tell you what, I'll go halves with the consolation prize if it's a disaster.'

Maggie winced. 'Oh no! I wouldn't dream of it. Honestly, Celia, I got myself into this, it's not a problem, really.' Celia looked doubtful, but she could see that Maggie was upset by the idea, and let it go.

In the event, the first meeting had turned out surprisingly well. Primrose had been her usual taciturn self, which made things simpler as at least if she didn't say anything she could scarcely say the wrong thing. Mrs Draper had been unusually understanding.

'Young girls of her age can be very shy and self-conscious,' she remarked the following day to Maggie. 'It's obvious that Primrose minds about her appearance. She doesn't take after you, does she?'

Maggie instantly thought that she should have said that Primrose was adopted. It was true that neither in facial structure nor in colouring was there any resemblance between herself and her supposed daughter.

'No, she's more like her father,' she said cautiously. 'I'm sorry she wasn't very communicative – I sometimes think all I ever hear from her is grunting.'

'Nonsense, it's just a stage.' Maggie, with an inward laugh, thought again how astonished Celia would be to hear her so-called Mugger being so understanding. In fact, she had been agreeably surprised by Mrs Draper's suggestion of a trouser-suit, and even more so by Primrose's acceptance of the idea.

'Something smart,' she said, if not eagerly at least positively. 'I saw one in Covent Garden, once, in one of those designer shops. I could get a Saturday job in a shop, maybe.'

'That's right. If you're well turned-out, they're far more likely to take you. Now, how do you like this jacket? Or this? I like those vertical seams and the longer length. I think they would be most becoming.'

'Becoming what?' muttered Primrose, but with a lift of her eyebrows that showed it was a joke.

'Becoming an elegant young woman, of course,' said the Mugger briskly. 'Now, most people would tell you to go for green, with that hair, but why should we be like most people? What I'd like to see you in would be a very dark navy, or a charcoal grey.'

'Not navy.' Primrose was positive. 'The school uniform's navy. I was thinking of black.'

'Black is good, too. It's one of those things you can't go too far wrong with, with your colouring. But then practically every girl you see is in black. I thought – not that I know you well enough to judge, but from what your mother has told me about you – that you'd like to be different. Charcoal grey is just as smart as black, but perhaps a bit more subtle.'

Primrose glanced sardonically at Maggie. 'What've you been saying about me . . . Mum?' The pause before the final word was infinitesimal, for Maggie alone. Maggie returned look for look.

'All mothers like to talk about their children,' she responded sturdily. 'It's natural.'

'Yeah,' said Primrose, and Maggie hoped she was the only person

107

who had heard the sadness in her voice, the voice of a girl whose mother had long since abandoned her.

Now, after two fittings at which it had been impossible to judge how the suit would look, Maggie saw with a lift of her heart that Mrs Draper had more than lived up to her promise. The fine charcoal-grey wool set off Primrose's pale skin, that was actually looking much clearer since her visit to the Spa with Stephanie. Against it her hair, now kept cleaner than before and less tightly confined, glowed like autumn beech leaves. Her figure, though still on the generous side, looked less lumpy, smoothed and flattered by the dark colour and the long lines of the collarless jacket.

'Oh Primrose, that *does* look nice!' Maggie surprised herself by finding her throat tight and her eyes prickling. 'And it's so beautifully made! I ran myself up a few dresses when I was young, but I've never tackled anything like actual tailoring.'

Mrs Draper pulled back the front of the jacket so that Maggie could admire the inside.

'All hand-finished,' she said proudly. 'I must say it's worked out even better than I'd hoped. So, what shall it be next? What about a skirt to go with the jacket, and then maybe a dress?' The Mugger, clearly, had got the bit between her teeth.

'You really shouldn't' said Maggie feebly.

'Nonsense.' The old lady was brisk. 'You can't think I'm going to stop now, when this has worked out so well. I've really enjoyed doing it. Now, let's have another look at those magazines, Primrose, and I've got a new one here, too, which might have something in. I thought perhaps a contrasting skirt . . .'

The month of March, Maggie decided, had obviously been brought up on the same poem that she had learned as a child. Why was it that she had to struggle to remember any of the things she had studied so hard for her A levels, and yet those early exercises learned by heart at primary school and in the first year at secondary seemed engraved almost on the inside of her skull? She could still recite, without any effort, the list of French adjectives that precede the noun, in alphabetical order. '*Ancien*,' she found herself reciting, '*beau, bon, cher, digne, gros . . .*' Each word fitted the forward thrust of her arms as she went down the pool. It wouldn't work so well with crawl; that had more of a two-four time, very suitable for music, whereas breast-stroke had a slower rhythm, ideal for waltzes – or poems.

Another violent gust of wind struck the long wall of the swimming-pool building, flinging abandoned crisp packets and empty cans against the low windows.

'*March* brings *breez*es *loud* and *shrill*, Stirs the *danc*ing *daffodil*' said Maggie's mind. 'Though these could hardly be called breezes, and it's just as well the spring has been too cold to bring more than a handful of daffodils out.' It seemed as though winter was never going to end. There had been another fall of snow the previous week, and yet April was only days away.

Reaching the far end of the pool, Maggie saw a pair of unmistakable legs – long, slim and dark – and stopped to speak to Stella.

'I hope the weather's going to improve soon. How long is it until the wedding?'

'Only about six weeks. But I'm sure it will be all right.' Stella was serene, with the untroubled smile of a child who has never known anything to go seriously wrong. Maggie, in spite of the warmth of the water, felt her skin rise in chilly goose-bumps. 'After all,' said Stella happily, 'the hotel people are in charge of everything. They'll make sure nothing goes wrong.' Her body curved off into the water, and she did a length of butterfly that was as elegant as everything she did.

'Lovely, isn't she?' Celia paused by Maggie.

'Yes.' Maggie shivered.

'Are you cold? You should keep moving.'

'No, not cold. It's just . . . oh, I'm being so silly. It was just a sort of goose walking over my grave feeling. She's so sure that nothing can go wrong with this wedding.'

Celia was puzzled. 'But why should anything go wrong? Surely that's the whole point of having that arrangement with the hotel – that they see there are no problems?'

'Yes, of course.' Maggie could not voice her anxieties, which in any case were too formless, based on her instincts and her knowledge of Turner. 'Ridiculous of me. Just one of those superstitious things.'

'That doesn't sound like you.' Celia looked at her closely. 'Is everything all right? I know, it's the Mugger. What's the old witch been doing – putting an evil spell on you?'

Maggie laughed. 'Not at all. Rather the reverse, if anything. She's been so good to Primrose – she's got a Saturday job in a shop now, and is looking a thousand times better. I know she'll be sorry when Mrs Draper goes back to Spain.'

'I know, I'm such a bitch.' Celia sighed, and pulled a face. 'Actually, she hasn't been nearly as bad as usual – largely thanks to you, and Primrose. Honestly, Maggie, if she'd only put a quarter the effort into getting to know the boys that she puts into making clothes for Primrose, things would be quite different at home. Still, at least the dressmaking has kept her amused, and she can't moan about the chaps leaving their toys about when she's littering the place with patterns, and scraps of fabric and pins. Not to mention the sewing machine being permanently set up in the study. Thank goodness she doesn't find the light good enough in the evening, or we'd never get to watch the television at all, and the boys would be staging a palace revolution. As it is, Phil's under a lot of stress at work, and I seem to spend my whole time keeping the peace so that he doesn't snarl at her.'

'Stress at work? I thought when you worked for the Council you were like some sort of minor god, with everyone bowing and scraping and making burnt offerings and human sacrifices?'

'Not exactly!' Celia chortled. 'Though in fact . . . I don't know much about what's worrying him, because it's something he's not allowed to talk about at home, but I do get the impression that one of his colleagues has caused some kind of huge problem. Misuse of his position, or something.'

'And Phil's got to sort it out?'

'Yes – and preferably without any scandal. In fact,' Celia grimaced, 'I think he's expected to do some kind of a cover-up, and he doesn't think it's right, which is why he's such a grouch at the moment. It wouldn't be so bad if he could talk it over at home, but as it is he just spends hours going through piles of old paperwork, and snarling when he's interrupted.'

Maggie thought, with sympathy, that it sounded remarkably like Turner. She resolved to try, once again, to find out what was troubling him.

That evening she cooked his favourite meal, rack of lamb with a coriander and apricot stuffing. He smiled when he saw it, but after a few mouthfuls Maggie saw that he was scarcely doing more than pushing the food round his plate.

'Turner, what's wrong? I wish you would tell me.'

'Wrong?' The expression of astonishment on his face would have fooled anyone but Maggie. 'Nothing's wrong.' As if to prove it, he launched immediately into an animated story of an incident that had happened during the day. He was a natural mimic, his face falling easily into the lines of his lugubrious site foreman, or with a lift of his eyebrows becoming the shocked face of a prim receptionist. Maggie couldn't help laughing, but when he had finished the tale his subsequent conversation seemed forced. There was a pause, and Maggie searched her mind for a new topic.

The thought of one anxious husband led naturally to the memory of another.

'I've heard there's something peculiar going on at the Council offices,' she mentioned casually.

'What sort of peculiar? Satanic rituals in the Council Chamber – or have they finally noticed that the Mayor is a Martian?'

'That one seems to have passed them by. No, it was just a bit of gossip I picked up from one of my swimming friends. She said someone was being investigated – misuse of his position, or something. Taking bribes, I suppose.'

'Mm.' Turner gave an indifferent grunt, and put a piece of lamb in his mouth. 'Which department – Housing? That's the usual one.'

'No, Planning, I think. Careful, Turner!' Maggie jumped up and ran round the table as Turner choked on his mouthful of meat. She thumped him hard on the back.

'Uh!' He dragged in a breath, and then coughed. Maggie stood over him until the paroxysm subsided, then fetched a glass of water. He wiped his eyes and nose, and sipped it.

'Thanks.' His voice was husky. He cleared his throat, and tried again. 'Sorry about that. Went down the wrong way.'

'I should think it did! Goodness, Turner, you gave me quite a fright! I was just about to do that thing I can never remember the name of, when you put your arms round a choking person and squeeze. I've always wanted to try it.'

'You don't have to wait until I'm choking to put your arms round me.' His eyes were still bloodshot and his face unusually pale, but Turner was making an effort to appear normal. Maggie gave him a quick hug, and dropped a kiss on his head before returning to her chair. Turner continued to sip at the water. After a few moments he pushed his plate away.

'Sorry, Mags, but I don't think I can eat any more. I had too much lunch, or something, and that choking thing seems to have shaken me up a bit. If you don't mind, I'll just go and sit quietly for a little while.' He was already standing up as he spoke.

'Oh, Turner, you poor thing! I'll come and sit with you.'

He shook his head decisively. 'No, love, you finish your meal. No reason for you to miss out – and it was delicious, as usual.' He left the room, and Maggie heard the study door shut. It was only because of the slight squeak that the handle made that she recognised it – really, she must put a bit of oil on that tomorrow – for he did it so gently. Turner's normal method of shutting a door was to give it a firm push, without bothering to touch the handle at all. This time he was as careful as a fifteen-year-old coming home two hours after his curfew and hoping not to wake his parents.

When Maggie had finished her meal she stacked the dishes in the machine then made coffee and went through to the sitting room. On the way she hesitated outside the study door, but heard Turner's voice coming faintly through the solid panelled wood, and knew he must be telephoning. He would smell the coffee – he had an extraordinarily sharp sense of smell, and often knew who had been visiting the house just from a whiff of perfume.

He came through for a cup of coffee while Maggie was watching a documentary, but took it away with him with a murmur of apology. When Maggie went up to bed she hesitated outside the study door. It was firmly closed. In the past the door had almost always been left ajar, so that Maggie could put her head round. A closed door had only been for something secret, which usually involved a gift or some other treat for her, or for complicated financial negotiations, when Turner needed one hundred per cent of his concentration without any interruptions. Then, the closed door had been a shield. Now, it had the implacable air of a barrier. Maggie had the feeling that if she tried it she would find it locked and bolted, though rationally she knew there was no means of fastening it.

She thought she heard a movement and started guiltily back, not wanting to be caught, as it were, with her ear to the keyhole. This is ridiculous, she thought. I should just gently open the door and give him a word or a wave, just so he knows I'm going up to bed. Why can't I do that? It's only Turner, who I've been married to for twenty years and who has always treated me well. What am I . . . worried about? Even in that moment, she could not use the word 'afraid'.

The door opened, and she started nervously. 'Oh – Turner! I was just wondering whether to come in. I didn't want to interrupt you.'

He smiled, but it was an automatic grimace that did not warm his eyes.

'You off to bed? Don't wait for me. I'm just getting myself a drink – I've not finished yet.'

'Can I get you anything?' Maggie wanted to help, but didn't know how to say so.

'No, I'm fine. Just a bit more sorting out to do. I might be pretty late, so I'll say goodnight.' He kissed her, and Maggie was surprised by the warmth and softness of his lips against hers.

'Turner . . .'

'Night, Mags.' He turned away from her, not looking at her or responding to the question and the appeal in her voice.

Chapter Eleven

'Y ou wouldn't be free on a Sunday evening, would you? The one after next, to be exact.'

Maggie turned with a smile to answer Stella. 'It's a long time since anyone asked me that! Me on my own, that is. What is it – a rave?'

Stella giggled. 'Not exactly. It's the Swimathon. You know, that sponsored swim in aid of charity – they've got the posters upstairs.'

Maggie remembered seeing them and dismissing them from her mind.

'But that's a five-thousand-metre swim! How many lengths is that? I'd never make it!'

Stella laughed again. 'Don't panic! I wouldn't ask you to, not at this late stage – though you'd be surprised what you can do, if you get into training a bit. No, I'm doing the full swim – it's a hundred and fifty lengths, by the way – and Jane upstairs who's organising it here suggested I should get together a team of people, just for fun, to do it between them. Brenda and Iris have said yes, and Primrose, and I wondered whether you'd be able to join us?'

'Oh, I see.' Maggie was tempted, not so much by the prospect of the swim as because she felt rather flattered to be asked. 'Well, I'd love to, but I'll have to check that my husband hasn't got anything on. And if nothing else, I'd be happy to sponsor you and them.'

'Great! And do you know anyone else who might be prepared to join in?'

Maggie thought about it. Celia? She might welcome an evening away from her mother-in-law. And what about Dawn? She was certainly a strong swimmer, and now that Tom was helping her brother with the farmwork, she might have more time as well as more energy. In any case, it would be worth asking her.

'There's a couple of people I can ask, if you like. When did you say it is – Sunday week?'

'Yes. It's rather a last-minute idea, but Jane really wants to make it a big success this year, so even if they can only drop in to watch for a while, and cheer people on, it would help.'

'I'll see what I can do. Will it be all right if I tell you tomorrow?'

'Yes, fine, and don't worry if you can't manage it. It's only an informal extra. All the proper entrants have signed up with the organisers, but there's still some space left and it's more fun if there are plenty of swimmers. Speak to you tomorrow!' Stella did a sideways dive away from the side, and shot down the fast lane in a swift crawl. Maggie lifted her goggles, to see better, and waited for Celia and Dawn.

Celia was disappointed.

'What a shame, we're already booked to go out. Supper with some old friends that we hardly ever see – mainly because we really don't have anything much in common any more, but he was at college with Phil and they used to play rugby together. It'll be pretty deadly, but I must say they've been very kind and asked the Mugger as well, and she's dead chuffed. The boys are relieved, too – she'd have been babysitting them otherwise, and that's always a recipe for disaster! I'll sponsor you, though. So much a length, or a lump sum?'

'I've no idea, I don't even know what it's in aid of.'

'I think it's one of the cancer charities – I saw it on the poster. Well, I'm good for a tenner for the whole thing, all right?'

'That's very generous. Only if we finish it, of course! Oh, there's Dawn, I must catch her.'

'Is that her name? I've noticed her, she's got such a good swimming style, but she seems very shy.'

'She is, but when you get to know her . . . Oh, Dawn! Sorry to interrupt your swim, but I didn't want to miss you.' Maggie dived under the ropes and through the fast lane – mercifully free – to catch Dawn as she came to the turn. Dawn, who didn't wear goggles, blinked pink eyes at Maggie, then smiled.

'Sorry, Maggie, I was miles away. Swimming always makes me go blank.'

Maggie laughed. 'Not blank – meditating! Look, Stella, the pretty girl in the fast lane, the one who lost her engagement ring, is trying to organise a team to do a sponsored swim for charity on Sunday evening – not this week, the one after. I've said I'll do it, as long as we haven't got anything fixed up that I don't know about, and I wondered whether you'd be able to join in? We have to do a hundred and fifty lengths between us, and to be honest I don't know how many I can manage, so we could really do with some extra people.'

'Sunday evening? Well, I don't know, there might be . . . And I don't know whether Gordon . . . But it would be fun. I haven't done anything like that for . . . Um . . .' The unexpected request had obviously thrown Dawn straight into her inconclusive mode.

'Well, you don't have to make your mind up straight away,' said Maggie encouragingly. 'I could ring you this evening, when you've had a chance to think about it.' 'To ask your brother' was what she meant, but didn't like to say. Perhaps something of her meaning filtered through to Dawn though, because she straightened her sagging shoulders.

'No,' she said. 'No, I don't really need to think about it. I'd love to join in, and after all, it is for charity.'

'Yes, Celia – that's her over there, I was just talking to her – she can't manage the swim but she's promised ten pounds if we do it. I know my husband will give me something, but there aren't many more people I can ask for sponsorship. What about the other people in your office?'

'Oh, I don't know, it's not very. . .' Dawn was thrown into another instant dither. 'They don't know I go swimming, so . . .'

'Well, going swimming's nothing to be ashamed of – I should think they'd be impressed. Still, not if you don't want to. I know how awkward it can be asking for money, even when it's for a good cause.'

'Come to think of it, I've sometimes sponsored them, or more often their children. Perhaps I could ask . . .'

'Well, if you can, there's a poster up by the door which will tell you more about where the money's going – I'm afraid I don't have much idea. Anyway, I'll find out about times and so on, and tell you tomorrow. I don't even know for sure that I can do it yet, but I will if I possibly can.'

'Swimalong? What's that?'

Maggie realised that Turner hadn't been listening to a word she said. He had been eating her glazed duck breast, one of his favourite dishes, without apparently noticing what was going into his mouth.

'Swimathon, not Swimalong – though I don't know that it's not a better name! Like the Marathon, only it's swimming. For charity, you know.'

'Oh, right. Put me down for fifty.'

'Fifty lengths?' Maggie attempted to tease his attention back to what she was saying. He looked at her as though she was speaking an unknown language.

'Fifty pounds. If that's enough.'

'More than enough, it's very generous. But what I really want to know, Turner, is whether we're free next Sunday. The one after this one, that is.'

'Sunday week? I don't know. I'll probably be going to the site.'

Maggie tried not to feel impatient. 'I meant, in the evening. So I can go to the Swimal . . . the Swimathon.'

'Oh, that. Yes, I think so.'

'No one coming to dinner? No meetings?'

'Nothing. I'll probably do some work on the books.'

'I suppose you wouldn't like to come along? Oh, not to swim, don't worry!' Turner was a poor swimmer, and was in fact rather nervous of the water, which was the main reason why the building of their own pool in the garden had never taken off. 'Just to cheer us on, give us some support.' Too late, Maggie realised that an evening with Turner at the Leisure Centre, where it would be quite clear that she was well-known, might considerably complicate her life, so it was a relief when he shook his head.

'I don't think so. I've got quite a bit to do – end of the tax year coming up, and so on. Sorry, Mags. Some other time.'

Although she knew it would have been difficult to keep her deceptions going, Maggie still felt disappointed.

'Some other time,' she echoed. 'It's a good thing–' She stopped, appalled by what she had nearly said. A good thing that they had no children, because Turner would always be too busy to go to their school play, or match, or parents' evening. She bit her lip. For the first time that evening, Turner actually seemed to have listened to what she said.

'What's a good thing?'

'Oh, nothing,' she said lamely. 'Just, it's a good thing that we haven't got anything fixed, that's all.' Unsuspicious, he nodded, satisfied.

When the Sunday came, Turner was out all day and had still not returned home when it was time for Maggie to leave for the pool. She banked up the fire and placed guards round it carefully, imagining with a shudder a spark falling on the rug, catching fire, and burning the oil-painting by Turner above. Her husband's supper was ready on a plate in the microwave – rather a good meal, to make up for his having to eat it alone – and Maggie herself had her new swimming costume, and a second pair of goggles just in case. She felt nervous and excited, like a child going to a birthday party, and laughed at herself as she locked the house and started up the Morris. She was early, having promised to collect both Dawn and Primrose.

With three of them in the car it was quite a squash. Primrose, as the youngest, went in the back, which meant she had to bend double to creep in and sit, her legs folded up almost under her chin, on the narrow back seat. She was more cheerful and forthcoming than usual, however, and unlike Maggie and Dawn, who were both wearing baggy tracksuits, was smartly dressed in the trouser suit that Mrs Draper had made her. Maggie found herself unexpectedly touched by this, and realised that for Primrose this Sunday-evening excursion was the nearest she had ever come to having a teenage social life.

Dawn, too, was unusually talkative.

'I've managed to raise twenty pounds in sponsorship,' she announced, as she climbed into the car. 'Much more than I expected.'

'That is good. Was it from the people in the office?'

'Yes. They were all quite astonished when I said I was doing it – of course, I told them I wasn't doing the whole thing, just part of a team, but still! They were really quite friendly about it, and I've said I'll take in a cake, on Monday, to have with our coffee. As a kind of thank-you, you know. With cream, and some of my strawberry jam. They're always on diets, but whenever they have a celebration, that's what they seem to buy.'

Maggie guessed that this was the first time that Dawn had been the donor of such a cake, and that generally she was the recipient of a slice, given in a spirit of grudging charity – 'Better give a bit to poor old Dawn, don't want her to feel left out.'

'Home made jam and real cream – they'll be begging you to do sponsored swims every week!'

The Leisure Centre car park was almost full, and when they went into the building there seemed to be people milling about everywhere. Maggie felt both Dawn and Primrose shrinking back, and realised that it was up to her to organise them.

'Come on,' she said briskly, 'it says that registration is downstairs. Oh, look, there's Stella!'

They followed the dark girl down the stairs. The hall there was even busier, and they fought their way through to a table where Jane was sitting. Stella was already there, talking to her, and they both looked pleased to see Maggie.

'You made it – well done!' Stella's voice was warmly welcoming. 'And Primrose, and . . . Dawn, isn't it? It's so good of you to come along, and I think it's going to be fun. Brenda and Iris are already here, in the changing room. What colour are their hats, Jane?'

'Green. Here you go.' She handed over bright green swimming hats with the Swimathon logo on them. 'That's to help the people counting to keep track of you; you'll be in a lane with a group wearing orange hats, and another wearing white. Do you know what order you want to swim in, and how many lengths?'

'No, I'm afraid we're almost completely disorganised. Do you need to know?'

'Not really, just work it out between you. Who's your strongest swimmer? It's probably best to start with the weaker ones, let them do what they can manage, and work up to the best who can finish off what's left.'

'Dawn, or Primrose, I should think,' said Maggie. 'What do you reckon, Stella?'

'Oh, make it Primrose,' Dawn put in hastily. 'I really don't think I can bear the responsibility of finishing, I'm not really fit, and I just can't . . .' She glanced round, as if searching for a line of escape.

'All right with you, Primrose?' Maggie broke in hastily, anxious to reassure her.

'I don't mind, if Stella thinks it's okay.' Primrose spoke in an off-hand tone, but she was obviously pleased by Stella's enthusiasm for the plan.

'Right then, let's go and change. We can catch up with Brenda and Iris, and decide how we're going to organise the rest of us.'

In the changing room, Brenda and Iris were living up to Maggie's nickname of 'The Gossips', which as they were in neighbouring cubicles made it easy to find them. Maggie knocked on a door.

'Is that Brenda or Iris?' she asked boldly.

'Iris. Who's that?'

'I'm Maggie. We're swimming in the same team.'

'Oh good!' Both the cubicle doors were flung open simultaneously and the occupants popped out, reminding Maggie of a Swiss clock she had owned as a child, so that she had to suppress a giggle.

'I'm Iris, and this is Brenda. Isn't this exciting!'

Maggie quickly introduced Dawn and Primrose. Iris's enthusiasm was infectious, and they were soon eagerly discussing how they would swim.

'So, I'll go first, and then Brenda,' said Iris. 'I know we can both do at least twenty lengths, so that's forty accounted for. Then the rest of you have about a hundred and ten lengths between you. What can you do, Maggie?'

'I usually do twenty in the mornings, but I could probably do a few more. Say twenty-five? Eighty-five left. Dawn?'

'Thirty or forty. Will you manage the rest, Primrose?'

'I think so.'

'Well, we'll all do as many extra as we can manage. I'm sure it will work.'

The crowd on the poolside, though less than in the hall, was still considerable, and looking up at the viewing gallery Maggie saw that it was more than half-full.

'My dad says he'll try to come along a bit later, when he's been to the supermarket. He always goes Sunday evening, says it's his social life.' Primrose, who at thirteen found it impossible to imagine that someone her father's age should want or even think about a social life, spoke indulgently, as one recounting a not very funny joke. Maggie, thinking of how she had got to know Dawn during a shopping trip, smiled wryly.

Since both ends of the pool were shallow, it had been decided that everyone should start their swim, and that the people counting should sit, at the far end. There were six lanes, the first two for fast, individual swimmers – Stella was one of those – and the rest for teams. Maggie and her team were in number six, with two teams of children from the swimming club and a local school, and a team set up by a local business, which consisted of three young men who were laughing too loudly and posing to hide their self-consciousness, and three girls who were giggling together, modestly wrapped in their towels. The noise, to one used to the decorous hush of early morning, was tremendous, and it was hard to imagine that so many people could be organised to swim orderly lengths at the same time.

With five minutes to go, the atmosphere settled into a hum as serious swimmers stretched their muscles and carefully adjusted their goggles, and teachers and instructors shepherded teams of children to sit along the side to await their turn.

'Where's Primrose going?' Dawn's quiet question made Maggie, who was watching the fastlane swimmers warm up, jump. Looking round, she saw Primrose, identifiable by her orange hat and the huge green towel she had draped round her, heading for the changing rooms at a run. Turning back she saw that Stella, too, had noticed the sudden departure and was about to go after Primrose.

Maggie went swiftly over to her through the crowds. 'Don't you go,' she urged Stella. 'You've got to warm up, you'll be in the water in a moment. I've got ages, Iris and Brenda are swimming first. She's probably just dashed to the loo. Nerves get me like that, too, and there's quite a tense atmosphere, isn't there?'

'If you're sure ..'

'Of course I am. Good luck, swim beautifully. I'll come and cheer you on for a while when I've done my bit.'

Primrose had disappeared. Maggie went to the shower area, expecting to find that she was in one of the lavatory cubicles, but none was occupied. The changing cubicles were similarly empty. Maggie began to worry – surely Primrose wouldn't have run out clad only in swimming costume and towel? Finally, she went into the female group changing room.

Primrose was huddled in the corner, still wrapped in her towel. 'Go away.'

Maggie ignored her. 'What's the matter, Primrose?' She sat down next to her, not too close because there were almost visible prickles surrounding the girl.

'You know perfectly well!' Primrose scrubbed furiously at her eyes with a corner of the towel.

'I wouldn't be asking you if I knew. I promise I haven't a clue what's wrong, so please do tell me.'

Primrose glanced swiftly sideways at her without turning her head. 'There's a school team here. And *he's* in it – Dez. I saw him.'

'I didn't notice him in all that crowd. And I can assure you I didn't know that your school were sending a team along – how could I have done? After all, you didn't know, and you go to the school. But is it such a disaster? You swim much better than he does, for one thing.'

Primrose pulled the towel more tightly around her. 'I don't want him – *them* – to see me.'

'With a hat and goggles on, they probably won't even recognise you. Besides, have you *looked* at yourself recently?'

'What do you mean?'

The sound of a whistle, and a burst of shouting, came through from the pool. The swim was starting. Exasperated, Maggie grasped Primrose by the wrist and pulled her to her feet.

'Come on. Nobody's here, they're all watching the swimming.' She dragged the girl, who was too startled to resist, through to the row of wash basins and stood her in front of the mirrors. 'Take off your towel. Come *on*, Primrose, you can see there's nobody here.' Maggie pulled the towel off Primrose, who crossed her arms and lowered her head. 'Don't do that. Stand up straight.' With her hands on Primrose's shoulders, Maggie pulled her upright. 'Straight, I said. Shoulders back. Head up. Now, *look* at yourself.'

Primrose looked. She had recently bought herself a new costume, plain black and practically cut for swimming rather than sunbathing, with a high neck and a zip up the back. The Lycra fabric fitted snugly to a figure that was, in fact, not unattractive. Regular exercise had firmed her muscles and honed away some of the puppy fat, and although she was still a large girl she looked feminine rather than flabby, her newly growing breasts giving emphasis to what was now a discernible waist.

'White slug,' she muttered. Maggie gave her a shake.

'Don't be daft. Everyone's skin is white at this time of the year, and you're certainly not a slug. You've got nothing to hide, even if they do recognise you, which I doubt. If you don't come back Stella will be very disappointed, and so will your father if he's coming here specially to watch you. And so will I, as a matter of fact.' Primrose wriggled, in impatience or embarrassment. 'Now, are you going to come back and support your team, and Stella, or are you going to sulk out here? Because I want to enjoy this, and I'm not spending my evening in the changing rooms.' Without looking to see whether Primrose was following her, Maggie turned and walked back to the pool. When she reached the far end of her lane she was greeted in some relief by Brenda.

'Thank goodness you're back! Iris has started, and I suddenly realised that you and Primrose had vanished. Oh, there she is, that's all right.' Maggie looked back. Primrose, her towel round her shoulders and her head down, was nevertheless walking towards them down the side of the pool.

'Well done,' said Maggie quietly. Primrose gave her a sick look, then sat on the floor so that she would be hidden behind the chair where the person counting sat.

Iris was swimming well. Without the distraction of Brenda beside her to chat to, she was revealed as a strong breast-stroker, and held up for twenty-four lengths before Brenda took over. The two children from the club teams seemed to slip effortlessly through the water as though frictionless, and the worst of all was the young man from the last team, who was splashy and erratic.

Brenda tired more quickly than her friend, and Maggie suddenly realised that it was going to be her turn quite shortly. Dawn, beside her, was sitting quietly, watching the crowds and seeming to enjoy the bustle without being part of it. Maggie took a few deep breaths to calm the quivering feeling inside her, adjusted her goggles, and slipped into the water. Primrose leaned forward and touched her on the shoulder.

'Good luck,' she muttered, 'you'll be fine.' Maggie realised that it was an apology, and smiled back. Then Brenda was clutching the rail beside her.

'Over to you,' she gasped.

Maggie took a deep breath, and pushed off. Ahead of her a froth of bubbles showed where one of the young men was threshing through the water, and to her right the children flashed past her like minnows, and beyond them four other teams were battling it out. Turning at the far end, she kicked out with more confidence, and found that she was actually catching up with the young man ahead.

After three lengths she had passed the young man, and though she herself had been overtaken by both the children she still felt that she was going well. At the turn Primrose was bending down to shout encouragement, and Maggie was swept by a feeling of euphoria that was as strong as anything she had ever known.

At twenty lengths she was still going strong, but on the twenty-fifth she became aware that she was weakening. The strength seemed to be oozing from her, and by the time she came to the next turn she signalled to Dawn that she would be stopping. She did two more lengths to finish off, but the last return seemed to last for hours, and she was relieved to touch the end and to see Dawn's unhurried but speedy crawl.

'Twenty-eight! Well done!' Primrose had recovered her equanimity, and sounded quite excited.

Maggie climbed out, thankful that they were in the side lane by the steps. Iris offered her a plastic beaker of water, and she drank it thirstily.

'That's better! How are we doing?'

'Just coming up to halfway,' Primrose answered. Your twenty-eight brought it to seventy, and Dawn's already done four. She's nice, isn't she?'

'Very nice. And a super swimmer.'

'She said Steph and I could come out to the farm some time, see all the animals,' Primrose chipped in. 'I should love that – I've always wanted a pet, but Dad says we're not at home enough, and he's right, I suppose. It wouldn't be fair on it. And Dad's here – look, up there – can you see him? He's got a blue and green sweatshirt, right in the front by the fat lady in red.'

As Maggie looked up Primrose waved, and her father waved back, signalling a thumbs up and a clap to Maggie.

'He looks nice. It's good he could be here. I'm going to see how Stella's doing – want to come?'

Primrose hesitated, but only for a moment. They threaded their way through the other swimmers, but everyone's attention was on the people in the water.

There were only three swimmers in Stella's lane; the other two were both men who, though they swam strongly, were clearly outclassed by the girl. As Maggie and Primrose watched, Stella executed a neat tumble-turn and went off again so fast that she overtook one of the men without any apparent effort.

'She's nearly finished,' said the person counting in response to Primrose's question. 'Ten more lengths. She'll probably get in at just over the hour.'

'Have I got time to stay and see her finish? I'll go and check how Dawn's doing.' Primrose hurried off, her previous worries quite forgotten, and Maggie crouched down to call encouragement to Stella as she came to the end.

'Only ten to go! Keep it up! You're doing brilliantly!'

Stella's teeth flashed white as she smiled, then she was gone again. Primrose was coming back, and Maggie saw her stop to speak to someone – Dez, surely? Oh dear, thought Maggie. Should I go over? Is he going to say anything to upset her? She saw Primrose shrug and shake her head before returning to Stella's lane.

'Plenty of time. Dawn says she's good for at least another twenty.'

'Um . . . was that Dez?'

'Who? Oh, yes.' Primrose spoke carelessly. 'He was quite surprised to see me here, especially when I told him I was my team's anchorman. They're only a few minutes behind us, and he's swimming last too, so we'll be racing it out.'

Maggie smiled. 'He's going to get a shock. His swimming isn't a patch on yours.'

Primrose grinned. 'I know. I pretended to be really nervous, told him he was bound to beat me, did the helpless female act for all it's worth. He *loved* it.'

'Good for you!' Maggie laughed. 'Now, let's see if we can encourage Stella for her last few lengths.'

Stella, whose energy appeared to be undiminished, responded to their shouts with even greater effort. As she went down the pool for the last time Primrose again waved up to her father, who was hanging over the edge of the balcony.

'Last length!' she shouted, and he nodded violently. The last tumble-turn was as tidy as the first, and Stella put in a last flourish by doing her final length in her faultless butterfly, so that all the spectators had their attention riveted on her. As her hands touched the pool end a great cheer went up. Primrose was jumping up and down, clapping her hands above her head. Maggie, remembering her own thirst, grabbed a bottle of water and a beaker. Stella drank, and gasped for breath, and drank again.

'Showing off,' she said with a smile, still panting. 'Couldn't resist it.'

'It was wonderful!' said Primrose. 'My dad nearly fell off the balcony, it was so exciting.'

'Your turn soon,' Maggie reminded her.

Primrose looked conscience-stricken. 'I must get back. Well done, Stella.'

'I'll come and cheer for you, when I've got my breath back.' Primrose smiled, her face lit up as Maggie had never seen it. Maggie went with her, feeling guilty about Dawn, and was able to encourage her for the last few lengths.

Dez was in the water before Dawn stopped. He was looking confident, posing like a body-builder to make his friends laugh. As usual, his swimming was more splash than speed, and Maggie could see at once that he had never learned the secret of the glide that Stella had taught Primrose. She found herself rather looking forward to Primrose's swim.

In the event, it worked out even better than she could have hoped. To Maggie's amazement, not only was Primrose swimming fast and neatly, but she had obviously been learning tumble-turns from Stella. The first one was a bit untidy, but after that she relaxed and did them, if not as beautifully as Stella, at least with the minimum of splash and fuss. The two teams of children finished, and the other team dropped out – their last swimmer had bad cramp, and was unable to continue. Primrose had the lane to herself.

Maggie saw Dez pause at the end, and glance into their lane. He frowned, then set off with renewed determination. Checking with the counters, Maggie found that his team were only two lengths ahead of hers, with fifteen to go. As Primrose approached, Maggie bent low to call to her.

'They're two ahead. Think you can do it?'

Primrose's thumb came up in a swift gesture before she turned. Maggie could see that she was swimming harder. After four lengths the lead was down to one length, and in five more Primrose was ahead. Dez kept glancing at her. His legs were threshing like pistons, raising mountains of spray, and his arms beat the water as though he were angry with it, but Maggie knew that all this sound and fury merely slowed him up. Stella was beside her, and Dawn, while Iris and Brenda were at the side of the pool, all cheering, when Primrose finished triumphantly, just over a length ahead of Dez. Her schoolmates in the other team watched in astonishment as Stella, the heroine of the evening and the fastest finisher, jumped into the water to hug Primrose.

Dez floundered up, his face red. Politely, Maggie turned to applaud his finish. He stood up. Primrose, still with Stella's arm round her shoulders, smiled at him.

'Well done, Dez,' she called.

'Friend of yours?' asked Stella.

'Sort of. Same school.'

'Well done, then.' Stella put out her hand and Dez, bemused, shook it. His hand remained out, and he looked at Primrose, who after a moment's hesitation put her own in it.

'Great swim, er, Primrose,' he said, and Maggie guessed it was the first time that any of her schoolmates had called her by her real name for many years. 'Um, those tumble-turns. D'you think you could teach me to do them?'

'Well . . .' Stella gave Primrose a little shake. 'Well, I suppose so. If you like.'

Chapter Twelve

In the changing rooms everyone got slightly hilarious. All the team – Maggie's Marvels, as Stella had immediately dubbed them – went together into the group room. They all had certificates and Stella, as an individual swimmer, had a large shiny medal on a bright turquoise ribbon. The rest of them had badges, which they pinned onto their clothes. By common consent, it was Primrose who was the heroine of the hour.

'I knew we'd finish all right, but I never thought we'd beat a team of students!' Iris was jubilant.

'They weren't very good,' Primrose pointed out modestly. 'And one of them got cramp, so that held them up.'

'Even so, they must be half our age. Well, our average age, anyway. I wouldn't have cared if that boy hadn't been so cocky. You really brought him down a peg! Lovely!'

Upstairs it was almost as chaotic as it had been when they arrived. Most of the younger children had been taken home, but all the contestants had been given tokens for a free soft drink from the bar, and most had stayed to use them. Maggie was introduced to Primrose's father. He was a Jack Sprat to his daughter's plump form, skinny and drawn of face, but he had the same hair, cut very short so that the springy curls, faded in him to a sandy beige, covered his head like the frilly swimming hat Maggie remembered her mother wearing. He gripped Maggie's hand, his look of habitual anxiety dissolving into a broad grin.

'Didn't she do well? All of you, of course, but I've never seen her swim before, not since she was little, and learning, and it was just . . . I had no idea! It's wonderful!'

'Nothing like as good as Stella,' Primrose growled, failing to hide her gratification. 'That's Stella, Dad, I told you about her.' She dragged him to meet her idol, who had her arm twined around a young man even taller than herself, and equally elegant. Maggie, who wanted to meet Colin, followed them. Stella's smile eclipsed the brightness of her medal, and the rest of the group, drawn as if by a magnet, drifted up.

'I was saying to Colin,' said Stella when introductions and

congratulations were done, 'that we should all go out and celebrate with a curry.'

'She's on a high,' said Colin, his voice slow and deep as hers was quick and light. 'Up in the clouds.'

'Oh, yes!' Primrose, quite obviously, would have agreed as happily to walk barefoot over hot coals, if Stella suggested it. She tugged at her father's arm as if she had been a small child. He glanced at his watch, frowning. 'Dad!' Primrose's voice expressed all the anguish of a thirteen-year-old who is about to be treated as a child in public. 'It's not that late.' He looked at her helplessly. 'I'll pay my share, out of my Saturday job,' Primrose cajoled, never realising that her words were as cruel to him as those she had feared he might say to her.

'It's not that,' he muttered to her, obviously unable to voice his fear that he, and perhaps his daughter also, would not fit in with this diverse group. Stella's smile swept over him like the beam from a lighthouse.

'Do come,' she said simply. 'You will, won't you, Maggie?' Four pairs of eyes turned to Maggie: Stella and Colin with simple invitation, Primrose imploring and her father worried.

'Of course,' said Maggie, wondering inwardly what Turner would say. 'What about you, Dawn?'

Dawn looked utterly surprised, having presumably not expected to be included.

'Oh! Well, I don't know... I ought to get back... Gordon...'

'He wouldn't mind, would he? You could ring him, so he wouldn't be worried.'

'Yes, I suppose... It would be nice... Haven't had a curry for...'

'The phone's over there, near the entrance. I'll come with you; I ought to phone Turner too.' Without giving Dawn a chance to back out, Maggie began weaving her way through the elated crowds. 'He won't mind really, will he?' she asked again, as quietly as was feasible. 'I mean, don't come if it's going to be difficult.'

'No, he... It's just that I don't usually... Good heavens! There he is!'

'Who?'

'Gordon – over there, look. Near the stairs!'

Maggie looked. Gordon, appearing more unsure of himself than Maggie would have imagined possible, was hovering on the edge of the crowd, his good arm clasped over the plastered one. He was scanning the people with the helpless air of someone who feels sure he won't recognise the person he's looking for, and when he caught sight of Dawn his face relaxed into something that was almost a smile.

'Roar!' His voice, used to calling across paddocks, made those near him jump. 'Rora,' he said more moderately. 'Over here!'

'Gordon!' Dawn sounded breathless. 'What are *you* doing here?'

'Came to watch you swim,' he said simply. 'You did well.'

'Oh, Gordon.' Her eyes filled with tears. 'How lovely of you. How did you get here – you surely didn't cycle?'

'Tom came round, gave me a lift. Have to get a taxi back, I'm afraid.'

'Not at all,' Maggie broke in. 'I promised I'd take Dawn back, and you too, now you're here. The only thing is, we were planning to go out for a curry first, to celebrate.' She saw Dawn open her mouth, and hurried on. 'Dawn thought she'd like to come, so we were just going to the phone to call you. I know everyone would be glad if you'd join us.'

His face took on a hunted look. 'No, I think I'll just slip away . . .' He glanced at Dawn, then with an effort stiffened his back. 'Well, I suppose I could. I've never been one for Indian food, but I expect there'd be something . . .'

'That's wonderful,' said Maggie warmly, wondering what kind of an evening this was likely to end up being, and hoping that Stella's smile would be able to work its magic even on this solitary farmer. 'Why don't you take Gordon back to meet the others, Dawn, while I phone Turner? I won't be a moment.'

Obediently the brother and sister, looking absurdly like a pair of elderly babes in the wood, made their way back towards Stella. Maggie fished out a coin and dialled her number. There was a short pause, then it rang.

There was no answer. Did I forget to switch on the answering machine, Maggie wondered? It was so much second nature to her now that she had no recollection of doing it, but on the other hand she almost never forgot. Turner was liable to be very irritated if he missed calls. Perhaps he was home, and not answering? That, too, was most unlike him. Turner had the American habit of snatching up the phone before it had rung more than twice.

Maggie let it ring, counting the numbers. Ten, eleven, twelve . . . after twenty-five the answering machine, even if switched off, would activate itself. The rings seemed interminably slow; it was hard to hear over the cacophony of chatter and Maggie had to keep the receiver pressed hard up to her ear. On the eighteenth ring there was a click.

'Turner? Turner, are you there?'

There was a short, echoing pause. Maggie was so confidently expecting Turner's breathless voice, explaining that he had been down the garden, or in the bath, that when she heard the careful tones of the recorded message it was like getting a bucket of cold water over her head.

'*Unable to take your call . . . please leave your name . . . after the*

tone . . . get back to you . . .' Maggie spoke over the voice. 'Turner!'
she said again more loudly, as though by shouting she could make
him hear. 'Are you there? The message finished with a beep. Maggie
took a breath.

'Turner, it's Maggie. Just to say I'm going out for a curry with
the others I swam with, so I won't be home for a while. I'll put my
mobile on when I get back to the car, in case you need me.'

Putting the receiver back down she stood for a moment staring
at the silent telephone. It was wrong. She knew it was wrong. The
answering machine was set, if switched on, to answer after three
rings. If off, it took at least twenty-five before cutting in. The only
way it could have answered, then, was if someone switched it on. A
burglar? Surely not. Any sensible burglar would simply ignore the
telephone. Turner, then.

Maggie had a powerful mental image of Turner standing over the
phone, his hand hovering above it then withdrawing. Of Turner
listening to her voice, his face shuttered, and turning away. Could he
be angry because she was going out with the others? But until she
had spoken, how could he have known? In all their years together
she had never known Turner not to answer a ringing phone, and yet
she had the strongest conviction that he was in the house.

Should she go back? She felt that she ought to, but felt even
more strongly that she didn't want to. After all, she rationalised to
herself, Turner would have heard what she said. If he had wanted
to talk to her, he would have picked up the phone. She wouldn't be
very late back, she could find out what was wrong later. Meanwhile,
she was enjoying this evening more than she would have believed
possible. The prospect of a curry, so different from the meals out
she had with Turner and his business associates, was more enticing
than the most luxurious of restaurants.

The rest of the groups were working their way towards her. Iris
and Brenda had produced husbands, both looking sheepish and
out of place but clearly making an effort to fit in. It occurred to
Maggie that she, alone of all of them, was without a supporter.
Primrose had her father, even Gordon had turned up to see Dawn
swim but she, who could have afforded to take them all out for a
meal without even noticing the expense, had no one, and a husband
who wouldn't answer her telephone message.

They reached her, and Maggie pushed all self-pity to the back of
her mind, determined to recapture the euphoria of their success.
Stella left Colin, who was talking to Primrose's father, and put her
arm round Maggie's shoulders.

'All okay? Your husband didn't mind, did he? Why doesn't he
come and join us? The more the merrier.'

'No reply,' said Maggie succinctly. 'I left a message. I know he
won't mind.'

'Fine.' Stella gave Maggie's shoulder a squeeze. She smelled of shampoo and baby powder, like a nice clean child, and her unaffected warmth had the same childlike appeal. She bent to murmur into Maggie's ear.

'Look, there's the boy that Primrose fancies. Shall we ask him to come along too?'

Maggie looked around, puzzled. 'Which boy is that?'

'Over there, look, the one she beat.' Stella's nod indicated Dez waiting at the top of the stairs that led down to the main doors.

'Him? Oh, no, she doesn't fancy him. In fact, she can't stand him.'

'Oh, yeah?' Stella lowered her eyelids and smiled. 'Whatever you say, Maggie.'

'You think . . .?' Maggie pondered. She remembered that Primrose had said that Dez was 'clever, too'. Probably they competed in lessons, the competition giving rise to antagonism when Primrose, plain and unpopular, outsmarted the boy. Certainly Primrose clearly minded what Dez might think or say about her, so perhaps . . . 'Well, he was certainly impressed with her swimming tonight, and managed to say so, which was brave after the way he'd been boasting.'

'Primrose is looking good tonight, anyway. That outfit suits her.'

It was true that Mrs Draper's expert tailoring had made a flattering job of the trouser-suit, and the silky lilac blouse Primrose wore with it made her skin, still faintly flushed with exercise and excitement, glow creamy pale, and set off the rich colour of her hair which for once was not dragged back with a rubber band but allowed to curl exuberantly round her head. She was walking between her father and Colin, her head was raised to listen to what they were saying, and she was laughing.

'*Match-maker, match-maker, make me a match,*' hummed Maggie, and Stella giggled. As she came level with Dez she stopped and smiled with her usual dazzling effect.

'You're Primrose's friend, aren't you, the one who wants to learn tumble-turns? We're going for a curry. Want to come along?'

He blinked at her. 'Uh . . . Primrose . . . Uh . . .'

'What's your name?'

'Uh . . . Uh . . . Dez . . .'

'Dez, I'm Stella, and this is Maggie, who was in Primrose's team. So what do you think?'

'Um . . .' Maggie thought that he could seldom have been at such a loss. Stella's directness, which made the phrase 'up front' seem positively repressed, had obviously thrown him into total confusion. Stella smiled again as the rest of the group caught up with them. Primrose, seeing Dez with Stella, hesitated, her face wiped suddenly blank. Stella turned to her.

'I thought Dez might like to come with us, seeing as he's a friend of yours. Someone to talk to apart from us old fogeys!' Stella's youth robbed her words of any malice.

Primrose looked haughty. 'He's no friend of mine,' she said coldly. 'Just someone at school.'

Dez, who would obviously have rejected any claim to friendship, nevertheless didn't care to have it denied by someone else, particularly in front of this beautiful black girl.

'I'd like to come,' he said to Stella, 'but I can't. I've got to get back.'

Primrose gave the tiniest of sniffs, which everyone present immediately translated into 'Mummy's boy'. Maggie's lips twitched, but Stella carried on regardless.

'Is someone coming to pick you up, then? Your mum? Shall we ask her?'

'Well . . .' He took a breath, his shoulders hunched. 'Not my mum,' he muttered. 'House-mother. From the Home.'

Stella glanced at Primrose, who relented.

'Come if you like,' she said ungraciously. 'I don't mind.'

Dez glanced back at the stairs. A brisk-looking woman was coming up, forging her way through the flood of departing swimmers without difficulty.

'I can't,' he said hurriedly. 'Not this week.'

'Grounded?' asked Stella, with a sympathy that robbed the word of any patronising overtones.

'Uh,' he agreed, relieved from the need to explain any further. Maggie thought that it was not the grounding, but his submission to it, that was embarrassing him.

'It happens,' Stella said philosophically. 'Oh well, another time, perhaps.' He glanced sideways at Primrose. His look expressed the hope that she wouldn't spread his subjugation to official discipline round the school, the dismal certainty that she would, and the rueful acceptance that he would have done the same, and that it was no more than he deserved. He hurried to intercept the woman before, presumably, she could cause him any further embarrassment.

It was midnight when Maggie crept back into her house. She went in through the lobby to the kitchen, as she usually preferred to do, although Turner always used the front door. The kitchen was bare and clean, the air smelling of coffee. Automatically Maggie went to the coffee-grinder, and screwed it together properly; Turner invariably put the coffee receptacle on askew so that the slightest touch sent the cup flying, scattering freshly ground coffee all over the worktop. Turner had been home, and made himself some coffee. Feeling rather foolish she peeped inside the dishwasher. A dirty plate, and a cup and saucer. He had eaten supper, then. Or, of course, it was an incredibly tidy burglar.

Giggling to herself, Maggie went to the sink. She felt light-headed, not with drink – having to drive, she had restricted herself to half a pint of lager – but with the memory of her evening. It had been a long time since she had eaten Indian food, as she had never particularly liked it, but it seemed to have improved a great deal since she had last tasted it. Stella and Colin, who knew the restaurant well, had ordered, covering every combination of hot to medium to mild, including chicken, prawns, meat and vegetables. Everyone had piled into the dishes as they arrived, even Dawn and Gordon abandoning restraint and tasting a mouthful of everything. Gordon surprised them all by his ability to eat a whole chilli without turning purple and gasping for breath, though he did mop his face several times with his napkin.

Maggie felt stuffed with food, her mouth tingling with the taste of garlic and chilli and other spices, her mind equally stimulated not so much by the conversation as by the novel experience of being with such a diverse mixture of people. Although physically tired by the swim, she felt far from sleepy. Thirsty, she ran herself a glass of water, but after a couple of mouthfuls poured it away and went to the fridge for a beer. Never a drinker, she generally preferred wine if she had anything, but the lager she had drunk earlier had the bitterness to cut through the spicy heat of her mouth.

Sipping the beer, she opened the door and went through to the hall. The lights were on, but the silence was profound. Swiftly she glanced into the study and the sitting room. Both were dark and empty, the logs in the fireplace beneath the Turner painting burned away almost completely to ash, with only the scented memory of their warmth lingering in the room.

Restless, Maggie prowled back to the hall, and checked the answerphone. No messages, it said, so Turner must have listened to her call and re-wound it. In the study Turner's desk was empty, the polished leather surface unmarred by even a single piece of paper. It was tidy even by Turner's meticulous standards. Idly Maggie opened the top drawer, and was faintly startled to find it empty too. She frowned. Surely this was where Turner kept his office account books? She quite often helped him with the routine paperwork of VAT returns and the entering and filing of invoices, and she had never known him to put them anywhere else.

Maggie finished her beer, thought about having another, and decided that she was too full to swallow anything else. An enormous yawn ambushed her, and she was suddenly aware that her legs were aching. Pushing the drawer shut she fetched a large glass of water to take upstairs, and switched off the lights. She knew the house well enough, by now, to find her way to the bedroom in the dark. When she got there, a glow of light from the ensuite bathroom door was enough to show her the hump under the duvet that was Turner. He was breathing slowly and regularly, so she tiptoed to put her water down on the bedside table, then shut herself in the bathroom to get ready for bed.

Looking in the mirror, she thought it was probably just as well that Turner hadn't opened his eyes. Her hair, which she had dried hurriedly at the pool, was wispy and limp, her eyes slightly bloodshot from a combination of chlorine, a late night, and the smoky atmosphere of the Indian restaurant. She cleaned her teeth vigorously, in the forlorn hope of banishing some of the garlic from her breath.

After the brightness of the bathroom the bedroom was impenetrably black. Maggie shuffled her away across to the bed, guided by the sound of Turner's breathing and secure in the knowledge that his tidy nature would not permit him to have left clothes or shoes where they could trip her up. She got into bed, sliding carefully under the duvet. Lying on her back she tried to relax her tired limbs, but the muscles in her legs and back seemed to twitch and throb all the more now that they were no longer being used.

Turner, beside her, was very still, and she wondered again whether he was really asleep. Generally, Turner was almost as active in sleep as when he was awake, turning constantly, flinging out an arm or a leg, muttering and snuffling. Maggie was so used to it that it no longer disturbed her, though in the early years of their marriage she had often found herself so far to one side that she was clinging to the edge of the mattress. Fortunately, for all the suddenness of his movements, the sleeping man seemed to retain some instinctive feeling for where she was, for she was seldom hit by a flailing limb.

Maggie found herself matching the rhythm of his breathing with her own. It was too slow, uncomfortable for her to sustain. She found herself having to draw in a long gasp of air, and felt her heart pounding. Her eyes, hot and gritty though they were, refused to stay closed, and she found herself straining against the unrelieved darkness. She held her breath, listening. The long slow breaths continued.

I must go to sleep, thought Maggie. Carefully she went through the relaxation routine she had once learned, tensing and relaxing each group of muscles, trying to empty her mind or at least to calm it. As she often did now, she pictured herself swimming in clear blue water, the most soothing image she could conjure.

'How did it go?' Turner's voice, pitched low but sounding wide awake, startled her and she jumped.

'I thought you were asleep!'

'Only dozing. How did you get on?'

'Oh, fine. We finished in good time, beat one of the other

teams, and they were school-kids! It was fun.'

'Good.' She could feel the warmth of him across the width of the bed – an extra large one to allow for his restless sleep. Even in the coldest weather Turner was always warm. She rolled towards him, and found that he was lying on his back, as she had been. Turner, who always slept on his side, who could never sleep on his back without snoring, was stretched out as still as a tomb figure, his arms down by his sides. He turned to meet her, and their bodies fitted together in comfort with the ease of familiarity.

'Do you remember when we were first married?' Maggie asked inconsequentially, wriggling her head into that place on his shoulder where there were no hard bones. 'I was always waking up with pins and needles, because there never seemed to be anywhere to put my arm where one of us wasn't lying on it.' Turner gave the kind of vague grunt that Maggie could interpret as she wished.

'Down at the Leisure Centre, wasn't it?' Maggie felt a little shiver, like a small electric shock, run through her.

'Yes, that's right.' Her voice sounded too bright in her own ears. 'I don't think the Club pool would have been big enough. There were so many people there.' He grunted again.

'Everything all right at the Club? Enjoying it? People okay, are they? Running it, I mean. Looking after you properly?'

'Oh, yes!' Maggie hated to lie to him. Why didn't I tell him right at the beginning, she wondered? 'How was your evening?' she countered. 'I tried to ring you, did you get my message?'

Was it her imagination, or did Turner, too, give a kind of nervous twitch at her question, or was it just her own guilty conscience?

'Yes, I got the message, thanks. Why didn't you come to the hotel to eat?'

It was a reasonable enough question, Maggie thought, if one assumed that the swimmers in her group were all members of her club.

'I don't know, really. Some of the people weren't Club members, and probably aren't too well off. Someone else suggested the Indian, and I just went along with it.'

'Mm. That was the only reason?'

Maggie was surprised. 'Yes, of course. Why?'

She felt him shrug slightly. 'Just wondered.'

They lay in silence, and Maggie felt him relax, the muscles shifting infinitesimally. He gave a sudden galvanic jump, and she knew he was falling asleep. Gently she eased away from him, knowing that he would give two or three more of these violent twitches as a prelude to deeper sleep, and she found them unsettling.

Turner muttered, and turned over. Maggie lay, more wide awake than ever. Turner, she was sure, hadn't been asleep when she first came home, only pretending. She was as convinced of that as she was that he had been there listening to her voice as she spoke to the answering machine. She felt strange, unlike herself, unreal. She tried, again, to imagine her body floating in blue water, but all she could feel was a depth of blackness, like being sucked down into bottomless mud.

Chapter Thirteen

When Maggie opened her eyes the following morning, she was already aware that she felt awful. She had been awake for some time – or rather, she had not been asleep for some time but had been lying with her eyes shut longing for oblivion but unable to reach it. Her body had been informing her, with increasing urgency, that her bladder was full. It was also demanding a drink, and a wash, and a fierce application of toothpaste and brush. At the same time it was telling her that even after she had done all these things she would not feel substantially better. Her mouth, she knew, would still taste horrible, her head and legs would still ache, her eyes would still feel as though she had spent the night in a dust-storm, and however much scented talc she might dust over her body her skin would still feel clammy and unwholesome. It seemed rather unfair that she should feel this bad when she had only had two beers the night before, but she assumed that the combination of the exertion and excitement of the swim, the large spicy meal eaten late on an empty stomach, and the late night itself, had combined to make her body rebel.

Maggie looked at her bedside clock, groaning when she saw that it was already seven o'clock. No point in trying to go back to sleep, then. Even if she decided to skip her swim, she would still have to get going soon.

Suppressing a groan, she rolled out of bed and dragged herself through to the bathroom. She had no need to look back to see whether Turner was up. However late a night they had had, he was invariably up by six o'clock, and out of the house by quarter to seven. Maggie washed, and feeling no better than she had expected to, decided that she might as well go swimming, after all. The cool water and the exercise might clear some of the cobwebs from her head, and it would be cheering to see the others.

By the time she reached the Leisure Centre, the entrance was empty, the queue having disappeared down to the changing rooms already. She meandered down and undressed slowly, soothed by the routine. In the water she swam gently, humouring the stiffness of her muscles and enjoying the feeling of the water holding her up.

The pool was much less busy than usual. Maggie realised that most of the people who had swum so hard the previous evening would be unlikely to want to swim again in the morning. There was no sign of Primrose or Dawn, but Maggie exchanged smiles and greetings with Iris and Brenda. In the fast lane she was surprised to see Stella, who had put in so much effort the night before. She was swimming quite slowly, but with a dogged determination that was somehow apparent in every fluid movement.

Maggie thought, as she swam, how much she had enjoyed the evening. The memory had been tarnished by Turner's strange behaviour, but here in the water she was able to push that disquiet away from her, and recall the earlier pleasure.

She herself had said little during the meal; her enjoyment had come from observing. It had been pleasant, for her, to be able to take a passive role for once. Generally, when she and Turner ate out with clients or business associates, she was in the position of hostess and as such responsible for the smooth running of the evening. She was always on watch for others' comfort, whether it was the service of the food and wine, or the maintaining of conversation so that no one was excluded, and all were amused and interested.

The previous evening no one had been in that position; the meal simply progressed quite naturally, with everyone sharing the dishes that Stella and Colin had ordered. Stella had been bubbling with happiness, her eyes sparkling with the mental and physical high of success, her cheerful, outgoing nature seeing no problem or incongruity in the mixture of ages and interests of the others. She was, Maggie thought, the ultimate product of liberal thinking. To Stella, everyone she met was a potential friend, regardless of age, sex, class or race. Maggie found herself praying passionately that nothing would ever happen to mar that shining friendliness.

The result, as Maggie saw, was that Stella brought out the best in everyone. Dawn, in general so shy, was more relaxed than Maggie had ever seen her. Her diffidence evaporated like morning mist in the bright sunshine of Stella's interest, and she talked freely without stopping halfway through incomplete sentences as though her own thoughts were not worth repeating. She even disagreed with her brother on the subject of fox hunting.

'I certainly don't want to hunt myself, but I don't think that gives me the right to stop other people from doing it,' she said robustly.

'Just because the fox took your pet cockerel—'

Dawn cut through his bluster. 'That has nothing to do with it. It's a fox's nature to hunt birds, and though I don't like it I don't want to punish it, just to prevent it if I can. I just don't see why people should be forced to stop doing something traditional, something that is part of our history. In any case, I'm quite sure that most of the people who are so violently against hunting dislike it because they think it's elitist, something only rich people do. Which isn't really the case.'

Maggie, with secret amusement, saw Gordon eyeing his sister with a kind of horrified fascination, rather as though one of his farm animals had suddenly asserted itself and started arguing with him. She guessed that Gordon had never suspected, or even contemplated the possibility that his sister might actually have opinions that differed from his own. She saw, with pleasure and relief, that although surprised he was far from being annoyed. There was even a measure of respect on his weathered, country-man's face. Dogmatic he might be, but not unreasonable.

Primrose, too, showed a different side of her character. Like Gordon and his sister, Primrose's father was watching his offspring with amazement. Maggie, who had seen the prickly side of Primrose's nature and guessed that her father rarely saw anything else, was fascinated.

The confidence engendered by her successful swim, and by the knowledge that her new clothes suited her so well, together with the friendly presence of the object of her hero-worship, combined to make Primrose blossom into a girl who, though no one would call her beautiful or even pretty, was certainly attractive. Her confrontational, aggressive style was softened, not to insipidity, but to a kind of feisty quick-wittedness, so that she several times had them all laughing at her sharp ripostes. It was rather a pity, Maggie thought, that Dez hadn't been able to be there to witness this sudden flowering, though of course his very presence might have inhibited it from happening.

Did I ever change like that? Maggie thought back to her own adolescence. The Swinging Sixties had given way to the early Seventies, a time when the first novelty of the Cult of Youth had worn off, the idealistic libertarianism of the Flower Power genera-tion had faded to New Romantic fantasies, politics to pirates in one fell swoop. Maggie, too lacking in confidence and perhaps too down-to-earth to want to float off into that colourful dreamworld, had felt isolated from many of her contemporaries. Adolescence, beyond the incontrovertible changes to her body, had seemed to affect her little. She had no memory of being rebellious, in the sense of suddenly turning against her parents' ideas and values. In many ways there was nothing to turn against, for their emotional distance from her meant that she had always rebelled inwardly. Outwardly she continued to conform to her parents' standards up to and after their deaths, but this was more from inertia than from any deeply held philosophy.

The only time she had really blossomed, as Primrose was blossoming now, was when she met Turner. In those first few months, she remembered, it had suddenly seemed so much easier to talk, to be amusing and interesting and interested. To find, for the first time in her life, that there was someone to whom she was important had changed her whole self-image. So was love, then, the key? She had felt reborn at that time, and though they had later settled into the more humdrum habits of an enduring marriage, that recreation of herself had never disappeared. Turner had made her what she was, and in return for that unconscious gift she would always feel love for him. Her own need for balance ensured that. In the past she had been worried by the fact that she felt so little love for her parents, until she learned to rationalise it by acknowledging that she gave them no less than they gave her. She had never rid herself of this desire for an emotional trade-off, though she wondered how it would have worked out if she had had children of her own.

Lost in her reverie, Maggie failed to notice how late it was until it dawned on her that she was almost alone in the pool. She climbed out, showered quickly, and hurried through to get dressed. As she went into the group changing room she thought at first that it was empty, until she rounded the panels that screened the room when the door was open, and saw Stella sitting in the far corner. She was only half-dressed, having progressed no further than her underwear; the rest of her clothes were hanging ignored on the peg behind her. She was frowning down at the floor and appeared not to notice Maggie's entrance.

'Stella! Are you all right?'

Stella jumped. 'Oh, Maggie! I'm sorry, I didn't realise you were there. Yes, I'm fine.' She made no move to finish dressing, however, and continued to sit while Maggie dried herself and rubbed moisturiser onto her skin.

'Want me to do your back?' Stella was holding out her hand for the cream. Maggie gave it to her gratefully, and turned round. Stella's hands on her back, smoothing and rubbing the moisturiser, were firm and warm. Maggie felt soothed, rather as she imagined a horse must feel when being groomed by someone experienced.

'Thank you,' she said as Stella handed back the bottle. 'That feels much better.'

'I did an evening class once, in massage. It was quite fun,' the girl said absently.

'I should think you could do it professionally, if you wanted to.'

'Mm.' Stella had taken her shirt off the peg, and was looking at it as though she couldn't remember what she was supposed to do with it. Maggie saw that Stella had dark shadows under her eyes, and that she was still frowning a little.

'You shouldn't have come in today,' she said gently. 'You must be exhausted after swimming so hard last night, and then our evening out on top of it. Thank you for suggesting that, by the way – everyone enjoyed it so much.'

Stella's lips curved up, but it was a pale version of her usual flashing smile.

'It was a good evening, wasn't it?' She spoke with more enthusiasm. 'A really happy time.' A happy time, her tone said, that is over and gone.

'You're tired?'

'Yes. I didn't sleep very well.'

'Nor did I. Too much excitement.' Maggie tried to joke, pushing away her worries about Turner.

'Mm.' Stella was silent for a moment. 'I had a phone call when I got home. It was a bit worrying.'

'A phone call?' Maggie's thoughts brought images of anonymous threats, of racial harassment such as one was always hearing of, but hoped did not exist in this calm little backwater of society. 'An unpleasant one? Oh, Stella.'

The girl shook her head, and even smiled a little. 'Not *that* kind of phone call! No heavy breathing, or telling me to go back to the jungle. Oh yes,' she saw the look on Maggie's face, 'it does happen, you know, from time to time. I don't let it bother me. No, this was an anonymous call, but I think I know who made it, and it was to warn me, not threaten. She said . . . I suppose it's silly to let it worry me, but she said that something was wrong at the wedding place.'

'The wedding place?' Maggie felt her blood run cold.

'Yes, at The Grange. You remember, we've been paying into it for months, and it's all done now – the dress, and the flowers, and the reception and everything. The trouble is, I couldn't ring them, of course, as they're not open yet, and it did rather keep me awake last night. We're relying on them for everything, you see, except the actual church service and the bridesmaids' dresses, and we've paid more than we could really afford. It seemed worth it, to know that it would all be done beautifully, and to have the photographs and the memories, but if it doesn't work out I don't know what we'll do. We couldn't afford anything else. As it is, we're going to Colin's aunt's cottage in Devon for our honeymoon, instead of anywhere abroad.'

Her lips trembled, and she put up a hand to cover her mouth. 'Sorry,' she said shakily. 'I'm being silly. Of course it will be all right. I mean, nobody's said anything about any problems at the hotel, have they?' She looked trustingly at Maggie, not knowing of her connection with the hotel but trusting in her as someone older and more experienced, perhaps more in touch with local things. Maggie put an arm round her shoulders and patted her reassuringly, her mind spinning.

'You said you thought you knew who it was who rang you?'

'Yes, that was really why I let it bother me. I think it was one of the girls who work there. She's really nice, she helped me choose the flowers and the menu and things, and we got on well. The trouble is that it's really difficult for me to make calls from work, and we're extra busy today so I shan't get much time at lunch, so I don't know when I can ring them. Colin's gone to Manchester for a couple of days, so I'm stuck. Still, if something has gone wrong, I suppose it won't really make much difference whether I can speak to them today or whenever. It's not as if we can do anything about it. Anyway, I expect it's nothing. I mean, a place like that hotel – it's been really successful, hasn't it? There can't be anything wrong.'

'I wouldn't have thought so.' Maggie spoke soothingly, attempting to calm and convince herself even more than Stella. 'I always thought The Grange was doing well, I must say. Tell you what, do you want me to see if I can find anything out for you? I've finished work by lunchtime, so I've got all afternoon . . . I could go round there on my way back, ask around, see what's what.'

'You don't want to waste your afternoon on that . . .'

'It wouldn't be wasted if it sets your mind at rest. And if there is something wrong,' Maggie swallowed, clenching her stomach muscles against the spasm of panic that set them quivering, 'then it's better to know. There must be something we can do about it.' Even, she thought, if I have to pay for it all myself. Oh Turner, is this what you were worrying about? Is this the thing I've been feeling, that something had gone horribly wrong somewhere? Is that why you asked me about the Spa? She gave a shiver. At once Stella turned to her.

'You're getting cold, you must get dressed. Are you sure, Maggie? I know that if anyone can find something out, it's you.'

'Because I'm old and tough?' Maggie attempted a joke.

'Because that's the way you are,' said Stella with simple faith. 'You're the kind of person who does things properly.' She looked so much happier that Maggie was more alarmed than ever.

'I'll do my best, of course I will. I just hope it will be good news.'

'If it isn't, I'd rather hear it from you. Oh Lord, look at the time! I must rush, I'm going to be late for work.' She began to drag on the rest of her clothes. 'Can I ring you when I get home from work? Are you sure you don't mind, Maggie? It's so kind of you.' She wriggled into her skirt, and zipped it up. Stuffing towel and costume into her swimming bag, she gave Maggie a swift kiss and was gone.

Maggie finished dressing, then sat down rather in the same pensive attitude in which she had earlier found Stella. Her first thought was to telephone Julie and ask her about the Club, but then she remembered that Julie wasn't working that week. One of her children was having some polyps removed from his nose, and Julie was going to the hospital with him.

It would have to be Turner himself, then. No other roundabout measures could possibly be taken. Impossible to approach the hotel or the wedding shop unless she used a false name, and she couldn't bring herself to do that. Besides, if by any wonderful chance there really was nothing wrong, it would do no good to stir up speculation and anxiety among the staff.

The door burst open and a group of small children in school uniform appeared. Maggie glanced at her watch, realising that it was much later than usual and that the school swimming class, which took place in the learner pool while the geriatric hooligans disported themselves in the large one, would soon be starting. Maggie was thankful that she had finished dressing, and was able to gather up her things and leave quickly as the children stared at her, affronted to find an adult in the changing room.

In the car, Maggie rummaged for her mobile phone, praying that the battery wouldn't be flat. For a wonder, as she hadn't remembered to check it for days, the display showed more than half-charged. Swiftly, before she had time to think about it and panic, she punched in the numbers. It rang, and she felt her heart give one enormous thump as though it were trying to break out of the cage of her ribs.

It rang. And rang, and rang. Maggie frowned. Turner hated a telephone to be unanswered, and all his office staff were trained to answer before the third ring, if humanly possible. Such a slow response argued that nobody was there. Almost relieved, Maggie disconnected and tried the home number, only to be instantly answered by the answering machine. Last of all she rang Turner's own mobile phone, something she rarely did. Very few people had the number, and although he often used it to telephone out he hated to have it ringing when he was occupied. This time it rang five or six times, then was switched through to an answering service. Glancing anxiously at her watch, Maggie tried the office again, this time gritting her teeth and letting it continue to ring.

After about the twentieth ring, when Maggie was beginning to wonder whether the world had suddenly come to an end and nobody had thought to tell her, the phone at the other end was picked up.

'Whittington Construction?' It was Turner's secretary, sounding a little out of breath.

'Angie? It's Maggie. Is anything wrong?'

'Oh, Maggie!' There was profound relief in her voice. 'Thank goodness. I've been so worried. Where are you?'

'At the Leisure Centre. Angie, is Turner there?'

'Here? No, we haven't seen him at all today. Isn't he with you? No, of course he isn't, or you wouldn't be asking me. I'm sorry, Maggie, only it's all been so strange and I'm not really coping. It's ridiculous, only I've *never* known Turner to be late without telephoning, and as for missing an appointment . . . well, it's just unheard-of!'

Maggie caught the panic in her voice. She could understand why the other woman was so worried. After more than six years of working for Turner, such a thing had never occurred before. Turner was meticulous in his business arrangements, a fanatic about punctuality and courtesy, and he would no more have forgotten an appointment, or skipped it without informing anyone, than he would have taken off his clothes and danced naked through the hotel.

'Could he have had an accident?' It was the only explanation that Angie could think of.

'He might have done. He's a very careful driver, but nobody's safe all the time. And he's been very preoccupied lately.'

'What shall I do?' Her years of working for Turner had taught Angie that, while he liked her to use her initiative over anything to do with the office, he very much disliked any form of interference with his private life.

'Oh, dear.' Maggie looked at her watch again. Feeling, as she did, that something was very wrong with some aspect of Turner's business life, she did not believe he had simply been involved in a car accident. In all their years together he had never had so much as a nudge or a dent. However preoccupied he might be, his reaction times were always phenomenally quick, and he had a kind of instinct for the aberrations of others that protected him from erratic drivers. At the same time, it was better to be sure.

'Could you ring the police, and the hospital? Just to check if there has been an accident. I'll be home by lunchtime, but I'll ring you in a little while to check. If there's anything urgent, you can get me on my mobile, but it's probably better if you don't ring it unless you have to.' Maggie wondered whether she should still go to Celia's house, but seemed unlikely that she could do any good, or find anything out, by going home. She could not telephone Julie, since the operation was scheduled for that very morning and she would certainly be at the hospital. If she failed to turn up at work, Mrs Draper would get into a state and start telephoning round and bothering Celia. On the whole, it seemed best to carry on as normal, while she could.

As it was, she was very late. Mrs Draper was inclined to be irritable – she was down in the kitchen making her own breakfast when Maggie let herself in.

'I'm sorry I'm so late, Mrs Draper, I'm afraid I was held up. I would have telephoned, but I didn't want to get you out of bed, but I see you already did.'

'I'm sure I can manage to make my own breakfast, for once. I'm not completely helpless, you know,' the old lady sniffed.

'Of course you aren't! But breakfast in bed is never quite the same if you have to come down and make it for yourself, is it? Do you want to go back upstairs, and I'll bring the tray?'

'No, I might as well have it here, now I'm down. Not that I

approve, in general, of people eating downstairs in a dressing gown. Slovenly, I've always thought. Still, I wouldn't want to make more work for you.'

Maggie saw that the Mugger was determined to be a martyr.

'How kind of you. And really, that's more of a house-coat than a dressing gown, wouldn't you say? Perfectly respectable, at any rate. I'll go and start on the sitting room, so you can eat in peace.'

As she had expected, this was not at all what Mrs Draper wanted.

'No, I don't think one should vary one's routine. You may start on the washing-up in here. Certainly there's always plenty of it, when my son's family have been eating. So, did you have trouble with your car? Or is it Primrose? I hope she isn't ill.' Her eyes were bright with interest. Maggie saw that she was rather pleased to have a break in the routine, and was hoping for some little excitement. Maggie toyed with the idea of telling her that Primrose was pregnant, just to give her a real shock, but decided that a limited version of the real reason would do very nicely.

'It's a friend from the swimming pool, such a lovely girl, she was very upset and I stayed to see if I could help her.' Mrs Draper made a little movement, settling in her chair like a broody hen over an egg, ready for a good gossip. Maggie told her about Stella, and her worry over the wedding arrangement.

'Now that is really too bad,' said Mrs. Draper with relish. 'How long did you say it is to the wedding?'

'Less than a month. Of course, there should be some kind of compensation. The place must be insured.' Maggie had made very sure, in fact, that it was. Assuming, of course, that the payments had been kept up.

'That won't give her a wedding though, will it? Much too late to book anything else. Poor girl, what a disappointment.'

'Yes,' said Maggie miserably, scrubbing at a dish that had been left in soak since the night before. Half her attention was given to listening for the sound of her mobile phone, which she had left in her bag in the lobby. She found it difficult to think about Stella without her eyes filling with tears. The more she thought about it, the more she felt sure that something had gone very wrong at the hotel. She supposed that she could use her own money to pay Stella back, or even top up the insurance payment if it could be claimed, but as Mrs Draper said, it was far too late to re-book the dress, the florist, the caterers, and the photographer, and above all find a suitable place for the reception.

At home, she thought suddenly. I'll do it at home! God knows the house is big enough, and if by some miracle we can rustle up some kind of marquee for the garden . . . and I could find some caterers and so on, and get the flowers done . . . it would cost a fortune, but so what?

143

'. . . so where is it?' Mrs Draper's raised voice broke through her reverie.

'I'm sorry, madam. I'm afraid I didn't hear what you were saying. Where is what?'

'The material, of course.' Mrs Draper's voice was sharp. 'You obviously haven't been listening to a word I was saying. The material for Primrose's dress. You were going to bring it in with you today.'

Maggie's heart sank. New clothes for Primrose had been the last thing on her mind this morning, and the material was still sitting at home.

'I'm sorry, Mrs Draper, I'm afraid I completely forgot it.'

'Well, really!' The Mugger's temper might be greatly improved, but it didn't take much to bring the sharp edge back to her voice, or the tight downturn to her lips. 'I don't like to criticise, Maggie, but I must say that when I'm going to the trouble to make something nice for Primrose, I do think you might try to be a bit helpful.' The words 'ungrateful' and 'taking it for granted' hovered in the air like horse-flies.

'I know,' Maggie agreed. 'It's too bad of me, and Primrose will be annoyed, too.' Primrose, with Stephanie to give advice, had chosen the fabric for a dress. Rather than bring it to the pool, where it might have got splashed in the changing rooms or even forgotten, Julie had brought it round the previous Friday when she came to work. Maggie, worried that Turner might notice it and ask questions, had stuffed it into a cupboard and then forgotten all about it.

'I've got a nice free day today, the boys aren't coming back until late because they've got a football match or something, and Celia is going to watch too. As I was going to be all by myself I thought I'd make use of the time by cutting out the dress. You know I can't concentrate when those boys are around, so noisy, and always dashing about the house in the most exhausting way.'

'Still, now you could go to the match after all, if you ring Celia at the College.' Maggie knew that Mrs Draper had used the excuse of doing the cutting out to avoid the football match, although she was now trying to make it sound as though she had not been invited and was cruelly excluded from all family events.

'I wouldn't dream of it,' said the Mugger acidly. 'I know when I'm not wanted.'

Maggie thought it wasn't worth arguing with her.

'I'll tell you what, why don't I run home and fetch the material? It wouldn't take very long, and then you'd be able to get on with it. I'll make up the time, stay on a bit later.'

Mrs Draper, who rarely did anything in a completely straightforward manner, went through the charade of reluctance and having to be persuaded, before doing as she had always intended and agreeing to the plan.

Chapter Fourteen

It was a relief to Maggie to jump into the car and head for home. Generally she found Mrs Draper easy, even entertaining, but today her head was too full of other things. She wondered whether she might, against all probability, find some clue to what was going on while she was at home. It was true that Turner never left anything about – no pieces of paper with scribbled notes, no unanswered letters or unfiled receipts. If only she had time to go to the hotel – but that would have to wait for later.

She pulled up outside the back door. It seemed quite strange to be there at that time of day – she had quickly become accustomed to her regular working hours – and as she unlocked the door she saw the place where Julie usually left her bicycle, and remembered that the operation might have started by now. Julie would be pacing the corridor or prowling in the visitors' room, convinced that her offspring would inevitably die under the anaesthetic. Maggie spared a sympathetic thought for her, convinced as always that such effusions of good will had virtue.

The kitchen felt empty and cold, although the heating was on. Maggie had the strange feeling that she was somehow unwelcome, that the house had its own secret life while no one was at home, and that she was interrupting it. She found herself almost tiptoeing across the floor to the door to the hall. As she touched the handle she heard the sound of a voice.

In that well-built house, with its solid walls and heavy wooden doors, she could not distinguish the words or anything much about it, except that she was almost certain it wasn't Turner's. His voice she would have known anywhere. Something about this one – the depth, or the rhythm of speech, was profoundly unfamiliar.

For a moment, she felt paralysed as if someone had hit her hard in the solar plexus and deprived her of breath. A burglar, she thought. Two burglars, because of the voice, unless it was a burglar who talked to himself. She must telephone for help, dial nine nine nine. The telephone was in the hall, unreachable, but she had her mobile in her handbag which was . . . back at Celia's house. How could I? she thought. I came out in a rush, and didn't bother to bring it with me. I must be mad. Now what?

Back to the car, she thought sensibly. Presumably they hadn't heard her drive in, so it should be all right – but even as she told herself that, the thought of getting into the car, turning the key in the ignition, was like a dash of cold water in her face. The Morris always started with a few hiccups, not infrequently a backfire, and sometimes stalled. Could she risk it? The idea of being trapped in her car was more than she could bear.

She would have to go for help on foot. Out of the back door, down the drive – overlooked by all those windows, any one of which might have enemy eyes staring out of it – and along the road to the nearest house, where there might not be anyone at home because they both went out to work . . .

There was silence from the other side of the door. Had they gone? Scarcely aware of what she was doing, Maggie turned the handle and eased the door open a few inches. Peering through, she could just see into the sitting room. The fireplace was dead and cold, the ashes of yesterday evening's fire still sitting greyly, and above them – above them, nothing!.

The precious Turner, her own Turner's most cherished possession, was gone – stolen! Without a second's hesitation, Maggie snatched the kitchen door open and catapulted through it and across the hall into the sitting room.

She was conscious, as an animal is, of a presence behind her even before he spoke, yelling: 'You silly cow!' She began to turn, her arms lifting, though whether in attack or defence she could never have said, but then almost immediately something crashed onto her head, and she was falling – down and down and down – into a blackness filled with echoing voices that came and went, swelling and shrinking like the reflections in a hall of distorting mirrors.

'YOU SAID she wouldn't BE here . . .'

'What have you DONE? My God, Maggie, MAGGIE!'

'She's all RIGHT, don't fuss, just a little tap on the head, I KNOW WHAT I'm doing.'

'Oh God . . .' The voices tailed away into the black mist. Maggie could not move or speak. Even the desire to save herself seemed to have gone, and she welcomed the rolling waves of darkness.

When she came back to herself it could have been days, hours, or minutes later, and she had no memory of what had happened. At first the pain in her head dominated everything else. Then, slowly, she became aware of the discomfort of the rest of her body. Because of the pain, she had assumed that she must be lying down – in a hospital bed, or at least in her own bed at home – but she soon realised that she was sitting upright, fully dressed, in a hard chair.

Her head, unsupported, was hanging forward, like someone who has fallen asleep on a train. Even the thought of lifting it made her feel sick; instead, she concentrated on trying to work out where she was.

Very gently she moved a foot, and felt carpet beneath it. Good carpet, too, with a thick pile like . . . like her own. She knew that she ought to open her eyes and look around, but somehow she couldn't. Partly because the thought of moving her head still made her feel dizzy, and partly from some instinct of danger that told her not to show that she was awake. It seemed odd that she should feel threatened in her own house – and surely it was, for she could smell the scent of the lilies she had arranged a few days earlier, and the dying fragrance of woodsmoke from an old fire.

She made a new, and unwelcome, discovery. Her wrists were tied together behind the back of her chair. Her body was tied too – a broad band of something round her waist and ribs binding her to the chair and keeping her upright.

She must open her eyes. It couldn't be put off any longer. When she did so, the light seemed so bright that it stabbed through to her brain, and she immediately shut them. Three slow breaths, and then she tried again.

A pattern of bright roses jumped into view – familiar, but not something she connected with home. Her overall, of course. Beneath it, her old tweed skirt and its matching jumper, and below them the familiar carpet of her own sitting room. She hadn't been wrong about that, at least, and she was sitting on one of the dining-room chairs that must have been brought through. But why was she wearing her overall, that she kept at Celia's house? Her mind, still in shock, fixed on this minor problem and worried at it like a terrier at a rat.

Then she remembered. She had been at work, and had come home. In a hurry, obviously, because she hadn't taken off her overall. So she had come home to fetch – yes! – to fetch the material for Mrs Draper. She tried to visualise herself parking the car, coming into the kitchen, going, presumably, to the sitting room because . . .

'Oh, no!' It came out as a groan as her head jerked up. The agony of moving was forgotten in the pain of seeing that the painting was gone. At the same moment she heard a stirring behind her, and cringed away until she realised it was Turner's voice, muffled but unmistakable.

'Maggie! Maggie, are you all right?'

'Oh Turner, your painting! Your lovely painting's gone!'

'I know. Don't worry about that now. How do you feel? Are you all right?'

'Yes, I think so.' Maggie spoke more to reassure him than anything else. 'My head hurts, but I can move everything. At least, I think I can. I'm tied to a chair.'

'Me too.' Painfully, Maggie turned her head. Turner was sitting on a similar dining-room chair, back to back with hers, but his head and shoulders were just a formless shape against the light from the window. Something had been tied over his head, something incongruously patterned and familiar. Of course! Maggie almost laughed. It was the slip-cover from the back of one of the armchairs.

Gritting her teeth, Maggie shuffled her chair sideways, turning it far enough so that she could see Turner properly. The pain in her head was already subsiding to manageable proportions, subsumed in her anxiety for him. She peered at the slip-cover. There was no sign of any blood soaking through it, but it was a heavy, densely woven material and the colours were dark enough to make it impossible to tell. Like her, his hands were tied together behind him, and fastened to the rung of the chairback. Maggie even recognised what had been used – a piece from the new washing line she had bought a few days earlier, that had been sitting in the lobby outside the kitchen. By twisting her fingers she could feel that her own hands were similarly tied, and her heart sank. The new cord, not a slippery plastic-coated kind but a strong cotton rope, would be well beyond human strength to break. She gave a little sob of frustration, and at once he twisted wildly against his bonds.

'Maggie! Oh Maggie, I'm so sorry. If only you hadn't come back . . .'

'It's all right, Turner. Don't panic, I'm fine.' Maggie could see the rope cutting into his wrists as he pulled against it, the new white threads already staining with his blood. 'Don't do that,' she said practically, 'you're just making them tighter.' His fists clenched tight, but she could see that he was making an effort to be still. 'They weren't taking any chances with you, were they?' His ankles, unlike hers, were tied to the chair legs, and his torso bound round and round with the rest of the rope.

'No, no chances. After he hit you . . .'

'You saw that? Were you there?'

'Yes. He . . . they . . . had already got in. I had a phone call, came home, they jumped me in the garden, made me open up, switch off the alarms.'

'Oh, Turner! They didn't hurt you, did they?'

'No, just threats. Oh, not against me. It was you . . . They said they'd . . . Well, anyway, I let them in, and then you came back, nobody heard you – and they hit you, and I thought . . . I didn't know what to do. I couldn't help you, I wanted to . . . oh, kill them. Bastards! Oh, Maggie.' She heard how the breath caught in his throat and felt her own eyes fill up in sympathy. She shuffled her chair back, moving it up to his so that her reaching fingers could touch his, and for a moment they clung together like children holding hands in the dark.

Then Turner pulled his fingers free and felt for the knots at Maggie's wrists. She kept still while he picked at them, but she could tell that his fingers could get no purchase on the smooth cord.

'I can't do it,' he cursed. 'I ought to be able to!'

'Wait.' Maggie twisted experimentally. 'My arms are only tied together, not to the chair, and my feet and legs aren't tied at all. If we could undo . . .' She squinted down at the band that held her body tied to the chair back. She hadn't looked at it before, but now that she did so she could almost have laughed. It was the length of fabric for Primrose's dress!

Lifting her hands again, she felt for the knot. The strain across her shoulders and in her arms was intense, but she could do it. The fine, silky fabric was easy to undo. Once she had found which bit to tug at, the knot loosened almost at once and she had soon released it. The material had been wrapped round her several times, but by jerking her body forward she could loosen it enough to be able to stand up and slide the whole thing off the chair back, after which it simply slithered down to her feet.

'What's happening? What are you doing?' Turner could hear her moving, could hear the little grunts of effort and the way her breath caught when a too-strong movement sent a thud of pain through her head and down her neck.

'I'm free from the chair,' said Maggie. 'Now I've just got to . . .' She sat on the floor, then lay on her side. 'Bother it,' she said breathlessly. 'I'm sure it's possible. Come on . . .' Curling her back round as much as she could, she wriggled and pushed to get her bottom through the circle of her arms and hands. 'Pity I haven't lost more weight,' she muttered. 'Oh, go *on!*' The nylon overall, being slippery, was probably the thing that finally made it possible, and Maggie found herself lying with her linked wrists behind her knees.

Even then, it wasn't all that easy. Taking her shoes off helped a bit, but when she tried to lie on her back – which would have been the ideal position – the bump on her head was too tender to allow her to stay there.

Finally, one leg was through; the second was comparatively easy. For a moment she just lay there on the carpet, breathing long breaths. Her arms and shoulders felt as though they were on fire, her head as though it was about to explode. She knew she should be doing something about Turner, and calling the police, but for the moment she had to take a few minutes to rest. She closed her eyes and tried to breathe slowly and deeply.

'Maggie!' Turner's voice was hoarse now. 'Are you still there? Are you all right?'

His voice boomed and whispered through the roar of pain in her head, bringing memories floating up from the depths like monstrous deep-sea fishes. Memories of voices . . . 'You said she wouldn't be here.' A stranger's voice, speaking to . . . 'What have you done? My God!' *Speaking to Turner, and Turner answering him.*

'Oh,' Maggie moaned. 'Oh, no. Oh *no!*'

'Maggie! What's happening?' Turner was twisting so violently in his chair that only the fact that it was large and solid stopped him from crashing the whole thing to the ground.

'Turner.' Maggie's voice was quiet, but something in it silenced him at once. 'Oh, Turner. You were there.'

'You know I was. I told you, they jumped me.' Maggie longed to be able to believe him, wanted it so much that it hurt, but she knew every nuance of his voice, knew that blustering tone. She dragged herself to her feet, and went slowly to where Turner sat in frozen stillness, like a child playing statues when the music stops.

Maggie gripped the fabric of the slip-cover with her bound hands, and tugged at it. It was partly caught under the cords round his chest, but most of it was loose and after an initial tussle she was able to pull it off. Turner sat still, his head raised but looking straight ahead, not at her. He wore an expression that she knew very well, but had never thought to see when they were alone together. To outward appearance it was a blank look, the ultimate poker-face. Maggie knew that it meant that Turner was backed into a corner, that he was in the wrong but was finding it impossible to admit it.

The chair she had been tied to was still there. A little while ago she had thought that she would never sit in it again. Now she slumped into it with gratitude. She made no move to release Turner, nor did he ask her to. They just sat, he staring straight ahead, she looking down at her hands in her lap, and the greying cord that still tied her wrists together.

At last Turner drew in a long breath, and looked at her. She could feel his gaze upon her as if it were a physical touch, but her head felt so heavy she couldn't bear to move it.

'It was a put-up job.' He spoke quietly, reasonably, as if he were discussing the weather or the price of fish. 'I needed the money. I was going to claim from the insurance. I'd have paid it back later on, arranged to "find" the painting. A short-term thing. I'd have borrowed against it, used it as collateral, but I can't borrow any more without the banks knowing there's a problem.'

Maggie made a little noise in her throat, to signify that she was listening but that she was disinclined to speak.

150

'I thought you'd be out.' He was not accusing, just stating the fact. 'It never occurred to me that you might come back; I know you've been out all morning recently. If I'd thought for one moment that you'd get involved in this, that you'd be hurt . . . Mags, I'm – oh, sorry doesn't begin to say it. I'd rather have lost everything else than . . .' He stopped, and she heard him swallow. 'Please say something,' he begged.

Maggie frowned at her hands. 'The problem,' she said. 'The one the bank mustn't know about – is it the hotel?'

'No, why?' In her peripheral vision she saw his hands twitch, and knew that he was trying to run his hand through his hair and down to his neck, as he so often did when he was worried and trying to explain something. 'It's to do with the Mall. Or rather, to do with the land it was supposed to be built on. Do you remember, the other night, saying that you'd heard there was some problem at the Council offices, in the Planning Department?'

'But I thought the planning was already in place?' Maggie couldn't help jumping in. 'When you bought the land, you said building permission was already granted.'

'Not exactly. I knew consent hadn't been formally given, but the chap at the Planning Department said it was a certainty. If I'd waited for formal permission, for the rubber stamping, the land would have been even more expensive. It seemed worth the risk. The Planning man – some kind of friend of the farmers, I think, or a cousin – would have swung it for them and for me, only someone caught on. It wasn't the first time he'd done something like this, by any means. Like a fool I jumped in with both feet. It seemed such a perfect site, near enough to the main road, not particularly valuable farming land . . . God, I was such a fool! So sure I couldn't put a foot wrong, so bloody *arrogant* . . .'

His hands jerked against his bonds, but still he didn't ask Maggie to try to free him. He squeezed his eyes tightly shut, then with an effort opened them again and assumed his previous blank expression.

'I borrowed up to the hilt. There wasn't much time, you see, it had to be done quickly. The lawyers said I shouldn't rush into it, I should wait until formal planning consent was granted, but would I listen?' He laughed without humour. 'Of course not. After all, I was the great Turner Whittington, wheeler-dealer *extraordinaire*. Stupid bastard. Stupid, arrogant *bastard*. And then, after what you said the other night, all those things I'd been closing my eyes to, all those hints and signs, suddenly fell into place and I knew, I just knew, that it was all blowing up in my face.'

He paused again, and hunched his shoulders, trying to wipe his face but reaching only his cheeks and chin. His forehead was wet, and so were his eyes. Maggie reached for the slip-cover, and silently

151

lifted it up to him. He scrubbed his face against it.

'Thanks,' he said. 'Well, like I said, I started thinking properly at last, and did some asking around. It turned out that guy in Planning had been taking bribes for several years, in exchange for arranging to get building consent through without too many questions being asked. I think the farmers had given him money to keep me sweet, but had done it in such a way that it looked as though *I'd* given it to him. He was already under investigation, and my only hope was to pull out at once. I had to be able to pay off some of what I'd borrowed. The minute there was any hint of scandal, the bank would start demanding their money back, and they'd take everything – the hotel, even this house, and I just couldn't *bear* it. The bank won't stand for having any kind of connection with something possibly criminal.'

'But you hadn't done anything criminal yourself, Turner.' With an effort of will, Maggie managed to make her words sound like a statement, not a question.

'No, absolutely not. Not in terms of giving bribes, that kind of thing.' The relief that flooded through Maggie was like a gulp of neat spirits, warming her stomach and sending the blood coursing round her body. 'The trouble is, who'd believe it?' Turner went on moodily. 'Property developers are only one degree away from the devil, in most people's minds. And that goes for bank managers, too. Any suspicion of involvement in something shady would stick like tar; I'd be a business leper, as far as the banks and commercial money people are concerned. So I had to be able to pay off the loan on the land, as far as possible, distance myself from it. And I had to do it without it looking as though I'd sold something on purpose, if you see what I mean. I couldn't put the Turner on the market, because . . . well.' He paused and shook his head as if rearranging the words inside it. 'Because everyone knows how much the damned thing means to me. Selling it would be like putting out huge banners with "I'm desperate" on them. I suppose I just panicked. I know you love this house, I hated the thought of having to tell you it had to go.'

To Maggie, knowing him as she did, this didn't altogether ring true. She knew, and thought that he did too, that the house was more important to him than to her. Was he trying to persuade her to go along with the insurance swindle? For the first time, she looked him full in the face.

'I don't care about the house! I mean, of course it's a lovely house, but it doesn't mean *that* much to me.'

He glanced at her, and then away. 'No, I suppose I'm still making excuses, aren't I? What I meant was, I didn't want to admit to you or to anyone else, that having bought this house I couldn't afford to keep it. Pathetic, isn't it?'

'Not really.' Against her will, Maggie responded to the bitterness in his voice. She stood up and walked round behind him; although her wrists were still tied together, she started to pick fruitlessly at the knot at his wrists. 'Just mistaken. What a muddle. And now they've got the Turner.'

There was a long silence. Maggie waited, knowing that there was more. At last Turner drew in a long breath, and now looked her properly in the eyes. For the first time his face lifted into a little grimace that was almost a smile.

'As a matter of fact, they haven't. That's why I went about things this damn-fool way. It's a copy, the one we had done when we went on that long trip to Australia, and didn't want to leave the real thing in the house. I sold the real one on the quiet some while ago.' He looked weary. 'Didn't even get a very good price for it, because of the secrecy problem. I always hoped that one day I'd be in a position to buy it back.'

Maggie sat down again, limply. 'So,' she said slowly. 'You would have claimed the insurance and paid off the creditors. And then?'

'There'd have been enough left over to look for another bit of land, have another go at the Mall. Here or elsewhere. I'd have paid back the insurance company as soon as I could, you must know that.'

'Yes.' He would have done, if only so that he could display the painting again. Then he would have moved heaven and earth to buy back the real thing. He would have rationalised it, quite happily, by saying that he had been paying high insurance premiums, that the company had been repaid and that it had been no worse than taking a short-term loan from them. Maggie, probably, would never have known anything about it.

Now that she did know, he wouldn't go ahead. There would be no arguments, no attempts to persuade her. Once he had come out with the truth, he had already mentally abandoned his plan.

Maggie felt very odd. She supposed she was still in shock, because nothing seemed quite real. It occurred to her that it was time to be practical, to free herself and Turner. I won't think about this for a few minutes, she decided. In a little while, perhaps I can begin to sort out how I feel. She went to the kitchen and awkwardly fished out the large sharp scissors that she kept for household jobs. With a great deal of effort and concentration, she managed to cut all the way through the rope round Turner's arms. Her bound wrists hurt with the strain of slicing through the washing-line without injuring her husband in any way.

When Turner's hands were free he made to take the scissors from her but his fingers were numb and they dropped, narrowly missing Maggie's foot.

'Blast,' he said shakily. 'Blast and bloody damn.' He flexed his fingers, wincing as the movement brought a renewed blood supply to his swollen hands. His shoulders, too, seemed locked solid after sitting with his arms stretched behind him. He shrugged them, rolling his head from side to side. Maggie retrieved the scissors, and this time he was able to hold them steady against his leg while she rubbed her wrists on either side of the blade, then with an effort he chopped at the cords.

'Lucky he didn't tie me too tightly,' said Maggie. 'And not to the chair, except for that bit of material round my body.' She crouched down to free her husband's feet, and the rest of cord that ran round his torso. Turner beat his fists on his thighs, partly because they ached and partly out of frustration and anger.

'I told him not to tie you at all. I *told* him. I'd have stopped him, only he'd already tied me up and I couldn't *do* anything. When I saw him tying you, I . . .' He compressed his lips for a moment. 'That's when he put that damned cover over my head, and then I couldn't even see what he was doing to you.'

'He didn't do anything – well, apart from hitting me, and I suppose that was just a panic reaction. He obviously meant me to get free without too much difficulty. That was the plan, I suppose – that you'd be tied up, and I'd come back and find you?'

'Yes.' Turner's voice was harsh. 'Maggie . . .'

'I need a cup of tea. And a brandy,' said Maggie firmly. 'I'm going to put the kettle on. You get the brandy.' Meekly he went to the table where the decanters stood on a silver tray. When he came through to the kitchen he was carrying one clasped to his chest with his forearms, unable to support the weight in one hand.

'Should you drink brandy when you've had a crack on the head?'

'Probably not, if I'm concussed. But I'm going to anyway, just a small glass.'

'We should take you to hospital, get you checked over.'

'And tell them what, exactly?' Maggie spoke with the kind of exasperated patience that she remembered hating in her own mother's voice. She made an effort. 'I think I'm all right,' she said more gently. 'My head aches, but not unbearably, and I don't feel sick or dizzy, or anything like that. I'm not seeing double. If you're worried, get the torch and see whether my pupils are reacting properly, but I really don't want to spend the next three hours sitting waiting in the X-ray Department. I'd rather take my chance that your – friend – knew what he was doing, and that my skull isn't fractured.'

Turner sighed, but gave in. 'All right, though we could easily have said you'd fallen against something. I just can't bear to think that I've harmed you.'

'Don't fuss.' Maggie tried not to snap. 'I'll skip the brandy, if it's going to worry you that much.' She tipped boiling water into the teapot, and found that her hand was shaking so much that half of it splashed onto the worktop. Assembling mugs, milk, sugar, teaspoons and the teapot all on the table seemed an almost insuperable task, and although Turner tried to help he seldom did anything in the kitchen, and didn't know where anything was kept. Maggie found it so irritating to watch him opening drawer after drawer hunting for spoons that she told him to fetch the milk – at least he knew where the refrigerator was – and then sit down out of the way.

The first mouthful of tea – hot and strong, the way she liked it – tasted wonderful. Turner had tried to put sugar in it – 'for shock' – but Maggie hated sweet tea, and had prevented him.

'That's old hat, all that hot sweet tea stuff. I know you can't drink it without sugar, but I'd rather have what I like.'

He nodded meekly. Maggie sipped her tea. It was so hot that it burned her mouth, and she could feel it scorching a pathway down into her stomach. The pain was good, clean: it made her feel alive and normal again. Even the throbbing in her head subsided a bit more. As a result, her brain felt clearer.

'Insurance companies don't pay out that quickly,' she said, neither accusing nor questioning, but as a statement of fact. Turner said nothing, but continued to stir his mug of tea. 'Particularly not on a big claim, and not one where there'd have to be a police investigation. You wouldn't have got the money in time.'

Turner was still silent. All his attention seemed to be concentrated on his mug of tea, which he continued to stir. He had the habit of doing this, creating a little whirlpool with his spoon for about ten times the length of time required to dissolve the small half-spoonful of sugar which was all he now allowed himself. Maggie generally stirred it for him, and took the spoon away. Now the sound of the metal scraping and clinking on the bottom of the mug made her want to scream.

'What were you going to do? Borrow against it? Hope that the bank would go along with it? For goodness sake, stop stirring that bloody tea and *drink* it!'

With great care he took the spoon from the mug. Without a saucer to put it in he looked hesitantly at the clean table-top, then stood up and went to put it in the sink.

'Something like that,' he said, his back to her, standing at the sink. He attempted no excuses, no self-justifications. Maggie shuddered.

'Thank God I came home, then. You must know that it would never have worked. A claim like that, they'd have been months investigating it, especially when they found you were in financial difficulties.'

'I know. I was mad. But I had to do *something.*'

155

He rinsed the spoon under the tap, turning the water on too hard so that it shot forcefully from the spout and splashed off the curve of the spoon bowl. She strove to keep her voice level.

'Do come and sit down. Your tea will be cold. And there's no reason why you shouldn't have a brandy with it.'

He sat down again, sipping the tea but ignoring the brandy. Maggie saw the raw places on his wrists, but her heart was hardened against sympathy. Not because she had been attacked – curiously, now that her headache was fading she found herself able to dismiss that quite easily as a kind of accident, rather as if she had tripped and fallen. No, the anger and shock she felt was due to Turner's behaviour, which she found astonishing. It was as though a familiar path, a place she knew so well that she could walk it blindfold, had suddenly become quicksand beneath her feet. She thought that if she were to look in a mirror she might find that her own reflection was suddenly changed, unrecognisable. The feelings of fear that had always spun themselves through her feelings for Turner had suddenly become, not an incidental thread in the fabric, but the very warp and weft of it.

The telephone rang, and they both jumped. There was a moment's pause, then Maggie saw that Turner was unwilling – or afraid – to answer it. She thought she needed to get away from him for a moment, even if this should prove to be some other disaster. She went to the hall.

'Hello?' She was surprised to find her voice sounding so normal.

'Maggie, is that you? Are you all right?'

'Celia?' Maggie' mind was so full of Turner and his problems that her own affairs were as insubstantial as a mirage. 'Yes, I'm fine, thank you.'

'Thank goodness! I've had Ma-in-law on the phone to me at College, insisting on getting me out of a class because she was sure you must have crashed the car or something, daft old trout.'

'Mrs Draper? Oh dear!' Maggie was full of contrition. She thought quickly. 'I came home to fetch that material, as I expect she told you, and there's a bit of bother here – nothing desperate, but my husband's not too well so I won't be able to get back, I'm afraid. I'll give her a ring, put things right with her.'

'Oh, poor you!' Celia was quick to sympathise. 'Is there anything I can do?' Little do you know, Maggie thought, that you've already done it – telling me what your husband said about the problems in the Planning Office.

'No, but thank you. I'll do my best to get to work tomorrow, but if I can't I'll let you know.'

'Don't worry about it. Do the old bat good to have to look after herself for a day or two, stop her taking you for granted. I'd better go, I've a class in two minutes. Don't forget – if there's anything

I can do, just give a shout.' She rang off before Maggie could answer. Maggie kept the receiver to her ear, clinging to Celia's straightforward kindness as something solid in her shifting universe. Reluctantly, she disconnected and punched in Celia's home number.

'Mrs Draper? It's Maggie. I'm so sorry, I should have rung you straight away, but there's a bit of a crisis at home.'

'I've been *worried* about you!' The Mugger spoke with the ponderous weight of one performing an almost unnaturally selfless action, which in her terms, Maggie thought, she probably was.

'I know, and I do apologise. It was so good of you to be concerned, and to ring Celia.' Maggie spoke sincerely. At that moment she was grateful for any crumb of kindness, however selfishly motivated. Perhaps Mrs Draper heard it, and the wobble in her voice that Maggie could not control, for she spoke more gently than Maggie would have believed possible.

'Are you sure you're all right? Would you like me to come round? I could get a taxi, and pick up the material at the same time.'

'No!' Maggie spoke with unthinking sharpness, the prospect of Mrs Draper turning up to wonder at her house being the very last straw. 'No, please don't worry,' she hurried on, softening her tone. 'I wouldn't like you to be put to that trouble, when it's so nasty out. I'll drop the material over later, if that's all right. And I shall hope to be with you tomorrow, as usual.'

'Well, I did want to get on with the cutting out, as I told you, but if you can't manage it . . .' The old lady paused, presumably summoning all her small reserves of generosity '. . . then don't worry about it.' Her tone was longsuffering, but Maggie was genuinely grateful, and said so. Mrs Draper, fortified by the warming effects of her selfless act, rang off quite cheerfully.

'Who was that?' Turner, too, was happy to be distracted for a moment. 'Your charity-work friend?'

'You could say that. Since this seems to be the moment for truth-telling, I'd better admit that it's not exactly charity work. I've been cleaning her house for her, the one who rang first, and that was her mother-in-law who's staying there.'

'Cleaning her house? You mean, like looking after a Stately Home? National Trust, that kind of thing?'

Maggie laughed out loud. 'Far from it! Nothing so genteel, I'm afraid. I've just been working as her cleaning lady for six pounds an hour, cash in hand, five mornings a week.'

'But – why? I mean, six pounds an hour . . .' For once in his life, Turner was bereft of words.

'Honest toil,' said Maggie grimly. 'At least, honest except in the taxman's eyes. But I didn't do it for the money, as you must know. If I needed more than you already give me, the odd ninety pounds a week wouldn't make much difference. I've been giving it to charity, to square it with my conscience. No, I did it because she's a friend, to help her out, and because I rather enjoyed it. I don't mean I want to do it for ever – and I didn't anyway expect to be doing it this long, only her mother-in-law didn't go back to Spain and her usual cleaner refused to come back while she was there. And while we're at it, the mother-in-law thinks I've got a thirteen-year-old daughter called Primrose.'

Turner, still speechless, gaped at her.

'The mother-in-law misunderstood something I said, and I went along with it to keep her amused, and then she wanted to make some clothes for my daughter so I had to rope in a girl from the swimming pool.'

'From the swimming pool – the Spa, you mean? One of the pool attendants?'

'No, of course not. None of them could pass for a thirteen-year-old, specially not a fat one with a bad skin. No, Primrose really *is* a thirteen-year-old I met at the pool, and it wasn't at the Spa.' For the first time, Maggie felt awkward. 'The thing is, I didn't feel comfortable when I went to the Spa. I mean, it's a lovely place and I really appreciated having the membership, but I didn't seem to fit in there, so I started going to the Leisure Centre instead. That's where I met Primrose, and Celia who I work for, and several other people, too.'

Turner groaned. 'No wonder you didn't say anything about the Spa. I was so relieved, when you said everything was all right there . . . but you haven't a clue, have you?'

'Not really. I could ask Julie, but not until she's back from the hospital.'

'Julie? Julie who cleans here?'

'Yes. I – well – I gave her my membership. Not to waste it, you know. And she was so thrilled, Turner, I'm sure she appreciated it twice as much as I would have done. I know you wanted me to meet people, useful people, but . . . I just hated it.'

He scrubbed his hand over his head in the familiar gesture.

'I don't want you to do something you hate, I'm just sorry you didn't like it. And don't feel I only did it so that you'd meet useful people. I don't want to use you like that. But if you had been there, you see, you might have had some idea of what was going on. The manager I put in to run it, and the Wedding Service – I've got a feeling he's been up to something dodgy. A faint whiff of the sea, if you get me.'

Turner, Maggie saw, was beginning to return to his normal self. She wished she could do the same.

'Fishy? That's not like you, Turner.'

'I know. Normally I'd have kept a far closer eye on the hotel, but

I've been so preoccupied, I couldn't really think of anything but the Mall.'

Maggie's heart sank. 'I think there is something. I don't know about the Spa – Julie hasn't said anything – but I'm pretty sure there's a problem with the Wedding Service. One of the girls I swim with has her wedding booked there, and she was given a hint that something funny was going on. I've been so hoping . . .' Maggie broke off, her eyes flooding and her throat closing so that when she tried to take a sip of tea she could scarcely swallow it. 'Oh dear. Poor Stella. They've put everything they could afford into this wedding.'

Turner's head went down, and his hands on the table bunched into fists again.

'I'll make it up to them, when things are straight again. I promise.'

Maggie knew he meant what he said. Turner had always been generous. The smallest of obligations, whether financial or in kind, never went unpaid without a substantial bonus. It was a matter of pride to him. He was not particularly interested in other people's feelings, their pleasure woke no answering response in his emotions, but it was necessary to his self-image that he should see himself as a benefactor. Born in a previous century he would undoubtedly have been known as a philanthropist, endowing orphanages or almshouses and bestowing his name upon them.

'When things are straight again will be a bit late.' Maggie didn't feel inclined to let him off the hook too easily. 'They want to have a wedding on their wedding day, not a year or two later.'

'Christ, Maggie! What do you expect me to do, walk on water?' Maggie was almost relieved to see the old Turner resurfacing. The meek, apologetic version, though doubtless appropriate in its way, had been making her feel nervous. The explosion was shortlived, however. Turner put his hands flat on the table and spoke more calmly. 'We're facing ruin. If that happens, not only will we have nothing, but the people I employ will find themselves without a job. There are worse things than having to do without a fancy wedding.'

'I know, I know. It's just . . . I like Stella – love her, even. If you'd met her, you'd know what I mean. She's so – so *nice*. Good, and innocent, and happy. Nothing's ever really hurt her, not enough to disillusion her, and I know it's bound to happen in the end. I know she'll maybe end up just as cynical as the next person, but I can't *bear* that we should be the ones to make it happen.'

Turner shook his head helplessly, but said nothing. Maggie could see that whatever she said, Stella's problems seemed trivial to him. Rationally, she knew that he was right, but somehow being rational seemed beside the point. She felt a bubble of pure, white-hot fury growing inside her, felt it physically as a burning sensation that spread outwards until every inch of her skin seemed on fire. Her face felt swollen with heat, her clothes too tight and she glanced down, almost expecting to see her sensible working clothes splitting like the Incredible Hulk's or bursting into flames of spontaneous combustion.

The wave of anger reached its peak without breaking into words or action, and ebbed. It left behind it not flotsam and jetsam, but a new Maggie. A kind of shell or mould that had formerly contained her was gone, broken or burned or washed away. The Maggie that emerged knew, with absolute certainty, that she would never go back to being her former self. Without being aware of it she had been chafing against her bonds, pushing at them to test their rigidity. The small gesture of going to the Leisure Centre rather than to the Spa had been the toe in the water – literally as well as metaphorically. From it had come the other things, and now Maggie knew that she was herself in a way that she had never been since babyhood.

It seemed extraordinary that Turner, still sipping his tea, had noticed nothing. Maggie's internal explosion had both shaken and illuminated her so profoundly that she thought the whole room should have been shuddering and lit by it. Even now, with the initial incandescence gone, she thought that in a darkened place she would still emit a luminous glow.

'Right,' she said. Her voice rang round the kitchen, and she moderated it as Turner looked at her in surprise. 'Right. I must think what to do. What *we* should do,' she amended, after a second's thought and another stare from Turner.

'About the wedding? I don't see that there's much we can do, if it's that soon.'

'Nonsense, of course we can. Not just the wedding, though. The whole mess. It's not going to sort itself.'

'I'll deal with it. You don't have to worry.'

It was Maggie's turn to look at him in astonishment. 'What do you mean, I don't have to worry?'

'I'll look after it. I can sort it out.'

'Forgive me, Turner, but your last idea for sorting it out involved something that would probably have landed you in jail.'

'It could have worked.' Turner hated to admit he'd been wrong.

'But it didn't. As it is, we've got a little bit of time before the shit hits the fan. As I see it, our only hope is to come to some kind of agreement with the bank.'

'Bloodsuckers. They'll take everything.'

'So what? At least we've got something for them to take, and it may be enough to satisfy them for the time being. Look, it's a setback, but we can survive it. There's work around, you can get enough jobs to keep the company going, cover the wages and keep things running while you look for a new project. And don't tell me you can't come up with a new project, Turner, because the day that happens will be the day they screw you down in a box.'

He gave a reluctant grin, acknowledging the truth of this, but was not to be sidetracked.

'You realise that all we can offer them is the house and the hotel – both mortgaged up to the hilt?'

'Of course I do. You're surely not telling me you can't part with the house, are you? Because if so, Turner, I have to say that it's me or the house, and you're going to have to choose.' Her voice was calm as she spoke, but Turner looked at her as though she had suddenly sprouted horns and a tail.

'Maggie!' he stammered. 'Maggie!'

'I'm sorry, Turner.' But Maggie's words were not an apology. 'I'm sorry for you, Turner' would have been nearer to what she meant. Turner was still looking at her as though he had never seen her before. Maggie looked back at him. Her anger had passed, she felt quite cool now, and she was watching her husband with the detached interest of a naturalist observing a familiar but unpredictable species. It was so outside his experience of her that he had no ready response. If Maggie had wanted revenge – which she did not – she would have had it in that moment. As much as she had done, he experienced the emotional earthquake of finding his basic assumptions about their relationship suddenly shaken to their foundations. Maggie thought that it might even have a more profound effect than it had on her, for it had never occurred to him that he didn't know her through and through.

Was this, Maggie wondered, what I always feared? This, or something like it? That his ambition was so powerful that he would overstep the limit in some way? There was a kind of relief in the idea that it had finally happened, the thing she had always vaguely feared, and like the nightmare figures of childhood it was less terrible in its reality than in her imagination.

When Turner finally spoke, his voice was bewildered. 'I don't care about the house,' he said. 'Not like that. Surely you know that?'

'Oh, not the house itself. Not as an object. But what it stands for – that's what you have to give up. Your . . . well, your pride, I suppose. And that's a lot for anyone to part with.'

'Aren't you proud of what we've done?' He was lost.

'Of course I am. I'm proud of your success, of your skill. Of the way you've worked hard, and taken chances, and built the business. I'll always be proud of those things, but I want to be proud of the future things too.'

'All this, for one missed wedding?'

'Not just for that – of course not! That's just one little apple in a whole treeful. But one rotten apple can infect all the rest. That's trite, but it's how I see it.'

Turner shook his head, not disagreeing but acknowledging that there was to be no compromising. Maggie, watching him, knew that she had won. She took no pleasure in it, for in winning she had also lost something, that image of Turner that she had sheltered behind all these years. She shivered, then straightened herself. There could be no turning back.

Chapter Fifteen

A t five o'clock in the morning Maggie gave up the struggle to get some sleep, and got out of bed.

The previous day had stretched to an unbearable length. Turner, his agile mind looking for ways out of his dilemma, had paced and talked until Maggie's neck ached from watching him go back and forth and her head from the barrage of words. His mood had veered from anger to despair, from despair to wild hope, and back to anger again. He railed in turn against the bank, the Council, the farmers, his own misjudgment, Fate, and Maggie herself. Through it all Maggie sat, letting his words wash over her, unmoving though not unmoved. When, finally, he was exhausted she took him back with inexorable patience to the essentials.

'We've got to settle with the bank. Offer them as much as we can. The Turner money, the house – all the furniture should fetch a good price, goodness knows we paid enough for it. My jewellery, too.' She raised a hand to silence his objections. 'Not all of it. Not the things you gave me early on. But some of the recent stuff, it must be worth quite a lot. I don't need it, Turner. And if the time should come when I do, you can think about buying some more. We only need it if we can afford it.'

By then it was mid-afternoon. Maggie heated some soup which they ate in a spirit of truce, not tasting a mouthful but taking comfort from the ordinary actions of a meal. Then Turner telephoned the bank and arranged to see the manager straight away. He was gone for several hours, and on his return was leaden-faced and grim.

'Well, that's it,' he said with an attempt at lightness.

'How did it go?' Not the most tactful of questions, but there was no easy way of asking.

'We should be able to swing it, if I can get a good price for this house, and for the hotel. That's the difficult bit. It's not been running for long enough to show any kind of profit, and it's going to take a miracle to find a buyer – at least one who's prepared to pay anything other than a knockdown price.' He scrubbed his face with his hands. 'He's not very happy about it. They're all the same, bank managers. When things are going well they throw money at you like they're kids at a coconut shy, but the minute you've got any kind of problem, they grab the ground out from under your feet so they can sell off the turf for a few bob.'

'What happens next?'

'They're sending a valuer round, some time tomorrow. Make a check on what's here. It'll all have to go, unless . . .'

'Unless?'

'Well, if there are things you can't bear to part with, we can say that you bought them, and that they belong to you. Then they won't take them.'

Maggie waved the words away. 'There's nothing here I'm that bothered about, except sentimental things that aren't worth much.' She saw that he was hurt by this casual dismissal of the carefully chosen, and very expensive antiques and paintings that filled the house, but such considerations were beyond her at the moment. All that she could focus on was the pressing need to raise as much money as possible, to repay the bank and keep the business going. Without that there would be nothing she could do to help Stella.

'We need to be able to pay people,' Turner said moodily. 'No good getting jobs if we can't cover the wages.'

'There's money in my account – several thousand,' she told him. 'Enough to last a few months, if we're careful.'

'I can't take that.' The response was becoming automatic. Maggie said nothing. 'I'll have to, I suppose. Oh, bugger it all, Mags. And we'll have to use it to live on. Food, pay the telephone and electricity and so on.'

'Yes, of course.' Maggie had already faced this one, realised that her healthy balance in the bank must be hoarded for such things. Impossible to let Turner sack any of the skilled workforce he had picked and trained so carefully. Lying in bed, Maggie reviewed the men in her mind. All were known to her, some were even old friends. However much she might want to use her money to pay for Stella's wedding, their livelihood must come first.

Turner was asleep, his breathing settled into the gentle semi-snore that meant he was deep under, not merely pretending to sleep. With his boundless energy he had never needed more than a few hours a night, but during those few hours nothing roused him once he was asleep. Maggie had often envied this ability. It was as if, however much was on his mind, he could switch himself off at will, and fall instantly into a profound and refreshing slumber.

Maggie fumbled for her slippers under the bed, and unhooked her dressing gown from the inside of the bathroom door as she passed. She went down to the kitchen, putting on the kettle from habit rather than need, and made herself a cup of tea. It tasted sour in her mouth, but she made herself drink it.

Stella's wedding, she thought. If only I could think what to do about that, I wouldn't mind about the rest of it. I ought to feel guilty about that. Turner would think so. Poor Turner, I should be sorry for him – I *am* sorry for him. At least, I will be when I can get my mind sorted out. At the moment I can't feel anything about him, not even angry. Surely, after all these years together, I should feel something? Maybe when I was hit on the head, it damaged the part of my brain that is concerned with Turner. Will it come back? Do I care? And if it doesn't, what then? Separation? Divorce?

Shock, she thought. That's it. I'm still in shock. Don't they say that people who are badly injured don't feel the pain at first? That you can lose a limb, and hardly feel anything? This must be the same. After all, in emotional terms I've certainly lost at least one limb, maybe even two. Could be terminal. End of the line for me and Turner.

Perhaps, thought Maggie, the important thing was what she did *not* feel. There was no anger, or disgust, nor dislike in her for him. It was impossible not to dislike what he had done, but she felt sure that he had reached and even passed the limits of what he might have been prepared to do. She guessed that he was glad that the scheme had been stopped. It was his nature to fight as hard as he could and with every weapon he could command, and she was quite sure that he would soon be struggling his way out of this quagmire.

He had been surprised, not by her opposition to his insurance scam, but by the strength of her motivation to make sure Stella had her wedding. Well, she was surprised by that herself. Maggie could see that fixing her mind on the wedding could be a way of coming to terms with other, more insuperable, problems. It was a distraction, certainly, but it was also a kind of test for Turner. Irrationally, she saw his commitment to helping retrieve Stella and Colin's wedding as an indicator of a similar commitment to rebuilding their own marriage on the foundations of their new knowledge of one another.

In her mind, the wedding was the key to it all. Sitting at the kitchen table, the remains of her tea congealing in the mug, Maggie once more went over the options that had kept her from sleeping.

Was there any chance that the hotel would be able to fulfil its promises? Not from what Turner had said. Maggie suspected that no deposits had ever been placed with suppliers of flowers, music, clothes or anything else. What's more, any potential buyer of the hotel might decide not to continue with the Wedding Service, and if there were no buyer, the place could well be closed by then. It wasn't yet clear whether the money had been stolen or simply used to prop up others parts of the business, but the police were actively involved.

165

The most obvious choice was to have it here, at the house. There was plenty of room, the garden was looking pretty; all in all it wouldn't be so very different from The Grange. Except, of course, that much of the furniture would have gone by then, and the house now technically belonged to the bank. More importantly from her point of view, how would she explain to everyone? The thought of Stella seeing this house, even depleted of furniture, made her cringe. To be seen as a woman who had everything, but whose husband was responsible for the loss of their carefully planned wedding, was almost more than she could bear. The fact that Stella was so sweet-natured that she would probably be more sorry for Maggie than for herself made it even worse.

Maggie's mind whirled like a roulette wheel, alighting on one image or another: dresses, flowers, food, cake, transport . . . Taken individually, none of these was insuperable. Maggie thought that Mrs Draper might well jump at the chance of making a wedding dress – surely the most feminine and romantic of all garments. Even bridesmaids' dresses, if there was time – or hadn't Stella said something about the bridesmaids' dresses already being bought? As for flowers and food, Maggie thought that she could probably cover most of that herself. It might not look quite so professional, but she was used to catering for large numbers. Their own store of wine, well stocked by Turner, could be raided for the champagne.

On that thought Maggie, glad to have something concrete to do, fetched the keys of the Range Rover and of the store, and went to remove as much as possible before the bank representative laid eyes on it. Julie, she thought, would let her store the cases of wine in her house for the time being.

By the time she was finished it was getting light. Maggie went back to the kitchen, put her mug from force of habit into the dishwasher, and ran upstairs to get dressed.

Turner was in the bathroom, shaving. His eyes met hers in the mirror, eyebrows signalling greeting, apology, question. His lips, covered with shaving foam, parted fractionally.

'You okay?'

'I suppose so. I couldn't sleep. I've been putting champagne and wine into the Range Rover to take to Julie's.'

He finished shaving round his mouth, rinsed the razor, and started under his chin. His voice came awkwardly, distorted by the position.

'Good idea, if we get desperate it's easy enough to sell, make a bit of cash. What about whisky, brandy, all that?'

'It's not for us. It's for the wedding.'

Turner grunted, an indeterminate sound that could have been acceptance, irritation, or agreement. Maggie didn't trouble to discover which, but stripped off her night-clothes and turned on the shower. Turner rinsed off his face and dried it.

'If we sold the spirits, it would be money to put towards the wedding,' he suggested, his voice neutral. Maggie spoke over the sound of the water.

'Some of it, perhaps. But the wine store's already looking pretty bare. Don't you think whoever's coming from the bank might be a bit suspicious?'

'Maybe.'

Maggie put her head under the shower then so that her ears were full of water. She knew her husband was trying to be helpful, which was what she had wanted, but perversely she now found herself resenting his suggestion.

Turner looked at himself in the mirror. To anyone other than Maggie his face would have appeared expressionless. If Maggie had seen it she might have been reassured and comforted by the determination she would have seen there. He gave a little nod, then left the bathroom.

Dressing, Maggie found herself putting on, out of habit, the clothes she normally wore to go swimming. Glancing at the clock, she saw that it was early still – only just after six-thirty. She could easily get to the pool, and be back long before Julie arrived. Julie, at least, must be told what was going on, and she would need to tell Celia that she wouldn't be able to go on working for her, for Turner would need her help in the office again, as he had done in the early days. Julie would soon be out of a job: could she, perhaps, take over at Celia's? That way, neither of them would be left in the lurch. On this, feeling that she had salvaged something from the wreck, Maggie felt encouraged to go for her swim.

Turner was in the kitchen. He had made coffee for himself, and tea for her, leaving every cupboard door ajar in his search for what he needed. He was smartly dressed in a charcoal-grey business suit, and looked rather blankly at her casual clothes.

'It's all right,' said Maggie. 'I'll be back before nine, and put on something respectable for the bank assessor. Unless you think sackcloth and ashes would be more appropriate?'

He thought about it. It was one of the things that Maggie had always liked about Turner, that he never dismissed any idea, however idiotic, out of hand.

'No, I think neat but not gaudy is what we're aiming for. Good quality – that kind of thing. You know.'

'I know. You don't mind if I go for my swim? I mean,' Maggie knew that he would understand that she wasn't asking for permission – when did she ever? – but simply being considerate. 'I mean, is there anything helpful I could be doing here? Or at the office?'

He shook his head. 'No, nothing. I'll deal with the office end. You have your swim, if you feel up to it. I'll be off in a minute, and I may be . . .'

'Some time?' Maggie saw him hesitate over what had been a kind of family joke between them. 'Just don't get lost in the snowdrifts, Captain Oates. I'll expect you when I see you.' Turner looked relieved that his little attempt to lighten the atmosphere had not been taken amiss. He is trying, Maggie told herself. I must try too.

At least, thought Maggie as she started up her car, Turner was the kind to see it through. Not for him the head in the sand, or the flight to South America. For Turner, at heart an eternal optimist, there was always another chance, a new way out, a change in direction that would lead to resolution. Which was probably another reason why Maggie found it hard to get too worried about the business. Even if they had to sell everything, and live on a shoestring for a year or two, Turner would start some project, find some new outlet for his energies, and they would fight their way back up.

Driving down the road away from the house, Maggie drew in a long breath of relief. It was all so blessedly ordinary. The familiar drive to the Leisure Centre, past trees that had been lifeless for so long and were now beginning to break into bud. The morning skies that had been iron grey when she first went to the pool had passed through rosy dawn to full day. Summer was coming, season of sunshine, holidays, flowers . . . season of weddings. Maggie pushed the thought away. For these few minutes she would cling to the normal, hide in its cosy safe depths, rebuild her strength.

Since she was the first to arrive and therefore at the head of the queue, Maggie was down and changed before any of the others. Forsaking her usual place in the women's changing room, she shut herself in a cubicle. It was claustrophobic but private. She shoved her clothes into a locker without bothering to put in a coin and lock it, and pulled on her hat, wincing as it touched the bruise on the back of her head. The tightness of the rubber set up a dull ache, but Maggie ignored it.

For the first time for weeks she reached the poolside while the surface of the pool was still mirror flat. Maggie slid in gently, trying to disturb it as little as possible, but standing waist-deep by the wall she could see the ripples spreading relentlessly down to the other end. A patch of sunshine, about two thirds of the way down the pool, shifted and shimmered as the wavelets passed. There was the sound of other people splashing through the footbath to the poolside, and Maggie quickly pushed off. For some reason she had to reach that area of brightness first, to see and feel the intense blueness of the water beneath the gilding of light.

The water welcomed her tired body, caressing skin that had felt thick and hard as old leather and softening it to flesh and blood again. It held her, buoyed her up. She maintained her glide for as long as her breath lasted, her body straight, arms and legs stretched to as streamlined a shape as the human body is capable of achieving, and for those few seconds she felt at one with the water. Her goggles, unmisted as yet, were no barrier to her vision. It was almost impossible to believe that she could not open her mouth and breathe in the water, make it part of her being as much as she felt part of it.

As she reached the sunlight there was a controlled splash as someone dived in from the side – it wasn't allowed at the ends, where the water was shallow, but the lifeguards closed their eyes to people jumping or diving in the deep middle section, as long as the pool was relatively empty. Maggie took as large a breath as she could manage, so that she could prolong her stroke into another glide. As she slid through the sunshine, feeling its warmth on her back, she saw below her the slender dark form that was Stella. It must have been she who had dived, and now she was crossing the pool deep down, almost touching the tiles on the bottom. Her arms stretched before her as Maggie's did, tapering to slim, long-fingered hands innocent of rings. Her body undulated as if boneless, legs moving together in a dolphin flick that was as effortless as it was elegant.

Maggie felt as though she had been kicked in the stomach. She had known that Stella would probably be there, but the water had momentarily lulled her into a state of trance-like peace. Now she abruptly stopped swimming and hung in the water. Almost at once a body collided with hers, and an arm hit her head on the sore patch with a blow hard enough to dislodge her goggles. Maggie gasped, swallowed water, and choked, struggling all the time to free herself from the other person. A hand grasped her arm and held her steady.

'Maggie, I'm so sorry! Are you all right?'

Maggie coughed painfully and nodded at Celia, who was looking at her in worry.

'Are you sure? The lifeguards are longing to earn their keep and dive in to save you. Can you make it to the side?'

Maggie looked round. It was true that one of the lifeguards had come down from his high seat and was standing on the edge, watching her and Celia. She coughed again, forcing the water up from her lungs. Her nose and eyes were streaming, and her chest felt as though it was burning, but she didn't need rescuing. She nodded again and looking in both directions to avoid another collision swam to the edge where she clung to the rail. Celia swam sidestroke beside her, ready to help if needed, and the lifeguard squatted down to speak to her.

'That was some pile-up. You all right?'

'It's my fault,' said Celia. 'I was swimming on my back and I should have checked more often. I was sure you were further ahead than that.'

'No,' croaked Maggie, 'my fault. I stopped. Saw Stella.' Her eyes filled with tears and she coughed again to cover the way her mouth was pulling down into a tearful grimace. She faced into the wall, hooking her left arm over the ledge and scrubbing at her eyes with the other. 'My goggles . . .' she muttered.

'On the bottom. Someone'll dive for them, I'm sure.' Celia looked up at the lifeguard. 'I think she's okay,' she said. 'We'll just rest a few minutes. Thanks.' She watched as the lifeguard stood up and returned to his vantage point, then turned back to Maggie. 'He's gone,' she said quietly. 'Look, there's obviously something wrong. You don't have to tell me if you don't want to, but if you'd like to talk . . .'

Maggie drew in a long, shaky breath, and was pleased to find she had stopped coughing.

'No, I've got to tell you anyway. It's pretty bad, I'm afraid. My husband's company's got big problems, it might even fold up completely.'

'So he'll be out of a job? Oh Maggie, I'm so sorry. I wonder if Phil could help? He knows a lot of builders, he might hear of something. And I've been meaning to tell you, but my Mrs Tomsett – you know, Tommy who used to work for me – says she doesn't think she's up to coming back, as her feet are worse than ever, so you can carry on as long as you like. If you wanted any more work, I've got friends who'd give their eye teeth to have someone like you. I'm sure we can work something out.'

Maggie was warmed by her eagerness to help, but she shook her head. 'No, it's not like that. When I said his company, I meant *his* company. His own.'

Celia put her feet against the tiled wall and pushed her legs to stretch her calf muscles. 'Not really a cleaning lady, then,' she said thoughtfully to her knees.

'No,' said Maggie miserably.

'I never really thought you were. I just didn't say anything because it was so lovely having you there, and I didn't want to spoil it. You're probably a lot better off than us, aren't you?' Her question was neither envious nor carping, but simply interested.

Maggie nodded. 'Probably. But not any more.' The thought was oddly pleasing. 'That doesn't matter, the money. And I think we can save the business, even if it means selling everything else. And I'm really sorry about not working for you, because I've loved it, but I won't be able to do it now. There is someone, though . . .' Unconsciously Maggie found herself copying Celia, bending and straightening her legs and enjoying the stretching in calves and spine. Their movements made a little area of turbulent water that slapped against the wall, drowning their voices still further. 'Julie, her name is. She cleans for me, and she's super, a really good friend. I dread having to tell her I can't employ her any more as much as I dreaded having to tell you.'

'It wouldn't be the same, but if you recommend her . . .'

'Oh, I do. Can I tell her to give you a ring?'

'Yes, of course. Oh, Maggie, I'm so sorry. It must be horrid for you. Is there anything I can do to help?'

Maggie let her legs drop down. She rested her forehead for a moment against her hands as they clasped the ledge, and shut her eyes against the threatening tears that kindness summoned.

'It's my own fault, really. I've been living in a kind of fantasy world – working for you, and all that business about Primrose – and I didn't realise how far Turner had committed himself. Not that I could have done anything to stop him, I don't suppose, but I might have prevented some of the, well, the fall-out. As it is . . .' Maggie shook her head, and winced as the bruise throbbed.

'As it is?' Celia prompted.

This was the bit that Maggie didn't want to say. She took a deep breath and spoke in a rush, as if to trick herself into getting the words spoken before she could stop them.

'One of the things Turner was involved in was the wedding place – the one where Stella's fixed her wedding. He was so preoccupied with the other business that he didn't realise the guy there was fiddling the books, and now it looks as though nothing's been paid for, and the money's gone. It's so awful, it's the worst thing of all, and I can't bear it.' Her voice died away and once again she let her head drop onto her hands.

'Oh dear,' said Celia inadequately. 'Oh, Maggie. That's awful.'

'It is. And I'm going to have to tell her. Tell Stella.'

'Tell Stella what?' The voice would have made Maggie jump, but she was already warned by the changing expression of Celia's face. Stella had slid unheard through the water towards them. She pushed her goggles up onto her forehead and smiled her radiant smile. 'Someone said Maggie had swallowed some water, and as you were still at the side I thought I'd come and check you were all right. And what do I find? You're gossiping about me!' She pretended anger, secure in the certainty that they would never be saying anything nasty about her. Stella, who never said or even thought unkind things, could not imagine that anyone else would either.

'Oh, Stella!' Maggie looked at the happy face, and quailed.

'Not here,' said Celia swiftly. 'Let's get out, and go back to the changing room. There won't be anyone there now.'

'All right,' said Stella serenely. 'I'll just finish my lengths, and I'll join you. Only twenty more!' Her body curved away and down into the water and she was gone before either of the others could stop her. Maggie and Celia looked at one another.

'Twenty lengths won't take her long. We might as well get out.'

Maggie realised that her hands were so cold she could scarcely grip the ledge, and she was shivering. She pulled herself hand over hand along the wall, with Celia behind her, and dragged herself up the steps. They were silent in the shower, warming their bodies under the hot water and, in Maggie's place at least, searching for words that would soften the shock of what must be said.

Back in the changing room Maggie looked round helplessly.

'My bag,' she said stupidly. 'My clothes. They've gone.'

'They weren't in here,' Celia reminded her. 'I remember being surprised. I'd seen your car outside, and when I came in your things weren't here. I thought it was a bit odd. Where did you undress?'

'In a cubicle,' Maggie admitted, remembering. 'I couldn't face seeing anyone. They're in a locker, I'll go and fetch them.'

Maggie stared blankly at the wall of lockers, which stared blankly back at her. She had no recollection of which one she might have used, and ended up going up and down the row checking each one. She assumed she would have chosen the middle row, which at waist-height was the easiest to use, but moved perhaps by some dim feeling of unworthiness she had actually crouched down and shoved her bag in an out-of-the-way floor-level one, one of the last she checked. She thought that later she might find that memory mildly amusing, but at the moment it was simply irritating. She was shivering again by the time she returned to the changing room, where Celia was already dressed.

'Found it?' the other woman joked. 'I was just about to send out the St Bernards.'

'Sorry. I couldn't find it. I think my brain's going.' Maggie pulled off her damp costume and huddled her towel round her. Celia rubbed her back briskly and Maggie had a sudden memory of her mother doing the same thing to her on a seaside holiday when she was five or six. She had stayed too long in the water and got thoroughly chilled. Her mother had scolded as she rubbed her dry, and Maggie had cried because the towel, stiff with seawater and encrusted with sand, was so scratchy and her skin so cold and tender. Her tears made her mother scold more and rub still harder, but strangely the memory came back now as one of being cherished.

Maggie was half-dressed when Stella ran in, beaming and dripping.

'All done!' she said cheerfully. 'Now, what was it you wanted to tell me?'

Maggie flopped down on the bench in her petticoat and blouse, with the buttons done up crookedly. Automatically she undid them, and did them up crooked again.

'It's your wedding,' she said baldly. Stella stripped off her costume and scrubbed herself vigorously with a towel. Her body, as Stella had noticed before, was perfect, the chocolate-coloured skin smooth and unblemished, moulded like silk over long slender bones. She bent to dry her legs and feet, then put down her towel and stretched up, uninhibited as a child.

'Don't tell me you're not going to be able to come!' Her voice was warm with concern. 'Oh, Maggie, you know I was relying on you being there, in case the Best Man loses the ring.'

'I'm afraid you won't want me there anyway, even if . . . Oh dear, Stella, I don't know how to tell you this. I'm afraid that it looks as though there isn't going to *be* a wedding. At least, not the one you've planned.'

'What do you mean? What's wrong? Not something with Colin?'

'No, no, nothing like that. It's the wedding place at the hotel. You know you said you'd heard something was wrong? I'm afraid you were right.'

Stella picked up her towel with shaking hands and wrapped it round her like a sarong, as though she suddenly felt her nakedness made her more vulnerable. She sat down on the bench, and Celia sat beside her, a gesture which Maggie didn't feel able to make until she had confessed. Stella looked up at Maggie.

'How do you know?' As always she was simple and direct. Maggie took a deep breath and responded similarly. Stella's eyes were on Maggie with the fixed regard of a rabbit before a snake, and as Maggie went through the damning details her face seemed to get visibly thinner, the flesh appearing to melt away from her bones. The rich brown of her skin paled and greyed to a muddy colour, and the pupils of her eyes shrank down as though to filter out what she was seeing of the future.

The sorry tale was soon done, and Maggie stood waiting. She didn't know what she feared most – an outburst of fury or of tears, but neither happened.

'Oh, well,' said Stella. 'It's not the end of the world. Don't look so worried, Maggie. We'll manage something.'

It was Maggie who burst into tears, and Stella who ended up comforting her.

'I'm sorry,' Maggie wept. 'I'm so sorry! I can't bear it, Stella! Your lovely wedding!'

'It can still be lovely,' comforted Stella. 'We'll just have to delay the reception for a bit, that's all. Go ahead with the church, and do the celebrating later when we can get something sorted out. Please don't feel so bad, Maggie. It's not your fault, after all.'

'I feel as though it is. I'd do anything to make it up to you, but I don't know how I can. I've got money in my account, but I daren't use it. We've got to be able to pay the wages, you see. I could manage a few hundred pounds, but it's not enough to hire a place even if we could find anywhere free at this stage. It's all such a mess.'

The door swung open and Primrose came in. She always changed in the group room now, partly because she was less shy than before and partly so that she could talk to Stella. She stopped dead as she saw the three women clustered together.

'What's up? Something the matter?'

Celia explained.

'What, the whole thing? All of it?'

'Except the church,' Celia confirmed.

Primrose frowned. 'Bummer. That's a real bummer.' She thought for a moment. 'Couldn't you have it at your house? It's big enough.'

'It's not my house any more. It belongs to the bank, and they're going to sell everything.' Primrose grunted, a sound which Maggie recognised as sympathetic. Stella smiled, a pale reflection of her usual glowing beam.

'It'll be all right. We'll have the reception some other time. Next summer, maybe.'

Primrose glowered at her. 'We can't give up that easily. How long is it till the wedding?'

'Just under five weeks.' Stella's lips were trying to turn down, and she put a hand up to cover her mouth. 'Four weeks next Saturday,' she finished in a husky voice.

'Plenty of time,' said Primrose crossly, 'if you don't all get limp and defeatist. What about your place?' She turned almost accusingly to Celia. Stella tried to protest, but Primrose ignored her. Celia thought about it.

'The rooms aren't very big, and nor's the garden. I'd be happy to do it, though.'

'How many?' Primrose fired at Stella, who looked at her blankly. 'How many people have you invited?'

'About a hundred and fifty. That's why . . .' Stella stopped, glancing at Maggie.

'That's why it was so much money,' completed Maggie grimly. 'Food and drink for that many people . . . But I've got the drink!' she suddenly remembered, cheered. 'Champagne, and wine. I've loaded it all into my car, so the bank don't see it.'

'Oh, well *done!*' Celia was delighted. 'Do you need somewhere to hide it? We could make room in the shed, that's pretty secure. But a hundred and fifty people . . .' Her voice tailed off as she tried to imagine cramming so many into her house. 'It would be all right if it didn't rain, but the weather's still so chancy, and we haven't a hope of getting a marquee at this short notice, even if we could afford it.'

174

'Then we'll just have to think of something else, won't we?' said Primrose crossly. 'Somewhere with space, and shelter . . . there must be *something*.' She beat at her forehead with the heel of her hand. 'What does that remind me of? Oh! Oh *yes*! Of course! That's the bollocks, the absolute *bollocks*!' She turned round, tugged the door open, and disappeared. The other three looked at one another.

'What does she mean?' asked Maggie, bewildered. 'She hasn't gone off her rocker, has she? She was always a bit strange, but I've never known her quite this odd.'

Stella managed a wan smile, and Celia grinned.

'You obviously don't spend enough time with the younger generation. The bollocks, short for the dog's bollocks, is a term of the highest approbation at the moment. Don't ask me why, it's just one of those mysterious phrases that they all suddenly start using, and just as suddenly drop. I think Primrose has had an idea.'

The door crashed back against the wall before anyone could say anything else, and Primrose came back in, pulling a dripping Dawn behind her like a determined tug towing a larger, sluggish ship. Dawn stood in the middle of the changing room, looking nervously at the three women who sat in a row on the bench like presiding magistrates.

'Um . . .' she said. 'I don't really know . . . Primrose said . . . something about a wedding . . .' She looked round helplessly. Primrose, who had deposited Dawn in front of Stella with all the proud pleasure of a mother presenting a toddler to recite a nursery rhyme, shook her head and stepped forward.

'Dawn's place,' she said patiently. 'Steph's been there with her dad. She says it's great, and there's a huge barn for if it rains. Dress it all up, rustic-style, foliage, flowers – oh, come *on*!' She was dancing with impatience at their slowness.

'You know,' said Maggie slowly, 'it might work. It really might be all right. Better than all right, in fact. It's brilliant, and you're a genius, Primrose!'

'But surely poor Dawn doesn't want her place invaded like that! And what about Gordon?' Stella's expression was, if anything, more worried than before. Dawn looked down at her. The water dripped off her sagging costume as she stood foursquare, feet planted slightly apart with the toes turned inwards, her swimming hat slipping up so that her head was curiously cone-shaped.

'Well, why not?' she asked, more firmly than Maggie had ever heard her speak. 'And if Gordon doesn't like it, he can . . . he can . . . boil his head!'

'Yay!' Primrose punched the air, then gave Dawn a pat on the back that was almost a slap. 'That's right, Dawn ma man! You just tell 'em!'

Chapter Sixteen

'Heavens, look at the time! I'll be late to College if I don't get going.' Celia's words had everyone glancing at their watches. There was a flurry of towels, and the silent struggle to pull clothes on over imperfectly dried skin. Primrose, who felt less anxious about getting to school than Celia, Dawn and Stella did about being late for work, stopped while still in her underclothes and spoke before Celia could rush out of the door.

'Hang on a minute! There's a lot to organise, we can't just leave it like this. What are we going to do next?'

Celia paused, her hand already grasping the door. 'You're right – we should get together later. What time does everyone finish work? Five-thirty the latest? Then let's meet at my house at six. Bring anyone who might be useful. Tell them where it is, Maggie. Hang on – will you be able to make it?'

'I'll make it,' said Maggie grimly. Celia whirled out of the door. Maggie scribbled address and directions on a piece of paper torn off a publicity leaflet for a charity swim that was stuffed in the side pocket of her bag, and gave it to Stella, who still looked stunned but had lost the greyish tinge that had alarmed Maggie. As Stella left she turned and smiled, a candle glow to the usual sunshine she dispensed, but still an earnest of hope. Dawn packed her swimming things neatly into her holdall. She looked bemused, her face pinker than usual, and Maggie eyed her nervously as she gave her Celia's address.

'Dawn, are you sure? This was flung at you rather suddenly. Don't commit yourself to something you're going to regret later.'

'I'd like to do it,' she said, 'as long as Gordon doesn't object. Stella's such a lovely girl, and I think it would be fun. I love weddings, and I never thought I'd have the chance to help organise one.' In her wistful voice Maggie heard the slow, reluctant death of a younger Dawn's dreams of her own wedding, perhaps even of a daughter's too. Maggie wondered whether Gordon would be sensitive enough to perceive it. It was difficult to imagine how he could refuse to humour so harmless a sublimation.

'Will you bring Gordon this evening?'

Dawn glanced at her watch. 'If I can. The trouble is, I'll need to go straight to Celia's from work, and it's a bit difficult to explain it to him from the office. He hates the telephone anyway, he wouldn't have one if we didn't need it to call the vet in an emergency, and when I'm not there he often doesn't answer it.'

'We can't very well make any plans without at least telling him about it. How do you think he'd be if I went to talk to him?'

Dawn put her head on one side, considering. 'Well he's so grateful to you for putting us in touch with Tom, it might actually be better coming from you than from me. Are you sure you don't mind? I know you've got some kind of trouble at home.'

'I don't mind at all. I'd be glad to be able to *do* something. If I go and see him around five-ish perhaps I could give him a lift to Celia's.'

'That would be good. I'll see you there, then.' Dawn was gone, and only Primrose remained.

'What's going on?' she asked curiously. 'I thought you were stinking rich.'

'So did I,' Maggie answered wryly. She found Primrose's direct approach refreshing. 'Unfortunately, it turns out not to be true any more. I don't really mind all that much – I mean, we're not going to starve or sleep rough, exactly – but Stella's wedding is a casualty of the whole collapse, and I feel I must make it up to her somehow. Will you be able to get to Celia's tonight, or shall I pick you up too?'

'No, I'll be all right, Dad'll take me. He's still talking about that evening when we all went to the Indian together – he really enjoyed it. He'll probably want to stay.'

Primrose seemed quite happy to stand and chat, but Maggie was getting worried. 'You're going to be late for school. Want me to drive you?'

'No, I'll be all right. What about you?' The question was so casually tossed over Primrose's shoulder that Maggie misunderstood at first.

'Well, I've got the car . . . Oh, I see. Yes, I'll be all right. Thanks, Primrose!' But she was speaking to the swinging door.

It seemed strange to be going home after her swim instead of to Celia's. As she walked in through the back door Maggie felt that the house was surprised. She found herself creeping in furtively, as if she had no right to be there. The thought made her nervous. After all, only yesterday she had been attacked here, in her own home. Feeling ridiculous, she nevertheless went through the house checking that it was empty before going to change into the 'neat but not gaudy' clothes Turner had recommended. Then she went down to the kitchen to await Julie's arrival.

It was not a long wait, but time enough to get Maggie thoroughly jittery, so that when she heard Julie's bicycle wheels on the gravel outside – a small sound she would never normally have heard – she felt her stomach lurch. She went straight to the back door, and opened it as Julie was still scrabbling in her bag for the key. The younger woman jumped.

'Maggie! Grief, you gave me a start! You in today, for a change?' She stepped over the threshold, then stopped to peer into Maggie's face. 'What's the matter? You're not ill, are you?'

'No, not ill, but it's bad news, I'm afraid.' Maggie took Julie to sit in the kitchen, then embarked once more on her explanations.

'Oh, Maggie!' Julie's eyes filled with tears. 'Oh Maggie, I am sorry. This lovely house!'

'I don't mind that much about the house,' Maggie said, still surprised to find that it was true. 'I feel bad about you, though, Julie. I've really enjoyed having you working here. I shall miss you a lot.'

'Why, where are you going?' Startled, Julie stared at Maggie with bloodshot eyes.

'Nowhere – at least, I don't exactly know, but I suppose we'll stay round here.'

'Thank goodness. I thought you were going to say you were emigrating, or something. So we can still be friends, then?'

At this, Maggie nearly burst into tears. 'Of course.' She cleared her throat. 'Meanwhile, I've got another friend who'd love you to work for her. I think you'd like her, and I know she'd like you.'

'It won't be the same. But I'd rather do that than go back to answering advertisements. Oh dear, just when everything seemed to be going so well. If only I'd told you sooner about the Spa!'

'It wouldn't have made any difference. Poor old Turner really over-reached himself this time. The whole thing was a time bomb waiting to explode. I just feel so awful about all the people caught in the fall-out.' Since it was so much on her mind, Maggie told Julie about Stella, and this led them via Primrose back to Celia again.

'We're all going to Celia's house this evening, to see what we can sort out about the wedding. Um, I don't suppose you'd like to come with me, would you? You'd get a chance to meet Celia and see the house. Oh, and be introduced to Mrs Draper, that's Celia's mother-in-law; she's a bit difficult but okay if you treat her right. In fact, she'll probably end up making clothes for Stephanie, and I can tell you, she's brilliant! As a matter of fact, I'm rather hoping to persuade her to make Stella's wedding dress.'

'If she's the one who's made the things for young Primrose, then I know what you mean. Yes, I'll come along. I've got a cheesy vegetable dish in the freezer I can get out for the kids' and Tom's supper.' She looked round the kitchen. 'So, what next? Shall I give the kitchen a quick go, and run the vacuum over the downstairs?

Make it nice for the bloodsuckers from the bank? Don't worry about the money. With all I've had from you, one way and another, I owe you big time.'

'Oh, Julie! I can afford to pay you for a few days – a couple of weeks, I should think – only I reckon Celia needs you more than I do, really. But if you can stay for this morning it would be lovely. How about you make a start on the kitchen, and I'll do the hoovering?'

'Sounds good to me,' said Julie cheerfully. 'Tell you what, if the worst comes to the worst, you and I can open one of those home-help businesses – you know, where you go in and blitz a house once a month, that kind of thing. Make a fortune, we would.'

'Yes,' said Maggie. 'Yes, I think we could really clean up on that one.' This childish joke sent them both into giggles which served to relieve some of the tension each was feeling. Julie set to work on the kitchen floor with even more vigour than usual, and Maggie vacuumed her way from room to room. Even the sitting room, where the space left by the painting grinned like a missing front tooth in a cover girl's smile, was just another room to be cleaned and set to rights.

When the two valuers from the bank arrived, Maggie was able to greet them with equanimity. In fact, she soon found that they were far more embarrassed than she was, which made her want to giggle again. They went from room to room, writing busily on their clipboards. Furniture, paintings, silver, jewellery, porcelain – all was checked against the insurance list. Maggie obligingly opened cupboards and drawers into which they peered unwillingly, standing as far away from her as was compatible with actually seeing the contents, their whole body language expressing discomfort. It reminded her of when her parents died, and how she had ended up behaving in an unnaturally cheerful fashion to ease the awkwardness of people who tried to find comforting words to say.

Turner didn't come back for lunch, but he telephoned at two o'clock to see that Maggie was all right. By then the valuers had departed in a cloud of hushed sympathy, like mourners at a funeral who have never met the deceased but are constrained by the occasion to preternatural solemnity. After Julie left, Maggie spent part of the afternoon making sandwiches and snacks. It looked as though there would be more people turning up at Celia's than was originally planned, and since many of them were coming straight from work then something to eat might oil the wheels a bit. Then, with the trays of food loaded into the Land Rover along with the cases of wine she set off to visit Gordon.

It was half past four when she got to the farm. Gordon was nowhere to be seen, but through the opening in the hedge she could see Tom busily hoeing the vegetable garden, where neat rows of burgeoning green testified to his skills. He glanced up and saw her. Maggie went through to meet him.

'Mrs Whittington! Is everything all right? Julie? The kids?' Maggie remembered Julie saying that Tom lived in constant expectation of disaster, and the better things were, the more he worried.

'Everything's fine,' Maggie said quickly, if erroneously. 'I haven't come to give you any dreadful news. I just had something I wanted to ask Gordon, if he's not too busy.'

'I think he's just doing the milking and the feeding. Do you want me to go and find him?' Maggie followed his glance down at his muddy boots, and guessed that they wouldn't be welcome in the immaculately scrubbed shed that was used as a milking parlour.

'No, I'll go and look for him, if you think he won't mind.'

Maggie crossed the yard. The temptation to assess its potential as a setting for a wedding was irresistible. She peeped into the big barn, picturing it cleared and swept, garnished with flowers and with tables set with food like an old-fashioned Harvest Home. The courtyard, too, which would also need clearing and sweeping, offered a relatively sheltered place for people to drink and chat, or even dance, and as for photographs . . . Since Maggie's earlier visit spring had finally arrived. The orchard behind the bottom wall was bursting into life, fat buds giving promise of blossom and leaf, and below them the daffodils carpeted the bright new grass. Oh please, thought Maggie, please let it be all right. Even if nothing else works out, just let this one thing happen. The thought itself was formless and wordless, addressed to no particular deity but cast desperately out into the unknown.

There was a clatter of hoofs on paving, and Gordon appeared through one of the doors in the long wall. He was carrying a covered bucket in one hand, and leading the Jersey cow with the other. His trousers, baggy and stained, were tied up with baler twine, and the holes in his ancient brown pullover showed glimpses of a khaki shirt that must be army surplus, above which the bright red knitted hat perched on his head was surprisingly reminiscent of a paratrooper. He hesitated when he saw Maggie, but the cow at least knew where she was going and pulled him inexorably onwards.

'Gordon, I'm Maggie Whittington, Dawn's swimming friend. We all had supper together after the Swimathon.'

'I remember.' He nodded a greeting. 'You sent Tom along to us. I'm grateful.'

'You don't need to be. I'm just glad it's working out so well.'

'You come to see Dawn? She won't be back until after six.' It was not that he was unwelcoming, but he clearly didn't know what to do with an unexpected visitor, particularly a female one.

'No, it's you I came to see. I need to ask for your help.'

He nodded again, acknowledging her right to ask and his duty to listen.

'You'd better take the bucket, then. I'll just put the cow back in her box. She's only out during the day with her calf, I keep her in at night, and the calf in a separate pen. That way we get a good milking in the morning.' He was surprisingly voluble, and Maggie realised that she was accepted as someone who belonged. She took the bucket, and followed Gordon.

He listened in silence to her explanation. She told him the whole thing quite plainly, as she had done with everyone, only leaving out the attempt to steal the painting. Gordon strained and cooled the milk, then set it in its pan in the fridge for the cream to rise before scouring and sterilising the milking equipment. He worked methodically, his movements so efficient that they appeared slow until one realised how much had been done. He listened without comment, exclamation or question, almost as though Maggie wasn't there, but she felt that he was assessing every word before storing it away in his mind.

When the bucket, the strainer and the cooler had been set upside down to drain under a spotless tea towel, he turned to Maggie.

'Cup of tea.' It was more a statement than a question, and he didn't wait for an answer before heading for the kitchen. There he put on the kettle and assembled teamaking equipment with the same economy of movement he had displayed in the dairy. Maggie kept out of the way and said nothing. She felt that no persuasion from her would sway him one way or the other. While the tea brewed in the pot he stared out of the kitchen window, then he poured three mugs and passed one to Maggie.

'So, they won't be building that shopping mall, then,' he said, looking at the view over paddocks and fields beyond the courtyard.

'No, they won't. I don't know what he'll do with the land but it's pretty certain it won't be built on at all.'

'Good.' There was a wealth of satisfaction in the single word. 'That's good.'

Maggie wondered what Turner did intend to do with the land. It was worthless to him as it stood. Could Gordon and Dawn afford to buy it from him? He would certainly be reluctant to sell it back to the farmer who had diddled him. She wondered whether to mention the possibility to Gordon but decided against it, thinking it might sound a bit too much like a bribe.

'Barn'll need clearing out,' said Gordon casually. Maggie, in the act of sipping her tea, choked. Gordon gave her a slap on her back as if she were a recalcitrant horse, and only the fact that Maggie had put her mug down to cough saved her from being drenched with tea.

'You all right?'

'Yes,' wheezed Maggie. 'Did you mean that you don't mind?'

'Mind what?' Gordon opened the window and leaned out,

bellowed the single word 'Tea!' and slammed the window shut again, cutting off an answering shout from Tom.

'About having the wedding here.' Maggie wiped her eyes and blew her nose.

'I don't mind, long as they don't upset the animals. And I don't have to make a speech or anything.'

'Oh Gordon, that's wonderful!' Maggie saw that her enthusiasm was alarming him, and tried to moderate her excitement. 'And you don't need to worry about clearing out the barn, There are plenty of people who will come and lend a hand.' Tom came to the window and Gordon opened it again, handing out the mug of tea and shutting the window without a word being spoken. Maggie perceived that she had brought about a meeting of soulmates.

'Sit down.' Maggie did so. Gordon sat opposite her. 'Nice girl, that Stella.' This time, the statement was more of a question.

'Very nice,' said Maggie warmly. 'I've never known her to say an unkind word about anyone. She's – oh, special somehow. That's why I couldn't bear it that she should be robbed of her wedding, because of my husband's crazy money-making schemes.'

'Nice smile,' said Gordon laconically. 'And she's kind. Kind to that girl, Primrose. Kind to Dawn, and me. People her age, they don't always bother.'

'Yes, that's it,' agreed Maggie eagerly. 'She treats everyone the same. My husband doesn't understand why I'm making such a fuss about her wedding, when there are so many other things to worry about, but it's just . . . oh, I can't really explain it, but it's like hitting a child, or something. A kind of betrayal.' She was surprised to find herself talking like this to this taciturn man, but he nodded agreement.

'Yes. I knew someone like that, once.' Abruptly he stood up and went out of the room. Maggie finished her tea and glanced at her watch. Twenty past five, and she had to pick up Julie as well. She took her mug to the sink and rinsed it out.

Gordon came back in. He was carrying a parcel, a long sausage shape, cradling it in his arms like a sleeping infant. He set it down carefully on the table, moving his mug of tea well out of the way, then stood for a moment looking at it warily, as if it might explode. Then, slowly and methodically as in everything else, he began to unseal the brown paper that covered it.

It was well wrapped. Once the sticky tape, brittle and brown, had been split or unstuck, the brown paper unrolled until it covered the table top. Inside was more paper, layers of white tissue, which he peeled back sheet by sheet, unrolling as he went. Maggie wondered, slightly hysterically, if there was anything in the middle at all, or whether it would prove to be some kind of joke package masking something tiny, like a fountain pen.

The last sheet of tissue fell back to reveal a roll of fabric, wide as the table. The cardboard cylinder in the middle stuck out at either end. Gordon brushed the loose end of fabric down as delicately as if it had been a butterfly's wing, then holding the cardboard ends he unrolled the cloth. Maggie gaped down at the table. She had not known what to expect, but certainly it had been nothing like this.

Shimmering across the table like moonlight on still water, the fabric lay light as gossamer on its protective layers of paper. Against the stark white of the tissue it glowed the warm, living cream of ivory. It was silk – no other fabric could match that ineffable sheen that caught and held the light from the window. An embroidery so fine that it lay like a cobweb over the surface was done in thread that must have come from the same spinning as the fabric itself, so precisely did it match in colour and texture. Garlands of leaves and sprays of flowers, so finely wrought that they disappeared in the shadowy folds, made what was already a beautiful fabric into something so rare, so rich and yet so delicate that Maggie held her breath lest she should sully its perfection.

Gordon's hands hovered over the table, not quite touching and yet seeming to caress. Against that perfect cream they were an incongruous sight, the hands of a countryman who had worked all his life outside: stained and calloused, the skin thick and cracked, the nails short and ingrained with soil.

'What do you think?' he asked gruffly.

'It's beautiful,' Maggie whispered. 'I've never seen anything so lovely.'

'Have it, if you like. For her dress.'

'For Stella's wedding dress? But Gordon, you can't just give it away. It must be priceless!'

'It is. There's no money that could buy this from me. But I don't mind giving it. It's been sitting there in the chest, wrapped up like that, for more years than I can think, and what good is that? It should be used. You give it to her.'

'If anyone does that, it must be you. Where did it come from?'

'India.' He was searching for words. 'It was a girl I used to know. Years ago, we were only nineteen. Or she was. I was twenty.' He paused again, a private man who found it hard to talk about himself. 'She was another one, like Stella. Always happy, smiling, kind. But tough, too. Not one of those wishy-washy milk and water girls who's always laughing because she hasn't got two thoughts to rub together in her head. Gold, that's what she was. Her father was out in India, he'd worked out there, stayed on after Independence. Her mother had left him when Mary was quite little, brought her back to England. They lived near us, we went to the same school, and we always knew. Me and Mary, Mary and me, that's how it was, and we thought it always would be.'

He shook his head, more in wonder than in sadness, contemplating across the years the certainties of two children who know nothing of life. Maggie listened as he had listened to her, making no sound.

'We planned to get married. They said we were too young – and we were, of course – but we didn't think so. Who does, at that age? We talked to them, Mary talked to them, not arguing, just talking and talking, and we knew they'd come round. We'd have had to live with her mother, but we knew we'd soon get a place of our own. Mary's mother was coming round, then her father wrote, from India. Said he wouldn't give his consent, she was too young to know what she was doing. Of course, he didn't have any rights, really. He'd sent a bit of money back from time to time, but never really bothered about her much, until then. Now, suddenly, she was his little daughter and he wanted to keep her that way.'

He brushed the edge of the fabric with his fingertips, and Maggie heard the slight snagging sound as his rough skin caught in the silk.

'Well, she could just have ignored him, but Mary wasn't like that. He said he wanted to see her, wanted to get to know her. Offered to pay her fare, give her the chance to see a bit of the world before she was tied down with a family. Well, how could she refuse? An offer like that, and to turn it down would hurt his feelings, something she couldn't do to anyone, so she went.'

Maggie kept her eyes fixed on the table, subduing her own emotion.

'She had a wonderful time. He was generous, I'll give him that. Took her everywhere – the Taj Mahal, all the sights, he even took her to Kashmir. I've still got all her letters. And all the time she was enjoying herself she was still looking forward to coming home. She sent this back to me, said I was to keep it for her and she'd have it made up into her wedding dress, with enough left maybe for a christening robe. Then I knew he'd come round, that she'd persuaded him. He'd bought it for her, you see. Though you could almost have put down a deposit on a little house for what this would have cost in England then, he wanted her to have it, and who was I to complain?'

Gordon began to roll up the fabric. His face and voice were as calm as though he were reciting the history of the Battle of Hastings. Maggie, looking back at her own earlier days, thought that he viewed both Mary and his younger self as if they were separate from himself, old friends to be regretted and to pity, but with a detached sorrow that made no connection to the present day.

'She didn't come back?' she prompted gently, when Gordon showed no sign of taking the story to its obvious conclusion. He looked at her in surprise, as though it was so obvious it hadn't occurred to him to say it.

185

'No. No, she never did. She died, you see. Just an insect bite, in Kashmir, but she neglected it and in that climate you can't afford to do that. It got infected, and she died of blood poisoning. It was all very quick. By the time I got the last letter she'd sent me, she'd been buried for days. I couldn't believe it, not for a long time. You can't, you know. Not when it's someone as alive as Mary was. I thought it must be a mistake – I even wanted to go out there, see for myself. It would probably have been a good thing if I had done, but of course I had no money for the fare, and in those days travelling was different, difficult . . . not like the kids nowadays, hopping on and off planes and setting off into the wilds the way they do.'

'Thank you for telling me,' Maggie said. Gordon began methodically re-wrapping the bolt of cloth.

'Funny,' he said. 'I've not spoken of Mary for more years than I can remember. Not even thought of her, if truth be told. Funny, there was a time when I couldn't think of anything else. I never saw anyone else I could fancy, after her. I suppose you could say I couldn't see past her, for some years. She blinded me to other women. I can't say I regret it. Better no marriage than second best, I'd say.'

'But you kept the silk.'

'Of course. What else could I do with it? If Rora – if Dawn had married, I'd have given it to her gladly, but she never did, so here it is. Pity to let it go to waste, I'd say, and one thing's for sure, you can't take it with you!'

He fetched a roll of tape and sealed up the brown paper, then pushed the parcel across the table to Maggie. 'There you are. They'll be needing to get on with it.'

'Won't you come with me? We were hoping you would.'

He stretched, arms wide, joints cracking.

'No, you don't need me. Tell them it's fine, just let me know what's wanted, all that. Reckon I'll walk up to those fields before it gets dark – the ones they were going to build on. What would they be going for, d'you think?'

His eyes, guileless as a child's and just as misleading, twinkled at her for a moment. Maggie grinned.

'I've no idea. They're not worth more than the agricultural price, I wouldn't have thought.'

He nodded. 'That's what I reckoned. Good land, that is. Take a few years, mind you, to get it clear of chemicals and passed as organic, but still, now I've got Tom here helping, it'd be worth taking on.'

'Well, if I have anything to do with it,' said Maggie, gathering up the parcel in her arms, 'you'll definitely get it!'

186

Chapter Seventeen

I t was a curious collection of people that finally assembled in Celia's sitting room. Maggie, with Julie to help her, carried the food she had made into the kitchen. Julie looked around her with interest, viewing it all as a prospective workplace. Maggie laid a tray with cups, warmed the largest teapot, made some coffee and filled the milk jug.

Banished from the sitting room and dying to know what was going on the twins burst in. Maggie had scarcely met them. They nevertheless felt warmly towards her, for she never disturbed vital Lego models or experiments, and was brilliant at finding those stray football socks and bits of homework that tend to go AWOL in a juvenile bedroom.

'Mrs Maggie! What's in the sandwiches? Wow! Sausage rolls!' They had arrived at this sensible compromise on her name when Maggie had said 'Mrs Whittington' was too formal, but Celia felt that just 'Maggie' from the boys was disrespectful.

'You can have a few,' said Maggie, unable to resist. Julie, used to her own tribe, cut in swiftly.

'Only one each of everything, and only if your hands are clean,' she said firmly. They eyed her with wary respect, and went to the sink to wash.

'This is my friend, Mrs Corre,' Maggie glanced questioningly at her, 'Julie. I can't come and work here any more, and she might do it instead, if you're lucky. Julie, this is William and Edward. Or should it be, these are? Anyway, I won't attempt to tell you which is which, because hardly anyone knows.'

The boys turned back from the tap, and looked warily at Julie. They considered her carefully, exchanged a glance, and seemed to reach a mutual decision.

'Okay,' said one, Maggie had no idea which. 'Do you mind caterpillars?'

Julie accorded the question the dignity of some consideration before answering seriously. 'Not as long as they're in something. Like a tank, I mean. Not a lettuce.'

They nodded in unison, like porcelain mandarins.

187

''Course.' They looked at the trays again. 'One of each?' they checked. 'What about the crisps?'

'A sensible handful each. And when you've eaten them you could earn your keep by taking everything in, and passing it round. Deal?'

'Deal.' No need, clearly, for consultation on that one. 'What's it all about?'

'A wedding.' They gave theatrical groans, slightly muffled by sausage rolls. A hideous thought crossed Will's – or was it Ed's? – mind.

'We won't have to dress up, or anything, will we?'

Maggie allowed her mind to toy with the prospect of identical page boys, but abandoned it without much reluctance.

'Absolutely not. Unless you want to?'

They accorded this the contempt it deserved.

'No, yuk! We did it once, when we were little. Awful little blue velvet trousers and frilly shirts, but we were too young to mind, then.' The one who'd spoken eyed the trays thoughtfully. 'We could help with the food, though. Pass it round, like now.'

Maggie and Julie laughed.

'Perhaps you could, at that! And before it happens there's a barn to clear and a farmyard. Does that sound more your sort of thing?'

Celia came in, looking faintly harried. 'I offered wine, but most of them seem to want tea or coffee. I must – Oh Maggie, you've done it, thank you. And all this food! It looks lovely.'

'It is,' said a twin, swallowing the last mouthful. 'Shall we take them in now, Mrs Julie? And pass them round?'

Julie nodded. Celia watched in some amazement as her unusually docile sons gathered up a tray in each hand and made for the door, which she opened for them speechlessly.

'Goodness,' she said. 'I hope their hands weren't too disgusting.'

'Julie got them to have a wash,' said Maggie, amused. 'Celia, this is Julie. She's the friend I told you about, who used to work for me. I hope you don't mind, I brought her along so that you could meet her. Her husband works at Dawn's farm, and her daughter is a friend of Primrose's, so I thought it was an idea to bring her.'

'Of course.' Celia came forward and shook Julie's hand. 'I do hope you are able to come to us, Julie. Having Maggie has been wonderful. I don't know whether she's explained to you about my mother-in-law? But of course she won't be with us for ever, though sometimes it does feel like it. We'd better take the tea and coffee through, I think everyone else is here.'

'Just one more thing,' said Maggie, hurrying back to her car to fetch the parcel of fabric, which she carried through to the sitting room. Dawn's eyes slipped past Maggie and she gave a little frown of disappointment when she realised Gordon wasn't there, then she saw what Maggie carried and her face cleared. Maggie raised her eyebrows in a question, and Dawn smiled back.

The room had been rearranged for the meeting, so that all available seating was grouped round the large central coffee table where there were glasses and two bottles of wine, and where Celia was pouring tea. Mrs Draper, as befitted her seniority, had taken the large armchair that she preferred, since it was not too low. Primrose was next to her, wearing the trouser-suit and looking remarkably sophisticated. There were no other free chairs at that end of the room, and her father was sitting on the other side, next to Dawn. He had pushed his chair slightly back, as if he wondered whether he really ought to be there. At Primrose's feet, much to Maggie's astonishment, sat Dez. He had a sandwich in one hand and a sausage roll in the other, and he was scowling at Colin, who sat side by side with Stella, rather close together. Colin was looking serious, and when his eyes met Maggie's they clouded, and he looked away. The third seat on the sofa had been left empty, perhaps for Celia.

In a little group between Mrs Draper and Primrose's father sat Jane, the lifeguard from the swimming pool. She was chatting to The Gossips – Brenda and Iris. They glanced at Maggie and smiled. Maggie thought rather humbly what a tribute it was to Stella that so many people should want to help organise her wedding.

Steeling herself, Maggie went to speak to Mrs Draper, wondering what kind of reception she would get.

'Well?' snapped the older woman. 'And what have you got to say for yourself?' Feeling about as young as the twins, and rather younger than Primrose, who was carefully not listening, Maggie apologised.

'I know it was bad of me to mislead you. I never expected things to get so out of hand. I thought I'd just be working for a few days, and that would be it.'

'And you're not coming back at all?' Mrs Draper couldn't keep a plaintive tone from her voice. 'Just till I go back to Spain?'

'I'm afraid I really can't. There's going to be a lot to do at home, and I must help my husband if I can.'

The Mugger sniffed. 'Men!' she said crossly. 'Nothing but trouble.' She glared at the twins, who were approaching with the trays of food. 'Take it away! This is *not* the time of day when I wish to eat, or to drink tea. If I have a cup of tea now I won't sleep all night. I'm very sensitive to caffeine. But of course you can't expect *men* to know about that kind of thing.' Fortunately at that moment Julie came up with a glass of sherry.

'There you are, Mrs Draper. Your daughter-in-law thought you might prefer this to tea, at this time of day.'

'And who are you, pray?'

Maggie performed the introduction. 'This is my friend Julie. She's going to come and take my place, and do everything better than ever I did. Her daughter is a friend of Primrose's.'

'A daughter? A *real* daughter?'

'Yes, a real daughter. And three real sons.' Mrs Draper ignored the three sons as unworthy of consideration, but Maggie thought she looked at Julie with something approaching approval. Maggie went across the room to sit next to Dawn, and laid the parcel of fabric down on the floor.

'That's Mary's silk, isn't it?' Dawn asked.

Maggie nodded. 'He insisted on me bringing it for Stella. I think he was embarrassed at the thought of doing it himself. Dawn, it's so beautiful – are you sure he really means it?'

'Of course he does. Gordon never does anything he doesn't mean. It can be maddening, but you always know where you are with him. So he's all right about the wedding?'

'I think he feels rather like the twins do about it. As long as he hasn't got to dress up and make an exhibition of himself he's fine. And he's already scheming to buy the land where the Mall should have been. I hope he'll get it, too. I'm sure he could make much better use of it than Turner.'

Dawn looked down at the package on the floor between them.

'Do you know, I'd completely forgotten about that silk, but as soon as I saw you carrying it I knew what it must be. Poor Mary! She really was a lovely girl. In a way, Stella is like her. The same sunny character.'

'Yes, that's what he said. He told me the whole story.'

'If they'd married, they could have had a daughter of their own by now – not as old as Stella, but getting on that way. I think he'd like to see that silk put to good use, instead of sitting at the back of a cupboard.'

'Has everyone got tea, or a drink?' Celia's voice, pitched to carry across a noisy classroom, interrupted them. 'If you want more, just help yourselves. Now, we all know why we're here, so shall we start? Anyone want to say anything?' As is usually the case, all present were instantly stricken dumb by this question. 'First things first, then. The venue. If we haven't got that, we can't do much else. Dawn?'

Dawn looked helplessly at Maggie, and flushed unhappily. Maggie came to her rescue.

'I went to see Dawn's brother, Gordon, this afternoon. He's happy for us to use the barn and the yard.' Celia, Julie and Stella smiled and looked relieved, but Colin stared moodily at his cup. It was Mrs Draper who unexpectedly put his thoughts into words.

'A barn and a yard! It doesn't sound at all suitable for a wedding to me.'

'I think it could be made very attractive,' said Maggie. 'Not sophisticated, of course, but a country wedding, like – oh, Thomas Hardy or something. *Far from the Madding Crowd*, that kind of thing.' She started to describe the place, trying to draw pictures in the air with her hands, until Celia produced a large pad of paper and a felt-tip pen.

'Borrowed it from the boys,' she explained succinctly. 'Sketch it out for us, Maggie.'

Maggie did so, showing how the open-fronted barn gave onto the yard, how the sides were sheltered by wall and hedge, and she described the outlook through the blossoming orchard to the fields behind. Colin began to look more hopeful, and even the Mugger nodded.

'Hmph – it sounds more promising than it appeared. And is the barn big enough to hold everyone, if the weather should be bad?'

'Oh, easily. If we can get it all cleared out, we can set up a long table for the cake and the buffet along the back, then have a scattering of smaller tables inside, and more outside if it's fine. Obviously we can't have everyone sitting down to eat in the barn – if it's raining, most of them will have to manage without a table, but people do that at parties all the time, it shouldn't be a problem.'

'Where will all the tables and chairs come from?' Colin was not to be won over too easily.

'The village hall,' said Dawn, too quietly to be heard. 'The village hall,' she repeated more loudly, blushing again. 'They hire them out quite often, they've got a whole lot of them. They're a bit basic, but they're quite solid. And with tablecloths . . .' She stopped and looked at Maggie for help.

'White linen sheets,' Maggie supplied. 'I've got a lot of them I never use.'

'So have I,' said Celia. 'And I'm sure I can borrow more – my mother has a cupboardful she's always trying to get rid of onto me.'

'Couldn't we decorate them?' asked Primrose. 'Stencils, or something?'

'Not stencils,' said Celia firmly. 'Nothing that can't be removed.'

'Garlands would be nice,' mused Maggie, 'but they'd be expensive unless we did them ourselves, and we'd never have time. I know – how about little posies, pinned on? The sheets are almost certain to be a bit too big for small tables; we could loop the fabric up at the corners or the sides, safetypin it, and fasten a little bunch to cover the pin. We could use plenty of leaves – something evergreen, if possible, that won't wilt too quickly – and one or two nice tough flowers like carnations or roses to match the colour scheme. It was deep red, wasn't it, Stella?'

'Yes. That's the colour for the bridesmaids' dresses – the grown-up's ones. We bought them in the sales in January. And the little

191

ones have cream dresses – they've been passed on to us – with matching red sashes.'

'Very nice,' said Mrs Draper approvingly. 'Practical, and a good strong colour.'

'I could do the tables,' Primrose offered, 'if Stephanie would help me. What about some ribbon, too? Not too fussy, but if we could find something the right colour just to bind round the stalks of the posies, and hang down? If Stella likes the idea, that is.'

Stella's old smile shone out. 'I think it sounds lovely. It's so good of you all. It's going to be even better than at the hotel, isn't it, Colin?'

She nudged him, and he managed to smile in his turn, but everyone could see that he was unhappy about it. Maggie's heart sank. She ploughed on.

'I think we should consider the food next. Obviously we can't cope with anything hot, but a cold buffet would be quite possible. The service is at two-thirty, isn't it?'

'Yes,' Stella said. 'And we'd been planning on having just sandwiches and little cocktail things, not a proper meal.'

'You want more than that,' the Mugger put in firmly. 'People don't eat much lunch before a wedding – there's no time, and they don't want to risk spilling anything down their clothes. Consequently, once they get started on the champagne it'll go straight to their heads, unless there's a proper decent snack available.'

'I'd be happy to do the food,' said Maggie, 'and Julie, I'm sure, will help me.' Julie beamed in approval. 'If I make things like mini-pizzas, they can go in the freezer. Those little kebabs, too, and savoury profiteroles . . .' Colin, she saw, was suddenly looking a bit happier. 'I can't do the cake, though. At least, I could do the baking of it, but not the icing. I've never got beyond that rough finish you do with a fork on a Christmas cake, before you put the sleigh and the reindeer on.'

'Iris is good at cakes,' said one of The Gossips of the other. 'She went to classes.'

'I can't do anything very fancy,' said Iris anxiously. 'Not all that free-standing lace-work and things. But I could make it look pretty, and the instructor at my class might give me a bit of help. There's not much time, though.'

'I'll make the cakes tomorrow,' Maggie promised, 'and bring them round to you as soon as they're cool. What were you having, Stella? Three layers?'

'Yes,' she said, 'but you mustn't worry. It really doesn't have to have all that icing and stuff. After all, nobody ever really wants to eat it, do they? It's just a formality.'

'But an important one,' put in The Mugger, who had obviously cast herself in the role of Wise Woman of the Tribe. 'It's not the eating of it that matters, it's the look of it, and watching you and your young man cut it. After that, you might as well feed it to the birds. Now, I don't suppose you young girls put pieces of wedding cake under your pillows any more, do you?'

'Whatever for?' asked Primrose. 'The False Teeth Fairy?'

'In France,' Celia volunteered, momentarily sidetracked, 'they have mice. Instead of the Tooth Fairy, I mean,' she added hastily, in case anyone should think she was denigrating French hygiene. 'It's supposed to be a mouse that leaves a coin in exchange for the tooth.'

'Disgusting,' said Mrs Draper firmly. 'And beside the point. What about flowers?'

'I thought I could do them,' offered Celia. 'There's quite a bit of greenery in our garden, and Maggie says she's got masses. What we really need is a source of not too expensive flowers.'

'My Tom could go to the market for you, early Thursday morning, say,' Julie said. 'That way the flowers can stand in water for a few hours before you start using them. Only you must tell him *exactly* what you need, or if you're not careful, he'll come back with a couple of boxes of ornamental cabbages and a bunch of asparagus fern.'

'I can help with the flowers,' Brenda volunteered. 'My sister-in-law brought me two boxes of Oasis last time she came down – she gets it wholesale. And I've lots of little dishes, too, that would be just right for the tables.' Her cheeks were pink with excitement.

'Wonderful!' exclaimed Celia. 'I did wonder if I could do it on my own, but I've only got the evenings, really, and Saturday morning, of course.'

Everyone was relaxed now, and involved. Celia scribbled furious lists on a notepad.

'Venue, tables and chairs, food, cake, flowers,' she muttered to herself. 'We're coming on. I really think this is getting off the ground!'

Dez stirred. Perhaps the word 'ground' had made him realise how hard the floor was.

'Cars,' he growled. 'Transport.'

There was a thoughtful silence as people contemplated their own vehicles, and found them wanting. Maggie thought of the array of large, shiny gas-guzzlers that had so often filled the drive and turning circle at home when Turner had invited potential investors back. Any of them, only a week ago, would have been lent without a second thought if Turner had asked. Now, of course, it was very different. Unlikely that any of those former buddies would lend Turner a bicycle, let alone a car.

'There's my Range Rover,' she said, 'only I'm not sure I'll still have it by then. And it's not very romantic.'

'It doesn't matter,' said Colin unexpectedly. 'We don't have to have big white hearses. I never liked those things, anyway. Can't we just use our ordinary cars, put some ribbons on them, something like that?'

'What about Stella's dress?' Maggie was dubious. 'It would have to be a pretty big car, or she'd get to the church and the reception crushed to a rag.'

'What dress?' Mrs Draper asked immediately. 'No one's said anything about a dress yet. I *had* thought you might need my help.'

'We certainly do,' said Maggie. 'In fact, we're relying on you. And here's the best thing of all. You remember I went to see Dawn's brother, Gordon, this afternoon? He sent this, for Stella.' She picked up the parcel. Julie and Primrose hurried to clear and wipe the coffee table, and when it was clean and dry, Maggie put the package down on it. She glanced at Dawn to see whether she wanted to tell the story, but the other woman gave a little shake of her head and gestured for her to carry on. Maggie knelt by the coffee table, unpicking the sticky tape as Gordon had done. When the brown paper was undone to reveal the layers of tissue, she paused with her hands on the rustling parcel.

'It's a bit of a tragic story, but a very beautiful and romantic one. This material was bought by Gordon's fiancée Mary, when they were both very young, to use as her bridal gown. Sadly, she died . . . Gordon never met anyone else after Mary, so he kept this safe all these years, and now he'd like Stella to have it.' Stella opened her mouth to protest, but Maggie silenced her with a look. 'Dawn and I believe it would make him happy, after all these years, to see something so exquisite put to such a good use. So if you like it – and I can't imagine anyone *not* liking it – then it's yours, Stella. Gordon says you remind him of Mary, and Dawn agrees, so . . . here it is.'

Gently, holding the dramatic moment, Maggie peeled back the tissue. In the silent room the rustle of the paper seemed loud as gunfire. Everyone was leaning forward to see. Maggie unrolled the fabric as Gordon had done, lifting the bolt by the ends of the cardboard roll and letting the shimmering stuff ripple across the table. There was a moment of complete silence broken only by a collective indrawing of breath, then a babble of voices. Stella put out a hand, and stroked the silk.

'How beautiful,' she breathed. 'So beautiful. Does he really mean it?' It was Dawn that she addressed, and she nodded.

'Gordon never says things he doesn't mean. I know he wants you to have it,' she said, more firmly than Maggie had ever heard her speak.

'You'd be mad to turn it down, girl,' said the Mugger in her usual forthright fashion. 'You might be having your reception in a barn, and going to it in a wheelbarrow, from the sound of things, but you'll have a dress fit for a princess. What about the style? With silk like that you don't want anything too fussy. Let the fabric speak for itself, keep it simple and classical, that's my advice.' She said advice, but it sounded like an order.

Stella, looking dazed but happy, took the notepad that Celia offered and went to sit by Mrs Draper. Primrose gave up her chair for Stella and moved to help Julie, who was collecting up mugs and plates. Dez pulled himself up from the floor and went over to Maggie.

'This clearing up in the barn,' he mumbled. 'What's going to happen about that?'

'We need to get started as soon as possible,' she replied. 'A lot of it is farm equipment that could be stored in other buildings for now. There's a stack of bales – hay and straw – that will need moving, but I'm not sure where to.'

'Couldn't we make a wall of them along the back, from the ground to the ceiling? One layer deep, say, and then put a row all around the sides of the barn, to make like a bench – people could sit on it. Might need something over it, more sheets or something.'

Maggie was impressed, and showed it.

'That's a brilliant idea, Dez. Let's see, it's Tuesday today, we can't do much before the weekend, but how about Saturday morning? Do you think any of your friends would come along? We can't pay them, but I'll bring some soft drinks and food – pizza, perhaps, or maybe . . . Dawn, do you think Gordon would let us do a barbecue? We could make a bit of a party out of it.'

Dawn turned from speaking to Primrose's father.

'There's a lot of old lumber in the barn – most of it's only fit for burning,' she said thoughtfully. 'Why not have a big bonfire out on the bit of rough ground in the far paddock, and do a cook-out? I've still got potatoes from last year we could bake in foil, and chops and sausages in the freezer. We've always got more meat than we know what to do with, and you'd be amazed how many sausages you can make from one pig, even when the best bits go for joints.'

'Sounds okay,' shrugged Dez, his grudging words belied by the brightening of his eyes. 'Could we have a bit of music? Fireworks?'

'No fireworks,' said Dawn and Maggie almost as one. 'It would terrify the animals,' Dawn explained. 'But music – well, there's no one within earshot to mind, and I expect we can survive it for once.'

'It won't be an actual party though,' Maggie pointed out. 'Definitely no drink, and nothing too late. If your friends will come under those conditions, we'd welcome their help.'

'They'll come if I tell them to,' Dez said, looking tough. Primrose, nearby, cast up her eyes. Then Dez, with a grunt to Maggie that might have been goodbye, walked out of the room.

'Will he turn up, do you think?' Maggie asked Primrose in a low voice.

'I think so. After all, he insisted on coming this evening when he heard me talking about it at school. They all teased him for coming to a thing about a wedding, but he just gave them a look – you know – and they all shut up. He fancies Stella, of course.' She sounded quite nonchalant about it and Maggie, who remembered that Stella had said Primrose was keen on Dez, was surprised.

'You don't mind?' she asked tentatively. Primrose gave her a look that was as old as the hills, one woman to another expressing amused tolerance of those simple children, men.

'Of course I don't. Stella's got Colin, she's not remotely interested in Dez. While he's dazzled by her, he won't be noticing anyone else either. It's good for him.'

'A civilising influence?' Maggie had to admit that Dez had become much nicer since falling under Stella's spell.

'Something like that. At least he's prepared to help. I hate to admit it, but people *do* do what he says, most of the time. He'll bring plenty of mates along. Anyway, it sounds fun, clearing out the barn. I'll tell my Saturday job I can't work that day so I can join in. And Sunday's free. We might even get Dad to help.' She saw Julie approaching the door with a tray, and went to open it for her.

Iris came to speak to Maggie.

'I was thinking, I could do the cake to match the dress – the pattern of the silk, I mean. If Mrs Draper gives me some scraps after the cutting out's done, I could make a template from the embroidery. What do you think?'

'I think it's a lovely idea. Why not have a word with Stella?'

'I will. The only thing is, I'm a bit worried about doing more than one layer. Not doing it, I mean, that's all right, but getting them strong enough for the bottom layer to support the weight. It's going to be several days before the basic icing can be done, and I don't think there'll be time for it to harden thoroughly. I'll ask the instructor, of course, but it would be awful if the pillars went through the icing and the whole thing collapsed.'

'Yes, I see what you mean,' said Maggie. 'You know, I remember my mother telling me that during the war, when rationing was really bad, people had fake cakes at their weddings, made with cardboard and plaster. Suppose you made fake top layers out of boxes or something, and iced them to match? You could do real ones as well, and keep them out of the way until they need to be cut. After all, it's the bottom layer they use for the ceremonial cutting, and that could be the real thing.'

'Yes, and I could use the box ones to practise on, so it wouldn't be such a disaster if it went wrong. Brilliant! I'll go and talk to Stella.'

Celia edged her way through the talking groups to Maggie and Dawn.

'I never thought we'd do as well as this, did you? And all thanks to you and your brother, really, Dawn. I know he doesn't want to be thanked, but you will tell him how grateful everyone is, won't you?'

Dawn nodded. 'To tell you the truth', she confided, 'he's been meaning to get the barn cleared out for years, but somehow there never seems to be time to do it. He'll be glad to get it done, even if it does mean a bit of noise and upheaval!'

'Noise and upheaval sounds about right,' chuckled Celia. 'I suspect my boys will want to come and help when they hear about it.'

'The more the merrier. Old clothes, of course.'

'Of course. Maggie, your friend Julie is great. I never thought anyone else would be able to deal with, you know, *the situation*,' she glanced swiftly at her mother-in-law, 'but she's got her eating out of her hand. Is it me, or is she nicer these days?'

'I think she's thrilled to bits to be making a wedding dress. Not that anyone asked her – she just took it as read that she'd be doing it! Thank goodness, though – that lovely fabric, it's got to be someone who really knows what they're doing.' Maggie looked at her watch, and pulled a face. 'Goodness, look at the time! I must get back – Turner will wonder what's become of me.'

Celia put her hand on Maggie's arm to detain her.

'Is everything all right?' she asked quietly. 'Are you all right, I mean?' Maggie felt her throat tighten at the sudden kindness.

'Yes, I'm all right,' she said, a bit huskily. 'I'm just so thankful we've got something organised for Stella. That bothered me more than anything else. It will work, won't it?'

Celia gave the arm she still held a little shake.

'Of course it will! The Mugger will see to that, you wait and see! She'll have us all running round in no time, you bet. No, I really think it's going to be wonderful, really unusual and special. Even Colin's come round, hasn't he? He looked pretty grim when he arrived, and look at him now!'

They looked. Colin, banished by Mrs Draper from any discussion over The Dress ('You can't see anything until the wedding day – in fact, you probably shouldn't even be looking at the fabric!') was talking to Primrose and her father. He certainly appeared quite cheerful, and as Maggie watched he glanced round and caught her eye. The smile he gave her was as open and uncomplicated as Stella's, and Maggie felt the last tension slide from her.

It was dark when Maggie got home. Only the kitchen light was on, and she went in that way to find Turner sitting at the kitchen table. It was neatly laid – the best china, Maggie noticed – and a handful of flowers from the garden arranged carefully, if ineptly, in a glass. Some kitchen dishes held, variously, two lobsters (halved and garnished), a mixed salad, some little fresh rolls, and a pile of asparagus. Turner jumped up as Maggie came in. He looked relieved to see her, and it occurred to her that she had never before been out late like this without telling him where she was going, or leaving him a note.

'Sorry I'm late,' she said politely, as to a stranger.

'That's all right. I thought I'd do supper.'

'Yes, I see.' Maggie examined the table again. 'Funeral baked meats?' she asked wryly. He grimaced.

'Something like that. I got them from the hotel kitchens. Last chance. It doesn't belong to me any more, after today.'

'I'm sorry.' We sound so stilted, Maggie thought. Now he'll say 'So am I.'

'So am I.' Maggie burst into hysterical laughter. Turner looked at her as if he didn't know whether to comfort her or slap her.

'Sorry,' gasped Maggie, wiping her eyes. 'I just knew you were going to say that.'

'What else can I say? Oh Maggie, I thought you'd gone.'

'Gone where?'

'How do I know? Just gone, for good. I wouldn't blame you if you had done.'

'I wouldn't do that, Turner. You should know that.'

'I don't know anything. Not any more. I thought I did. I thought I was in control, that I knew what to do and how to do it. Now . . .' He shook his head.

'But you know *me*, Turner,' said Maggie. As she said it, she wondered whether it was true, whether even she herself knew the Maggie who seemed to be emerging from the chrysalis of this trouble.

'Yes,' he said. 'Yes, I know you. But Maggie, you know me, and would you have expected me to do anything as mad as that stunt I tried to pull yesterday?' She shook her head, feeling the throb of her bruise that she hadn't noticed for several hours. 'Nor would I. I mean, it's just not the kind of thing I do! So if *I* can do something like that, which I would have said was completely against my character, then how can I know what to expect from you?'

He looked so miserable that for the first time Maggie felt profound pity for him. She went across the kitchen and put her arms round him. It must be her imagination that made him feel smaller and thinner. At first he was stiff within her embrace, but after a moment his arms moved to hold her. She leaned against his shoulder, and felt his cheek resting gently against the top of her head.

'I thought I'd lost you,' he whispered. 'I've never been so frightened. If you went, Mags, what would be the point of it all? I don't care about anything else – the Mall, the painting, the hotel, this house – as long as I've got you.'

Maggie realised that in all the years of living and working together, she had always assumed, and accepted, that the business was more important to Turner than she was. Deep within her something shivered, like the ripples on the calm, still water of the empty pool when it was first touched. It was as though Turner's words had broken through a barrier of which she herself had been unaware, to reach a more profound emotional layer of her being. While there was still a part of her that said, coldly, that she wanted nothing more to do with him, her inner core told her that something new had been planted within her. As some women, she had heard, were aware of a new life even at the moment of conception, so she felt that there was something, so small as to be almost invisible, that might yet grow through her being and change both her and Turner. At that moment, the cobwebby tendrils of fear that she had thought were an integral part of her, shrivelled and vanished like a tangle of threads in a fire, gone to dust and nothingness in an instant.

Chapter Eighteen

M aggie left early on Saturday morning to go to Dawn's. It was a relief to be out of the house. She had spent the previous day, after an early-morning shopping trip, in the kitchen. The cake had been the first priority. She had baked the bottom, largest layer first, an anxious process since she seldom made fruit cakes and was worried about overcooking or undercooking it. It had seemed to work out all right, and the second two layers, which she had been able to fit into the oven together, had been simple by comparison.

While they were cooking in the slow oven, she had made tiny individual pizzas, little pastry cases ready to be filled with savoury mousses, roulades that could be filled on the day, and managed to find space for them all in the freezer – a more difficult task than the actual baking. A valuer from a big firm of London estate agents had arrived to take details of the house, with a downtrodden photographer in tow who looked as though he didn't think much of any of the rooms and took his pictures in a lackadaisical fashion so that Maggie was surprised, later, to see how good they were.

'We're lucky the bank are allowing us to handle the sale ourselves,' Turner had pointed out. 'We should get a much better price. When people know it's a bank selling they always think they're going to pick up a bargain, and of course the bank don't mind accepting a lower offer – they know they'll get the money out of us in the end, anyway. I've stipulated a London agent, too. Not quite so much local gossip, that way.'

Maggie could see that this was better, from a business point of view, but she would have preferred to go back to the local agent they had originally bought from, who had been pleasant to deal with and not too pushy. The London valuer had been condescending, implying that he was accustomed to more imposing residences and that this one was rather beneath him, almost slumming. Maggie punished him by giving him coffee in the kitchen, and refraining from offering him a biscuit with it, though the table was loaded with little cakes and biscuits cooling on wire racks.

Saturday dawned fine, with only a few high clouds making the sky look more intensely blue. Maggie assembled everything she thought might be needed – mostly of an edible nature, including a large bottle of ketchup and several bags of rolls. Turner, applying himself to a bowl of muesli in the kitchen, watched in surprise.

'Doesn't look much like wedding food,' he commented tentatively. Maggie added silver foil and a roll of kitchen paper to her basket, and started to wrap a big rectangle of chocolate cake, made in her largest roasting pan to be cut into squares later. She answered his unasked question.

'There's a big group of kids – at least, I hope it's a big group – coming to help clear the place where we're having the reception, so. I may be a bit late back. It's at a little farm – a smallholding, really – near where the . . . where the Mall was going to be. We're having a bonfire and a cook-out as a reward at the end. I've left you some food in the fridge for lunch, if you're here.'

'Thanks. I don't know when I'll be back. There's a lot of paperwork to go through at the office. So is this the same smallholding you told me about? The one where they want to buy the land?'

'Yes,' said Maggie shortly, aware that Turner was reluctant to sell the land at a huge loss, partly to save face and partly in case there was ever any chance to reverse the planning decision. She knew that this was a reasonable attitude, in terms of business, but she had still been irritated by it and preferred not to discuss it.

'I'll see you later, then,' was all Turner said. Maggie noticed that he rinsed his bowl and stacked it in the dishwasher – something he would never have thought of doing a week earlier – and she was softened by this evidence of New Man-ism.

At first sight, the barn presented a daunting prospect. Maggie had only glanced in it on her earlier visit; on closer inspection she saw that it was not only full of bales and farm implements, but also mounds of discarded pieces of wood, dustbins brimming with baler twine, boxes of empty plastic bottles and tins, and all the other detritus that gets kept in case it turns out to be useful one day. Walls and rafters were festooned with cobwebs and crusted with bird droppings, and every movement stirred up a cloud of dust.

'Looks dreadful, doesn't it?' Dawn fretted. 'I don't really know if we . . . Perhaps it's a bit . . . but what else can we do?'

'Nothing,' said Maggie grimly. 'I just hope we get plenty of helpers.'

'So do I. I've defrosted a mountain of sausages and chops, and they can't be refrozen, though I suppose when they're cooked . . . but then what would I do with them? Oh dear . . .'

They needn't have worried. Primrose and her father were the first to arrive, followed by Julie and Tom with all four children plus Celia's twins crammed somehow into the back of their car. Dez arrived with no less than six friends, all on bicycles, racing one another into the drive and skidding to a halt on the gravel. Dressed in uniform black, the sunlight glinting off studs and earrings, they looked more of a threat than a help, but Maggie soon discovered they were harmless enough. At her suggestion they wheeled their bikes through into the yard and propped them against the wall by the orchard, out of the way. Four sheep, with their lambs, were in the orchard, and to Maggie's amusement all seven boys stood against the wall and watched the lambs playing. When one of them, essaying a foolhardy leap onto a high stump, missed its footing and tumbled off, there was a concerted groan of dismay, and a general relaxation of tension as the tiny creature picked itself up and shook itself before bounding off again.

By the time Stella and Colin arrived an hour later, the clearance was well underway. Gordon had retreated, at the start of this invasion, into impenetrable silence, but Tom had everyone organised into three teams. Gordon, at what might be termed the coal face, could indicate with gestures which team was to take what. One lugged inflammable rubbish to the corner of the field, out of sight but not too far away, where the bonfire was to be set up. A second group loaded unburnable things into a trailer, for transport to the dump, and the third stored things to be kept in other outbuildings. Everyone was filthy, but the floor space was already clearer and Gordon had found several useful things he thought he'd never see again; this put him in what was, for him, an expansive mood which helped him to endure Stella's heartfelt thanks and her hug with more equanimity than might have been expected. He was still silent, but he smiled.

Colin turned out to be an expert in bonfire building, and immediately took over the rearrangement of the collection of cardboard boxes, feed sacks, rotten fence-posts and assorted offcuts of wood. Stella fetched and carried with the rest, and by the time they stopped for lunch – soup and a huge slab of home-made pizza from Maggie and Julie – more than half the barn had already been cleared. Under the layers of straw and dust, the floor proved to be not concrete, but old bricks, worn in places but still close-laid and almost seamless.

'Cleaned up, that's going to look a real treat,' said Julie happily. 'Look at that colour – can't you just see it with the white tablecloths, and the flowers? Set them off a treat, that will.'

Celia, who had been to the church in the morning to plan the flowers and had now come to investigate the barn, agreed.

'It could look stunning. And what about those beams! I've always wanted to have a go at those hanging decorations like big balls of flowers, and this is just the place! You've got plenty of greenery, haven't you, Maggie? Though what I'd like to do in here is some big branches of new leaves – pussy willow, say, and hazel, with perhaps some flowering cherry to lighten everything up. Or even copper beech, if we could get it. The colour would be just right.'

By this time the floor of the barn was clear of everything except the bales. Gordon brought out two sets of steps and some brooms, and the teenagers were taking it in turns to climb up and sweep down the rafters and the wall at the back and sides, before moving the bales there. Cobwebs, the remains of old nests and the occasional dead and mummified bird showered down, greatly to the amusement of the sweepers though those underneath found it less funny.

'I see cobwebs are in this year,' said a voice in Maggie's ear as a hand picked bits out of her hair.

'Turner!' Maggie spun round. 'What are *you* doing here? And how did you find it?' She need hardly have asked, she thought. You could trust Turner to know every inch of the land surrounding his own purchase, and he would have had detailed maps to help him. It was the why, rather than the how, that was intriguing.

'I'd done as much as I could in the office. I thought I'd come and see how it was going, lend a hand. I've got a cold-box of ice creams in the car for the workers, if you think they'd like them?'

'I'm sure they would. It's time we had a break, anyway. Dawn went a few minutes ago to put the kettle on – I'll go and give her a hand.' As she left the barn Maggie heard Turner give what she called his 'building-site bellow', a wordless call of command that had the power to stop every worker in his tracks and engage instant attention. In spite of everything, Maggie was amused. Turner could no more help taking charge of a workforce than he could stop breathing.

The tea-drinkers and ice-cream eaters split themselves neatly by age group. They sat around on the loose bales that were about to be moved.

'What are you going to do with them?' asked Turner, kicking the bale he was sitting on. 'There's a fair few.'

'Dez – that tall boy standing over there – suggested stacking them along the back wall, and in a row down the sides for people to sit on. Then we can put the tables against them, on the back wall, with the food on. At least, not right against, so that Stella and Colin can go behind them to cut the cake, but not too far forward.'

Turner cast a knowledgeable eye over the uneven wall. 'Trouble with stacking the bales there, though I agree it would give a good backdrop, is that in a single layer they're likely to be unsteady. Anyone going round to the back of the table could knock into them, bring two or three down on top of themselves. Wouldn't do them much harm, but it wouldn't improve the buffet much.'

Maggie nodded. Turner, with his builder's eye, was right.

'I wonder whether we can fasten them somehow, with baler twine? Or – I know, Tom's trellis!' Maggie swallowed the rest of her tea, and went to fetch the pieces of trellis that Tom had found earlier and saved from the bonfire. Extended, it was at least six foot high. 'If we could fix this along the front it would be just right.'

Turner flexed the trellis. 'Just the job, I'd say. You could decorate it with flowers, leaves, that kind of thing. Make an arch behind the cake, to frame the bride and groom when they're cutting it.'

'Too fiddly,' said Maggie regretfully. 'It's going to be hard enough for Celia to do the church flowers, and some for here, without that kind of thing.'

'Taking my name in vain? And who's the new helper?'

Maggie jumped. 'Celia! I thought you were still foraging the hedgerows. Have you had a cup of tea?'

'Julie's daughter's just gone to fetch me one. What's that about the flowers?'

'Oh, just an idea that Turner had – this is my husband, Turner. This is Celia. I used to work for her,' explained Maggie quickly.

Celia looked at him, reserving her judgment for the moment. 'So,' she said. 'You're the one.'

'I'm the one,' he agreed ruefully. 'Sorry I've done you out of your cleaning lady.' Used to sizing people up instantly, Turner judged that Celia would prefer the direct approach. Sure enough, her eyes narrowed with amusement.

'Me too, but I'm glad to say I've done you out of yours. Julie's working for me, now. So, what was your idea?'

When Turner had explained, Celia agreed enthusiastically. 'We could stand two of the barrels of branches on either side, to frame it, then have the archway and fill it in with that reflective foil. I saw it on one of those makeover programmes on the telly – you stretch it tight and it looks like a mirror. It would reflect the outside, lighten up the wall. Someone – Tom, perhaps? – could knock up a frame to tack it to, and then we could decorate it with something long and twiny, ivy and that wild clematis, there's masses of it in the hedgerow, and a few fresh flowers . . . We could push bits of Oasis in plastic bags into the bales themselves, that way it could be done the day before and the flowers would keep fresh.' Her eyes were sparkling, her hands shaping the archway in the air. 'Well done, Turner!'

He nodded acceptance of her thanks, aware that he had only gone a small way towards redeeming himself. He had a further card up his sleeve, however.

'You'll want some lighting,' he pointed out. 'Even if it's sunny and you get the reflected light a lot of it will be blocked by people, and it's still fairly dark back against the wall. I can bring some spotlights we can string up on the rafters, put them to shine down on the table. There must be power in here, isn't there? Yes, I thought so. That shouldn't be a problem. But I'll tell you what *will* be a problem.' He paused for dramatic effect while both women frowned at him, trying to think what it might be.

'Loos,' he declared. 'People drinking, people who've travelled a long way here, they're all going to need lavatories.'

Maggie and Celia looked at each other, horrified. It was true that neither of them had given it a thought. Of course, there was a cloakroom and a bathroom in the house, which they and the other females there had used that day. Most of the helpers, however, were men and boys, who had been perfectly happy to take themselves out to the midden at the back where, screened by walls, they had been able to pee when necessary. Such arrangements would scarcely do for a wedding.

'Damn,' Celia muttered. 'How could I not have thought of that? It's the first rule, isn't it? What goes in must come out. What can we do?'

'Don't worry,' said Turner. 'I've got two of those mobile ones we use on sites. One of them's in the yard, the other one can come back the day before and they'll have to manage without for Saturday. They'll just have to walk down the road to the public one, it won't hurt them.'

'Won't they be a bit, well, smelly and nasty?' asked Celia.

'They needn't be. They're both pretty new, and I'll have them scrubbed out, make sure they're spick and span, and get them down here Friday night. They've got water tanks, but it's better if we can fit them up to a tap and a hose. I'll have a scout round in a minute, see if I can find a place.'

'Round the back by the milking shed – there's running water there, and electricity,' said Maggie. 'I'll find Gordon, he can show you.'

'Ah, Gordon. He's the farmer.'

'Yes, that's right. You and he can have a nice talk,' said Maggie with meaning. 'Look, he's over there, by the tractor.'

'Right. I'll catch up with him. He's probably the only person here who'd really like to talk to me.' Turner raised a quizzical eyebrow at Celia and Maggie, and went.

'Quite an organiser, your old man,' said Celia carefully.

'Mmm.' Maggie watched Turner go up to Gordon and introduce himself. The two men eyed one another up for a moment. Turner waited, then Gordon gave a nod. Maggie smiled. Gordon might want to buy the land, but he wasn't one to enthuse. Turner might well find that he had to make all the running. She wondered whether he'd end up suggesting that Gordon buy the land as his own idea, and talking Gordon into it.

'Lucky he said about the loos. And it's good of him to lend us his.' Celia seemed determined to see the best in Turner. Maggie, who was determined not to be won over too easily, smiled inscrutably.

'It's no skin off his nose, he'll just tell someone to organise it. Celia, how much do you need for the flowers? I mean, Brenda's Oasis might not be enough if you want to do your hanging things, and then we simply must have some of those dark red lilies. I know they're what Stella has set her heart on. Some for the church, and some for here, and other flowers too. Carnations for the posies for the tables, and roses. Do you have any idea how much we need? In numbers, and in money too, of course.'

'Not a clue, really. I can probably work out numbers, but I've no idea how much they'll cost. Look – why not just give Tom what you can manage, and I will too, and we'll tell him to get whatever he can get with it.'

'I don't see why you should have to pay, when you're doing all this work,' said Maggie gruffly. 'It's my responsibility, and Turner's.'

'But I'm fond of Stella too,' Celia pointed out. 'As a matter of fact, I'm rather enjoying all this. It's one of the silly little things I've always slightly regretted, having just the boys, that I'll never get the chance to do a wedding. And this is ideal, because I can have all the fun of arranging things without the emotional hang-ups of a daughter getting married. So don't grudge me my contribution, Maggie. I know you want to do the sackcloth and ashes bit and put everything right by walking barefoot over hot coals, but it can't be done. No time, for one thing. And don't you think Stella will be happier knowing that a lot of people have done a bit for her, rather than just one person, however guilty they feel, martyring themselves in the cause?'

Such plain-speaking was like a slap in the face with a cold flannel. Maggie blinked.

'Yes,' she said. 'I suppose I was trying to punish myself. But I'm not used to having people help. I've always just muddled through on my own.'

Celia looked as though she thought this a bit sad, but said merely: 'Well, it won't hurt to get used to it, for this time, at least. There's such a thing as being too independent, you know.'

'In that case, how about helping me scrub the potatoes and wrap them in foil? I think it's time they went in the bonfire; it should have burned down nicely by now.'

Celia grinned. 'Lead on, Macduff. What else are we having?'

'Sausages and chops, I think. Dawn's got them out of the freezer; they always have masses of meat – she said she's glad to use some up.'

'Great. How are we going to do them? Sharpen some sticks and spear them?'

Maggie shook her head. 'I don't know. What do you think?'

'It's what my lot always want to do, but I have to say that we mostly end up fishing things out of the fire, and washing the bits off. It's surprisingly difficult to keep a sausage or a chop on a stick, especially if the fire's hot, and you have to have a long stick. I should say we'd do best to find a rack, and build some brick supports for it. I could run home for the one out of our barbecue, if you like.'

Fortunately Dawn had already sorted out a big metal grid. She had also scrubbed the potatoes and wrapped them.

'Oh dear, I meant to do that for you. Sorry, Dawn.'

'It's all right.' Dawn smiled shyly. 'I was quite glad of an excuse to escape to the kitchen for a while. I'm not used to having so many people here, it's a bit of a shock.'

'Be more of a shock when we have the wedding. You're not having second thoughts, are you?'

'No, of course not. Though I do wonder about Gordon . . .'

'Gordon's fine,' Celia reassured her. 'He's gone with Maggie's husband, to see where to put the loos.'

'Heavens, I hadn't thought of that!'

'Nor had we. Fortunately, Turner is more down to earth, as you might say. He's going to lend us two of those mobile ones. And some spotlights for the barn.'

'That is good of him.'

'Not at all,' said Maggie firmly, 'it's the least he can do, under the circumstances. And now he's talking to Gordon, and I hope Gordon screws him down to a rock-bottom price for the land.'

'By the way, Dawn, do you castrate your ram lambs and your bull calves?' Celia asked calmly.

'Yes, of course.' Dawn looked puzzled at the change of subject. 'Except that the vet does the calves – we usually wait until they're a few weeks older. Why?'

'I just wondered,' said Celia primly, glancing at Maggie. 'Perhaps our friend here might like to borrow your implements, whatever they are . . .'

Maggie giggled, her moment of crossness subsiding. Dawn looked faintly shocked. 'Stop!' She put her hands over her ears in mock horror.

'They bullying you, miss?' Dez put his head round the door. 'Teachers, they're all the same. Power-crazed, that's what it is. Like a disease – they can't help it, but you have to watch 'em.' He winked at Celia. 'Need a hand with the food? Colin says the bonfire's just about right, now.'

'And you're hungry again, I suppose.' She handed him a tray of foil-wrapped potatoes. 'Those need to go in the hot ashes, they'll take a while. And if you're seriously famished, there's a bit of pizza left over from lunch. Though not, of course, if you're going to be rude about teachers.'

'Wonderful people,' he said at once, taking the piece of pizza. 'Dedicated. Caring. Hardworking. Undervalued.'

'Easily irritated,' added Celia, 'by cheeky kids. My God, if you're like this now, what will you be like when you get to the Sixth Form College?'

'It's just a phase I'm going through,' he assured her blandly. 'I'll be a reformed character by then, you'll see. That Colin, he's an okay guy, you know? I thought he wasn't good enough for Stella, but I reckon he'll do.'

'She *will* be relieved. Now for goodness' sake get those potatoes cooking, or we won't eat before midnight.' He swallowed the last mouthful of pizza, and left.

'Ah, lurve,' Celia joked. 'Amazing what it can do. He was all set to be madly jealous of Colin, but he's obviously decided he can afford to bow out to a worthy rival.'

'I'm astonished,' said Maggie. 'I didn't know he could speak whole sentences. I thought he only grunted. Poor kid, he's in some kind of home, it's a shame. I should think he's quite bright, wouldn't you? Primrose said he was, but I didn't really believe her.'

'Being bright, or being seen to be bright, isn't cool,' Celia informed her. 'And cool is all, at that age. He's university material, though, if he can keep out of trouble. With that kind of background, it's not easy. How long's he been in care?'

'I don't know. Is it really that bad?'

'Well, it's not great,' said Celia sadly. 'Not that we see many of them. They tend not to bother with Sixth Form College. Anyway, however good it is, it's never the same as being with a family. But there's not many will foster lads of that age. I mean, would you?'

'I don't know. I suppose not.'

'Still, he's certainly enjoying himself today – mostly thanks to Colin. Have you noticed how men never grow out of wanting to make bonfires? Phil's just the same.'

By the time the potatoes were ready and the rest of the supper cooked, the bales had all been re-stacked and the trellis erected. The newly cleared floor had been roughly swept, and Maggie was amazed by the difference in the whole place.

Tired and filthy, the motley collection of wedding workers lounged on spare bales or the ground. The potatoes, with Dawn's home-churned butter liberally smothered on them, were pronounced perfect, and if the sausages and chops were slightly burned nobody minded, since in any case it was now too dark to see them. Wine for the adults (brought by Turner) and fizzy drinks with peculiar names in brightly coloured cans, were greatly appreciated, and even the music wasn't too bad, since the only available means of playing it had to run on batteries, which successfully damped its carrying power.

Maggie and Turner drove home in silence, though the silence was less charged than before.

'Nice girl,' said Turner as they wearily carried the empty food trays into the kitchen. 'I see what you mean.' In the mysterious way that long-married couples understand one another, Maggie knew that he meant Stella. She made an indeterminate sound signifying assent without commitment.

'Got everything sorted now?' he pursued. 'What about transport?'

'We thought we could just use ordinary cars, decorate them up. It's more a thing of not crushing Stella's dress, though.'

'I might be able to find something appropriate. No promises. Want me to?'

'It's not a dumper truck with ribbons on?' She was only half-joking. One of his men had asked for, and got, permission to leave the church with his bride in a JCB. Turner shook his head, smiling. Maggie knew that smile; it meant he had come up with one of his wilder schemes which he wouldn't discuss with her yet. She sighed. There was no stopping Turner when he looked like that. Maggie felt her spirits lift. This was the old Turner, the man who had amused and beguiled her when they first met.

She yawned suddenly and uncontrollably. Turner grinned sympathetically.

'You must be exhausted. Do you want a drink or anything? Something hot?'

Maggie shook her head, though she was touched by his concern. 'No, I just want to have a shower and get to bed.'

Nevertheless, when Maggie emerged from the bathroom and climbed into bed, she found a tray of tea on her bedside table.

'I made it weak, so it wouldn't keep you awake. Don't drink it if you don't want it.'

There were two cups on the tray. Maggie realised that it was exactly what she wanted. She poured the tea.

'Lovely. Thank you.'

They sat side by side, rather primly sipping from their cups. Maggie felt strangely shy, like a teenager on a first date. She glanced sideways at Turner, and found that he was doing the same to her.

When she had finished she lay down, not turning away from him but unready to bridge the physical gap between them. He put out his light and went through the familiar ritual of punching his pillow, as he always did. She knew that he would not instigate any contact, that any attempt to re-establish a physical relationship between them must come from her.

'Thanks for your help today.' She spoke into the darkness.

'No problem. I hope it works out.'

'Yes.' They said no more. Maggie was too tired not to sleep; she drifted off almost immediately. But in the night she half-woke, and found that they were holding hands.

Chapter Nineteen

T he days went by strangely, sometimes so fast that Maggie felt she could blink and miss one, at other times in slow motion like walking in treacle. Maggie moved through them without minding either, unaffected by it although the perception must surely, she knew, come from her own state of mind.

Her morning swim was the only thing that seemed real. It was true that at the moment very little swimming seemed to get done as the early session became a time for planning and co-ordinating efforts. People met and clustered along the walls, sometimes kicking their legs or doing stretches in token of taking exercise, but most of their energy was focused on Stella's wedding. Several other helpers volunteered their services including, surprisingly, Body Beautiful, who turned out to be the owner of a private off-licence, and who offered to lend the glasses as long as they were returned clean.

Although she was central to many of these discussion, Maggie still swam as much as possible. She sometimes felt that she was only properly alive when she was in the water, pulling herself through it, feeling how it resisted and yet held her up. Her eyes and mind would focus on the way the blueness intensified as she reached the deeper middle of the pool, and paled to a tender aquamarine in the shallow parts. She longed, sometimes, to be a part of that blueness, to open her mouth and fill her whole body with it, not suicidally, but as if it were another world, a Narnia or a Wonderland, where she herself would be changed into something that belonged there.

At home she moved silently through empty rooms, the only noise the hum of the vacuum or the distant whir of the washing machine. She no longer had any inclination to sing as she worked, as she had done when cleaning Celia's house. Not, she thought, because she was unhappy. It was more that she felt almost an intruder in the house. The rooms waited, garnished and shining, for new owners to bring them to life again. They were in stasis, and Maggie drifted through them like a ghost. Do I really exist here, she wondered? If a tree that falls in an uninhabited jungle makes no noise because no one is there to hear it, am I not also invisible and inaudible? She rather liked the idea, but wondered whether she would continue in this limbo state for ever.

People came to view the house. Couples, mostly, several of them surprisingly young. Most of them treated her as the housekeeper, which made everything easier. People who poked around in her cupboards and came out with remarks like: 'Well, of course, this kitchen would have to go, I couldn't live with that,' or, 'Naturally, the bathrooms would have to be stripped out,' or simply: 'Place could do with jazzing up a bit,' could not grate on her feeling when she was 'that Mrs Thing who comes and does'. The only time she got upset was when someone wanted to bulldoze her lovely old garden and 'theme' it. She was deeply relieved when the agents never heard from them again.

She saw Turner rarely. He was spending more and more time in his office, coming home only to shower, to snatch a bite of food and a few hours of sleep. They co-existed easily enough, as they had always done, a civilised veneer being preserved by means of polite enquiries such as: 'How are you?' or, 'Would you like more supper?' Maggie wondered occasionally whether their life together had always been like this, except that she had only recently noticed. Certainly such a superficial companionship was easy to slip into. Looking back, it was no more than a continuation of the kind of relationship she had experienced with her parents, whose care of her had never extended beyond the provision of food, clothes, and a roof over her head.

I want more than this, Maggie thought. And I'm sure Turner does too. Surely it's only because there's so much going on outside, with the business and selling the house, and the wedding, that we don't seem to be able to talk about things. She felt that Turner was waiting, but didn't know whether it was for some signal from her, or for other things to be settled. She, too, was reluctant to push things. She was still unsure of what she wanted from the future. That it must be more fulfilling than her previous life was certain: that it should involve Turner was certain, too, now, but she was unwilling as yet to commit herself.

The following weekend Turner spent all of Saturday checking out bits of work he hoped to be able to pick up, which involved a fair amount of driving around. Maggie went back to the farm, and spent several hours with Dawn going over the food, and what, if anything, could be served hot. The barn looked empty and dusty, but Maggie told herself that when the floor was properly scrubbed, and the whole place decked with flowers, it would be transformed. Dawn was getting cold feet about it all, and the effort of encouraging her made Maggie more positive herself, so that she went home feeling cheerful. Unfortunately Turner was too late home to benefit from this, as Maggie was fast asleep by the time he came in.

On Sunday Turner got up, put on some old gardening-type clothes and disappeared while Maggie was still in the bathroom. Maggie, who was stuck in the house because there were three lots of people coming to look at it, didn't know whether to be relieved or peeved. It was true that the thought of Turner being at home all day, and worse still helping to show prospective purchasers round, was dispiriting. Turner, quite definitely, would not react well to even the mildest criticisms of the house or anything about it.

At the same time, Maggie had been telling herself that she must make an effort to have some kind of meaningful discussion with Turner about their future. For one thing, she had no idea where they might live once the house was sold. She didn't worry greatly about it, assuming that they wouldn't be sleeping under a hedgerow, but it was one of the things that she thought she ought to take an interest in.

The three couples were coming at widely spaced times – eleven in the morning, two o'clock, and half-past five. If it hadn't been for the two o'clock, Maggie thought, I could have gone to the farm again. As it was, some people seemed to want to inspect every power point in the house and shrub in the garden, so that a viewing could take anything up to an hour. Maggie resigned herself to a day of solitary cooking.

By half-past eleven the first couple had still not arrived. When the telephone rang Maggie vaguely assumed it would be them with an apology or a request for directions – forgetting that they would scarcely have been given her telephone number. When she picked it up, however, it was Primrose.

'Can I come round?' she asked without preamble. 'I want to try out pinning up a sheet and putting the flowers on it. Dad's going out to some deadly engineering exhibition and wants me to go with him, but I told him you needed me. He's so old fashioned, he's got this thing about not leaving me alone, as if I were going to start playing with matches and set fire to myself, or something.'

'Of course you can come. I'm on my own, too.'

'Good, then you can explain to me just exactly what has happened with your husband's business. Everyone's all "whisper, whisper" about it, treating me like a baby again, but it's not a secret, is it? I mean, you don't mind me asking, do you?'

'Not really. It's not very interesting, but it's nothing criminal or anything. He's just over-reached himself and made an unfortunate investment, that's all. Now we've got to raise as much money as we can, as quickly as possible, to keep the bank quiet.'

'But why does that mean Stella couldn't have her wedding? Oh, never mind, tell me when I get there. Have you got a sheet, and a table?'

'Plenty of sheets, and I should think the folding table I used to use for wallpaper would be about the right size. How are you getting here? I'd come and pick you up, only I'm waiting for some people who are due to look at the house.'

'No, it's all right. I was going to cycle, but Dad said he'd drop me off, it's on his way.'

And make sure you're really coming here, Maggie thought with some sympathy for the anxious parent. Not that Primrose was exactly into wild behaviour yet, but there was no doubt that since Stella had been helping her improve her swimming, and since she'd acquired her new clothes from Mrs Draper, Primrose had lost weight, was beginning to look far more attractive, and had consequently gained confidence in herself. The doorbell rang, and Maggie went to let in her visitors.

The viewing didn't last long.

'I had no idea the house was so far from the town,' complained the elderly woman as she entered, with the distinct implication that it was Maggie's fault. 'I don't think I'd have bothered to come if I'd known.' Since she was carrying a copy of the agent's particulars, complete with a detailed scale map of the area, Maggie didn't feel very sympathetic. 'Come *on*, George, for goodness sake, don't be so slow. So this is the hall? I should think you find it rather cold in winter, don't you?'

As the couple entered, Maggie shut the front door behind the hapless George, who trailed limply behind his wife and said nothing, merely giving Maggie a deprecating glance. Maggie pointed out the two radiators in their covered alcoves, and mentioned the well-fitting and sealed-unit glazed windows that had been specially made to blend in with the style of the house. This was to no avail.

'All these old houses are draughty,' pronounced the woman in the voice of one who will not be nay-sayed. 'And this is the kitchen?' Maggie made no answer, since the question seemed self-answering. 'Hmm. An Aga. I always say they make a lot of work. They throw out dust and ash. Uneconomical, too.' Maggie started to explain that since the Aga was electric it made no dust at all, then thought, why bother? After that she agreed blandly with everything the visitor said, which seemed to irritate and disconcert her.

They had just finished going round the house ('I can't think why the agents have set such a high price on this') and were about to inspect the garden when Primrose arrived. Maggie, with a word of apology, went to the back door. She waved to Primrose's father who pointed to his watch and mimed a tearing rush before driving off with, Maggie noticed, a pleasant-looking woman beside him in the front of the car. Was this, she wondered, why Primrose had chosen to come to her instead? She hurried back to her viewers, who were inspecting her lawn. Primrose, feeling nosy, went with her.

'Your lawn is full of moss,' said the woman, prodding at it with the heel of her shoe. 'And daisies.'

'Yes, isn't it?' agreed Maggie affably. 'So soft to walk on, and the lawn stays green even in the dryest summer.'

'Lawns look better with daisies on them,' added Primrose helpfully. 'It shows off the green better.' The woman looked her up and down.

'And is this,' she enquired with ponderous venom, 'your daughter?'

'Oh no,' said Maggie brightly. 'This is Primrose. She's on day release from the local children's home. Well, they call it a children's home, but really it's a remand centre. For young offenders,' she added, to make everything quite clear. Primrose, after one startled glance, fell into a slouch and started to chew a piece of imaginary gum with her mouth open.

'Yeah,' she growled. 'They let us out, like, y'know, when we've been banged up a long time, like, for sumfin serious – drugs, like or prossichooshun. Kind of, get used to the outside world, like, so we'll know our way around when they let us out, righ'? We often come up here.' She leered at the man, who looked thoughtfully back at her, then fixed her eyes on the woman's large diamond rings. 'Nice,' she said appreciatively. 'Real, are they?'

'Well, really!' The woman put her hands behind her. 'I think we've certainly seen enough. Come on, George!' She made for the side gate in the wall that led back to the front of the house. Maggie followed her, trying desperately to suppress her giggles. At the car the couple were slowed while George tried to unlock it with the remote control, and Primrose was able to buttonhole them.

'You got a fag you can spare? Or a coupla quid? Come on, just a coupla quid – nuffink to you, is it? Or a fiver, even? Nice car like that, you can spare it.'

'Certainly not! Get away from the car, you dreadful girl. George! George! Get the car open! *George!*'

His fumbling fingers finally found the right button, and the doors unlocked with a bleep and a click. As was clearly his accustomed duty, George opened the door and helped his wife in, then slammed the door shut on her. His hand went swiftly to an inner pocket and with an economical movement, shielded from the car by his body, he pressed a folded note into Primrose's hand.

'There you go, love,' he muttered.

'Oh!' Startled, Primrose forgot her part. 'No, I couldn't possibly—'

'Go on, love, you've earned it.' He winked at Maggie. 'She doesn't want to move, anyway. She just likes an outing, and a good nose around. This'll give her something to talk about for weeks.' He climbed into the car and drove off, leaving Primrose staring down at a crisp new twenty-pound note.

'I never meant . . .' she stammered sounding just like Dawn at her most distracted.

'Of course you didn't. He knows that, it's why he gave it to you. That'll make up for missing your job last Saturday, anyway.'

'Ooh yes. Have you got any more people coming to look at the house today?'

Maggie laughed. 'I have, but I don't think we should push our luck, do you? Now, why don't we pick some bits of foliage while we're out here, to make some posies for you to practise with?'

They set up the pasting table in the kitchen, and Maggie continued to cook while Primrose experimented with a sheet.

'The trouble is,' she said in a muffled voice round the safety pin she held between her teeth, 'that you really need to have the sheet hanging down as long as possible, to hide the table legs because they're ugly, but if you have it too long people might trip over them.'

'Not to mention the fact that a lot of white sheets will get pretty dirty,' Maggie puffed as she beat eggs into choux pastry.

'Want a hand?' Primrose took over the beating. 'Oof, it is hard, isn't it? Couldn't we just buy whatever it is readymade?'

Maggie explained that the little cheese choux, which could be piped onto baking sheets and frozen, weren't easily available and besides would be much nicer freshly baked on the day.

'Yum. Do you eat like this every day?'

'Well, they're not exactly everyday food!' Maggie smiled. 'But I do like cooking, so we have a lot of homemade things.'

'I've never done much. A bit at school, only everyone messes around. At home Dad usually buys stuff to go in the microwave.'

'I don't suppose he's got the time or the energy to cook, when he gets back from work. And really, those ready meals are so convenient, and there's a lot of choice.'

'They all taste a bit the same though, don't they? Perhaps I should learn to cook, give him a treat sometimes. Could you teach me?'

'I could, but it's not difficult. If you can read a recipe, and follow it, then you can cook. The trick is choosing the right recipe.'

Primrose pondered this as she carefully piped the little blobs of mixture and sprinkled them with parmesan and paprika.

'We're having a roast tonight,' she remarked casually.

'Great. I love a roast, but it's never quite so satisfactory when it's just for two so I don't always bother. Your dad does roasts, then?'

'Yes, sometimes. Not tonight, though. Tonight he's got a friend coming to cook. You might have seen her.'

Aha, thought Maggie. The woman in the car. I wonder if that's why Primrose is showing this sudden interest in learning to cook. Worried about the opposition?

'In the car?' Maggie matched Primrose's offhand tone. 'I got a glimpse, yes. Well, it will make a change, won't it? Has she cooked for you before?'

Primrose bent over the second foil-lined tray, keeping her face turned away. Maggie wondered whether she had gone too far, but reflected that Primrose needn't have mentioned it in the first place if she hadn't wanted to.

'Not at the flat. He's been round to hers once or twice, I think. She may have cooked for him then.'

Her tone was cynical. Maggie, too, thought that a woman who invited a single, available man back to her home probably had more on her mind than feeding him. Difficult for Primrose to accept perhaps, but her father was, after all, an adult and also, as Primrose herself had once said, probably a bit lonely.

'Do you like her?'

'What's not to like? She's all right. Looks okay, smiles a lot, doesn't say much.'

Poor thing, Maggie thought with some sympathy for the unknown woman. She could imagine how daunting Primrose might appear, with her sharp tongue and habit of speaking her mind.

'She's probably terrified of you.'

'Of me? Don't be daft.'

'No, really. If she's . . . friendly . . . with your father, I should think she sees you as a bit threatening.'

'I hardly hit her at all,' said Primrose after a moment, 'and I kept the safety catch on the revolver.'

'Armed neutrality?'

'You could say,' Primrose admitted. 'So, you think I should be nicer to her? Pay her compliments on her gravy, that kind of thing?'

'Depends on what you want. I seem to remember you telling me you wished your father had a bit more of a social life. Well, this is it.'

'I did, didn't I? And I meant it, too. But it's different,' said Primrose with the air of one making a momentous discovery, 'when it actually happens. I mean, I'm not used to it. Since Mum left, it's been just the two of us.'

'Yes, but that was never going to last, was it? You're beginning to lead a life of your own, aren't you? Or were you planning on staying at home for the next forty years or so, to look after your dear old Dad?' Maggie slipped a small tin, with the last of the cheese choux mixture blobbed on to it, in the oven and set the timer. 'Tasters,' she explained succinctly.

'Mmm,' said Primrose. 'But she's dull.'

'There's worse things than dull. Presumably your father doesn't find her so, and he's not stupid. Get to know her a bit. Isn't that what your dad does when he meets your friends?'

'Mmm,' said Primrose again. The doorbell rang. 'Shall I get that?' It was obviously a welcome distraction.

'No, I'll go, it'll be the next lot of people to see the house. Goodness, is it that late? We should have had lunch. Take the things out if the timer dings, will you? Unless you think they need another minute.'

The couple who were on the doorstep could scarcely have been more different from the earlier pair: They were Asian, he tall in a well-cut suit and she diminutive in a flowing sari. Maggie at once felt elephantine and dowdy next to her, but the doll-like visitor smiled up at her.

'Such an imposition, on a Sunday,' she apologised. 'I do hope we haven't ruined your day or spoiled your lunch.'

'Not at all,' said Maggie politely. 'Lunch isn't really on the menu today, as you might say.'

They laughed in what appeared to be genuine amusement and followed her round the sitting room, dining room and study, murmuring politely.

'Such lovely furniture,' said Mrs Chaudhari. 'Are they family pieces? They suit the rooms so well. I suppose you will be taking them to your next house?'

'As a matter of fact, no. We'll be selling most of them. And they're not family things, so I don't feel particularly sentimental about them. We shall be moving to somewhere smaller, so we won't have room for all this.'

'How very practical. In our culture we regard it as a step forward, spiritually, to move beyond the ties of physical possessions. Like your Saint Francis, perhaps?' The tall man smiled gently down at Maggie, and she saw in his face that while he might not as yet have progressed to this unworldly stage, it still exercised a powerful appeal.

'I'm not very saintly, I'm afraid,' she said cheerfully. 'We shan't be selling all this to give the money to the poor. Unless you think of banks as the poor, that is.'

'Who can plumb the depths of spiritual impoverishment?' he murmured, with a twinkle.

'Well, I am not ready to cast off my earthly shackles yet,' said his wife firmly. 'Now, the kitchen?'

Primrose was on the floor by her pasting table, with her mouth full. On the visitors' entrance she stood up quickly, chewing and swallowing.

'This is Primrose, who has come to visit for a few hours,' said Maggie quickly, in case Primrose should think of making a repeat performance of the morning's antics.

'Something smells good,' remarked Mr Chaudhari. 'I like to see a kitchen being used.'

'As long as someone else is using it,' said his wife, without rancour. 'Hello, Primrose. Sorry to disturb you.'

Primrose swallowed again. 'That's all right,' she said. 'I was just trying these, they're lovely. Would you like one? They're cheese,' she added, proffering the baking tin. A child of her time, she had only a sketchy knowledge of the Bible, but was fully aware of the dietary restrictions of different religions.

'Delicious,' pronounced Mrs Chaudhari. 'Did you make them?'

'Yes. Well, I helped. I'm really meant to be doing this.' Primrose gestured at her table. The sheet was looking crumpled from her different attempts, and the posies of evergreen had wilted.

'I wondered what it was. I suppose it isn't usually here?' Primrose explained. Mrs Chaudhari examined the table, her head on one side like a very alert bird.

'Yes, I see the problem,' she said. 'To hide the legs as completely as possible, without trailing on the ground. Rather like a sari, in fact. Now, if I were doing it, I think I would start *here* . . .' She swooped on the middle of the long side, pinched the fabric about a third of the way from the hem, and lifted it until it just cleared the ground. She looked round, and Primrose quickly passed a safety pin. 'Then, you see, you can do the corners, like *this* . . .' Once again the smooth, boneless stoop, another decisive pinch, and the second pin was stabbed in, level with the first. The white fabric between swagged in a graceful curve, and the point of the corner hung down so that it was just higher than the bottom of the swag. 'Now, the flowers.' The little bunches of greenery were fastened with a swift turn of the florist's wire that bound them. 'So, Ribbons, to hang down, you said? That will be good, a bit of colour, and of course there will be flowers.' She smiled brilliantly at Primrose.

'You must excuse my wife,' said Mr Chaudhari with the air of one who knows it will happen. 'She always knows best how things should be done.'

'Not at all. A suggestion, merely. When we have gone, Primrose can do it the way she wants.'

'No, it's just right, thank you.' Maggie thought how affronted the woman from the morning would have been to see Primrose now, politely offering the cheese choux again. She drifted momentarily into a happy little dream where the Chaudharis bought the house and the furniture too, so that there need be no auction to deal with, no standing to watch people bid, lot by lot, for the things which, though she could part with them with equanimity, had still been chosen with care and love.

At four o'clock Primrose's father and his friend came to collect her. Maggie invited them in for a cup of tea. She saw, with some amusement, that The Girlfriend, as her mind had all too easily dubbed her, was indeed nervous of Primrose. She saw also that

Primrose, by showing off her table and explaining exactly how the draping was done, was making a serious effort to please. But by the time they left, having finished the sample of cheese choux and also the little blinis that Maggie had made afterwards, none of them seemed to have relaxed much. Primrose turned, in the doorway, to wink at Maggie. She then looked a question, flicking her eyes at The Girlfriend, and Maggie nodded vigorously. Primrose gave a little shrug and pulled a face.

The five o'clock viewers arrived soon afterwards, but did not stay long. They were effusively complimentary, but hurried, and Maggie strongly suspected that they had already made up their minds against the house, and didn't know how to say so. She had discovered, when selling previous homes, that the people who assured you that they would ring the agent first thing in the morning to make an offer, and who loudly planned how to fit in their furniture, were the ones least likely to buy. She was still pinning her hopes on the Chaudharis.

Turner didn't get home until after seven o'clock. He smelled strongly of white spirit, and his clothes were spattered with oil and paint. He looked remarkably pleased with himself, and far more like the Turner of the past. Maggie told him about the various viewers, and he laughed at her impression of Primrose as a young offender. He did not, however, respond with a description of his day, and Maggie stubbornly refused to ask. She had a feeling that he wouldn't tell her even if she did, and was meanly unwilling to give him that satisfaction.

At the swimming pool the following morning Celia asked Maggie about transport.

'Have you had any brainwaves? I did try ringing a few local firms, but all their cars were booked up for months.'

'Turner's got some kind of ploy afoot, but he won't tell me about it. He was out all day yesterday, and came back covered in paint. Heaven knows what he's up to. Still, if the worst comes to the worst they can always go in ordinary cars – lots of people do.'

'What about your Range Rover? It's nice and big.'

'Gone, I'm afraid,' said Maggie without regret. 'Turner knew someone who'd buy it, so I've just got my little Morris. Don't look like that! I love the Morris, and I never really liked the Range Rover much. I always think they look silly unless you live on a grouse moor or something.'

'I don't know about the moor, but there's plenty of grousing going on round our way,' said Celia grimly. 'Mother-in-law's taken over the little sitting room downstairs, where the television is, as a sewing room. Says there isn't room in her bedroom, and she needs to be able to have everything set up all the time. She's bought one of those dummy things – you know, those awful headless figures you can fit things on – and everything's swathed in sheets, including the floor. No one's allowed in there, so I've had to move the little television into the kitchen, which means the boys are always in there when I'm trying to cook supper.'

'I can imagine the joy. How's the dress coming along?'

Celia smiled. 'I have to say it's going to be stunning. The Mugger may be an old battleaxe, but she certainly knows her stuff when it comes to dressmaking. By the way, she says Julie isn't up to your standard, but she admits she's "quite pleasant." ' Celia mimicked Mrs Draper's acid tones.

Maggie shivered. 'It is going to work out, isn't it, Celia?'

'The wedding? Of course it is. It's going to be wonderful, you wait and see.'

Maggie hoped that she was right. And if the wedding went off smoothly, perhaps things would work out for her as well? And Turner, of course, she added quickly.

Chapter Twenty

'Someone's made an offer on the house.'

Turner had waited until their supper was over before telling Maggie. They had been eating rather well recently – Maggie had been trying to clear out the freezer, so all sorts of goodies bought and put by for a special occasion had been brought out. They had just finished a bag of langoustines, and Maggie had taken the trouble to make proper Hollandaise sauce to go with them. She and Turner ate in the kitchen, with their fingers, sucking out tender bits of flesh from the claws and getting thoroughly fishy and sticky in the process.

Their conversation while they ate had been confined to appreciative murmurs about the food (Turner) and trivia about the day (Maggie). They had an unspoken agreement not to spoil a meal, if possible, with anything that might cause a problem. Wrapping the pile of shells and claws in newspaper and stacking the plates in the dishwasher, Maggie felt more pleased than sad. Turner was the one who was upset by the loss of the house.

'Which ones have made the offer?' Maggie asked now, casting her mind back over the couples she had shown round. 'Let me guess – the Chaudharis?'

'Yes, that's right. You thought they were keen, and they were. It's not a brilliant offer, though the agents think they can chisel a bit more out of them. The thing is, they've said they'd like to buy everything. All the furniture, take it as it stands apart from our personal stuff, of course. I told them what it was all valued at, and they made quite a reasonable offer on that. They'll sort out what they want to keep, get rid of the rest. They're coming from Australia, keeping their house there, so they've got nothing in the way of furniture at all. It's convenient for them, and equally so for us. We might make a bit more at auction, but auctions are chancy and we could easily make less, and then there's the auctioneer's cut. Not to mention the stress of it all.' Turner paused. He obviously needed feedback, some kind of reaction from Maggie.

'They were a nice couple. I'd like them to have the house.'

He gave her a baffled look. 'It doesn't really matter whether they're nice or not. We're not finding a good home for a kitten, we're selling our main asset.'

'We're selling our home.' The house she lived in had never been hugely important to Maggie, but still this one had welcomed and sheltered her, and she had cared for it, kept it clean and attractive. Maggie had never thought of any place as a refuge: neither a burrow nor a nest. Perhaps if she had had children, the memory of their babyhood and childhood, the images of their growing years, would have tied her to the house where they grew up. As it was, her refuge was in her own mind. She thought suddenly that she was more attached to the local swimming pool than she was to her house. If that should be closed down, for any reason, she would mourn for it with genuine feeling. Not because the building was special or unique in any way, but merely because of the associations, the friendships she had formed there, the way it had made her look at life differently.

'They haven't got anything to sell,' Turner continued, still mulling over the Chaudharis. 'That's a big bonus. With a house like this you could have a chain ten properties long, right back to some youngster buying a studio flat. And they're cash buyers – they've sold a chain of restaurants over in Oz, apparently. They want to move quickly, that's another bonus. I think we should go for it.'

Maggie was surprised that he seemed to need her approval. 'I'm sure you're right,' she said equably. 'It would be a relief not to have to auction the furniture and everything. How low was their offer?'

'Not insulting, but not great. I was hoping for more, but it's swings and roundabouts. A quick sale reduces the interest I have to pay on the loans.'

'And the agents think they can get it up a bit?'

'Well, they said they'd try.'

'Can't you speak to them yourself? They seemed very straight-forward people. I'd have thought they might prefer to deal directly with you.'

'You think so? My grandad would have said, I don't reckon to keep a dog and bark myself, but I suppose I could.'

'I think you should. After all, you're used to buying and selling land and property. It's not as if you haven't got any experience.'

'True. I'll get on to the agents in the morning, ask for their number.'

'No need. He gave me his card.' Maggie went to the little decorated tin shaped like a house where she kept things like odd stamps and business cards. 'There you are. You can ring him tonight, at home. Better, when he's with his wife. I got the impression that she has a good say in things. She's certainly not the meek Indian wife walking three paces behind her husband.'

Turner took the card. 'Why not?' he said. 'I'll go and do it now,' and he went to the study. It didn't occur to him to ask Maggie if she wanted to be there too, but she noticed that contrary to his usual habit he left both the doors open so that she could clearly hear his resonant voice. She knew, before he came back to tell her, that they had reached an agreement.

'Nice chap,' he said. 'Very reasonable. Says he can move as fast as we like – has a solicitor friend who can get things organised in a few weeks. Easy as that.'

'The bank will be pleased,' said Maggie, seeing that he was looking uncertain.

'Yes. Yes, that's true. Keep the bank happy.'

Maggie put the kettle on for coffee. Turner fetched the brandy, and poured himself a generous helping after Maggie had shaken her head in refusal. They were still in the kitchen – now that the Turner painting was no longer over the fireplace Turner preferred not to sit in the sitting room, and Maggie was quite happy not to have the extra work of clearing and re-laying the fire every day.

'If the sale goes through that quickly, where . . . what are your plans?' She had been determined not to ask, but it was ridiculous not to know.

'There's the flat above the office,' said Turner neutrally.

'But what about Arthur?' One of the first men ever to work for Turner, Arthur, had lived in that flat ever since Turner had first taken on the building. Now an old man, he was given the courtesy title of 'Caretaker', because after all his years of teaching Turner everything he knew about building, he was a kind of mascot to the firm.

'He's not really well enough to stay in the flat,' Turner told her. 'That last spell of bronchitis was bad, and I suspect he may have had a slight stroke without realising it. His memory's suddenly beginning to go, and he's not safe on his own any more. He nearly burned the whole place down the other day, leaving a pan on the cooker. You know I've had his name booked in at that Air Force place on the coast for some years. Thank God the money is put by safely for that – there should be enough to see him out. He doesn't like it, but he's accepted the idea and in a way I think he's quite looking forward to the company. The flat's not very big, but as a temporary measure . . .' He glanced at Maggie, gauging her response. She nodded.

'It's convenient. On the spot.'

Between them, like a wall of glass, was Maggie's money, her share of the value of the house that was hers absolutely. Not a huge sum, but certainly enough to buy a small house. She had several times offered it to Turner, but he had been resolute in refusing.

'By rights, half of what we get for the house should be yours, not just that smaller amount. It's bad enough that everything else has to go. I'm not leaving you with nothing, no security.'

Maggie knew that he was right. While she did not doubt his ability to bounce the business back into a healthy position, they were neither of them young and nothing was certain. Meanwhile, the flat was small, but it was also free and would provide a breathing space.

It was a pleasure, the following day, to be able to go out. Until then she had stayed in, in case anyone wanted to come and see the house, but the Chaudharis had freed her from all that. She went into the town; Stella had given her the sash from one of the little bridesmaids' dresses, and Maggie had promised Primrose that she would spend some of the twenty-pound note on buying matching ribbon to use in the decorations. Primrose had tried the local florists, but nobody had been able to give her the right colour.

After hunting for a parking space, Maggie went to the department store where she generally bought such things. There were racks of ribbon – plain and patterned, wire edged, silky, ribbed, velvet . . . the choice was endless, but none of the colours was remotely possible.

Coming empty-handed out of the store, Maggie stood on the pavement and wondered what to do. She could go to London, but it seemed a bit excessive, just for ribbon. Just then, an elderly woman shuffled by, clinging to a Zimmer frame. Although the day was warm and bright she was carefully wrapped up in a wool coat, with a knitted hat like a tea cosy and a matching scarf. An almost visible aroma of camphor followed her down the pavement, and Maggie felt her nose twitch and tickle. Does she like the smell, she wondered idly, or simply not notice it? And you'd think she'd be roasted, too. She was probably wearing a cardigan under that coat, and a nice warm vest next to her skin – one of those pink lock-knit ones . . . Of course!

She hurried off, searching for the little shop where she had bought her overall, so long ago it now seemed, to wear when cleaning Celia's house. For a few minutes she was confused about where it had been, and she hunted down several little side streets before she remembered which turning it was. The shop was still there – just. Every other window in the street was boarded up, and a large paper sign in the window announced, depressingly, *Closing Down Sale*. Maggie went in.

To her pleasure the elderly proprietor hunted through a stack of boxes and produced a roll of ribbon that was exactly what she was looking for.

'I'm sorry to see you're closing down,' she said, with sincerity.

'Well, this place has had its day, my dear. People don't knit or sew the way they used to. I shan't be sorry to see it go. So many of my old customers have died recently, it's been quite sad. One of them left me that little sewing table, with an inlaid top. Said she

228

had no one to leave it to, and she wanted me to have it.'

'How lovely. That will be a good memento of your time here.'

'Yes. I went to her funeral, it seemed only right. Such a big house she'd had – Victorian, but what a state it was in! She'd been on her own for so long, hadn't been able to manage the stairs, just lived in two downstairs rooms. Nothing had been done to it for years. One of the relatives said it was a miracle the place hadn't burned down, the wiring was that bad, only she wouldn't have workmen in the house, you see. Frightened of them. I saw the house in the paper last week. It's been on the market for months and they keep bringing the price down, but nobody will buy it. Pity, really.'

Maggie's response was automatic, the result of all the years of living with Turner.

'Really? Which agent?'

'I don't remember. I just recognised the picture, and it was on the front of the property section so it caught my eye. Wait a moment though, I've still got the paper somewhere.' She bustled through to the back and returned, paper in her hand. 'There you are, my dear, it's that one there. You can keep the paper, if you're interested.'

'Thank you. My husband's a builder, so you see . . .'

'He could do it up! And would you live there yourself?'

'Oh no, it would be just a business thing. Do it up and sell it on, he does it all the time. I'm surprised he hasn't spotted this one, actually, only he's had rather a lot on his plate recently, one way and another.' Goodness, Maggie thought, I'm beginning to talk in clichés, like her. I'd better be going.

'Well, it's better than letting it rot, I suppose. And maybe a nice family will buy it.' Maggie remembered Turner saying that selling a house wasn't like finding a home for a kitten, but she nodded and agreed. She took her roll of ribbon, neatly packaged in brown paper and tied up with twine that ended in a little loop for her finger. The elderly woman's hands moved fast, creasing the paper briskly, lapping the twine round the parcel and tying it just so, not too tightly, and all with hardly a glance to see what she was doing. Maggie was irresistibly reminded of her childhood, of shops which had been considered old-fashioned even then which had had tracks on the ceiling that carried money to a cashier in little suspended cylinders.

'How beautifully you do that,' she exclaimed, sidetracked once again.

'It's how we've always done it, and our customers seem to like it. Salesmen were always coming round wanting us to have those plastic carrier bags with our name on, but they were so dear it never seemed worth it. Can't teach an old dog new tricks, eh?' Maggie left the shop with her little parcel dangling elegantly from her finger, feeling like the lady in the old Mazawatee Tea advertisement.

When she was driving out of the town, and accident in the High Street diverted traffic down a parallel road. Sitting in her car, moving a few inches every five minutes, Maggie realised that she was in the road where the estate agents clustered together for company. Birds of a feather, she thought. Then: I must stop this. A familiar sign caught her eye – the logo at the top of the page where the house had been advertised. On impulse she signalled and pulled into a side turning, parked recklessly on a yellow line and went into the agent's office.

'It needs a lot of money spending on it.' The agent spoke with the resignation of one who has almost given up hope of selling this particular hot potato. 'Wiring, plumbing – all the pipes are the old lead ones, have to be changed. No heating. Woodworm. And worst of all, some nasty cracks.'

'Great selling job,' Maggie murmured. 'Subsidence? Underpinning?'

He grinned. 'So the surveyors say – all four of them. We've had four sales set up on this, and every time the buyers read the survey report, they panic and run for the hills. And they always behave as though it's our fault for not telling them, though after the first time we made sure we did. Oh, and the roof's not that great, either.'

'Lovely. Can I see it?'

He looked at her dubiously. 'It's quite a mess. Are you sure you want to?'

'I know a good builder,' said Maggie evasively. 'And yes, I'm sure. You've got the key, presumably?'

'You want to see it now?'

'If possible. I'm parked on a yellow line. Unless you're too busy.' Maggie glanced round the office, where three men and a young woman were trying to look occupied. He grinned again.

'I think I can find a window in my diary. You go back to the car, madam, while I get the key. The ladies in black are pretty active round here – you don't want to get a ticket. My car's round the corner, a red Escort, if you'd like to keep an eye out and follow me?'

Maggie did so – no parking ticket, to her relief – and within twenty minutes she was drawing up on a drive where a few bits of gravel could just be seen amidst a healthy crop of weeds. In front of her the young man was opening the front door by barging it with his shoulder in a matter-of-fact way that showed this was a regular occurrence. Maggie stood back and looked up at the house.

It stood foursquare in its plot, not beautiful in any way, but functional, with the simplicity of a child's drawing. It was faced with pebbledash – of all decorative finishes Maggie's least favourite

– that had once been painted cream but so long ago that the colour was now a dingy beige, enlivened by patches of green where long-blocked gutters had overflowed. There was a suspicious sag to the roof, and the window frames had rotted.

Inside was no better. The place smelled of damp, and a faint but lingering tinge of urine. Maggie followed the young man from room to room, saying nothing, her eyes checking for cracks and bulges, damp stains, things crooked or damaged. At the end she wrote a few notes on the copy of the details that she had been given.

'Do you want to see the garden?' Maggie looked out of the grimy window at the tangle of weeds and brambles.

'Not just now. I'm not really dressed for it.'

'It could be lovely,' he said, without much hope but as one in honour bound to be persuasive.

'Yes, it could,' she surprised him by agreeing. 'I'd like to walk round once more.'

Tactfully, the agent waited at the door as Maggie wandered from room to room. Dilapidated though it was, the house appealed to her. It seemed to her to be crying out to be used again. Wordlessly, the generously-sized rooms begged to be home, to shelter not just one old lady and a host of memories, but a family, a future.

'It's no good looking at me,' Maggie spoke to the house in her head. 'I'm not a family. I'm just me, and I'm not even sure who that is any more.' The house, stubbornly, continued to insist. Maggie, who had seen many wrecks worse than this one restored by Turner, could imagine only too clearly the transformation that could be achieved. Somehow, it did not have the empty, dead feeling that long-closed-up and neglected houses usually have. It was as if the ghostly presences, not of past occupants but those of the future, already hovered in the rooms and ran silently on the stairs, just waiting for Maggie to given them corporeal reality. Maggie shook her head, and went back to the agent, who hastily put out a cigarette and straightened his tie. Maggie smiled at him, and brushed a cobweb off his shoulders.

'I'll be in touch. Thank you for showing me.' He blushed sheepishly, which amused her. The door jammed when he tried to close it, as though the house was fighting not to be locked shut again. At the gate Maggie looked back, knowing that it was a mistake. The house, its eyes closed with dirt, nevertheless looked pleased with itself.Maggie turned her back firmly, and walked to her car.

When Maggie reached home she realised guiltily that she had no recollection at all of her journey. She assumed, since she had arrived safely, that with some part of her brain she had stopped and checked at crossroads and roundabouts, but if so it had been an automatic process. Equally absently she let herself into the empty house, and made a sandwich for her lunch. She had eaten more than half of it before she noticed that she had used lemon curd instead of mayonnaise on the grated cheese and salad of the filling. It wasn't too bad, so she finished it, and made herself a cup of instant coffee.

As she drank it, she glanced through the newspaper the woman in the shop had given her – a copy of the previous week's local paper. Maggie skimmed through reports of burglaries and lost cats, scarcely taking in what she was reading until she came across one article which she read several times before fetching the scissors and clipping it out. The last time she had used them, she realised, was to cut the ropes round Turner's wrists.

The small piece of newspaper was put carefully into the National Trust tin. Then, moving like a sleepwalker, she went to the telephone.

'Hello – Hardwick's? This is Mrs Whittington. I viewed one of your houses this morning. Yes, that one. I'd like to make an offer.'

Chapter Twenty-One

On the morning of the wedding, Maggie was awake at four. She had set her alarm for five, but had woken earlier in a panic of anxiety that the clock hadn't worked and she had overslept. Reassured by the complete darkness outside, she tried to go back to sleep, but couldn't even lie still, let alone close her eyes. In the end she slipped from the bed and went to the window, pulling the curtain aside to peer out. It was so black that she blinked her eyes to make sure they were really open. Nothing. No moonlight from what should have been the last quarter of the moon, and not a star in sight. She had to accept that it was cloudy. She had been obsessively studying weather forecasts for the past week, long before it was feasible to predict anything accurately.

They had started out on the previous Sunday with a fairly optimistic view of the next week from the farming programme. This, as the week progressed, had steadily worsened and the evening before had offered no better than cloudy, with showers that might turn to rain. And what was the difference, Maggie wondered? When did a shower start being rain? She had flicked from channel to channel hoping for something more encouraging, tried Ceefax, even telephoned the weather number, but all were equally, smugly, depressing.

The window was open a few inches. Maggie unlatched the stay and pushed it wider, thrusting her arm out into the blackness. The air felt cool and heavy, pressing on her hand with an almost tangible weight of water, but it wasn't raining. Or even showering.

'What's it doing?' The voice from the bed made her jump. She had thought he was still asleep.

'Cloudy. At least, no moon and no stars.'

'It'll clear.' Turner's optimism, in the face of the dismal forecasts and of the evidence of her own eyes, seemed almost manic. 'You'll see.'

Maggie bit back a cross answer. There must be no angry words today, nothing that might open the way for discord or bad luck. She felt as superstitious as any peasant of ancient times, fearing bad omens and jealous gods.

'I'll make some tea. And I think I'll get up. There's plenty to do, and I feel wide awake.'

Once downstairs she felt calmer. In the middle of the table were her lists. A list of things to do, of food to take, of other things to take. Maggie's life recently had seemed to be run on endless lists, so that on waking in the morning her instinct was to put a tick against 'Have a night's sleep'. In the larder the trays of unfrozen food stood gleaming in their virginal clingfilm, and in the big freezer were more trays, layer upon layer of them, containing pizzas, blinis, savoury tartlets, the choux pastry with which Primrose had helped. In the cool of the utility room Maggie's largest roasting tin held the little posies of flowers and leaves for the tables, up to their necks in water and awaiting only the finishing ribbons. Maggie put the kettle on, and went through her lists once again.

Everything was as ready as it could be. Celia had spent the two previous evenings (and part of the nights) doing the flowers for church and reception. In Maggie's garden, and Celia's own, trees and shrubs had been cut and cut again.

'Do them good,' said Celia firmly. 'Nothing like a bit of pruning,' as she ruthlessly sawed small branches from a spreading copper beech. She had stood them in warm water for two days until the sharp buds unfurled into tender pink leaves. Now they were in the barrels that Primrose had painted, standing like trees on either side of the archway behind where the cake would be put. The archway itself was twined with variegated ivy and wild clematis, the flowers like wax against the shining leaves, admiring their own reflections in the mirror foil.

The eastern sky was just tinged with light as Maggie drove to the farm, the first of two journeys. As she carried the tin of posies through to the yard she heard the clatter of hoofs as Gordon finished the milking and led the cow out to pasture. A little while later he came back, carrying a covered bucket of milk to the dairy. He greeted Maggie with a shy smile.

'Morning, Gordon,' she said. 'Sorry I'm so early. I couldn't sleep, so I thought I'd start bringing things over.'

'Dawn's been up for a while, too. Want a hand?'

'No, you're busy. I'll put these down and go home for the next lot. Oh Gordon, such a shame about the weather. You don't think it will clear, do you?' Maggie retained the towndweller's belief in an inbred ability of a farmer to prophesy the weather. Gordon squinted at the sky.

'Forecast said showers,' he said dubiously. 'You going to set up those tables outside?'

'I think so. We've got enough to spare them, even if they get soaked and have to be taken down.' She hurried through to the kitchen, where Dawn greeted her with a harassed smile.

234

'Thank goodness you're here! Not that there's any panic, really, just that I feel better when there's two of us. I've got the stand up in the utility area.' With some of the old lumber from the barn, Gordon had built a kind of stacking unit, with flat, wide shelves to take the trays of food which, when no longer frozen, could not go one on top of the other. Maggie slotted in the ones she was carrying, and Dawn hurried out to the car to get some more.

By twelve o'clock, everything was as ready as it was possible to be. The tables, with their sheets artfully pinned and decked with posies by Primrose and Stephanie, stood dotted round the yard with chairs clustered nearby. The cake, iced to match the fabric of the dress, stood reflected before the flowered arch of the mirror, and nobody could possibly tell, Maggie thought, that the top two layers were really blocks of expanded polystyrene, iced to match the rest and topped with a silver vase of flowers. The barn smelled of flowers, the rich dusty scent of the lilies vying with the sweetness of lily of the valley which grew so plentifully in Maggie's garden.

Maggie took one last look around before she went home to change. At the last minute it had occurred to her that it was rather risky leaving everything open and laid out while they were all at church, and Turner had suggested bringing Arthur over to keep an eye on things. The old man, in a state of high delight, was seated in a chair in the corner of the barn with Turner's mobile telephone, ready to call for help should any passing vandal decide to desecrate the cake.

Back at home, Maggie had a quick shower and changed. She was thankful that she had an outfit that was eminently suitable – one she had bought for the opening of the hotel, and scarcely worn since. She wondered fleetingly whether it was an ill omen, seeing what had become of the hotel, but knew this was silly. There is nothing unlucky, she told herself, about a silk dress and jacket from Cerruti.

She stood in front of the mirror seeing, not herself in the Cerruti dress and the hat from Dickins & Jones, but the younger Maggie dressed for her own wedding.

If Maggie's mother had lived to see her only child married, Maggie had no doubt that she would have had the full-blown church affair, white frock and veil, bridesmaids, flowers, Mendelssohn's March, speeches and all. Not that her mother was a great believer – she went to church for Christmas, Easter and Harvest Festival because that was the Thing to Do. A white wedding was also, in her book, What One Did, and without joy or excitement she would have organised the entire performance.

Thankful not to have had to endure being transformed into a Wedding Baked Meat and sacrificed on the altar of the neighbours' opinion, Maggie had opted instead for a quiet Register Office. The suit she had bought – from an Oxford Street chain store and the most expensive she had ever owned – had been a similar colour to this, a deep peacock blue. Looking back at the young woman Maggie could scarcely believe was her, she marvelled at the certainty she had felt then. Where had it all gone, that calm belief in the future? When had it become the shivering uncertainty she felt now? It had happened so gradually that she hadn't become aware of it until recently.

I should have been terrified, Maggie thought, and yet I didn't have any of those pre-wedding nerves the magazines go on about. Now I'm terrified for a girl I scarcely know. If she were my daughter, would I feel like this? Worse? Huh – if I were any worse, they'd be carting me off in a straitjacket! Or is it *me* I'm worried about? That would be more logical, under the circumstances, but I just don't seem to care very much about my own future. Things will work out, or not, and I'll do my best but I shan't lose any sleep over it.

She adjusted the hat to a more becoming angle, and looked round for her handbag, which contained money, lipstick, compact, handkerchief, and a packet of confetti. Pull yourself together, Margaret, she said in the tone of a long-dead headmistress. Maggie took a deep breath and held it, to calm the feeling of having a stomach full of tadpoles, then went downstairs.

Turner was nowhere to be seen, but on checking in the wardrobe Maggie concluded that he must already be in his morning suit. He had told her he would meet her at the church, and Maggie had been too busy to question him. From time to time she had wondered about his mysterious car, or whatever it was, that was to carry Stella to the church and back, but he never offered any hints and Maggie was too stubborn to ask. She assumed that he had now gone to oversee it.

When she reached the church, Turner was waiting for her at the door. She thought, as she always did, how very becoming formal attire was on men. Turner's suit, made for him some years ago, still fitted admirably. He carried the office camera, with its wide-angle lens, which he used for taking publicity shots of buildings.

'You look nice. Everything all right?' he asked.

'I think so.' Maggie couldn't bring herself to say an outright yes. 'I just hope Arthur doesn't have to repel boarders, he's very wobbly.'

'He'll be fine. Now, let's go in and bag our seats, and then I want you to come back outside until Stella arrives.' He was fizzing with suppressed excitement. Maggie followed him into the church, where the scent of the flowers was even stronger than in the barn. She thought how good the dark red lilies looked against the creamy white roses and carnations, all set off by the foliage from her garden and Celia's. The church was already half-full.

236

Celia saw her come in, and waved. 'I've kept you two seats with us,' she said. 'How smart you look!'

'So do you – and the flowers are lovely. Were you up all night?'

'Just about, but I'm on such a high it hasn't hit me yet. I'll be a monster tomorrow. Speaking of monsters . . . did you see the Mugger anywhere? Phil took her to Stella's, some superstition about putting the last stitch into the dress, and he's supposed to be bringing her on here. I've never seen her in such a cheery mood since the day of my father-in-law's funeral. She even said the boys were looking smart. They were horrified, nearly changed out of their good clothes there and then.'

'Where are they?'

'Off with Primrose. She's got some kind of plan for something to do with when they come out of church. Explosive confetti bombs, I expect. Still, it's better than having them fidgeting in here for too long.'

'Turner wants me to wait outside for a bit. I'll check on them, if you like.'

They struggled back through throngs of arriving guests. Once outside the door again Maggie looked round for Primrose, and spotted her just appearing round the corner of the building, followed by Stephanie, the twins, Dez, and Stephanie's younger brothers. They looked alarmingly cheerful, and Maggie went to meet them.

'It's all right,' said Primrose before she could speak. 'We haven't been desecrating anything. And we're not going to do anything dreadful.'

'I wish you wouldn't mindread, it's quite unnerving,' said Maggie plaintively, and Primrose grinned. 'The twins' mum thought you might have exploding confetti bombs, or something.'

'Never thought of that,' said one of the twins regretfully. 'Still, this is going to be good.'

'Primrose?'

'Don't *worry*. I wouldn't do anything to spoil Stella's wedding, would I? It's just an idea we had, and it's going to be really good – you'll love it, I promise. We've just been rehearsing it. I mean, I'll tell you about it if you really want, but it'll spoil the surprise.' The boys and Stephanie looked downcast, sure that Maggie would insist on knowing, but Maggie trusted Primrose.

'That's all right, I'll wait and be astonished. Are you going in now?'

'Yes, but we're going to sit at the back so we can get out quickly. Will you explain to the twins' mum? She won't mind, will she, them not sitting with her, I mean?'

'I should think she'll bear it manfully. See you later, then.' Maggie and Turner watched them go into the church. The twins looked particularly angelic, their hair slicked back with water and their faces shining above white shirt collars and school ties. Even Dez looked clean and relatively respectable.

'What do you think they're up to?' Turner was amused.

'Heaven only knows. Strewing their path with swimming towels, or making an arch of floats for them to walk under? I honestly don't think Primrose and Steph would do anything dreadful, especially Primrose. Stella's her heroine since she helped her with her swimming. Can we go in yet? It's nearly time, and everyone else is inside.'

'Just another few minutes. I want you to see . . . ah, here they come.'

There was a stir among the bridesmaids, waiting in the porch and fussing with their dresses. Listening for the sound of an engine, Maggie was puzzled by the quiet of the seemingly empty road, broken only by a sound that carried her back to this morning, hearing Gordon leading the cow back to the field.

'Oh, Turner! I don't believe it!'

'Don't tell me you don't like it, after all. I thought it was just the ticket.'

'It is! It's wonderful! I never thought . . .' The bridesmaids, shrieking, were running down to the lychgate in a rustle of taffeta petticoats, their voices calling out high and shrill with excitement. Reaching the gate they hung back, fearful of the great hooves of the two shirehorses that were harnessed to what looked like an old-fashioned farm wagon. The wagon had been newly painted in deep maroon, toning with the colour of the dresses but darker and richer, the wheels picked out with cream and the shallow sides decked with flowers and ribbons which twined down the shafts and garlanded the horses. Their manes and tails had been plaited with red and cream ribbons, and a cockade of the same ribbons stood in the hat of the elderly driver, who drew the cart to a halt just by the lychgate.

Stella and her father sat high above them. Against the dark background Stella's dress gleamed like ivory. Her father beside her, resplendent in a morning suit and top hat, beamed proudly down at her. Beside Maggie, Turner was clicking away with the camera, recording the scene. As the driver climbed down and produced a set of steps, painted maroon to match, he moved to get pictures of Stella climbing down into the cluster of bridesmaids, then he turned and came back to Maggie.

'It's wonderful, Turner, thank you. Wherever did you find it?'

'The cart was hidden away in one of Gordon's sheds. He'd bought it years ago, but never used it because it wasn't practical to keep a workhorse on such a small acreage. I painted it up, scoured the countryside for horses – that was the difficult bit; you've no idea how much persuading and bullying I had to do to get the owners to lend me these two. They're from that farm that's turned itself into a kind of museum showplace; they actually use them for ploughing and so on and they never normally hire them out. Worth it, though, wasn't it?'

'Yes. More than worth it. It's the most romantic thing I've ever seen.'

Turner looked at her. 'It was for you,' he said simply. 'We didn't have anything like that, when we were married. Do you wish we did?'

'It wasn't what we wanted, at the time.'

'No, but now? Maggie, I realise this isn't the moment, but I must know. Is there still a place in our lives for this?'

'For a horse and cart?' Maggie's voice was trembling.

'For romantic gestures.' Turner was not going to let her escape so easily.

'I don't know, Turner. I just don't know. I think I would like there to be. Is that enough?'

He studied her face before answering.

'More than enough.' She saw that he was moved, that his eyes were glassy with tears. Her throat tightened in response, and she spoke huskily.

'Look, they're about to go into the church. We'd better get inside and find our seats.' He took her hand and gripped it hard. They hurried down the aisle, faces turning to watch them, a little buzz of expectation running through the congregation.

'Ssh! Here they come!'

Tall though Stella was, her father overtopped her by a head. They paused in the doorway for a moment. Maggie, looking round, saw them through a shimmering haze of tears. Mrs Draper had surpassed herself with the Indian silk. The dress had all the stunning simplicity of inspired cutting, flowing down in a smooth line from lowered shoulders and fanning out to a short train. By her own choice Stella wore no veil and her dark hair was crowned with a wreath of fresh flowers to match her bouquet.

Maggie turned back to look at her order of service (designed by a calligraphy class at the College and printed by the printing club). Stella reached Colin's side, and the service began. Maggie tried to concentrate, but only the occasional word penetrated her mind. The service, so familiar and yet so endlessly powerful, was almost painful to listen to. Stella and Colin had chosen to have the old service and the rolling phrases coiled into her thoughts like roots splitting concrete. Turner's hand reached for hers again, held it warmly. Maggie, her defences annihilated, allowed herself to think of the future she had tentatively planned. She saw the house, saw it repaired and made into a home, a real home that would be a refuge and a haven.

At the end of the service a different door was opened for the congregation so that the bridal party could pose for photographs outside the porch. Turner nudged Maggie.

'Come on,' he muttered. 'I want to see what those kids are up to, don't you?'

'Do you mind if we carry on, Celia?' Mrs Draper, who was sandwiched between Celia and Phil, had smart shoes on and could not be hurried.

'No, you go, I can't bear to look. Stop them if it's too dreadful.'

To Maggie's relief, since she doubted her power to stop Primrose from doing anything she had really set her heart on, there was no need to step in. The eight children had arranged themselves on either side of the porch like a miniature guard of honour. They carried, not upraised swords, but what looked like brightly coloured plastic guns that they were pumping vigorously. From the nozzle of each issued a stream of bubbles that shot upwards to form what was almost an archway before drifting off on the light breeze. At that moment, as the bells rang and the guests exclaimed and chattered, the sun came out and all the bubbles turned iridescent, catching the light and picking up colours from the bright clothes. Turner had his camera out, and was edging through the crowd. Because the camera was large and expensive people gave way to him, thinking he was some kind of official photographer. In no time he was organising them, and Maggie could hear his voice: 'And now one with just the bride's family . . . just close in a little – lovely . . . hold your flowers up, bridesmaids . . . that's right, hold that . . . perfect! Now with the groom's family . . .'

'Good grief!' Celia, reaching Maggie, was stunned. 'What will they think of next? I hope it doesn't do any damage.'

'I shouldn't think so, and it looks wonderful. I expect the vicar will prefer it to confetti; lots of churches don't allow that any more, though I can't see that it's really messy. I think it's rather inspired. Water, and all that.'

Turner's decorated cart was waiting at the lychgate, the patient horses receiving much attention from all the children present. Maggie saw Turner with his camera, getting ready to take pictures of Stella and Colin sitting in his fantasy conveyance. She grabbed his sleeve as he passed.

'I think I ought to get back to the farm. I want to put a few things in the oven that need heating. I'll catch a lift with Dawn and Gordon – you come on when you're ready, okay?'

He gave her a searching look, smiled and nodded, his eyes returning to the tableau of bride and groom.

'Fine. I'll see you there.'

★ ★ ★

The party was in full swing. The bubble blowers, in between recreating their triumph at the church with refills of washingup liquid, were assiduously passing the food round. Primrose insisted that she had proprietorial rights over the cheese choux – no one else was allowed to offer them, and woe betide any guest who refused to taste one. The sun shone from a sky that had cleared to just a few fluffy clouds, as decorative as the lambs below the apple trees. Their dams had all been decked with the last pieces of the ribbon tied round their necks in flouncy bows, but attempts to decorate the lambs had reluctantly been abandoned; they were too difficult to catch, for one thing, and if one did succeed in tying a ribbon on it was promptly nibbled off again.

Maggie stood at the bottom of the courtyard, her back to the low wall. Behind her the lambs, tired with play, had flopped down together in a patch of sunshine. Their dams, nearby, chewed thoughtfully on their cuds. In their ribbons, draggled but still rakeish, they resembled elderly gum-chewing tourists decked out for a spree, exhausted and somnolent with sightseeing. Maggie sipped her champagne, slightly wishing she could snuggle down against a nice soft sheep, and watched the shifting patterns of people; groups collecting and splitting, reforming anew. Stella's family, tall and good-looking as one might have expected, stood out like exotic birds. Her parents had thanked Maggie several times.

'So much better than the hotel – we thought that was very dull. Don't tell them that. But at home, in Trinidad, all our celebrations are very *colourful*. We were so afraid it would be all stiff, formal. But this – outside, the animals . . . the flowers . . . the bubbles . . .' Stella's mother described swirling motions in the air with her hands, somehow indicating pleasure. 'So joyful!'

'I'm so glad,' said Maggie simply. 'She's a lovely girl. She deserves the best.'

'She's a good girl,' was the judicious maternal response. 'But she tells me all this is because you have, your husband has, a problem with his work. So sad, so very sorry, such difficult times. But you have made the proverbial silver lining!'

Stella drifted through the throng to join them. 'You two look as though you're hatching a plot down here.'

'I am just thanking Mrs Whittington for all this, as you should be doing.'

'Maggie knows, don't you, Maggie?'

'Yes, of course. And please do call me Maggie, not Mrs Whittington! Really, we've all had so much fun, there's no need of more thanks. And it was something I *had* to do.'

Stella's mother nodded. 'I know. To make the balance.'

'Yes.' Maggie was grateful to be understood. 'Yes, exactly that.'

'And now, you move on.' There was only a delicate hint of a question.

'I have some plans. Not very definite ones, perhaps not even very sensible. I haven't discussed them with . . . anyone . . . yet.'

The older woman nodded. 'If it is what you want, I think you are one of the people who can make things happen.'

'I've never thought of myself like that.'

Stella's mother gripped Maggie's arm. Her hand was strong and warm and she looked earnestly into Maggie's eyes.

'You can do it,' she said. 'Trust me, I'm a doctor.' She and Stella burst out laughing at what was obviously a family joke.

'She really is,' said Stella. 'Not a medical one, though. But you can believe her,' she added more seriously. 'She doesn't often say things like that, but she's always right about people. Always.' Maggie, still in her superstitious mode, was encouraged.

They drifted off. Dez, a bottle of champagne in one hand and a tray of blinis in the other, approached her purposefully.

'Drink? One of these whatevers?'

Maggie eyed him. She hoped he hadn't been drinking what he was offering round. He looked relaxed – was that a good sign, or not?

'No, thank you, to both. Champagne is not my cup of tea, and to be honest I'm sick of the sight of most of this food. I seem to have done nothing but cook it, and freeze it, and think about it, for weeks.'

He put the tray down on the wall, freeing his hand to eat a blini.

'Good,' he said, slightly muffled. 'Fishy, but good. Never had smoked salmon before, thought I'd better try it.'

Maggie was impressed. 'That's good. Most people don't like trying new food. What do you usually eat? What do you like best?'

'Dunno. The normal stuff – pizza, burgers, chips.'

'Don't you ever get to cook for yourselves?' Maggie wanted to ask what they got at the Home, but didn't know how to.

'Yeah, but it's just stuff like baked beans, bacon and eggs. Spaghetti, once. That was okay.'

Maggie, realising that this would be true in many families, not just children's homes, still thought it sad.

'Primrose said she wanted me to teach her to cook,' she said casually. 'Want to join in, or is cooking too girly?'

He took up the challenge. 'Best cooks are men,' he said. 'They say,' he added disarmingly. 'I dunno. I might.' He ate another blini, picked up the tray and wandered off.

'Maggie! Are you all right?'

Maggie, lost in thought, hadn't noticed Celia's approach.

'Yes, fine. Just taking a break, that's all. It's rather fun just watching everyone. It's going well, isn't it?'

'Brilliantly, I'd say. All I hope is that none of the kids gets drunk, and that the bubble guns don't get too out of hand. Luckily they're running short of detergent, and Dawn's hidden the rest of hers away.'

'It was a lovely idea, though. So pretty, when the sun caught them! I hope Turner's photos come out. He's the nearest thing to an official photographer we've got.'

'Well, he's certainly taken plenty. He seems to pop up everywhere, clicking away. The cart was inspired, too. He's gone to a lot of trouble, hasn't he?'

'Yes.' Even with Celia, Maggie couldn't discuss what was happening between her and Turner. Partly because, she realised, she didn't really know herself. There had been many times, in the past few weeks, when she had thought that what she really wanted to be was just herself, just Maggie. Whoever that might be. Not just half – and the less important one – of a couple.

'Oh Lord,' Celia groaned. 'I must dash. The twins seem to be battling with the bridesmaids.' Fond of Celia though she was, Maggie was relieved to see her go.

The speeches were mercifully short and the cake was cut without anybody noticing that the top two layers were fakes. At five o'clock Maggie and Dawn were hailed with acclaim when they brought out trays of coffee and tea. Most of the adult guests were glad, by that stage, to sit down and all the children, including the brides-maids, had gone to watch Gordon milk the cow.

By seven o'clock, people were starting to leave. Stella and Colin, in an ordinary car and changed into everyday clothes, drove away in a shower of rice, confetti and good wishes, and a final burst of bubbles – Dawn had been persuaded to donate some of the hidden washing-up liquid. After that the families with young children loaded them, protesting, into cars. Stella's family left to return to London, where they had a family gathering for all the relatives who had come over from Trinidad. They were pressing in their invitation for Maggie and Turner to join them, but Maggie pleaded exhaustion, which was true, and promised to visit them soon.

At last only the original organisers were left.

'I'm going home to change,' said Celia, surveying the debris. 'No good clearing up in best clothes, and these shoes are killing me. They felt fine in the shop, but now they feel about two sizes too small.'

'Good idea. I'll do the same.' Maggie looked round for Turner. He nodded. 'I'll bring some more washing-up liquid. To be used,' she said firmly, 'for washing up.'

Chapter Twenty-Two

T he washing up, even with so many helpers, took for ever. The kitchen was too small for more than three to work comfortably together, and the hot water began to run tepid so that they had to heat kettles. In spite of the extra tea towels that Maggie had brought, every cloth soon seemed to be saturated, and by the time all the glasses were washed and dried – only two broken, to everyone's amazement – and fitted into their boxes, they all felt they never wanted to wash or even see another one.

Finally, the people whom Maggie thought of as the Early Birds group sat, or sprawled, on chairs or sheeted bales in the barn. Most of the adults had, like Maggie, slipped home to change out of wedding clothes and into something more suitable for clearing and washing up. The few remaining items of food were piled onto two large dishes from which people helped themselves, while a generous supply of drinks stood where the cake had once been, reflected raffishly in the flower-framed mirror.

The Gossips, Brenda and Iris, sat with their heads close together, engrossed in a low-toned conversation: what *did* they find to keep talking about, Maggie wondered? Their husbands, equally friendly, were sitting on the bales chatting about sport. Gordon was perched on one of the hard wooden chairs borrowed from the village hall, the backs of which seemed expressly designed to catch either the spine or the shoulder blades, according to one's posture. Dawn, on the other hand, was in a garden chair, several of which had been brought over by Maggie and Celia. Primrose's father had carried it for her, and put one for himself next to Dawn. She was quiet, but more relaxed than Maggie had ever seen her outside the swimming pool. Mrs Draper, in an upright garden chair, sat near her.

Celia and Phil shared a bale, as did Julie and Tom. Their collection of male offspring had joined forces and were out in the fields, fighting some kind of complicated battle with the bubble guns. Julie, with Dawn's permission, had given them the rest of the washing-up liquid.

'At the moment, I intend never to wash up again. Just don't disturb any of the animals, and don't squirt it into each other's

245

faces.' The sound of their voices, calling and shouting, was distant enough to make no more than a pleasant background to the rural silence.

Primrose, Stephanie and Dez, feeling that to join in the younger boys' games was beneath their dignity, were sprawled on a heap of straw – two of the bales had burst apart while they were moving them, and if Maggie suspected that the baler twine had been surreptitiously cut, she said nothing. They had worked as hard as anyone, and deserved the chance to relax in their own way.

Still full of energy, Turner photographed the group. They jumped as the flash went off.

'Not more photos,' complained Celia lazily. 'Haven't you taken enough yet, Turner?'

'Just to complete the set,' he explained. 'This is all part of it. A record of the day.'

'I don't think any of us is likely to forget it in a hurry,' Julie pointed out.

Maggie sat in another of her own garden chairs, part of the group but slightly withdrawn, not close to any one member. She felt that she was glad to be with them, that she was fond of them all, but that she needed to separate herself slightly from them. The future, that she had tried so hard to ignore, was now taking on substance and reality. No longer was it hidden behind the mountain ranges of The Wedding.

Where they sat, facing due west, they could see the full glory of the setting sun. The clouds, miraculously, had cleared from the sky for the whole afternoon, and only a distant bank of them stood on the horizon, a symmetrical mass of rounded forms, taller in the middle and dwindling to the sides. The sun was directly behind them, rimming the top edges with a blinding ribbon of yellow light and sending beams, like the idealised gleams rising from the head of a saint in an Old Master, up through a sky that shaded through palest lemon to a limpid blue.

'That,' said Philip idly, taking a healthy mouthful from a tankard of beer, 'is not a real sunset. It is a stage set. Probably from one of the more florid operas. Or an illustration from a children's Bible. Any minute now, Elijah is going to appear in a burning chariot, or the Angel Gabriel, or Jesus in a white nightie with a nice neat beard and a lamb.'

'Moses, with tablets,' suggested Dawn. 'I always used to think they were like the tablets people took for headaches, and I used to wonder how they got all that writing on them.'

'Too perfect to be real,' said Primrose. 'But it is real. Like today. I never thought it could go as well as this, but it was even better.'

The twins, darting in to collect a handful of pizza – how did they manage to keep eating? – put in their two penn'orth.

'Things can't be better than they actually are,' stated Ed – or was it Will? 'A thing is what it is, so it can't be more than that.'

'That's what you think,' Dez retorted, with the authority of his extra years.

'Well, squits to you,' said Will – or Ed – and retreated with strategic speed as Dez looked as though he might come after them.

'Stella said it was far better than it would have been at the hotel,' Dawn told them all. 'I think she really meant it.'

'Of course she did,' said Mrs Draper stoutly. 'The hotel would have done it very well, I expect, but it would have been just like every other wedding. This was unique. Unique!' There was a murmur of agreement.

'Funny that it's all over,' said Primrose. 'It's been manic, but I'll miss it.'

'We all will. We'll have to find new projects,' said Celia. All the adolescents groaned at this word. 'Well, not projects like school, but something to look forward to.' There was a silence, while they thought this over.

'I'm going to look for a working horse to buy.' Unusually, it was Gordon who spoke up first. His eyes were fixed dreamily on the sunset, and Maggie knew that he saw, superimposed in silhouette against the dramatic sky, a lone ploughman walking his plough behind the solid bulk of his horse.

'Great,' said Tom. 'Great'. His voice reverberated with satisfaction: there was no need for more words.

'You know,' said Julie, 'you could rent out that cart, now it's painted up. There was a guy from the local paper at the church this afternoon, taking pictures. I bet that'll be in the *Gazette* next week, and you'll be inundated. Even better if you had your own horse.'

'Someone asked me this afternoon, whether we would let other people use this place for parties. Rent it out, I mean.' Dawn spoke tentatively. 'I said I didn't know; it would depend on the parties. I mean, we couldn't really do the food, or the drink – well, we'd have to have a licence – but if people wanted to bring their own . . . It's a thought.'

'I don't know.' Gordon wasn't taken with the idea. 'Upset the animals. Fires . . . lucky hardly anyone smoked today. I wonder how much they'd pay?'

'Quite a bit, for something as unusual as this.' Turner, ex-hotel owner, spoke with authority. 'You'd need to check with the authorities, have a fire certificate, that kind of thing. I can put you in touch, if you like.'

Gordon grunted. He doesn't really fancy the idea, Maggie thought, but workhorses are expensive . . .

Mrs Draper shifted in her chair. 'My flat will be ready soon,' she said. 'I'll be going back to Spain.' Maggie was careful not to catch

Celia's eye. There was a slightly uncomfortable pause. People felt they should perhaps say 'Oh, what a pity', but nobody felt able to risk it. Primrose filled the breach with unconscious tact.

'I'm doing GCSE Spanish as one of my options,' she said. 'Perhaps I'll come and visit you.'

'I'd like that,' said Mrs Draper. She sounded startled, perhaps by Primrose or, more probably, by her own willingness to house a guest. 'Yes, that would be all right. And if you bring some fabric, I could make you something. I was thinking, I might consider doing a bit of dressmaking, just for friends. No alterations, of course. Just new garments.'

They all nodded, acknowledging the appropriateness. Maggie thought that when word got round, Mrs Draper would find herself popular as never before. Who knew, she might even welcome her son's family for a visit, one day?

'I'm going to join the swimming club,' Dawn announced with unusual firmness.

'Yeah,' said Dez. 'Thought I might, too. What about you, er, Primrose?'

'Good idea,' supported Primrose. 'We could all go together. Why don't you come, Dad?'

Maggie buried her nose in her glass to stifle a giggle. Primrose had confided to her, while they were setting up the tables, that the Sunday lunch with The Girlfriend had not been a success, and had not been repeated.

'Dad hasn't seen her since,' Primrose had said with some satisfaction. 'Just as well. She really was terminally wet. And the roast wasn't as good as Dad can do, even. I bet Dawn could cook a mean roast.'

'Dawn?' Maggie had been surprised.

'Why not? She's not that old, and I really like her. I think she'd be very suitable. And haven't you noticed, when we're all together, Dad's always talking to her?'

'I've heard of parents arranging their children's marriages, but not the other way round. I don't think you should interfere, Primrose.'

'I'm not interfering. I'm just being helpful.'

'Heaven preserve us. Well, just don't be too obvious.'

'Me? Subtlety is my middle name.'

Now, Maggie didn't dare look at Primrose's father. It was true that he was sitting next to Dawn – could anything come of that? And if so, would Dawn move out or would he and Primrose come and live at the farm? They could very well convert part of the barn, enlarge the house. Maggie gave herself a shake. Thinking of conversions, though . . .

'I've got a plan, too,' she said, then stopped. Was this the right moment? There was never going to be an easy time to do this. Perhaps better now, with everyone there.

'You're going to set up a business arranging weddings?' Celia suggested.

'Home helps,' said Mrs Draper decisively.

Turner said nothing, but she could feel his tension. She should, she supposed, have told him about it before. She took a calming breath.

'I'm going to buy a Victorian house, a real wreck. Do it up.' She saw Turner nodding. This was the kind of thing he knew all about.

'Something to sell on?' That was Phil, the practical man.

'No. I'm going to live there. Camp out, to start with. It really is a wreck – no power, not even a proper water supply, though I believe there's a well in the garden.'

'Cool! Can we come?' Ed – or was it Will? They popped up like jack-in-the-boxes.

'We could help.' Dez shuffled his feet, glancing sideways at the twins and then at Maggie.

'Thank you,' she said with grave courtesy. 'I shall need all the help I can get, as long as you don't mind camping.'

'Mind!' Obviously they could not imagine how anyone could object to such a thing.

'And then what? When it's done up?' Julie, who probably knew Maggie better than any of them except Turner, saw that there was more to it than just doing up a house.

'And then,' Maggie didn't look at Turner, 'then, I thought I'd like to use it. The house, I mean. There was a bit in the local paper, a scheme to find homes for youngsters who were too old to be in care, but not ready to live by themselves. A sort of cross between a landlady and a foster-parent. And I thought, why not? Be a bit of use in the world.'

She said it lightly, jokingly. She wondered whether anyone had noticed that there was no mention of Turner in all of this. Carefully, she turned her head and met his eyes. She tried, in her look, to express what she had not been able to say to him. That this was what she wanted to do, intended to do. That she was not excluding him, but that if he chose to exclude himself she would go ahead anyway. That she was not trying to fill a space in her life, that she did not feel the need to mother other people's children, merely that she wanted to make something positive before it was too late.

'You could foster, too. We could,' he said neutrally, a tentative offering.

'Oh, yes!' Primrose, leaping in. Primrose being helpful. 'Yes, you could, you could foster—' Maggie broke in quickly, before she could go any further and mention Dez.

'I don't know about fostering. I'm not sure I know enough about bringing up children.' She glared at Primrose, who subsided.

'I just thought . . .' she muttered.

'I think you'd be a wonderful foster-mother,' said Julie loyally. 'If you wanted to.'

'Yeah,' growled Dez, staring at the ground. He cleared his throat. 'Yeah. If you wanted to.'

'I might, at that.'

Might I? she wondered. He's what – thirteen? Fourteen? Just hitting the most difficult age of all. Could I cope? Might I make things worse? What do I know about teenage boys except that they're likely to be trouble?

Once again she looked at Turner. He saw the panic in her face, and the warmth in his eyes told her that his smile was not meant to mock her. He would do it, she thought. I never thought he would, but he'd take it on, give it his best. If I want him to. And do I?

That was the question. In her mind, she had seen herself doing this alone. Even now, the idea of camping out by herself in the ruined house was powerfully appealing. That, she thought, I will do. And he can take on the repairs, so he'll see the house, know what it's like, and then, perhaps . . . But it will be on my terms, this time. And I will not, under any circumstances, be Margot. Never again.

She stood up, stretched. Through the whole of her body she felt the certainty that she could do it. With Turner, if that was what he wanted, and that would be the best, but without him if necessary. She stretched again.

'What a day. What a day!' She looked round the group. 'And another one tomorrow. Now then, Early Birds, who's on for a swim in the morning?'

250